Praise for *The Wire-Walker*

"James Janko is a marvelous writer whose compassionate imagination spans worlds. The wire he walks on trembles with humanity and hope—it is not strung only between two peoples, but between all of us who care about justice in the wider world and safety for all human beings. His interest in the circus projects between Palestinian/Israeli communities, his willingness to listen, his gifts of description, render him a mesmerizing ringleader under the Big Top. This humane story of love, care, and dreaming could not be more timely."

—Naomi Shihab Nye, author of *Habibi* and recipient of the 2024 Wallace Stevens Award

"From the descriptions of every-day actions and thoughts to life-changing and tragic events, the novel is both magical and honest. As a Palestinian from Nablus, I appreciate the accuracy of the setting, plot and characters specifically, and more generally the way the occupation affects the lives of Palestinians, especially refugees, both directly and indirectly. It's clear that the author has fully absorbed both facts and feelings related to Palestinians and the occupation and through empathy and imagination woven a most wondrous story."

— Mahmoud Masri, Founder of the (actual) Nablus Circus School

"Amal [the narrator of *The Wire-Walker*] is Palestine's Anne Frank. Her presence in the world will make it better...The ending is breath-taking."

—Maxine Hong Kingston, author of *The Woman Warrior*

"When one is practically forbidden to support Palestine or to challenge the violence descending into genocide against Palestinians, or when the Israel war machine urges us to ignore Palestine's existence, Golda Meir, 1969, 'There is no such thing as Palestinians,' James Janko dares to introduce us to a luminous sixteen-year-old Palestinian wire walker living a courageous and compassionate life in a refugee camp in the West Bank under siege every day by the IDF. Creation means, bringing to life, and indeed these characters, particularly Amal Tuqan, are living, vital and wise and will be with the reader, as fine literature makes possible, for all time. May I dare to confirm, as the novel implies, that Amal Tuqan and Anne Frank would be companions of the heart if they had known each other? Here I am speaking of Amal as if she is alive, because she is. We must read this book so we understand the horrific, violent nature of the war against the Palestinians, and also the possibilities of alliances as lived through the circus, the Flying Kids of Tel Aviv. A character came to James Janko and he has the gift, heart and will to listen and tell her story and so we have this extraordinary work of literature and truth telling and vision."

—Deena Metzger, author of *What Dinah Thought*, *The Other Hand*, and *La Negra y Blanca*, winner of Oakland Pen Award for Literature

"A poetic combination of beauty and horror, disillusionment and hope. This novel provides an unforgettable perspective to a centuries-old conflict. I hope to read more novels from this author, a singular voice, a remarkable talent."

—Gabriel Bump, author of *Everywhere You Don't Belong*

"*The Wire-Walker* is so moving and the flow so good, I had a hard time putting it down. Janko did an absolutely amazing job as a writer."

—Nili Belkind, Jaffa, Israel, ethnomusicologist and author of *Music in Conflict: Palestine, Israel, and the Politics of Aesthetic Production*

"Sometimes words are worlds," says the narrator of James Janko's novel, *The Wire Walker*. Indeed, I was astounded by the fully realized worlds that Janko imagines through the words of his female teenage narrator, Amal, a Palestinian wire-walker struggling to carve out a meaningful existence in a West Bank refugee camp. The plot, which involves the mysterious fate of Amal's father, unfolds as a thriller in the hands of a most literary writer. Janko evokes with great feeling but without sentimentality the complicated friendship between his hero and an Israeli-Jewish girl, based upon their mutual passion for circus and, perhaps more importantly, their common humanity, flaws and all. Along the way, he trenchantly evokes the lives of various Israeli and Palestinian children and adults in both Tel Aviv and the West Bank, all beset with their own, often painful, pasts that bear down upon every

breath they take in the here and now."
—Andrew Furman, author of *The World That We Are*

"In *The Wire-Walker*, James Janko has found the perfect image to describe life in the refugee camps of the occupied West Bank, a life suspended with narrow balance above the land the Palestinians don't quite own. Janko has also found the pitch-perfect voice of a teenage Palestinian girl, Amal, to narrate the story. His research comes across, in Amal's voice, as lived experience. It is her voice that draws the reader in from the start, her voice that puts into the reader's heart a longing to see her set free, like 'a bird with strong wings,' to traverse without fear the land of Israel/Palestine. Janko's book makes a strong contribution to the trove of literature that has tried to come to terms with the seemingly eternal conflict of a troubled land. It is a powerful book, by turns warm and wrenching."

—Charles Hansmann, author of *Skylighting*

Also by James Janko

Novels

What We Don't Talk About

The Clubhouse Thief

Buffalo Boy and Geronimo

Poetry

Love and Catastrophe

The Wire-Walker

James Janko

Regal House Publishing

Published by
Regal House Publishing, LLC
Raleigh, NC 27605

ISBN -13 (paperback): 9781646035809
ISBN -13 (epub): 9781646035816
Library of Congress Control Number: 2024950445

Cover images and design by © studiochi.art

Printed in the United States of America

Regal House Publishing, LLC
https://regalhousepublishing.com

For Mahmoud Masri, Mohammed Shafee,
Nili Belkind, and Eden Fuchs,
and in memory of
Robert Ray Boeskool

"But let me see if—using these words as a little plot of land and my life as a cornerstone—
I can build you a center."

—Qiu Miaojin

Contents

Part One

The Balata Refugee Camp

Nablus, Palestine

2019

1

STILLNESS

I wake in the arms of my mother. Somewhere in the night men fire their rifles at the sky, the stars, or each other. Maybe there's a bride, a groom, many cousins, or maybe there are fighters in the mountains. An ambush? A wedding? A war? Words are slow near bullets or love.

My mother says, "Lie still. I shouldn't have to tell you."

She has faith in stillness, the safety of stillness. And it is true, or almost true, that every movement is a risk.

I would like to give all of Palestine the smells I love most: cardamom and coffee. These morning smells say to me, *You're alive, you're still here, and so is your family*. My grandfather invites me to sip his coffee. No sugar, no honey. Black mud at the bottom of the cup.

The morning has come to our alley, first light, almost no light, and two men of Balata have left us for Allah. My grandfather mentions the names of the martyrs. Unlike me, he knows them, remembers them, but how can this help? Eighteen years old and nineteen years old. Young men with moustaches, hard eyes. I can't see them, only imagine. They strayed beyond the alleys, the crevices and cracks of the camp, the passageways so narrow the walls hold their breath. But the martyrs have leaped to heaven. They are in heaven. Most of us believe this, or wish to believe. Mothers who lose their sons wail their grief and ululate their joy. *Lie still, lie still. Or leap all the way to God.*

I wonder if I will ever be ready to die. I'm glad I'm a girl because most of our martyrs are young men, or boys a few years older than me. I enjoy being alive even on mornings when I can do nothing but sip coffee that burns my stomach. Grandpa likes it this way. Bitter. He's skinny as I am, but his stomach is an iron basket. I would like to trade in my body for an iron one, a thick shell, or a body of light that neither bullets nor coffee can harm. Now I think light would be better than iron, far better. Iron can be melted, crushed, broken. Or die in a pile of rust. Light is beautiful. Light is difficult to harm.

"The Israelis will assume the worst," says my grandfather. "They'll find new ways to punish us. If not today, tomorrow. If not tomorrow, the next day. They always assume the worst."

The dead are being washed and prepared for burial as I sit with my grandfather before a small window. I smell sweaty; I too should be washed, but not now. Grandpa Saeed knows what I need, or what we both need—he lights the lamp over our window. The sun will take half the day to find us. Look. I can lean forward, extend my arm between iron bars, and touch the wall across our alley. How long is my arm? Not long. To light our alley, or the bottom of a well, or my face, the sun will need to rise over the camp and climb toward the highest point in the sky. A few minutes before noon, if no clouds pass over us, the sun will find our homes, our stone walls will turn white, and our pathways will shine like rivers. The sun will be ours a short while before it drifts toward Mount Jarzim and leaves us in shadows. My grandfather, who seldom complains, calls the Balata Refugee Camp "a sardine experiment, too many fish in one can." Thirty thousand of us live inside one square kilometer, in homes that rise up three or four stories. Few streets here, mostly alleys, some of them as skinny as I am. Thirty thousand. I don't really understand a number this large. I am just one and my grandpa just one and my mother and my brother, each of us one, though I have more cousins than I can count. Our homes are small, yes, but they are not coffins. As long as there's light in the morning, or even a lamp over a window, I feel somewhat lucky. Grandpa Saeed offers me another sip of coffee. Not bad, not bad. The second sip always tastes better than the first.

Issam, my twin brother, leaves the room he shares with our grandfather and slouches in the doorway to the alley. How long will he live, my brother? Unlike me, Issam is unafraid to die. There are many like him, boys too angry to be afraid. Why are they so sure that death leads to heaven, to gardens watered by streams, to the end of hunger, thirst, and all suffering? I haven't visited heaven, nor have they. What will we see when we die? We all wish to believe in something beautiful that never ends, but what will we see?

My mother and my aunts often ignore my questions. In part, I love my grandfather because I can ask him almost anything. He seems to have a lot of room inside himself, a place wide enough for all the words I can wonder. Maybe I don't have to stay small just because I live in a small space. Sometimes words are worlds—that's what I'm learning. I can ask questions, sometimes aloud, sometimes inside me, and I have a hunch I will not keep quiet till I die.

Maybe not even then.

2

SOMETIMES I WALK INSIDE A MOVIE

Late in the day, in the homes of the families of the dead, in the alleys outside the homes, the martyrs are remembered. Among the men, young and old, mostly young, there is much talk about what to do and what not to do in this fight against the Israelis. Does anyone believe this fight will ever end? I step away, choose not to listen. The sun has crossed to the other side of the sky and the light in our alleys is the color of smoke.

They always assume the worst. Maybe the Israelis will raid the camp tonight in search of weapons and explosives. What were those young men from Balata doing late at night on a road near Elon Moreh? Maybe trying to kidnap or kill a settler, or several settlers, or trying to leap to heaven. They are martyrs[1], istashhadeen. Soon their portraits will appear on posters on the walls of our alleys so we can celebrate them as long as our walls last, or as long as memory lasts. Maybe there will come a day or a night when our walls have no more room for faces. We will build stairs to our roofs and search for faces in the sky.

I am in my alley walking on a crack in the cement. Long before I learned of the Nablus Circus School, I began to play this game with myself, walking on cracks or on lines that I drew in chalk, or on thinner lines that I imagined. As a little girl I learned to wobble, then walk, and now I'm ready for the high-wire. I go to the Circus School when I can, but it's far away, on the other side of Nablus, so I mostly practice at home. I have ropes, wires, several of each, and sometimes I string one diagonally from my window to my friend Maysa's window some ten meters down the alley. Nobody pays much attention when I practice, but Maysa is all for me. She, too, is a circus girl. She often practices juggling while I rope-walk across our alley. For most of my life I have wanted one thing—to be an aerialist. I will try to explain.

[1] The vast majority of those called martyrs are non-combatants, including women and children caught in the middle of the conflict. The term istashhadeen refers to the self-sacrifice of fallen resistance fighters; they, too, are martyrs.

I was five years old when I saw a movie from Europe, from Italy, I think, and though it was about war, not circus, there was one scene that showed a beautiful woman, almost naked, walking across a wire strung between two towers, the twin steeples of a cathedral. I was not supposed to see this. My mother had dozed off in a soft chair. My grandpa and Uncle Sami were watching the screen, not me, my eyes peeking over a blanket. I lay on a green carpet, a hand on my chest, and for the first time I saw the life I wanted. Church bells rang. The beautiful woman seemed to walk one thousand meters over the earth as the sun shone on the towers of the cathedral, the stone so white I had to squint. Below, in a courtyard, a stout policeman stumbled this way and that, his arms open as though he could save her if she fell. Her face was the calmest my eyes have seen. Maybe God held her, a woman too beautiful to die, or maybe she was about to die in her own way rather than in a war, whatever war this was. Bombs began to fall near the cathedral, the streets, the alleys, as she kept walking, her pace steady, her balance perfect. I can't remember if she survived the walk or the war, though it doesn't matter. She was perfect every step of the way.

3

HOME

I live on the first floor amid four stories of cousins. My grandfather and my mother and my twin brother and I have the bottom floor because Grandpa Saeed is old and was already old when he was shot in the leg in 2002. My family shares one room with sleeping mats and kitchen things, but we divide it in three with plywood and curtains. I sleep beside my mother. If not for the partition, I could reach out and touch the bed where my grandfather and my brother sleep. In the homes over us, there are babies and kids and aunts and uncles, and an orange cat named Handala watches over us from our roof. Four stories of cousins lead to a ceiling, no opening to the sky, so I'm not sure how he gets up there. My grandfather named him after the most famous cartoon character of Naji Salim al-Ali.

On the wall opposite my home, you will see pictures of martyrs, but you will also see a drawing of al-Ali's Handala, a Palestinian boy who has grown too large for a newspaper or a book, a ten-year-old giant three meters tall, a silhouette in green and black. What makes him Palestinian? Well, he turns his back to the world that has turned its back to him. My brother drew the spikes of hair that stick up from his skull while standing on my cousin Ghassan's shoulders. Maybe a dozen alley kids took turns drawing Handala. I helped to draw the bare feet, the raggedy pants. Handala stands near a pile of stones (real stones, not drawings) in an alley too narrow for a tank or even a jeep. My brother says the Israelis are afraid of us, and I wish this were true. Soldiers enter our alleys and search our homes whenever they wish.

We have no land, no orchards or fields, but we have Naji Salim al-Ali, his name written over and over on our walls. Someday I would like to show you the Handala in our alley, and also a three-meter-wide drawing of Big Fatty, the self-satisfied Palestinian politician and deal broker who lives in comfort, and who—like the Israelis—looks down on us as from the distance of stars. We throw stones at Big Fatty. We practice our aim. Girls aren't supposed to throw stones, but sometimes a small one flies from my hand and means more to me than this flurry of words.

I want to live a long life, but I can't change where I was born. I wonder if walking on wires over the earth is as dangerous as drawing pictures, cartoons, or writing a story about the Balata Camp. According to my grandfather, Naji Salim al-Ali was assassinated, shot in the right temple in London, in 1987, at the order of Israeli intelligence. The Mossad killed a cartoonist on August 29th.

4

STONES

On a cool morning, after the first light has come to our alley, the planes arrive. My twin brother runs down a passageway to a wider alley to throw stones at a flash of wings. He is beautiful, my brother. A rain of stones arcs over rooftops and is gone. Maybe the rage, something harder than stones, reaches the wings, but the planes come again—three of them, or four—with a roar that seems loud enough to destroy the world. The Israelis often remind us of who is in charge. *We can kill you,* the planes say. *We can watch you disappear. Who will care? Will someone file a report?*

Our alley is too narrow for throwing at jets, so I hurry toward my brother, the wider alley, till my mother traps me in her arms.

The silence is as swift as the noise, but then my ears make whooshing sounds, back-and-forth sounds, echoes. The planes are gone, probably returning to their base, but my brother keeps throwing stones. He calls out, as if the vanished pilots can hear him, "Come back, you cowards! I dare you!" I watch the last of his stones disappear in light.

I slip free of my mother when she opens her arms. I start walking to make sure that my body is here, that our homes are here, that Naji Salim al-Ali and Handala are here, and they are, they are. No bombs have fallen, no missiles. But my mother and grandfather and Uncle Sami and many cousins scan the strip of sky overhead and worry the planes will return.

I picture myself walking on a wire over our roofs and up through the sky where the planes flew. Will they return? Will the sky remain quiet the rest of the day? Our prayers are often simple: *Sky, be quiet. Please be quiet. Stay quiet. Mercy. Inshallah.* None of us know what will happen in the sky or on earth. *We are here, we are alive.* Our day has begun.

5

FRIDAY

Fathers and sons and orphans burn tires and disappear in smoke. Israeli soldiers seem to retreat from the intersections of alleys, and maybe the drone operators sitting at computer terminals in Haifa or Tel Aviv or (none of us know where they sit) study plumes of smoke instead of spots (fathers, sons, orphans) darting across screens. An hour has passed since the midday call to prayer. My brother and three boy cousins—Ghassan, Naji, Mohammed—feed rotting tires to flames.

I slip into the room I share with my mother and wrap my face in a headscarf. Now I can breathe a small breath. I sit in a corner as black smoke billows over the walls of our alley. To breathe is enough. I will ask for nothing more till this is over. A small breath, then another, another…thank you. I will stay here till the tires melt into black glue that will stain my feet.

Lord…sustainer of worlds. A voice, a smudge of light. A prayer I can almost see. I listen hard till I know who's in the alley praying through smoke—Aunt Salma. "In the name of God, the compassionate, the merciful…" She sputters, coughs, and I don't know who besides me is listening. I call to her through my scarf: "Auntie, this way, this way. Come in out of the smoke."

I believe she could pray better inside, but she stays in the alley. Do we suffer more than we need to suffer? Do we need to breathe well to pray well? I am better at questions than answers. Maybe her coughs and sputters mean something to Allah or an angel. Or maybe we're alone.

6

FIVE QUIET DAYS LATER

"Hey, Wire-Walker! Where's the circus?"

The only foreigner I know with a wink and a laugh in his voice is Juan Ramon of Spain, an Oxfam infrastructure expert, a volunteer, who pauses now and then to watch me practice. He may never learn my real name (Amal) because I seldom speak with men outside my family, but Wire-Walker is beautiful and daring and—inshallah—please call me this forever. The Israelis call me 753085164. I hope to live long enough to outshine their wire-walkers and trapeze artists, the greatest stars of their most famous circus. I would like to show them what I can do in Nablus and the Balata Camp, and in Tel Aviv and Jaffa, Jerusalem and Haifa. I would like to be good enough to travel with a professional circus and go wherever we have an audience. Europe maybe, or even the U.S. My grandfather, the most knowledgeable man in Balata and perhaps the world, told me circus is "not integral to Palestinian history or culture." I believe him, I know he's right. But circus is part of the world and has been part of me since I saw that movie I already told you about.

I've visited the world beyond the Balata Camp and Nablus through YouTube. I've seen the Mediterranean Sea on a screen the size of my palm, but I will remain ignorant until I feel it on my body. My grandfather was born in Jaffa, his ancestors lived there for six centuries, but now he too is "a stranger to the sea." These are his words, and he is sad about being a stranger. I love my grandfather for many reasons. He's the only adult in Balata who believes me, or at least listens, when I promise I'll be in a professional circus someday, the best high-wire walker in the Middle East, if not the world.

I'm not always good, so now and then I steal looks at Juan Ramon. He has black hair, green eyes, a lean, muscular build, and his affection for us is greater than his pity. My hair's even blacker than his, wavy and long, but Juan Ramon may never see it since I have to keep it covered. Anyway, he's way older than me, so I shouldn't see him as a potential husband. My mother has hinted that Ghassan, the eldest son of my uncle Sami and aunt Salma, will one day be my husband. Although he's halfway smart and mostly kind, I hope many years will pass before I become his bride.

One morning before school, I listen to Juan Ramon talking in English with my grandfather. "I've spent the last week in Ein Beit al-Ma'," he says. "Their alleys are almost as narrow as your alleys."

"We should hold a contest."

"And the Askar Camp's crowded, and New Askar's crowded."

"We keep trying to make ourselves smaller."

"It reminds me of how little my team and I can accomplish."

"Yes."

"We can't widen the walls, the alleys, but maybe we can bring more water to the camps."

Juan Ramon is part of a team, mostly Spaniards, trying to improve the water supply in four refugee camps. I don't know how they can help because the Israelis decide how much water we receive, how deep we can dig our wells, and they rule the maze of checkpoints that encircle Nablus, the farms and orchards in the surrounding hills, and they sometimes close the road to the cemetery where my father is buried. He died when I was four. My mother has never told me what happened, but she nodded, almost bowed, when I begged her to answer one question: Was my father brave?

"Like Issam?" I probed.

"No, he was calmer than your brother. Issam lacks…" She made a basket of her hands to catch the right word. "Poise," she whispered. "Issam knows nothing of poise."

7

MY TWIN BROTHER

On a Friday night, I hear whispers through the wall that separates our bedrooms. "No," says Grandpa Saeed, "how will this help? You should take risks only when something can be gained."

Issam is about to slip into our alley and other alleys as he does on most nights to meet with his cohorts, the boys or men who devise plans to strike back against the settlers and soldiers who encircle Fire Mountain, the city of Nablus.[2] I doubt my brother carries a weapon other than rage. Grandpa says, "Have you forgotten who's in charge of you? I will be your grandfather till I die."

Issam remains silent.

"I'm too old to hit you. Your father, if he were alive, would take care of this."

"I don't want to disobey you."

"Then sleep, and allow others to sleep. There is nothing we can do at this hour."

Hundreds of Israeli soldiers protect the settlements, or maybe there are thousands, plus their tanks and assault helicopters, their fighter jets, and other gifts from America and Europe. Grandpa tells Issam what he already knows: "If you injure one settler, they will kill at least ten of us, and these may include your mother and your sister." My brother speaks of dignity, honor, and the worthlessness of life if it is lived in a prison. No voice is softer at this hour. I hear two words clearly—dignity, honor—but I know them all.

Grandpa Saeed says, "You imagine things can get no worse, but I assure you they can."

Issam grunts. I hear ruffling sounds. Maybe he's putting on his shirt.

"A boy disobeying his grandfather—this cannot be accepted. And what will you do? Throw stones at a guard-post? A jeep?"

"I am sorry."

"You'll be worse than sorry if you're arrested. Boys spend years in jail for nothing more serious than throwing stones."

---

[2] Nablus is also known as Fire Mountain.

But stones are serious. They are hard and have no room to breathe, but they are what we know best. When someone dies in our alley, the men pass the body through the windows of our homes till they reach a street wide enough for a funeral procession. The dead, washed and wrapped, pass through windows, as do brides on their way to weddings. Alive or dead, we can fit almost anywhere. A stone is serious, and so is a bride, a corpse. So is my twin brother who tries hard to grow a moustache. So am I. So is my grandfather, though he is very old.

Issam slips into the alley, and soon his footsteps are on some other side of night. Maybe Handala the Cat watches over him from our rooftop. I wonder who Issam is about to meet. Friends from school? Other stone-throwers? Or men who will give him guns?

Maybe an hour passes before I hear him come in. Grandpa Saeed is awake, as is my mother. No one says anything, but I believe I know what my mother is thinking. *I pray that no soldiers have followed you home. I pray that you wise up and live at least long enough to marry and give me a grandchild. Inshallah. I hope we will all be alive when the sun comes up.*

We are. After breakfast and dishes and laundry, I walk down the alley past two Handalas, the drawing on a wall of the Palestinian boy with his ragged clothes, spiked hair, and the orange cat who perches like a sentry at the edge of our roof. Cats have good eyes. I bet Handala sees the whole sky over the camp, over Mount Ebal and Mount Jarzim, but all I see from down here is a sky-rope, a blue line over our walls. Does every wire-walker dream of walking on light, or just me? I am more hopeful than angry as I kick up some dust.

If you think this alley is a sad place, you are somewhat wrong. No one's bothered us in over a week, so we've used this quiet time to draw and paint more pictures on our walls, even some flowers and trees. I am learning that what we see inside our bodies, our eyes, is—as Grandpa Saeed says—"true enough." He claims he's "not an artist, never an artist," but he teaches painting and drawing to me and Maysa and several other girls, and—at different hours—to Issam and some boys. This NGO, Project Hope of Canada, has helped us for years, and they've given us boxes of paint and ink, brushes of different sizes, and even an easel. Grandpa Saeed says things like, "Tell the truth, don't waste time. Just do your best to be honest." So, yes, boys mark our walls with fighter jets, soldiers, splashes of red, colors louder than blood, but there are also—an arm's reach away—tomatoes on vines, almond trees in bloom, olives, yellow suns in the sky, and a fig tree as tall as a man. We have no gardens or orchards in Balata, other than those we make with paint or ink, brush and memory. My grandfather, whose words stay with me because he often repeats himself, believes we have to tell the truth in different ways to tell any truth at all. You already know (because I told you) that most of our walls have pictures of martyrs. Yes, you'll need to look hard to find these other walls, but they are here. My brother draws nothing pretty, no flowers or trees, but he too is honest. A bomb, a man in a suit. A knife on a table. A frazzle of lines and colors that collide, implode. I have not yet painted a beautiful girl walking a tight-rope, but I will. She will have perfect balance even if there are drones spying her from above.

8

MEET THE PROFESSOR

In the last hour of light, Grandpa Saeed and my brother sit on plastic stools and sip lukewarm tea in the doorway to our alley. A jump away, or a body length (mine), I sit at our kitchen table, my forearms on the sill, and stretch my ears to hear my grandpa thinking, whispering, drawing words as from a well. *The poet writes his life on pages of water, the scientist too.* If the water goes silent, so does my grandpa. I catch other sounds—*click, scrape*—my brother grinding his teeth.

"We once more distinguished ourselves from other refugees," says Grandpa Saeed. "Almost no one in Balata owns a vehicle, yet we burn more tires per capita than any camp in Palestine."

Three clicks. Teeth loud as words.

"Aunt Salma's youngest daughter suffers from asthma," Grandpa continues. "Several children in our alley, including three babies, struggle with similar afflictions." He flicks a hand. "And what did we gain from all that smoke? Before it dispersed, the Israelis had what they came for—the fathers of the boys killed on the road near Elon Moreh. How long will they be in prison, the fathers? Can any of us estimate?"

Click.

"We will be sad if we count the days."

In single file—no room to spread out—four boy cousins pass by, the taller one carrying a soccer ball. They will play till dark when they reach Balata Street and the entrance to the camp.

Grandpa looks at Issam. "So what happened? How could the Israelis find the right homes, the right fathers? The air was black. We kept bumping into each other, bumping into walls. When the air cleared, when we could breathe without choking, we realized the Israelis had accomplished their mission." He holds up his hands. "How could they see through smoke? And not just any smoke, mind you, some lump of garbage on Al-Quds Street, but black smoke, *tire* smoke. How could they see through *that*?"

My brother's jaw bones stick out as he clamps his teeth.

"You're clever enough to figure this out in two seconds," says Grandpa, "but sometimes you're too angry to think."

Two seconds? I doubt Issam will live long enough to be as clever as Grandpa Saeed, who was once a professor. As a young man, he studied at An-Najah National University in Nablus and received a doctoral degree in physics at the age of twenty-six. He later taught at the university, and also in Cairo, but his formal teaching career ended when he was imprisoned during the Second Intifada. He and my grandmother used to live in the Old City, the heart of Nablus, but my grandmother has been dead for many years and the home—if it still exists—belongs to others. I think of my grandfather as the professor of science of the Balata Camp, and sometimes he is also the professor of history, poetry, literature, art, story-telling, should anyone care to listen. Some people in our alley, even some cousins, don't like him because he "talks fancy." I like his fancy talk and he likes mine.

He calls to me. "Amal, help us for a moment. Why is burning tires sometimes useless?"

"The smoke makes us cough."

"Yes, of course. It assaults the lungs. What else?"

"The Israelis have gas masks. They can breathe."

"Yes."

"And it seems they can still see us through the smoke."

He waits a moment, then nods. "They most certainly can see us," he says, "as can anyone who has the right tools. Drones, for example, are tools, and you can think of them as flying cameras, eyes in the sky, and they are most likely watching us now."

Issam flashes a finger at the piece of sky over our alley.

Grandpa Saeed looks up, winks, waves, and continues.

"You've heard of radar, yes? You can think of it as waves that are able to feel things: the outline of a body, the frame of a window, a wall—even the air we exhale has a discernable shape. Standard X-rays provide maps of our bodies, our bones. Smoke's just a gnarled-up ball of air, easy to see through compared to flesh."

Issam rubs his right eye with a knuckle.

"No wizardry," says Grandpa Saeed. "Any of us can see through smoke if he applies the right tools."

The right tools. Inside me it seems that I, too, am made of waves that can move outward and feel things: other bodies, especially those I love (Grandpa, Mother, Issam, Maysa), the frames of windows, walls, the ropes and wires I walk, the air around me, the narrow sky. *A hole in the wall was enough/ for the stars to teach you the hobby of staring/ into the eternal.* Grandpa Saeed taught us this poem, and many others. Narrow gaps—is that all we have? Will it be enough? The poem is true, though, whether or not any walls come down.

Issam points his chin at our grandfather. "So what are we, then? Insects under a microscope?"

"No, we're human beings. We are human beings."

"The Israelis don't think so."

"They will. They have to."

Issam shakes his head.

"They have to. Otherwise…" Grandpa tugs at his chin. "Yes, they have the power now, they can do as they wish. But they need to wake up if we are all to live."

My grandfather looks at our sky, a dull gray line over our eaves. I can't see any drones, but I hear a slight buzzing. *The right tools.* Handala the Cat watches over us, as do the Israelis with their gadgets. Eyes in the sky. Mechanical. Inhuman. No people up there, no pilots. Only machines are at risk. I'd like to kill a drone, crush its eyes, its lenses, its radar, its waves that feel things. No blood would come out. Maybe just crackling sounds—glass, metal—breaking apart. I would burn it and make soldiers breathe the smoke.

If I were a wizard, a magician.

A god.

9

THE PHYSICIST AND THE WIRE-WALKER

My mother once told me that my father, who died for reasons no one will explain, was different from his father, my grandpa, except for this—his tongue loosened at night. This somehow makes sense: loose tongues in the dark, and the chance for stories, even secrets. I have no memory of my father's voice, but I have my grandpa. After sundown, over glasses of tea, I help loosen his tongue.

Tonight I ask him about his role in the Second Intifada. Was he shot in the leg while fighting the Israelis?

"No," he says, "a stray bullet caught me. There's a good chance I was wounded by one of our neighbors."

"How could that be?"

"Chaos," he says. "People have guns and bullets fly."

We sip mint tea at a small table beside our window to the alley. Issam lies on his mat in the dark. My mother's gone upstairs, three stories, to visit cousins, so she can't chide me for bothering my grandpa. Nonetheless, I whisper, almost smother my words, because my question may seem rude even to him.

"Were you afraid you might never walk again?"

Grandpa Saeed scratches his chin. "Yes, I *was* afraid. I overheard the medics debating whether or not I would lose my leg."

"Did it hurt?"

He blows on his tea. "The pain was mild at first, but late in the night it was like being burned by a flame."

I'd hoped to hear something else because I fear certain wounds as much as I fear death. A wire-walker is an athlete. A wire-walker needs her legs, her arms, every part of her body. Sometimes I almost convince myself I'm powerful, un-killable, but I'm nothing compared to weapons. Or even a single bullet that burns like a flame.

My grandpa leans across the table to pat my arm. "No need to dwell on this," he says. "The worst pain was gone in a day or two. I was strong then, and still am. I'm from hearty stock, which means you are too."

I know I should shut up, let him keep his pain private, but I ask about his time in prison.

"That was long ago, and only for a few months."

"How many?"

He pauses to calculate. "Four months and three days, to be exact."

I worry about prison, too, so I ask about the food. Was there enough?

He shrugs. "I never complained."

"Did they interrogate you every day?"

"Only at first."

"What did you tell them?"

He flicks a hand. "Not much. They were disappointed with how useless I was."

"Did they think you were trying to make a bomb or something?"

He rubs his chest, as if something there burns or itches. "Yes, they were sure of it. They kept asking who else was involved."

"Did you tell them?"

"No, of course not. Because I taught physics at the university, they made certain assumptions. In the end, I told the Shin Bet the truth: I love science; it would be a sin to use science to destroy anyone, even the oppressor. I said, 'Let me speak with your scientists. Maybe two or three of them will understand.'" He winks. "I should have asked to speak with their poets, artists, musicians, circus performers. But so many bridges had become impossible to cross."

I restrain myself from asking the question at the front of my mind—Were you tortured? I'm afraid of torture; I want to prepare myself, but I don't want my grandfather to relive his worst memories. Instead, I ask how long it's been since he taught at An-Najah National University, the university I hope to one day attend.

He waves a hand. "Oh, that's a long, lost chapter of my life. Almost twenty years have passed."

"You miss it?"

"What do you think? The Israelis released me on one condition—that I not return to the university. I loved teaching, still do, and would teach for free if they gave me a chance." He grimaces. "No, I'm not quite telling the truth. I would pay to teach if I had a small classroom and a few shekels to spare."

I still wish to know if my grandpa was tortured, but I hold my tongue. Whatever the Israelis did to him was not enough to destroy his intelligence. I take comfort in this, and take more comfort in the fact that he loves me. The Shin Bet couldn't kill his mind or his love for me, though I hadn't yet breathed my first breath when grandpa was in prison. Can a girl be loved before she is born? I don't know, but I am certain he loves me now.

I go out to the alley and practice walking on a rope skinnier than my pinkie. My balance is perfect when I'm about one meter above the earth. How well would I walk if I were in the sky over our roofs, high over Nablus and the valley between Mount Jarzim and Mount Ebal? Would my nerve fail me, or would I walk with the confidence of one who believes death will not come for her soon?

A talented aerialist can do more than walk across ropes and wires. I bring out my foam mat and practice cartwheels, hand-stands, then front-flips and backflips. I know what I must learn in the coming weeks and months, or however long I live. On Grandpa's phone, on YouTube, I've watched high-wire artists do front-flips and backflips, and rise almost to the domed roofs of circus tents before they arc back to their wires and the glare of the spotlight. I've seen human frogs, two women in green tights, take turns leaping over each other, one crouching and the other leaping, flipping forward and back, this way and that, too lucky to die, or too agile. Well, yes, they were daring and beautiful and I love them. I could see, though, that their wires are wider than mine, plus they have tools to cinch them tight so they sway only a little. I will not complain. I will not waste time with excuses. If someday I can do what they do on *my* ropes, *my* wires, I will be ready for every circus in the world.

10

TALI GLAZMAN

My grandfather is helping me to organize a children's circus in the Balata Camp. Within a month, maybe two, he wants us to perform in our alleys, or at the Circus School in Nablus, or wherever we can clear a space. My friend Maysa can juggle oranges and stones at the same time. Nadir, her brother, wants to swallow swords that shoot flames, but he is not serious. I would like to have a long balance pole like Phillippe Petit, a great wire-walker I have studied on YouTube. Instead, I have my arms (I think of them as wings), and something else. Does a body stop where the skin stops? Sometimes yes, sometimes no. If I walk well, careful and quiet, I can feel all around me the shape of the air, the sky, and I grow larger than myself. Something I can't name, something shiny, moves inside me and beyond me. If people say I'm small, it's because their eyes are small. All they see is some skin that slips over me like a stocking. They're missing the light around the body, the part of me no bullet can harm. The calmer I am, the shinier I am. I believe Phillippe Petit and other great aerialists would know what I mean.

I can blog about wire-walking or whatever I want on Grandpa Saeed's phone. Anyone—a poet in Paris, an actress in Cairo, a senator in the United States—can read what I write. I'm startled that Tali Glazman, a Jewish girl in Tel Aviv, is my most faithful reader. No, let me tell the truth—she's my *only* reader. Tali's my age, sixteen, almost seventeen, and performs with The Flying Kids of Tel Aviv, a professional circus for Israeli and Palestinian children. Sometimes she calls me on Messenger, and sometimes I answer. Talking to Tali is more difficult than walking across the thinnest of wires.

She's well fed, chubby for a circus girl, with teeth as white as eggshells. Although she performs with Palestinians, she knows nothing about us. We mostly chat about circus because we get angry if we speak of other things. Once, on a Sunday afternoon, she tried to tell me about her side of the story which goes back many years, and which—for her—is not even a memory. Several of her ancestors escaped from the Nazis during World War II, but many others died in Auschwitz and Treblinka and elsewhere. The descendants of those who escaped are now among the millions who've displaced us, who've taken our life and our land, which they believe they deserve. I say to Tali, "Palestinians had nothing to do with the Holocaust. Why don't you surround German towns and cities with settlers, soldiers, walls, checkpoints? Why don't you give every German citizen an identification number? Why is my family in a camp?"

My uncles sometimes speak this way, but no one in Israel hears them. I expected Tali to end the call. Instead, she leaned away from her phone to make her face smaller and smaller on my screen. I could've done the same, but I wanted this girl to see me. I switched on a lamp and bent over my grandpa's phone so my face would appear as big and bright as the moon.

Tali made no effort to see. In a far-away voice, she suggested I read two of her favorite books: *The Diary of Anne Frank* and *Salt to the Sea.*

"No, I don't think so. Have you ever read a book by a Palestinian? Tell the truth."

"No, but my father had."

"One book? A short one?"

"No, he read dozens of books, maybe hundreds."

"Like what?"

She shrugs. "How would I know?"

"You know the titles of *your* books, the ones you want me to read."

"I only mentioned two. There are many."

"We also have many."

"Do you?"

"Thousands, maybe millions. But you haven't read one."

She set her phone on a table or something, face-down, to darken my screen. She was still with me, though; I could hear her breathing. A long time passed before she picked up her phone and let me see a wall or a ceiling, soft blue. The light shifted. Maybe she raised her phone to the sky out her window or the wide blue over the Mediterranean Sea.

Tali whispered her father's name: "Jacob, Jacob. He was a teacher," she said. "He could've taught literature and drama at Tel Aviv University, but he chose to teach at a public high school."

I said to myself, *Maybe he's half as intelligent as Grandpa Saeed.*

Her voice grew loud. "I want you to read certain books, but more than that I wish you could've known my father."

And my father? Will he ever matter?

"Are you listening?"

"Yes."

"You will need both your ears to understand where I come from and who I am."

I turn all red inside when I'm angry. Do Israelis have ears? Do *any* of you have ears? Before I could ask, Tali placed her phone face-down on a table or something, my screen went black, and a breath or two later she ended the call.

She sent me a text the next morning. *Sorry a little. I didn't tell you what I needed to tell you and shouldn't have even tried. I'm not sure there are words. If there are, I can't find them. I know this sounds stupid, but maybe all I can do is wish you well on the high-wire. These words probably sound like nothing, or next to nothing, but I mean them. I love circus. Nothing's better than circus. Most of my life doesn't make any sense. What about you?*

I didn't text her back for three hours. I told myself I didn't need her, never would, but I couldn't lie to myself for long. I began as she began—*Sorry a little. I wish I could find a way to show you who I am and where I'm from. Please know I want to be your friend. Maybe it's okay if we argue sometimes. We are girls from different worlds.*

11

PROJECT

I'm making a film called *One Alley in Balata.* I will include the drawings of Handala and Big Fatty and some poems and pictures on a link so Tali can see for herself where I live. If I show her one alley, our art and some of our words, will she know us a little? This phone—a gift from a former colleague of my grandpa who still teaches at the university—is a miracle. Tali will see Balata, see me and my alley, from her city by the sea.

Look. I stood on a ladder and drew this girl on a tightrope in blue chalk. Under her, in silver, are knives, swords; above her a drone and two fighter jets, and these words under everything—*Keep your balance, please.* Some day or night the rain will wash away the chalk, but I have my drawing on film and I can always draw something else after the chalk disappears. I've filmed Handala and Big Fatty and the poetry of Mahmoud Darwish and Samih al-Qasim. No one can film this whole alley, but it would be a sin not to try. Maysa and I painted a garden with cucumbers and tomatoes, and some cousins—I have many cousins—painted a fig tree, two olive trees, a stream of clear water. We have no garden, but I will show this to Tali because it's part of what's true. My brother painted a boy hurling stones at a fighter jet, smoke rising from the cockpit. We have wolves on the wall, wild dogs, a small farm, a pasture, a burning house, a graveyard, the names of the dead beside the names of the living. Some of us paint and write in black and white while others use colors. Juan Ramon said to my grandfather and my uncle Sami, "This alley should be in the Prado," which is this big museum in Madrid. I kept quiet, but I said to myself, "No, it belongs here, right here. Let Madrid come and see it. Let Tali come and see it." They won't, so I make my film.

Handala the Cat walks across a strip of wood thinner than his paws. I film him, I study him, and I also study people. I make videos of my family and cousins and neighbors when I feel quiet inside and they forget I'm here. I ask no one to pose for pictures. If my brother looks like he wants to murder someone—*snap*—I catch the flame in his eye before it dulls. If my mother surprises me with a smile, or if she glances into the sky over our alley as if Allah might appear, or a drone, a fighter jet, I catch wonder and fear. Truth is fast. So is my eye, my camera, as I try to keep pace. Everything shifts: faces, light, shapes, sounds, my eye, my touch, my movie that won't stay still. If I look, I mean *really* look, even a photograph of a chair looks like something about to leap.

My friend Maysa films me wire-walking between her window and mine. I film her juggling oranges and stones, seldom dropping any, but later she tells me she'd rather be a contortionist and twist her body into impossible positions. Grandpa Saeed films both of us: Maysa juggling as I jaunt back and forth on a wire in the background; Maysa sitting on the ground while trying to lift the soles of her feet to her shoulders. Sometimes Grandpa chuckles as he films, but my friend and I are serious. I walk across a wire so thin that Grandpa says he can't see it in the shadows of the alley. Good. It seems I have learned to walk on air.

12

FRIENDSHIP

One Alley in Balata includes seventeen minutes of circus performances. Tali has watched it twice, and has also met my family, some aunts and uncles, many cousins, and everything else I can film. She wants to know about the food. "I didn't see any," she says in a text, "except a few tomatoes and things painted on a wall."

So I film what appears on our table, though I wish I could film the smells. Taboon bread and mint tea, coffee and cardamom. Nabulsi cheese and melons and sweet fried onions. My grandpa takes me to the Old City, so I can show Tali the most impressive market in Nablus. A barrel as wide as a man overflows with olives, and others almost as large are stuffed with dates, almonds, black cumin seeds, the reddish-purple of sumac, the browns of cinnamon and za'atar. Necklaces of figs hang from rafters over mounds of pomegranates and apples, and a long silver fish (I feel so sad for him) breathes his last breaths on a butcher's block. Back home, after Grandpa buys almost nothing, I film my mother preparing a watery stew of onions and rice, strips of chicken. She says, "Where are we? Hollywood? Put down that phone and help me cook."

I resend Tali the link that shows "a few tomatoes and things painted on a wall." Look again, please, at Balata's only garden. Tomatoes and cucumbers. A fig tree, two olive trees. A stream of clear water. I wonder how quick she is. Not quick at all, I'm thinking. Tali will need to lose something dear before she can see our garden and understand.

She sends me videos and photographs of Tel Aviv's beaches and parks, her life of leisure. There's one picture I like, though, and have looked at many times. Tali, shopping in a market, leans over a barrel filled with red powder. Other barrels are capped with colors—green, yellow, black, ocher—small mountains of spices. The display is beautiful, and so is Tali as she sniffs a spice. Paprika, I'm guessing, or red pepper. She looks lovely breathing something fresh, her black hair shining in the sun.

I don't hate her.

I don't love her.

Does she feel the same about me?

❧

My brother will not talk to me. There is no privacy in the camp, so he and my mother and my grandfather and our cousins and all the people in our alley know Tali and me talk and text and exchange emails when this magic called the internet reaches from Tel Aviv to Balata. My grandfather thinks it's important to have an Israeli friend if the friendship is genuine, but others are suspicious. My mother worries that Tali will get me in trouble, maybe get us all in trouble. I always tell her what I half believe: This friendship is about circus, nothing else—*circus*. I brag for Tali and call her an artist, a professional performer in a children's troupe. I don't know how to pray, unless prayer is a wire in an alley. I want to be bold enough to tell my mother, to tell Balata and Tel Aviv, that I, too, am an artist, and feel no shame for doing what I was born to do.

❧

Today the skies are quiet and clear. I call Tali on Messenger in the late afternoon and we talk for a while, then argue. One thing we both need is circus, though I say my need is greater. We disagree about this, that, and everything. Tali is stubborn. So am I. She says, "You think you know me, but you don't."

I take a breath. "And you know *me*?"

"I'm not saying I do. I'm just saying you assume too much."

"Like what?"

"I'm lucky to be alive."

The Holocaust—that's what she's talking about. And it happened many years before Tali was born.

I tell her about the drones that hover over Nablus and the Balata Camp, and the fighter jets that sometimes scream over our roofs. "The planes torture us," I say. "The whole camp seems ready to explode."

"I have nothing to do with that."

"And at night soldiers sometimes throw stun grenades to frighten us, rob us of sleep, keep us off balance."

She plays a trick with her phone, backs away till her face almost disappears from my screen. "And that's *my* fault?"

"Well, what will you do to stop it?"

"And *you*? What will you do about the next rocket fired into Israel?"

She waves her phone around, blurs my screen. "And what will you do about the bombs strapped to the bodies of young men who believe they'll go to heaven for killing Israelis? The more they kill, the higher their place in heaven. Isn't that right?"

"You don't understand."

"Really?"

"The men of Balata have no weapons other than stones."

I have just told a lie. I'm afraid my own brother already knows a few things about rockets, explosives, a body waiting for a bomb. His rage and impatience frighten me, as does Tali's ignorance. I'm surprised we don't have more martyrs, those she calls terrorists, whereas my "friend" seems to wonder why we have any. If you leave us alone, I'm thinking, abandon the settlements, dismantle the checkpoints, go away forever, we'll leave you alone. A moment later I wonder if I'm lying to myself. So much hatred is in us. I've felt it as a current under the skin, a burning in the blood. I fear that no one in this camp—not even a child just born—will live long enough to know peace in Palestine. Salaam, salaam. Easy to say, but bring us some. Bring it from wherever it hides and push it under our skin near the fire. I hear a voice in my head that I won't let Tali hear, or even my own mother: *I don't want children.* Soon I will be a woman. I'll be encouraged to have children, lots of them, but I don't want any. None. If some morning I wake up in a safe world, okay, I'll think about having babies. Until then, I don't even want a husband. My mother had one who didn't live long enough for me and my brother to know him. Tali lives in Tel Aviv. One day she'll marry and have children and she and her husband will live many years and never go to jail. Why? Because Tali's people have the guns, they have America, they have the Holocaust, they have the story the world remembers. In Balata, we have a garden of memory and paint and portraits of martyrs. Palestine, Palestine. We have no story the world hears other than the familiar one on the front page when some of us explode.

Today I'm a stranger to myself. I went to bed hating Tali Glazman, wanting something bad to happen to her, but now I miss her bad enough to ache. What happened in my dreams? I don't know. Maybe my dreams took me to someplace warm and left this softness in my stomach. This much is clear: I don't want Tali to suffer. If she's as ignorant as the world, as arrogant as the world, that's not enough to harden my stomach. The morning sky is a pale line over my alley. Today I won't be jealous if Tali raises a window to sky and sea.

I send her a text: *Let's not talk about bad things for a while. Let's just think about circus, our love for circus. Maybe this is impossible, but maybe not.*

Three hours later she responds: *It is possible, or at least sometimes possible. We have a rule in The Flying Kids of Tel Aviv. We don't talk about politics at any time before or during practice. Ideally, this gives us the chance to know each other beyond the usual arguments. All our coaches, Palestinians and Israelis, gave us this rule. We mostly follow it, though sometimes we lapse.*

I'm surprised she wrote *Palestinians* before she wrote *Israelis*. But who thought of the rule first? Which coach? I bet an Israeli coach came up with the rule, but this is not the time to ask.

13

BASIC MATH

There are no tricks on the rope, the wire, or the long stick lain over the ground. My grandfather, a physicist, has no training in circus skills, but he is my coach. This morning, after I fell from a wobbly rope, he told me to take a more careful look at what's inside me and around me. "Watch a bird as it flies," he said. "Yes, there are wings and wind, but there is also intention. Maybe the latter is more important—I'm not sure yet. I wish we could ask the bird."

I have seen sparrows and hawks in the tightrope-sky over our camp. Wings, yes wings. Straight up over this alley. Skinny as a circus rope, or almost, our sky hemmed by walls. Birds cross our tightrope-sky into the open sky, the wide blue or gray, and I can only guess where and when they plan to alight. If I could rise with wings and ride the winds over our camp, over Nablus and its mountains, I would fly west toward the sea, the port of Jaffa, where my grandfather was born. "There are wings and wind, but also intention." But what if there's no wind? What if there is stillness? A bird or a wire-walker better be ready for anything. I have fallen many times. Sometimes even a bird falls to earth and must shake the dust from her feathers before she can rise.

I have studied Nik Wallenda and the Flying Wallendas on YouTube. Twice, I watched Nik walk blind-folded on a swaying wire, two hundred meters over the Chicago River. I wonder if anything can frighten this man. A bomb, for instance. Or a grenade. A bullet. Or the bark of a soldier giving an order in a language he may never understand. I know only a few words of Hebrew, but my English is good and I could talk with Nik Wallenda if I knew how to reach him. I want to ask about fear. His great-grandfather, Karl, maybe the most daring of the Wallendas, died at age seventy-three when he fell from a wire strung between two towers in San Juan, Puerto Rico. Some blamed the high winds; some blamed the rigging. I watched Karl fall to his death on YouTube. No second chance, none. He walked through wind and light, he was beautiful. And then he died.

❧

Nik Wallenda practices six hours a day, six days a week. He also trains with weights ten hours a week, and does at least five hours of aerobics. I lift weights with bricks. I run back and forth through alleys. I will one day be as disciplined as Nik Wallenda or any of the Flying Wallendas. My grandfather, my coach, says, "Balance is in the mind of the feet, the mind of the breath, the mind of the heart." Maybe he speaks this way because his wife, my grandmother, was a poet. If my mind misses his musings, my body understands.

"You could see this as basic math," he says. "The whole world is under the wire. Sky above, earth below. Walk the line between the two."

❧

In school, while my teacher discusses a math formula I learned more than three years ago, I make a map in my mind of Nik Wallenda's world, Phillippe Petit's world, my grandfather's world, *my* world.

Sky

Earth

Maybe I will paint this on a wall in my alley after I get home from school. Blue sky and green earth, a line between the two. This simple? Just this?

14

ARTISTS' PERMITS

Tali Glazman trains with coaches and with other kids her age, whereas I train with Maysa al-Sa'ih, the juggler who wants to be a contortionist, and sometimes my friend and I walk four kilometers to the Nablus Circus School to show off our skills. Tali, who has seen a peek of what we can do through film clips and live performances (Messenger), invited Maysa and me to come to Tel Aviv for training, which shows how ignorant she is. On some days we can't leave our alleys, and on *all* days—year in, year out—we can't enter Israel without special permission. Tali thinks the managers of the circus can help us to receive artists' permits. "No guarantees," she says, "but it's possible. Three acrobats from Ramallah once trained and performed with The Flying Kids. You'll have to fill out some forms and submit them electronically. The whole process may take a while."

The whole process may take forever. Tel Aviv, forty kilometers away, may as well be on the other side of the world. When my mother says, "Forget about it, you're not going anywhere," all I can do is nod. Inside myself I'm praying, *Inshallah, give me one chance. I'll walk a wire over Tel Aviv!* Is it possible to describe how badly I wish to go? A professional circus! If I'm not already better than Israel's acrobats and aerialists, I soon will be. How hard will I need to work? Will I have time to sleep this year?

Early one morning, I receive a six-page form electronically from Israel's special permits division. The Flying Kids of Tel Aviv Outreach Program is cc'd in the message, so Tali must have persuaded the managers of the circus to help two Palestinian girls from Balata. Is she our friend? Our Israeli friend from Tel Aviv? Happiness is confusing. Once, in a dream, I flew through the sky, and now, awake, I close my eyes and almost forget where I was born and where I stand.

My grandfather promises to help Maysa and me with the forms, the security questions, and so on. "Who knows?" he says. "Maybe something will come of this. You would have no chance if you were boys."

15

PRACTICE

My grandfather helped me to string this cable across one of the wider alleys of Balata. Three meters off the ground, it begins at the window of some second cousins and slants up to the window of a couple who longs for children and have none. We lack the tools and guy wires to make the cable as tight as it would be in a professional circus. There's too much slack, which means it will roll out from beneath me and leave nothing to walk on. When I tell my grandpa not even Nik Wallenda can weave the air into a rope, he says, "Yes, it's impossible, it's perfect. You might surprise us all!"

My alley is too narrow for a balance pole, but here I can use a metal rod almost three meters long. My grandfather rests his back against a wall and starts banging on a drum. "What are you waiting for? Start walking before your audience goes away."

Only my grandfather and the childless couple are watching. The drumbeat helps me to relax and wake something bright in my chest and stomach. My body shines, as if I carry inside me pockets of light and can show them off the way others might show off valuable jewels or rare coins. I breathe long and deep, take the first step, teeter, swing my balance pole, take another step, another, and three more before the cable swoops out from beneath me and I fly like a comet into the dirt.

The childless couple calls, "Mumtaaz, mumtaaz," which means wonderful, amazing. They adore every child, even one covered in dust.

Grandpa Saeed helps me up. "If you learn to walk on this," he says, "you can walk on anything. Next time try to grab the cable to break your fall."

16

ADMINISTRATIVE DETENTION

In the early evening, Tali calls me on Messenger to tell me I may have to wait months or even years to receive a permit to visit Tel Aviv.

"I already knew this."

"It's more complicated than I thought it would be."

I tell her I didn't expect much, but then I realize I'm lying. I want so badly to practice and perform with a professional circus that I half believed the force of my will would prove my innocence. I am sixteen. I am a girl. Israel should know I'm not yet a bomb waiting to explode.

Tali says, "Your grandfather was once in jail."

She could say this about almost every man in Balata.

"Without charges," I tell her. "He was placed under… I forget what they—"

"Administrative detention. They suspected that he incited violence."

"How do you know this?"

"The circus has a legal advisor. She's—"

"A lawyer?"

"Yes, she's doing what she can for you. Your grandfather was suspected—"

"He did nothing wrong."

"Maybe that's true, but there was an attack near Nablus. One settler was killed and—"

"He had nothing to do with it."

"Amal, how would you know? You weren't born yet."

"I've known my grandfather all my life."

We look at each other on the screen, but not for long. I turn away and glance out the door to the alley. Night is here. The brightest light is the screen of my grandfather's phone.

Tali says, "There might still be a way, but right now there are more questions than answers."

I won't look at her just yet, or talk to her.

"No one wants to see you punished for something your grandfather may or may not have done before you were born."

"He never hurt anyone."

"Maybe so. But one settler died when a bomb went off. Another—"

"My grandfather's innocent. Besides, that settler shouldn't have been anywhere near Nablus anyway."

"Amal, he was murdered. The man was murdered."

"Yes, but we're murdered all the time. And those of us who survive—we're trapped. We can't go anywhere."

"It's not that simple."

"All right, then. Israel can do as it pleases because everything's so complicated."

"I didn't say that."

"Yes, but you're here, aren't you? You're in Palestine."

She pauses before she corrects me: "Amal, I live in Tel Aviv. And I never had a choice."

I would break the connection if I'd lost all hope that I would one day perform in a professional circus. I say, "Tali, if you knew me, if you knew my grandfather, you'd understand that everything I tell you is true."

I ask if Maysa still has a chance to receive an artist's permit in "the near future."

"I'm afraid…"

"What?"

"She has little chance because her father's in jail."

The boys of our alley have a soccer ball as flat as a disc of bread. My brother tries to shoot air into it with a hand pump, but the ball—though it sounds like someone alive and breathing—stays flat.

My brother cuts it open with a knife. He finds some plastic bags, mushes them together, and fills the space inside the ball. He secures the sphere with a spider-web of twine, a bit of tape, and again he and my boy cousins have something to bang against walls.

17

WEDDING

The bride almost restrains giggles as she enters the front door of my home. Nour has come with her mother and aunties and sisters and girl cousins who pass single file through my back door and into the home of my aunt Lena and her three daughters. I can't show everything through the lens of a phone, so I'll soon tell Tali what no camera can reveal—Nour smells of lilacs and rain. Maybe no one has smelled real lilacs in Balata, only the perfume. Rain—this fresh smell that sometimes blesses us—is the smell we love most. No one can bottle it and offer it as perfume, so where did Nour or her mother find such sweetness? No dark clouds have come for days.

I remember when I ruined beautiful water. I was maybe four years old when I trapped raindrops in a bottle, tried to keep them forever, but soon they smelled like sewage. Rain has to be fresh. I want to ask Tali Glazman, "Can your soldiers and engineers build a wall around the sky, and also a roof? Can they bottle the rain, keep it for themselves, and make perfume sweet enough for weddings?" No, the sky is the sky. Even if fighter jets drop all their bombs, the clouds and the rain and the fresh smells will find ways to return. People can be trapped behind walls or bars or pressed into graves, but the sky has no bones, no flesh, no edges to its skin. Listen, Israel. Fire missiles through the blue and the wounds heal before the sounds echo and die.

The bride's mother also wears a white dress, but the dresses of the aunties and sisters and cousins are of every color. We pass through four more homes and two more alleys before we reach a street wide enough for a wedding procession. Young men prance around and bang drums. I hear tambourines, a violin, but I can't see the players. All the doors and windows of our homes are open. Women and girls ululate their joy for Nour and her family and all of us still alive. I keep quiet because I want other voices in this film I will send to Tali. Up ahead, four men in white suits wait for the bride to sit at the center of a palanquin so they can carry her like an offering to the home of the groom. Nour stumbles on the hem of her dress. Her mother and two aunties lead her to the stool where she sits alone. A white flower with a veil over her face.

The drums grow louder as the singers start up. Someone blows windpipes. The four men in white lift the palanquin and Nour rises in the air. She's such a skinny bride that they could as easily carry a bird down the street.

I keep the eye of the camera on Nour while I listen to ululations, the play of singers, drummers, blowers. The sounds bounce up from the earth. We invite the sky to hear the happiness of wedding sounds.

I duck into one of the homes and climb crooked stairs to the third story. From a window, I film the men in white suits and the bride in white, and the women and girls in reds, greens, blues, purples, all the colors I have known. I want Tali to see our clothing. Even little boys wear suits, or at least clean white shirts. Tali needs to learn at least two words of our language. *Nour* means light, and my name, *Amal*, means hope.

Near the home of Fadi the groom I smell bread and honey, yellow rice and lamb. Nothing makes me hungrier than a wedding. Today I will eat big. I will not try to walk across any ropes or wires till tomorrow. I would like to record the smells of our roast lamb, our rice, and our famous dessert—kanafeh. We make it from honey and pastry dough and boiled sugar and the best white cheese of Palestine. Tali will be hungry when she sees it on a platter, bright as an orange on top and a creamy yellow underneath.

That night I dream about *my* wedding. Fadi is cute and smart, but he's Nour's cousin, not mine, and now he is taken. I will never touch his hair or his waist, except in a dream, and even here my hand is too slow to feel what he is made of. Bye, Fadi. He turns away the moment I wave.

My cousin Ghassan is not pretty, but he is sweet. Once, and not in a dream, he made a green kite and taught me to fly it, toss it into the sky over Balata Street and the entrance to the camp. We were nine years old. In my dream, we fly the kite again, and then my mother and my grandfather take me aside and ask if I want to marry him. "Yes," I say, "if you wish." But my voice is small.

I see Tali standing before a white house with a red tile roof. Her dress is the color of the leaves of the orange trees lining a wide boulevard. I want to surprise us both—kiss her on the cheeks before I marry

Ghassan. I don't see my cousin anywhere. I don't see his mother or mine, or anyone in our family. A dream is real before the dreamer wakes. I walk a stone path to the white house. I breathe. I sweat. I see Tel Aviv. I think yes, no, maybe. Tali's cuter than some alley boys. Is she really my friend? I kiss her on the cheeks once, twice. My face shines, though it is one thousand times darker than hers. Asleep or awake, I feel my warmth and color. Tali's face is the moon when it can't grow any fatter. Plump and pretty—that's my circus friend. I'm pretty, too, in a bony way. Dark light and muscles like ropes. I'm all lightning under the skin.

18

HOUSE HALF FALLEN

Israel has no idea someone like me could exist. I'm the girl who weaves spiderwebs with ropes and wires, who learns a little more each day about how to walk in the sky. Grandpa Saeed believes I have a special gift, that I can "learn to walk on the narrowest spaces imaginable." He enjoys coaching me, giving me tips, which—in his words—"sometimes stray beyond the margins of science. By training, I'm a physicist, I respect the rigor of science. But my wife, your grandma, was a poet, and so I equally respect the rigor of poetry, the discipline required in finding a language that harms no silence. Science and poetry—are they not a marriage? As for your wish to be an aerialist, a professional, you will have to quiet both your mind and your body to know the sky as you know the earth. How well will you walk? How high? I believe there *is* a way to breathe all the way through the soles of the feet and into the rope, the wire, the points of contact. The body expands as one's concentration expands, yes? Empirical evidence suggests this is true."

I do my best to pay attention. I watch my breath become deep and calm, sometimes shallow and calm, and I understand a little about concentration when I walk the narrow spaces, or when I talk with Tali and we get angry but still need each other for reasons we may never understand. I can't say why I would be sad to lose her. Many in my alley distrust me now, even consider me a traitor, but I have one friend to hold in my heart—Maysa al-Sa'ih. Although we no longer speak of Tel Aviv, the chance to train and perform with The Flying Kids, we have not forgotten our dream. Maysa wants to be the best contortionist in Palestine. She's a juggler, too, but her #1 goal is to master contortion. I sometimes help her to twist her body and hold still in difficult positions. In one pose, she folds into herself, becomes a circle, and appears almost as small as the repaired soccer ball my brother and boy cousins bang against walls.

If you ask where I live, I might point to my alley or point to a wire.

Sometimes Maysa shakes the wire I'm walking, or tries to swing it out from under me, so I can test my limits, find new limits. I watch YouTube, study what the great aerialists can do, and afterwards I practice, copy, before I find my own way to walk, fall, jump, fly. Sometimes I set my wire less than a meter over the ground so Maysa can straddle it. I walk toward my friend, pause, crouch, her signal to hunch down so I can leap-frog over her and fly home to my wire. Sure, I fell in the dust one-thousand-and-one times before I learned how to do this. I can also jump-rope and do the splits on a wire. I've been taught not to brag, but I will say this in writing: *I am brilliant on a wire.*

Maysa and I have a new place to practice, a house half fallen near the south end of the camp. No one bothers us here. Four years ago, the Israelis began to bulldoze this home, then realized they'd meant to level a different home in a different alley. Anyway, I tie my ropes and wires to poles and pillars, a spiderweb of rigging, and walk back and forth in the ghost of a home the Israelis refuse to rebuild. Maysa practices her poses behind a wall that leans outward and will not crush her should it fall. Is she as good as the contortionists in The Flying Kids? I don't know, but she will be in time.

There is no roof in the ruined house. The hole through the front wall is wide enough for a tank. I could balance easily on the barrel of a tank, for it is one hundred times wider and more solid than any rope or wire on which I practice. Blindfolded, I could skate forward and back, spin and jump, and I wouldn't need a balance pole to keep from falling. It's easy to walk on something solid that stays put. A rope or a wire rolls a bit, swings one way, then another. I tell myself over and over, "Play the sway, play the sway." I'm a skinny girl, there isn't much of me to see. But I know I'm beautiful the moment I balance on a wire.

19

FATHER

Uncle Sami's taxi putters toward Al-Quds Street. He and my grandpa and my mother and me are on our way to visit my father's grave. My uncle has forgotten his glasses. An unlit cigarette in his mouth, he leans over the steering wheel as my grandpa, sitting in front, warns of potholes and ruts. Sometimes I wave my arms as if I'm wire-walking rather than riding on wheels. Swerve. Slide. Bump. My mother, beside me in the backseat, shuts her eyes to Nablus and the world. *I'm not here*, she seems to announce, *and never have been.* My grandfather says, "Excellent, excellent," each time Sami misses a bump.

I don't know the father I wish to visit. I know death only a little, though I have seen some. I don't know why light fills my body each morning unless this is the way of bodies, to catch light the way trees catch light, to shine even from a gray alley or the backseat of a car. My father has lain in a grave since I was four years old. His soul? I may never see it, or know if it shines. But I would offer him all my mornings if I could.

We pass a low wall marked with graffiti—a black fist, a red flower, the Palestinian flag, a sketch of Abu Salem, a recent martyr. A visit to my father's grave was my idea. My mother turned away when I mentioned it after breakfast, but Grandpa Saeed, who decides almost everything, called upstairs to Uncle Sami, "Got any gas in your car today?"

My brother crawled back to bed minutes later, complained of a stomachache, but I know when he's lying. Issam carries with him everywhere, even to bed, a wooden sculpture that fits in the palm of his hand, a map of Palestine before the Nakba, the Catastrophe of 1948. Our father's a mystery, but we know he was not a martyr. Issam inherited his name, maybe nothing else. He feels no love for a man who made no great sacrifice for Palestine, or none we know of, and who left behind no legends, or even a story for his children to remember. But how is it possible to leave no trace? I say most stories are buried. I say dig them up and invite them to speak. I wonder if our buried stories are more true than the ones we tell over and over. Issam lacks poise. I doubt he could sit still and listen for words and write them down to make a book for the world. My heart grows strong and quiet when I wait for words. It's like walking the high-wire—earth below, sky above. Words come from shadow and from light.

Uncle Sami's taxi has no air-conditioner. We bump along till we reach Al-Quds Street, smooth pavement, only to get stalled in a long line of cars. No breeze, no shade trees. The air white as paper. Maybe Tali Glazman is swimming in the Mediterranean Sea.

Uncle Sami and my grandfather get out of the taxi to try and see what's ahead. My mother scolds me when I begin to unwrap my hijab. "You know better," she says. The sun beats down on the roof.

Sami, standing on his front bumper, says to my grandfather, "Nothing's moving. This means they've put up a checkpoint."

"Can you see it?"

"Everything's sort of blurry. All I see is cars."

So we wait in the sun. Soon there are vendors selling bottles of water, sugar drinks, tea, oranges. I wonder if they knew in advance the road would be closed.

Now Sami walks ahead to talk with some other drivers. I wish I had my grandpa's phone so I could record our wait and forward the video to Tali Glazman. A typical morning, I would say. We don't know whether a road will be open or closed. We are on our way—or *were* on our way—to the cemetery where my father is buried. We haven't visited him in a long time.

Sami comes back and says to my grandfather, "No luck today. We're stranded."

"How long have people been waiting?"

"Some have been here for hours."

"Has anyone gotten through?"

"Tourists. A few tourists."

"What's the hold-up? What happened?"

"Nothing happened."

"When's the last time they closed this road?"

"Maybe a month ago."

"The cemetery's just up ahead, less than a kilometer."

Uncle Sami grunts. "A kilometer? Are you serious?" He whirls his arms in a circle. "The whole world's far away."

❧

As soon as we are settled in our home, I send Tali a message: *Tried to visit my father's grave today. The Israelis closed the road to the cemetery and no Palestinians were allowed through. Any tourist from Europe or America could have visited my father's grave. He died when I was four.*

Tali writes, *I too have lost my father, but I can't say more. Please know I am sorry. I've told my mother about your wish to visit your father's grave, and she too is upset. Your father is your father and you only have one. I won't ask you to forgive. I know how hard it is to forgive.*

Really? How would she know? Her father probably died a natural death. Someday I will tell her that a stroke or a heart attack is a luxury. Tali lives in a safe city, a safe world. Who would she forgive?

❧

I make up stories about what I don't know. No one will tell me how my father died, so I fill his grave with stories. I'm still searching for one I believe.

If I'm angry, I sometimes tell myself he killed a family of settlers in Elon Moreh, butchered them, or blew them up with a bomb strapped to his body. Well, I know this isn't true because we would remember my father as a martyr if it were. There would be T-shirts and posters to honor his sacrifice, and his photograph would be pasted to the walls of our streets and alleys. He would be remembered long after my own bones are dust.

I call my second story "The Collaborator." What if my father worked for the Israelis, shared secrets, and his own people had no choice but to kill him? No, this can't be right either. My mother once told me with a nod that my father was brave. She does not lie. A nod from my mother is a nod I believe.

I call my third story "Suicide." Maybe my father feared he would never find a way to help his family, his people, so he took his own life. Maybe he cut his wrist or his throat, or put a bullet through his brain. Maybe my mother and grandfather won't speak of it because it brings too much sorrow. I wonder if my father felt no light in his body, no home anywhere, and no love for his children. No, this can't be true. I feel numb inside when I think of my own father harming himself. Besides, I know of no one in Balata, or *any* camp, who has committed suicide. We don't do that. We suffer, yes, but we don't give up. The more they try to bury us with suffering, the more we fight. Why don't the Israelis know us by now? Would they stop tormenting us if they knew they could not succeed?

After dark, Grandpa Saeed and I sit in our alley with tea. My father was his son, his only child, so he must know everything. He will not speak of death, but he might tell me a little about how my father lived. I already know he was an engineer, a skilled mechanic. According to my grandfather, he could fix anything, the engine of an old car, a radio, a TV, but what he loved most was to hike in the hills beyond Nablus, the hills no longer ours. Story #4: Maybe settlers killed him when he tried to pass near their homes.

I don't want Grandpa Saeed to parrot my mother and tell me my father was "an honorable man." I want to know facts, what he did and didn't do, what he lived for and died for. If he was brave, as my mother once claimed, where's the proof?

I say to my grandfather, "Can you tell me something I don't know?"

He looks past me and shrugs. "Tomorrow the road to the cemetery may be open."

"Or maybe not."

"Yes."

"I can't remember when I last visited my father's grave."

I hear Handala the Cat walking on our roof four stories above us. This cat has seen many things, but he has a cat tongue, not a human tongue. I understand when he's hungry or happy, or when he's hurt. I wish I understood more of his language, or the language of our mountains, Jarzim and Ebal. Our mountains were here from the beginning. Although Handala the Cat watches over our alley, he's younger than I am. Our mountains are older than all cats, all humans, all stories. But we would have to be wizards or jinn to hear what they say.

"Can you tell me something about my father that I don't already know?"

Grandpa Saeed faces the wall in front of us. "I'm not sure what you know or don't know, but he was better than me. In some ways, he was my opposite."

"How?"

"Your father was more intuitive, more intelligent, but he seldom disappeared in a book."

"You've already told me this."

"Yes, but there's no harm in adding that he seemed to draw as much knowledge from the air or light as I do from the page. Your father grew up in a home overflowing with books, but he never needed them as I did, as I *still* do." He winked. "He once told me I'd found my Homeland in my library, in the parchment of poetry and literature and science. I began to argue, but your father was halfway right. I cried when I was released from jail to find my library had been ransacked." He shook his head. "All that was left was your grandmother's cookbooks. If the Israelis had once tasted her mansaf or her pastries, they would've left nothing at all."

I hold my breath before I ask my grandfather if he cried when he lost his son.

"What do you think?"

"I don't know."

"Of course I cried. He was my son, he was beautiful. He and your mother brought you and Issam into this world. You are my life."

I'm afraid to ask if he cried more tears over his books or his son, my father. I say, "If my father were here tonight, if he were sitting between us, what would you tell him?"

He looks at me. "This question is easy."

"Really?"

"I would say thank you. I don't know what else anyone could say."

Tali writes to me on a Sunday morning: *I hope by now you've had a chance to visit the cemetery where your father is buried. I am sorry, Amal, that things can be so unfair.*

The last thing I want is for Tali to feel sorry for me. Pity, I hate pity. I would like to spit on it, then let the Israelis run over it with their bulldozers, their tanks. How can Tali know me, or any of us? My dream of performing with The Flying Kids of Tel Aviv seems absurd, for I can't even reach my father's grave a few kilometers away.

I write back to Tali several hours later. *My father was born in Nablus. My grandfather and all my ancestors are from Jaffa. The nickname of Nablus is Fire Mountain. This is what I can tell you about my family today.*

That night I dream I hold a rifle in my arms. Awake or asleep, I have never held a rifle, but this one finds a home in my arms, a killing machine as light as a broom.

I aim it at dark figures at the end of our alley. *Pop. Pop. Pop.* There would be no Israelis left if dreams were real.

My throat is sore, so I stay home from school. My mother makes me drink glass after glass of hot water with lemon juice and a pinch of sugar. Does she ever get sick from anger? No, I think her faith protects her. Many find refuge in rituals and prayers and the wish for a better life when this one is dust. Me? I want the dust to shout. I want it to say to our gravediggers, "Drop your shovels; rifles shine brighter than spades."

20

WATCH FOR ME

Women make things grow:
Sometimes like the crocus,
surprised by rain, emerging
fully grown from the belly of the earth…
Women make things cold
sharp and hard
like a legal argument thrust
before the threat of detention;
or warm
and gentle like
justice in a poem,
like the suggestion of
the image of freedom
as a warm bath and
a long soak, in an undemolished home.

I am done with sickness. I must stop being sick because I have so much work and so little time. This morning I've come to school with Maysa and other girls from the camp. Words that are true find a home in me: *Women make things grow…* The poet, Hanan Mikha'il 'Ashrawi, is from Nablus, but she's old now and lives somewhere else according to my teachers. Where? I ask, but no one knows.

As I walk home from school through a maze of alleys, I place one foot in front of the other as if the earth has unraveled in a single thread. Maysa laughs and some other girls, too, but I walk with as much care as Handala the Cat, or as Phillippe Petit when one misstep, one loose seam in his concentration, would mean death. I walk as if I'm three hundred meters over the world, and I feel something inside me that would be difficult to explain to my classmates, or even to Grandpa Saeed. I will not accept a Palestinian death. No, I refuse. I understand my brother's rage, the strength of it, but I am not a martyr-in-training. I am learning to walk on the narrowest surface. Call it concentration. Call it survival. Call it what I have that is still my own.

Back home, after my mother forces me to drink two cups of hot water with lemon and sugar, I lift weights with bricks, one in each hand. I also do squats, hundreds of them, holding the bricks level with my shoulders. I'm a skinny girl with muscles. Tel Aviv Tali? She's sixteen and still has baby fat. She outweighs me by many kilos, but I bet I could lift her over my head if that's what it took to save my mother's life, my grandfather's life, my brother's life, or any life in Palestine.

Tali sends me texts and emails and asks, *Where are you, Amal? Why won't you write to me?*

Days pass before I write back: *I'm busy practicing. I'm getting better every day.*

Keep practicing, she says. *I want you to perform with us in Tel Aviv in late July. There's still a chance you'll receive a permit.*

Really?

I don't understand the bureaucracy, the regulations, but I would do anything to make this happen.

Anything? I ask.

You know what I mean, says Tali. *I would help you if I could.*

Maybe she really is sorry I couldn't visit my father's grave. Neither of us has a father, but can we build a friendship from loss? We go silent for three days. I'm beginning to miss her, but then she sends me a passage from Anne Frank's *Diary*. I wonder if this is a test, a "friendship" hurdle. Tali, by way of introduction, says, *Anne died at age fifteen, but she knew more than most adults. After you read this excerpt, let me know what you think.*

> I don't believe the war is simply the work of politicians and capitalists. Oh no, the common man is every bit as guilty; otherwise, people and nations would have rebelled long ago. There's a destructive urge in people, the urge to rage, murder and kill. And until all of humanity, without exception, undergoes a metamorphosis, wars will continue to be waged, and everything that has been carefully built up, cultivated and grown will be cut down and destroyed, only to start all over again.

I send Tali a text: *I appreciate this passage, but maybe some people in Tel Aviv need it more than I do.*

Anne Frank wrote to everyone.

Maybe so.

Forget the maybe. Anne wrote because it was all she had left. Sometimes a girl becomes very honest when she's almost dead.

Almost dead? What would Tali know about that? She'll probably be alive a year from now, or in fifty years, sixty years, and she can visit her father's grave whenever she wishes. I can't say why I want her to like me, or even love me. Israelis know nothing of Palestinians, nor do they wish to know. Tali, I'd show you who I am if you could see through the sky to Nablus. I weigh forty-two kilos. I am almost a woman. I am Fire Mountain. I am the wire-walker who walks in alleys so narrow the walls hold their breath. Maybe all of us in Balata are almost dead. I can't stop anyone from dying. I will walk as far as I can. I am born to walk. I will walk on wires so thin they cannot be seen.

Watch for me in the sky.

21

ARTIST'S PERMIT

We don't text or email for almost two weeks, but then I receive a message that I still have a hard time believing.

The subject bar says: Please open this! Respond!!!

> Dear Amal,
>
> Dagan, who coaches the aerialists in The Flying Kids, told me three minutes ago your artist's permit has been approved. You can—if you wish—come to Tel Aviv from July 21st till August 1st. Practice sessions can be grueling, but you'll receive a stipend—530 shekels. The Flying Kids will perform in Ha'yarkon Park on July 31st before an audience of hundreds.
>
> Call me, call me, call me! I'm awake!
>
> Tali

I couldn't visit my father's grave, but in July I have permission to travel to Tel Aviv.

530 shekels? I wonder if this is real.

Tali: *Please come, Amal. Why are you hesitating? The Flying Kids are mostly nice. No one bites hard enough to leave marks.*

I keep quiet, except for my heart.

Tali: *Coach Dagan wants you to perform with us. I've shown him clips of what you can do, and he believes you're more talented than our aerialists.*

I work harder.

Tali: *I never thought this would happen. I knew our legal team would try their best, but I never thought you'd win.*

Me (after a pause): *Can Maysa come with me? Did she win too?*

Tali (her eyes closing, her breath loud in her nostrils): *I'm sorry.*

Me: *Why can't she come?*

Tali: *They tried for her too. There's a problem with...*

Me: *What?*

Tali: *Her father's in jail. He tried to stab someone.*

Me: *A soldier who was very arrogant.*

Tali: *Maybe that's true, but—*

Me: *It* is *true.*

Tali: *I'm sorry. I know your friend's innocent.*

Me: *And the soldier?*

Tali (covering her face with her hands, her hair fanning out as she shakes it): *Amal, let's start over. I want you to come to Tel Aviv and join our circus.*

Me: *Really?*

Tali: *Really and totally.* (She rakes her fingers through her hair.) *Don't make this more complicated than it is.*

I shut my eyes, but not my heart. I want to walk every rope and wire in Tel Aviv, however high, however dangerous, but I want Maysa to come with me. She's a circus girl, too, and I love her as I would love a sister. I'll ask my friend if I should go alone, or if *she* would go alone if by some magic she had received an artist's permit. I'll ask her before I ask my mother and grandfather if I can board a bus and try my luck crossing checkpoints and perhaps road blocks on my way to Tel Aviv.

Me: *I will need to ask Maysa if I should go.*

Tali: *But why—*

Me: *I've known her since I was born. She's a circus girl, too, and talented.*

Tali: *She's not your mother.*

Me: *That's not the point. If Maysa says yes, I'll ask my grandfather, then my mother.*

Tali: *Okay, but if Maysa's really your friend—*

Me: *She is, she is.*

Tali: *—she will have to say yes.*

I jump across the alley to Maysa's. We sit for a while around a table with her mother, a younger brother, and three cousins. We drink tea with a squeeze of lemon. I don't know where or how to begin until these words fly from me: "Maysa, is it okay if I go to Tel Aviv? I mean… tell the truth. Will you still be my friend if I go to the circus and you stay home?"

She looks at me, open-mouthed.

"I'm sorry," I say. "They won't give you permission because your father, he's—"

"He should be out by now."

"No, he shouldn't have been in jail to begin with. But is it okay if I go to Tel Aviv? I don't want to go alone, but there's no other way."

Her mother and younger brother and cousins look at me as if I'm all at once foreign. Maysa looks too, or stares, but then her face softens. "Amal," she says, "you're so good at what you do. No one works harder at circus, or ever could." She slides her chair toward mine and rests her head on my shoulder. "You must go," she says, "you *must.* I might not be your friend if you don't."

There are only two people who know me in my heart: my grandfather and Maysa al-Sa'ih.

My mother makes me dizzy with questions. "Where will you stay? What will you eat? Who is Tali Glazman? And what about her family? Who are these people? Are there boys in this circus? How can I let you go?"

I reach Tali on Messenger and find out I'll be staying with her and her mother. I'm so confused I don't know whether to feel happy or afraid. I assumed I'd be staying in a home with Palestinian girls.

"Tali," I whisper, "are you sure about this? Did you ask your mother for permission?"

"Yes," she says. "Yes."

But I can tell she too doesn't know whether to feel happy or afraid.

I promise my mother that she will not lose me forever, only twelve days, two-hundred-and-eighty-eight hours. Grandpa Saeed, who can say yes or no, no further discussion, opens this new door in my life, but not before giving me a lecture. "Neither your brother nor I can protect you in Tel Aviv; no uncles can protect you. No one in our family can watch over your shoulder to be sure you are safe."

I claim I will be safe at all hours.

He winks. "How can a high-wire walker say such a thing?"

It was easy.

"Any other father or grandfather in Balata would keep you at home, but I've seen how hard you've worked. Ropes, wires, acrobatics—they are half your world."

Maybe three-quarters.

"Circus will be your career if such a thing is possible for a Palestinian girl."

I will find out.

"How careful will you be?"

On or off the wire?

"Answer me, child, how careful?"

"I will stay away from boys."

"You're sure you can do that?"

"I have no interest in them now."

Part Two

A Refugee on Vacation

22

TEL AVIV

If I could block my memory, forget how I'm supposed to behave, I would jump in the sea and ride the highest wave. I am far from home on a gold beach where young women wear almost nothing. The sea is less naked for one sees its surface, not its fishes and flowers, its hidden treasures. Fully clothed, my hair covered by a scarf, I walk beside Tali Glazman, a shapely girl in a two-piece bathing suit. She smells sweet, like the oils and lotions she rubs on her skin. The only moisture on me is sweat.

Tali speaks of "a beach to the south where Palestinian women bathe in the sea in all their clothes." I can tell she's trying not to judge us, though I believe she's smart enough to know we're beyond her understanding. If I could be a magician for a day or even an hour, I would become invisible to everyone, Palestinian and Israeli. I want to swim naked and let only the sea know my beauty. The sun knows me, but the sea has never had a chance.

My mother would scream if she saw me shake off my shoes, roll up my slacks, and wade in the shallows. I think I'm the only Palestinian on this beach. A policeman watches me. Others watch as I jump and splash until I'm soaked through and a delicious coolness seeps through my skin to the hardness of muscle. I'm telling the sea, "Here I am, here I am. This is your chance to know me." I wish I could take the smell of the Mediterranean all the way home to Balata. I want Grandpa Saeed and my mother and twin brother and everyone crammed in our alleys to smell the sea before they die.

Dripping wet, my clothes like another layer of skin, I walk beside Tali. I've hardly spoken to her because most words that cross my mind seem to belong elsewhere. Nervous, awkward, I smile a lot, or try to. Tali's nervous, too, but she talks and talks, and maybe the words blowing out of her release some tension. Sometimes she's funny. She points to a palm tree and tells me it's a palm tree. I won't be surprised if she points to the horizon and says, *Look, Amal, the Mediterranean Sea.*

Her city has mountains of food, mountains of everything. Tali treats me to an iced drink with lemon and honey. Before I can finish, she says no one should visit Tel Aviv without trying the roasted spiced yam and sabich, so she orders "the jumbo size" from a sidewalk vendor. I eat, I drink, and wonder about everything. Sabich? Tali tells me it's a mix of things—fried aubergine, boiled egg, cabbage, potato, humus, spicy mango—wrapped in a pita. We sit in the shade of a palm while we eat. Delicious. I could get fat in Tali's city. I must be careful or I will not be light enough to walk the wires of Tel Aviv.

I swallow my questions along with the food. Why is Tali kind to me, or to any Palestinian? And why do most Israelis hate us? I know why most of us hate Israelis, but does *she* know? Tali is so far from our world that she may understand nothing. Occupation? What would she know of it from her city by the sea?

We walk past tall white buildings that disappear in the blue. Skyscrapers. I'd thought this was a dream word, but these towers scrape against the blue like wild stones that broke loose from the earth and couldn't decide where to stop. What wizards built this city? The architects, the engineers—are they still alive? Will they build a tower to heaven? I'm curious, but also ashamed. Hours before I left the Balata Camp, my brother and two boy cousins scavenged scraps of lumber to make a table for Aunt Salma. We have few materials for building our furniture, or for raising the walls of our homes, or for fighting a war. Yet a bird with strong wings could fly from my home to Tali's in less than an hour.

I will soon have my first practice with The Flying Kids of Tel Aviv, so Tali's trying to show me her city in forty minutes. We pass from the shadow of a skyscraper to sunlight, the entrance to a park. Eyes down, watching my feet, I ask Tali if any of the performers in the circus are from the West Bank.

"No," she says, "just you. The other Palestinians live here, they're Israeli citizens."

Third-class citizens? I want to ask.

But each word feels fragile as an egg.

23

PRACTICE

For the first time in my life I step inside a beautiful ring, a circus ring with stage lighting and rigging and a low red wall, with mats softer than my mother's bed, with trampolines, trapezes, and of course the high-wire where I shall live or die. I am alert. I didn't sleep well last night in Tali's home, Tali's bed, but my body is electric. Dagan, the coach for the aerialists, leads six of us through drills, breathing exercises, stretching and strengthening routines. Calisthenics. The aerialists are two Palestinian boys, one girl (me), plus three Israelis, two boys and a girl. They tell me their names that I'm too excited to remember. The boys are tall and thin, and everything about them is quick: their muscles, their eyes, the shine of their hair in overhead lights. The Israeli girl has pouty lips, black hair, a body as slender as mine. She is beautiful and so am I.

❧

They have circus paraphernalia I have never seen or dreamed of. I watch as the two tallest boys of The Flying Kids, one Palestinian and one Israeli, lift what looks like a log with a flat cushion on one side. The Israeli girl with pouty lips—am I jealous already?—jumps onto the cushion and begins to bounce as on a trampoline. I'm thinking, *This is easy, this is nothing*, but then the boys raise their arms and she flies, spins into a back flip and comes down on the log with her knees bent, her feet parallel, as if she has landed on a wire. She was less than perfect because the boys lurched forward to catch her. Timing. Placement. Three players make a team.

Dagan asks if I wish to try. "No need to do flips," he says. "Just get a feel for the cat-walk for starters." I say the phrase in my heart—*cat-walk*. Handala the Cat, who walks the roofs of Balata's alleys, could out-perform even Phillippe Petit or Nik Wallenda. The boys lower the walk so I can hop-step onto a rubbery surface. I find my balance, then spin on one foot to face one boy, then the other. The Palestinian (Tali told me he's a trapeze artist) has the shiniest smile I've ever seen. I hear my mother's voice: *Don't look at him, don't you dare*. A refugee on vacation, I dare a close-lipped smile.

Light has its way with my body. I cannot stop it any more than I can stop the air from reaching my lungs. Inhale. Exhale. Jump. Bounce. Fly. I'm a cat on a cat-walk, a narrow trampoline. Each jump takes me a bit closer to the red dome I wish I could touch. I want to fly higher than the Israeli girl before she catapulted into a back-flip. Dagan says, "Enough, make your landing." But I pretend not to hear.

Look. The cat-walk and me fly apart and return to each other as if we are magnets. I catch the bouncy walk-way with my feet and spring far up over the ring. I can feel the Palestinian boy smiling, the light of him going through me the way my breath goes through me. I don't have to come down exactly where I plan to come down because the boys can shift their positions to catch me. Only later will I wonder why I trust the Israeli boy who holds one end of the walkway. Dagan calls louder, "That's enough, that's enough!" So I leap into a backflip and the walkway is right here to meet my left foot, my right, one in front of the other, as on a rope or a wire.

Dagan lectures me on safety and insists that I listen to his instructions if I wish to perform with The Flying Kids in less than two weeks. *I'm sorry, I'm sorry, I'm sorry.* I glance across the ring at the Palestinian boy. Does he always smile? His face is another kind of sun.

Dagan gives a final admonition before dismissing me with a curt nod. He worries for my safety, but none of my people are safe or ever have been. I am certain of one thing: I'm less afraid than any Israeli in this circus, including my coach.

The high-wire, cinched tight, is easy to walk. There's almost no wobble, and it's wider across than the ropes and wires of Balata. I know this wire after two steps, so I close my eyes and walk in the dark. Dagan says, "Open your eyes, *keep* them open," and I do so after a silent breath, a dark step. Three meters over the mat, I try to believe I would be as beautiful and calm if I were half way up the sky, alone on a wire between white mountains, the skyscrapers of Tel Aviv.

24

MRS. GLAZMAN

Tali's not as rich as I thought she would be. Her home's nice enough, two bedrooms for two people in a three-story apartment building, but there are no elevators, no maids, no Palestinians to take care of her or her mother, and she has to do chores like dishes and sweeping and washing dirty clothes in a machine that shakes and rattles like Uncle Sami's taxi. How many uncles and aunts and cousins live on her block? Zero. I almost feel sorry for Tali when she tells me her closest relatives live three kilometers away.

Mrs. Glazman's quiet, but my mother would also be quiet if a Jewish guest appeared in her home. She welcomes me with food—oranges, nectarines, red cherries, cheese. How can I put these gifts in a belly almost as hard as bone? I say, "Thank you, Mrs. Glazman, thank you," and she waves a hand and says over and over, "Have some more, have some more. You're so *thin*." She tries to smile, but there's no light in her face, her eyes, or none I can see. She reminds me of my alley, a tunnel of shadows on the bluest day.

My second night here, Mrs. Glazman and Tali grill a large fish for us, toss in handfuls of roasted garlic and pine nuts, and splash it with fresh lemon. I see why Tali's a chubby girl. The meal includes couscous with butter, a salad of pickled cucumbers, diced tomatoes, green and black olives. The fish tastes so fresh I wonder if it swam in the sea hours earlier. I, too, came up from the sea in the late afternoon. Twice in two days, I've rolled up my slacks, waded out, and splashed myself till even my hijab was wet. Lucky Tali, in her swimsuit, dove into a wave, began to wrestle with it, and was swept ashore. I, too, would wrestle the sea if I knew I would be released.

Mrs. Glazman nibbles at her food. I doubt there's much fat under that yellow dress. Why yellow? Gray would make more sense, or a black robe. I feel in her a kind of strength, though, or grace, that reminds me of my mother and certain aunts and cousins. I wait for Mrs. Glazman to ask about my family. After a long silence, I tell her my mother is very nice but worries too much. If not for my grandfather, his permission, I would still be at home.

She leans toward me over the table. "I'm glad you're here. I wish…"

I wait, but she cannot continue.

Tali, her voice too loud, says, "She wishes you'd eat more, take a second serving."

I know this isn't all her mother wishes.

Tali says, "We have ice cream for dessert."

My circus friend is sometimes a clown. Grilled Fish. Couscous. A delicious salad. Ice cream for dessert. Mrs. Glazman wishes for something we can't set between us on a dish or a platter. What is it? I don't know, but maybe Tali does. *I wish…* Had I shut my eyes, I would have heard a girl speaking, not a mother. But Tali seems relieved that the voice went dead.

My friend, who eats enough for herself and her mother, fills her plate a second time. A wire-walker needs discipline. I let Tali give me more salad, which—like me—is mostly water and light. I feel a brightness in my throat, my chest, and a quickness in my calves. I'm curious about Mrs. Glazman. She'd wanted to make a wish, but couldn't complete her sentence. I wish…I wish… The whole world could be in her next words, or nothing at all.

I can't resist a small bowl of coconut-almond ice cream. Mrs. Glazman seems able to resist anything. She is beautiful in a quiet way. The words inside me, the chatter that almost gets out, drift away like clouds. I will not speak until I can say something that matters. My silence is respect.

Tali praises my performance at practice. "You're off to a good start," she says. "What do you think of Coach Dagan?"

I hesitate. "He's nice."

"He had a lot to do with getting you a permit. After I showed him one of the video feeds you sent me, he really wanted you on the team."

I wonder if I'll have enough time to feel I'm part of The Flying Kids, part of "the team." I've been in Tel Aviv for about forty hours. I arrived late because of delays at Qalandia, a checkpoint between Ramallah and Jerusalem. I remember long lines, almost falling asleep on my feet, and then a white room where two female Israeli soldiers ordered me to take off my clothes and place them on a bright counter that reflected everything like a mirror. I said, as if it might matter, "Did you notice I have an artist's permit?" The soldiers conversed in Hebrew. The taller one, who seemed to be in charge, made a mark on her clipboard. "There's been a lot of activity in Balata Camp," she said in English. "Everyone from Balata has to be searched."

I stood naked and sweaty and silent. Anger smells, as does fear, and one of the soldiers kept brushing her nose with a hanky. I remembered—and remember now—Tali reminding me in an email the morning before I left for Tel Aviv of an important rule of The Flying Kids: "We don't discuss politics at circus." At the checkpoint I obeyed instructions, became very quiet, and let one of the soldiers touch me. *No politics, just a body. Smell me, go ahead. I'm naked. I stink. Smell me.* I don't mind the silence now. In fact, I welcome it because it comes from Mrs. Glazman and me. We sit still. I have no shyness or fear, only a desire to know her secrets. *I wish…I wish…* I want to hear her unspoken words, or see what she sees when there are no words.

Tali says, "Don't let your ice cream melt," so I reach for my spoon.

25

ALLEYS

Tali lives in south Tel Aviv, in Florentine. She describes her neighborhood as “a bit rough,” but I don’t think so. After I help her with the dishes, she decides to give me a tour of her alleys. I’d shown her my alley through photographs, video feeds, and now she claims *her* alleys may have more graffiti than all of Nablus. Prove it, I’m thinking. Do you have anything to match our Handala, three meters tall? Do you have poems? And why would you paint olive trees and fig trees and gardens on walls when you have green parks on the shores of the sea?

We pass along a street where clothes hang from lines on narrow balconies. The night is warm. Sweat trickles down my chest, my back, but Tali, in shorts and T-shirt, smells like the fragrant oil she rubs on her skin. She saunters along in thin-soled sandals, swinging her arms in the casual way of one free to go anywhere. I shadow her as we enter the dim light of an alley. She leads me to a wall, a mural, where a snake crawls from the skull of a beetle taller and wider than the Handala of my alley. The artist or artists painted a sky of faces, misshapen, half human, half beast, and the last man on earth is a prisoner in a shirt and tie, an orange blindfold, his mouth open to laugh or yawn, maybe both, a man surrounded by numbers rather than iron bars.

10010101 10010101
10010101 1001 0101 10010101
10010101 10010101 10010101 10010101
10010101 10010101 1001 0101 10010101
10010101 10010101
10010101 1001 0101 10010101
10010101 10010101
10010101

I know something about prisons of numbers. Once, about a year ago, Israeli soldiers took my uncle Sami’s ID and told him to wait at the entrance of Balata Camp until they returned. He waited almost four hours before he went home for dinner. The authorities supposedly ran a check, found nothing, but they detained him the next morning and held him for seventy-two hours for refusing to obey instructions. If I were less polite, I might mention this to Tali. The Israeli-issued ID that I carry at all times is 753085164. I am here, in Tel Aviv, because of my talent for walking on wires. Uncle Sami can't go anywhere, so I am his eyes to the world. I am the eyes for my mother, my grandfather, my uncles and aunts, my cousins, and my friend Maysa. I'm wide awake for my brother, too, though he will not wish to hear about Tel Aviv.

Farther down the alley, Tali and I stop beside a door. There's no window or handle, only a drawing of a man with long, rectangular teeth, sharp quills for hair, a dazzle of lines for face, mouth, cheeks, ears. The artist must have drawn this in less than a minute. A crisscross of brush marks curve, collide, explode. Why is Tali showing me this? A portrait of a suicide bomber before he rises, a million small suns. I look again and see my brother. I will still see him if I close my eyes.

"Do you like this?"

She nods. "Sort of. It's like something in a scary movie."

"I wouldn't know."

"I like being scared if I know it's not real."

But to me it *is* real. Look. Some crazy artist drew a man's thoughts. I mean, he made these teeth from thoughts, long ones that can chomp through anything. He made thorns that poke like hair from a soft skull. Yes, soft. I don't know why. As if bones are cheese. He made these frazzled lines spin and spin into a face, the skin pulled tight and ready to burst. Flesh and thoughts—is there a difference? What's strange, though, is that it feels lonely. The whole door, I mean. No handle. No window. No way in. Why bother to knock? And the face, the hair, the teeth, the thoughts—how do they stay in this narrow frame? One spark and the alley will explode.

My brother would see me as a coward because I don't wish to die.

He would hate me because I want no one else to die.

I know hatred, too—it is why I sometimes fall from wires.

An aerialist…a martyr. How much distance between the two?

We are about to turn up the alley when we hear a ruckus behind us. I make out three silhouettes—men, I think, though I can't be sure. They jangle and sway, clumsy boxes of noise, more mechanical than human.

Tali says, "Street theater, boring." But I fall to my knees the moment I see fire.

Nothing explodes. Nothing burns other than a stream of air. The figure in front waggles a hand, waves. He wears a mask ten times the size of a human face, metallic, almost featureless, with a spout that shoots a stream of fire every few seconds. Behind him, in shadows, someone holds a canister, propane, I think—I don't know what else could blow fire from a metal tube. Tali says, "Bad theater," then walks away from the performance. Maybe she expects me to follow her, but I won't, I can't. Not yet.

The Mask and the Fire-keeper pass by, connected by a tube. The third figure, in a white suit and a blue tie, carries an oversized computer strapped to his shoulders. Machine sounds pour out, gnashing and grinding, and there are photographs in black and white. The first one I recognize is the Qalandia checkpoint. Long lines of Palestinians appear frozen in a maze of metal. I see other checkpoints, road blocks, a cemetery, an Israeli guard post on a hill overlooking a mosque and minaret. The screen flickers, blinks off, before a film begins. A tank bounces over an embankment, uproots a tree, and flattens the walls of a shed. The screen goes blank, black. No machine sounds now, only the strain of someone small trying to breathe. I think the show's over, but then I hear rifle fire, echoes. A man shouting in Hebrew. Dim light on the screen, dawn or dusk. This lump near a dirt road could be a woman, a child, or an animal. I smell something soft, sour, newly dead. There are no corpses here, but I know this smell.

Tali calls my name. She calls again and pronounces my name correctly.

"I'm going home," she says. "*Home.*"

She calls once more. "Amal?"

Tali sometimes has a big voice, but not now. She becomes as quiet as the person or animal trying to breathe before the rifles roared. *Amal?* Tonight I hear small sounds best, so I turn to my friend, catch up with her, and wait for something to explode.

26

MACHINE ARTISTS

Tali won't tell me anything until we lie in bed late at night and neither of us can sleep. The three figures we saw in a Florentine alley are veterans of the Israel Defense Forces. At first I don't believe her. "No, it's true," she says. "They put on these shows, and sometimes they land in jail because they don't have permits. They don't even *apply* for permits. They often disappear before the police arrive."

I turn on my side to face her. "I've never heard of Israeli soldiers being arrested."

"*Former* soldiers," says Tali. "They can pop up anywhere, usually for a minute or two. But I hadn't seen them in more than a month."

I have to ask around twenty questions to find out anything else. Tali describes these veterans—maybe thirty in all—as members of Machine, an art and theater enclave whose mission, if they have one, is to shock and provoke. "Bad theater," she whispers. "They stage their shows in alleys and side streets, or in warehouses in Florentine and Jaffa. They don't advertise. Some people know when and where the shows will happen, but most of us don't. The warehouse shows sometimes spin out of control."

I ask for an example.

"There was a fire once. I think it was in Jaffa."

"Were you there?"

"No, I just heard about it."

"From someone who was *there*?"

I can feel her trying to see in the dark. "I can't remember who told me. It doesn't matter."

"Okay."

"Robots and video and conflagrations. It's violent and stupid. You want to see Israel's avant-garde theater? Well, you just did. We were very unlucky because the machine artists haven't been in Florentine for over a month."

I gnaw my lower lip. "Machine artists?"

"That's what they call themselves."

I roll over on my back. I am small, a shiver of light, but words are smaller and I make room for them all—the spoken, the unspoken, the words under the words. I'm afraid to lose the only Israeli friend I may ever have. Is Tali afraid to lose me? The right words at the wrong time…

Tali, I've never heard you say occupation, but you can say Auschwitz. Maybe you will never whisper a true word about Nablus, Jenin, East Jerusalem, Hebron, Gaza, or the Golan Heights. No, the occupation is not the Holocaust, I know this. But you're in a soft bed and will stay in a soft bed as long as you live. I'm a guest, a refugee on vacation. I will be a refugee all my life.

"What does your mother think of it?"

"Of what?"

"You know, the shows. The soldiers, what they're doing."

"*Ex*-soldiers."

"All right, ex-soldiers. What does she think of them?"

"My mother doesn't go out much."

"Why?"

"She'd rather stay inside."

I believe this. I remember her silences at dinner, her yellow dress that failed to brighten her face, her failed attempt to tell us something. *I wish…* Maybe Mrs. Glazman wishes she felt less strange in the presence of a Palestinian girl. No, she told me she was glad I'm here and I know she meant it. Maybe she wishes everyone had a home, a *real* home. Maybe she stopped because she was afraid she would sound naïve. Maybe she wishes she could wish for something that could come true before we die.

"Amal, you're here for circus. There's no other reason."

I wink in the dark. "I have an artist's permit."

"We'll perform in Ha'yarkon Park on July 31st. This will be our biggest event of the year."

I hold still.

"There will be hundreds of people," she says, "maybe a thousand."

I hope the machine artists come.

"Amal?"

"What?"

She rubs my hand. "Let's remember why you're here."

We hold hands a little while. Tali's sweating, me too, but I miss her when she pulls her hand away and we are each alone in a bed twice as wide as the one me and my mother share.

27

CIRCUS

Let them measure me. Three meters tall, maybe four, I stand on the shoulders of boys, one Israeli and one Palestinian, as Coach Dagan gives instructions. "Walk," he says to the boys, "as if you are carrying water. Slower, slower... Stop at the center of the ring."

Now my coach tells me to shift my weight, balance on one foot, lift my other foot free, and raise it toward the ceiling.

"What?"

He repeats the instructions.

"I'm not sure—"

"They'll catch you if you fall."

Boys will catch me. *Boys.* The Israeli on my right, the Palestinian on my left. My mother... I must not think of her. She would prefer that I walk alone on a wire one thousand meters over the earth.

If I had iron legs, anchors, I would shift my weight to the Israeli side. I am a feather, a whisper of light. A lost wing that flew free from a bird. The Palestinian boy, shiny and dark, lifts his face to smile, and if I could speak my mind, if this were proper, I would tell him what I think of him. *Your teeth are crooked, one is cracked, but you're the prettiest boy in the circus. You're shinier than sunlight, yes you are.* I would nod a few times. *I'm shiny, too, and dark. You make my nerves itch. Do I do anything for you?*

My legs wobble only a little. I lift free of the Israeli shoulder, put my weight on the Palestinian, and now my left foot rests in a basket of bones. The shiny boy—wish I knew his name—has wrapped a hand around my ankle so I'm like a tree with its taproot in the earth. Coach Dagan calls to me, "All right, you've got the idea. Now slowly raise your right leg straight over your head as if you're a dancer, a ballerina in a circus." A ballerina? I take a long breath to find the quiet inside me, and then I lift my right leg and stretch up, up, up, my toes pointed toward the trapezes and the high-wires and the red lights beneath the roof.

The boy who holds me in a basket of bones—will he ever stop smiling? He must believe the world, or at least the circus, is a funny place, but he has a long purple scar along the left side of his jaw. I could stand here all day, one foot in the earth of him, one in the sky of the arena, but Coach Dagan tells me the way to end this drill is to swing my right leg down, cross my arms over my chest, lean back, and let myself fall into the arms of the boys.

I try to smile.

"They'll catch you," he promises. "They've done this many times."

I need to stand still a small while before I'm calm enough to lean back and give myself away. Shoulders are small baskets. Arms are big baskets, but mostly it's the shiny boy who catches me. Does he know I tilted his way as I fell? One moment, half a heartbeat—that's all I can give him before I shiver a smile and slip away.

I have never learned the trapeze. I can only watch as the star aerialists of The Flying Kids, Miki and the shiny boy, swing and glide over a white net. They are kids and they are birds. I hear the rush of wind, of bodies, as they fly toward each other, and now she lets go, trusts him to catch her, and he does, his long arms dangling, his hands snatching her from the air. Dagan hollers instructions and I hear his name—Mazin. Give me a moment to quit my surprise. The name means rain and cloud, raincloud. But I have seen both turn shiny in a flash of light.

Dagan wants me to do nothing fancy on the wire, just get the feel of it. I'm less than four meters over the net. Calliope music plays in the background. One breath, one step. Balance will come easily if I quicken the pace, two or three steps for each breath, so I challenge myself, walk slower and slower, till I almost stand still. Dagan claims I have "natural ability." No, I'm thinking, I've worked for this. You have no idea how I've worked.

During a break, I step into a courtyard and watch Tali juggle eight torches, then exchange torches with another juggler, a Palestinian boy. They drop some, then relight them and keep going. The torches streak like comets beneath a row of palms. Fire and tree shade. The sun overhead. I can smell my sweat. I can smell trees. A gardener must have come by this morning. I smell water in the earth. I smell roots.

I've seldom gone up and talked to a boy other than my brother and little cousins. Mazin, Raincloud, might think I'm bad, but I only have a few days with this circus before I return home.

"Do you know my name?"

I whisper, but I'm sure he hears me. We're standing at the edge of the ring and watching an Israeli girl, a contortionist, twist and twirl her limbs as if she has no bones, no hinges. I've forgotten *her* name, but in my mind I call her Ms. Octopus. I am jealous for Maysa. This girl is far more advanced than my best friend in the world.

I wait in vain for the shiny boy to remember my name.

"I know yours." I shrug. "Mazin."

"Yes."

"My name is Amal."

I dare to look straight at him. "Why are you always smiling?"

He chews his lower lip, his smile crooked. "It's just how I am."

"Always?"

"No, the smile sometimes goes away."

"When?"

He glances at the contortionist. "Nobody can smile day and night."

Mazin catches me glancing at the scar along his jaw.

"That's old," he says. "More than three years ago."

"What happened?"

"I was in detention for several months. I didn't think I'd ever get out."

Mousa, a Palestinian coach, Dagan's assistant, shakes a finger at us. No politics at circus. All we can discuss is technique, style, and—in a general way—trust. Miki has to trust that Mazin will catch her as she flies through the air. Jugglers sometimes practice solo, but they also share their skills as a duo, a trio, and—I saw it once—a quartet. Our coaches want us to focus on our art, forget politics, and I believe this is easier for Israelis. One reason I love the wire is that I walk alone in what my grandfather calls "the mind of the body." Perfect concentration is effortless, but this only happens through work. I learned my art by walking on wobbly wires in Balata. In Tel Aviv I have well-cinched wires and a net.

28

THE SUN AND THE SEA, MAZIN AND ME

After practice, I walk along the shore with Tali, then skip ahead when she turns to talk with Miki and other Israelis. I want to catch up with Mazin, match his stride, but he is so tall that I would need to take three steps to his one, or else leap like a comic frog.

I call his name in a quiet voice. To turn this boy around, the sounds in my mouth must reach his ears, yet I can't go near him. This is more difficult than walking the high-wire. I say, "Mazin, Mazin, *Ma*zin," till he slows his stride and turns. I mustn't give him the wrong idea. He waits for me, smiling, but I stop before I'm close enough to touch.

I am blunt when I'm nervous. I can't do small-talk, especially with a boy.

"Do you know of a group called Machine?"

He gives me a look.

"Well, *do* you?"

He glances toward the sea as if it might help him remember.

I say, "Tali can't stand this group. She thinks they're violent and stupid."

He grins.

"Are they?"

He scratches the scar along his jaw. "Why ask me?"

A heartbeat later he tells me he's seen the group perform in alleys in Florentine and Jaffa. "They wander around and make noise," he says. "Most people run the other way."

"I didn't."

"Maybe you should've."

"Why?"

"It's just chaos. Machinery and fire and…" He looks past me. "It's stuff you already know."

He stays quiet when I ask about Machine's warehouse shows.

"I want to see one," I add, "before I return to Nablus."

"Good luck."

"Do you know anyone in the group? Anyone's name?"

He blinks his eyes as if to clear them.

"Jonathan," he says. "Everyone knows Jonathan, or knows of him."

"What do *you* know?"

"Just the name. He's sort of famous."

"Why's that?"

"Israelis hate him, all but a few."

"What about Palestinians?"

He giggles.

"Well?"

"I guess most of us like him, but he's sort of a clown."

This pleases me somehow. If Jonathan's "sort of a clown," maybe he doesn't hate anyone. If he's like my grandpa, if his mind is strong enough to turn hatred into something else, he is already my friend. By chance, Tali and I saw three machine artists in a Florentine alley. These men know something of my world. Most surprising, they proved to me that at least three Israelis want the occupation to end. Maybe they know it won't end, it can't end, unless millions of Israelis see it and hear it with their own eyes and ears. These former soldiers are bringing the occupation home.

Mazin can't tell me much. He knows Jonathan lives in a warehouse, lives among the machines that he and other ex-soldiers make, but he can't say where. "Maybe by the bus station," he says, "or some alley in Jaffa." He can't even guess where and when Machine will put on their next warehouse show. He tells me Jonathan and his "machine friends" sometimes hang out at a Florentine café.

"What's the name of the café?"

He grunts. "I don't know."

"What street is it on, or in what alley?"

He scratches his scar. "It's both a café and a bar. I'm not sure it has a name, or even a sign."

"How close to the sea?"

"I don't know."

I stand tall, or as tall as I can. "Well, what *do* you know? What's my name?"

His quick laughter sends a shiver through my body.

"Well?"

He looks beyond me to the sea.

"Amal," he whispers. "Your name is Amal."

29

HOTEL GLAZMAN

Tali's mother told me I can call her Rebecca. I'd rather call her Mrs. Glazman because she seems older than my aunts and I need to show respect. She walks hunched over, her eyes downcast, as if she has nothing better to look at than stones, rubble. Her windows open to light. Has she forgotten the sea is less than a kilometer from her home?

I've seen one photograph of Tali's father. The bright kitchen and living room are one open space, and the photograph of him holding baby Tali in his arms is on a table beside a blue sofa. He had wavy black hair, dark eyes, a relaxed smile. I've never seen Mrs. Glazman glance at the photograph. She and my mother will always have this in common—no husband—and Tali and I will have no father. My mother lives in fear that something bad can happen at any moment, but Mrs. Glazman is somehow sadder. I, too, would be sad if I married a beautiful boy and gave him a baby and then he died. Would it hurt too much to look at his picture? Would I forget the sea?

Mrs. Glazman enjoys giving us food. Maybe this is her sole pleasure, these feasts that leave bulges in our stomachs. Tonight we have homemade pitas, still warm, to go with chickpeas, tahini, pickled vegetables, and roasted yams. I eat more than talk not only because the food is delicious but because I feel awkward, tense. My voice, when it comes, squeaks like a cricket. Mrs. Glazman has the darkest smile.

Tonight they won't let me help clear the table or wash the dishes. Tali seems arrogant at times, but now she and her mother bend over the kitchen sink as if they are servants. I watch them out the corner of my eye. There's some sadness in their silence, but I can feel their love for each other. Sometimes my mother and me keep quiet at night. She rests her worries and loves me in silence. She, too, is dark, but no one feels darker than Mrs. Glazman. The yellow blouse, white slacks—they're just so many threads. I see shadows within shadows, pretty somehow.

Tali knows Palestinian girls from circus, but I doubt any of them have stayed in her home overnight, or that she has stayed with them. Why am I here? Maybe the Palestinian girls' homes are too crowded for a guest, or maybe they have brothers and worried mothers, so here I am at Hotel Glazman. They are especially kind tonight, mother and daughter, but I'm happiest when I'm on the wire, alone, where there are no servants or masters. Grandpa Saeed once urged me to see my work as basic math: *The whole world is under the wire. Sky above, earth below. Walk the line between the two.* People who praise my talent don't know where talent comes from. I love the earth, the sky, the wire between them, and they love me.

After the dishes are done and Mrs. Glazman retreats to her bedroom, I ask Tali if she'd like to show me more of Florentine, more graffiti.

"No, I don't feel like going out tonight. I've already shown you the best of the street art."

I glance at the photograph of her and her father. "I'd like to see more."

"It's mostly repetitive, the same artists."

"Circus is repetitive too. Especially at practice."

Tali says, "Maybe another night."

I can't tell her I want to wander the alleys of Florentine till I find Jonathan and other machine artists in a nameless café that is also a bar. How will I recognize them? I don't know, but I have a hunch they sit in back.

"You want to watch a movie?"

If I tell the truth, *No*, she might see me as a difficult guest. "All right."

"We'll need to keep the volume low. My mother's real fussy about noise."

So we watch an American movie about gangsters and detectives and fast cars and daredevil women who reveal half their breasts every time they lean over a bar or a table. In the final scene, the most handsome gangster, the anti-hero, is shot around twelve times, but there's no blood, only a bunch of holes through his suit jacket and shirt. He didn't smile for two hours, but now that he's almost dead he curls on his side in a junkyard for cars and smiles at the sun going down over a shack. We hear him breathing, little puffs of air, and then we hear the snarls and barks of an unchained dog. Big and black, this dog bares its teeth but shuts up long enough for the anti-hero to ask, "What's your name, boy?" This dog may kill the gangster before the bullets do. Maybe he smiles because nothing can hurt him anymore, or else nothing ever could.

Tali has kept the volume low, but not low enough. Mrs. Glazman comes out of her bedroom in a robe.

"Please," she says, "can't you find something better for your friend? Is that the only movie you can watch?"

Tali tells her it's over, almost over, and a moment later it is. The anti-hero keeps smiling as the credits roll down the screen.

Tali tells me she's sorry after her mother goes back to her room.

She should tell her mother she's sorry.

"I don't know why I like gangster movies, American movies."

I don't know either.

"My mother doesn't like any movies."

I could say the same about my mother.

"Did you like it?"

I shrug. "It's okay."

"I've seen it three times."

30

NIGHT FIVE AT HOTEL GLAZMAN

After dinner, Tali and I go out for a walk. My steps are careful, as if streets and alleys are wires, and my friend seems skittish. Her eyes are quick. Maybe she's afraid we'll see what I want everyone to see—street theater, machine art in an alley, because how else can Israelis catch a glimpse of where I live? We pass bars, cafes, a restaurant where a chef grills fish near the walkway. Tali and I round a corner and smell where fish live—the sea.

Before I return to Balata, maybe leave Israel forever, I want at least one more surprise. Machine artists, former soldiers, care enough about people like me that they stage performances, burst into alleys, make noise, flash images, as if to announce—*This is what's happening over the Green Line. Like it or not, have a look.* Tali calls it "avant-garde theater… robots and video and conflagrations." I call it a miracle. I saw Palestine from an alley in Florentine.

I don't want Tali to know my world so she can suffer. No, I want to ease the suffering, even end it, and live long enough to invite her and Mrs. Glazman to my home when my family *has* a home. Tali has seen my alley in Balata through photographs and film. The machine artists could show her more of Palestine if she dared to look.

I like her anyway, this circus girl, and she likes me. To walk with her in Florentine is something of a dream, except that everything becomes clearer on waking. I am *here*. My whole wire-walking body has arrived. A quiet joy spreads over me in the space of a breath.

I spot a café that serves desserts. The Glazmans offer me delicious food every night, so I say to Tali, "Can I treat you to ice cream or something?" I've hardly spent a shekel of the stipend The Flying Kids paid me because Tali and her mother take care of me. I begin to lead my friend to a sidewalk table, but she turns away and keeps walking. "Not here," she says, "too many people. Maybe somewhere else."

But all the cafes are crowded. Tali says she's not hungry anyway and would rather walk to the sea, then go home and watch a movie. "Okay," I say, "sure," but I'm confused. I've never seen her unnerved, almost panicky. We walk fast. Her eyes jump one way, then another. We slow down when we reach the Promenade, a wide path beside the sea.

"Tali, is…is something wrong?"

She waves a hand. "I'm fine."

"You sure?"

"I don't like crowded cafes. Some nights I don't even like empty cafes. *Period.*"

I nod, as if I understand.

"I buy food from street vendors. I almost never go to cafes."

I have questions, but maybe it's best I keep them to myself. We cross the Promenade and sit on the seawall. I don't know what to do for her, so I gesture to the horizon where the sun vanished minutes earlier and left behind a trail of pink ribbons over the water. Tali nods, almost smiles, but seems distracted. "You're nice," she says, and I don't know what to reply except, "You, too." I feel dumb because I can't see into her. Only the light over the water brings comfort now.

She points to a ship sailing out to sea, inky-colored, except for green, red, and white navigation lights. "Do you think the deckhands will hear us if we call to them?"

The ship will soon vanish over the horizon. "Tali, we would need to be giants."

"No, if we call together, strain our lungs, they might hear us."

"I don't—"

"It doesn't matter if we succeed. We have to try."

So she calls out, her voice strange, weak. "Amal," she says, "help me," so I call, too, and now a dozen or more shorebirds fly away. Tali lurches to her feet and grabs my hand. "Come on," she says. "We can shout louder if we're standing." So I join her, hand in hand, and we teeter on the seawall and call to the deckhands aboard the ship drifting away from us. The light from a lamp post shines on one side of Tali's face, her cheek long, her mouth stretched wide. We shout for maybe a minute, catch our breaths, and Tali says, "Not enough, not even close. Turn up the volume!" So we do. A juggler, a wire-walker, a circus of noise. We squeeze each other's hand as we yelp, yowl, bray, bawl—for I don't know what—but maybe we need this more than ice cream. I doubt the deckhands hear us, but people walking on the beach pause and gape and wonder. We must sound like girls in trouble because pretty soon a man hurries over and starts climbing the stairs that rise from the beach to the seawall. We calm down enough to hear him ask if we need help.

Tali, breathing hard, says, "No, but it's kind of you to ask."

He rises one step closer. "You sure you're okay here?"

"Yes. My friend and I…we're studying to be opera singers."

He tilts his head.

"Don't worry about us," says Tali. "Sometimes we come here in the evening to see if our lungs are powerful enough to reach the sailing ships."

The man, middle-aged, paunchy, sighs, mumbles, and turns toward the beach. Tali waves to his backside. I'm still holding her other hand.

On the way back to her home, I quiz Tali and learn only a little.

"Some nights are perfect for screaming," she says. "Some are not."

"And why tonight?"

She holds up her hands. "The night never needs to explain itself."

"Do you do this often? I mean, call to a ship sailing away? Or scream at the sky, the sea?"

She shrugs. "I wouldn't call it a habit."

"Does it help?"

"Help with what?"

"I don't know."

"All it does is stop me from trying to figure things out."

I know better than to ask, *Figure what out?* She yelped and yowled to empty her mind. Maybe calling to the sky and the sea is old medicine. Tali swings her arms in a relaxed way all the way home.

31

NIGHT NINE AT HOTEL GLAZMAN

In Tali's bed, I lie still and listen to her snore. I count the hours—fifty-one before I return to Balata. I don't want to sleep. I want to use every moment to see everything I can see. A guest, a refugee, I am almost gone and might never return.

I stare at the ceiling. Every night this week, Tali and I walked to the ocean, decided not to scream at ships or sailboats (the mood needs to be right), then returned to her home for ice cream and a movie. Last night we watched an adventure film, *Robinson Crusoe*. Tonight we watched gangsters running wild in Chicago. I think Tali's hooked on gangsters. Chase scenes, shootouts, tough guys in three-piece suits, women with painted lips, large breasts. I kept watching, only because the lead actor was more beautiful than his three Cadillacs. In the end, the cops cornered him in an alley, shot him dead, but there was no blood, no guts spilling out, and his hair—even his necktie—stayed in place. A handsome corpse, death without sorrow. Tali seemed less anxious after the film.

I roll onto my side. Thanks to Mazin, I know the name of a "sort of famous" machine artist—Jonathan. Maybe he was among the three artists who surprised Tali and me in a Florentine alley. I can see them still, as I calm my mind and concentrate. The first performer wears a mask with a spout that blows streams of fire. The second, faceless (or with no face I remember), grips a canister, propane, I think, and the last one—in a white suit, a blue tie—shoulders a widescreen computer. At first the screen is dark, but I hear machines gnashing and grinding, metal to metal, a factory gone berserk, no one in charge. The images come in fragments: photographs in black and white, a slide-show, and video, perhaps thirty seconds, a window to my world. A tank bumps over an embankment, uproots a tree, and flattens the walls of a shed. A body lies near a dirt road at dawn or dusk. Has Tali ever smelled someone dead? No, I don't think so. But maybe the machine artists have.

Mazin told me they hang out in a no-name café that is also a bar.

How large is Florentine? How many streets and alleys will I walk before I return to the Balata Camp? How many hours before dawn?

I ease out of bed. I know where Tali keeps the one thing I need—house keys on her nightstand. My friend is a sound sleeper. I doubt she's ever heard tanks at night, or stun grenades (what my grandpa calls "alarm clocks for Palestine"), or fighter jets swooping over roofs and alleys. Mrs. Glazman? She may wake to small sounds, so I must be careful. Only a ghost can match the quiet of a wire-walker. I barely hear the whisper of my feet.

❧

I walk down a street in Florentine. Others are about. Bars and cafes are open. Only I walk alone, though not for long.

My mother could be on the farthest side of the earth and still reach me, a voice in my head: *Who do you think you are? And where are you going at this hour? Have you no decency? Where's your hijab?* I love her almost as much as I love my grandpa, but I wish to be free of her for a minute, an hour, a night. Who do I think I am? Well, maybe I'm the only girl from Balata walking where she wishes to walk. Watch me. I may turn up this alley, or this, or this. I'm looking for machine artists. Okay, my hair's uncovered, long and black, pretty as night, but I'm good inside. Decent? I'm better than decent. I forgot my hijab only because I was in a rush to leave.

I edge up to the entrance of a café that is also a bar. *Any machine artists in here?* I'm too shy to ask.

A taxi driver pulls up in front of a tattoo parlor. The chatter on his radio is in Arabic. I skip across the street, the bar and café behind me. The driver thinks I'm his next customer, so he hops out to open the back door of his taxi. I talk fast in Arabic, not at all shy now. He winks down on me and I wish he were less amused.

Machine artists. He knows of them, but he won't say if he knows Jonathan. He lights a cigarette. "Does your father know you're on the streets tonight? And your grandfather—does he know? And what about your brothers, your uncles? Your mother? And can't you at least cover your hair?"

"Sir, I've done nothing wrong."

"You haven't answered my questions."

"Okay, my family doesn't know where I am. My family lives in a camp."

He tilts his head.

"It's true," I say. "But my grandfather would help me if he could. The men I'm looking for…I don't know their faces. They were once soldiers. Now they make machines."

He half smiles as he puffs on his cigarette. I have my stipend, more shekels than I've ever seen. What might he tell me for five shekels, or fifty? Unlike Uncle Sami, this taxi driver doesn't appear hungry. He's got some meat on his belly, a comfortable pouch.

He asks my age.

I lie a little. "Eighteen."

"You have no business wandering these streets at night."

I'm supposed to hush, let him scold me, but I tell this man what he needs to know. I come from Fire Mountain, Nablus, the Balata Camp. I'm a wire-walker in a professional circus, The Flying Kids of Tel Aviv. He asks again about my grandfather, my father, my mother, my brothers, and I tell him my father is dead and I have only my mother, my grandpa, my twin brother, and a thousand cousins. "Sayyid," I say, "I'm telling you the truth. My grandpa gave me permission to come here and he would help me tonight if he could."

I turn away and begin to walk toward an alley. Just when I think the taxi driver is useless, he calls to me, "Wrong way, try the next alley. Third door on the left."

I look over my shoulder and watch him draw hard on his cigarette, the ember glowing. Allah yerda alek. God bless you, sayyid, and may He grant you a long life. Shukran, a mere thank you, is never enough for a Palestinian when the gratitude is genuine. I don't really know how to pray, but I will do my best for this taxi driver in Florentine.

32

APARTMENT NUMBER 3

Skeletons on a narrow door, barbed wire binding their ribs. The artist scrawled an X on one of the foreheads; the other is vacant bone. Two bicycles—real ones, not swirls of paint—lean against a wall.

Someone is home because I hear voices, conversation, though I can't make out the words. What will I say if the door opens? *My name is Amal. You don't know me, but I come as a friend.*

I wonder if I can say this, or if I should. *I come as a friend.* What can this mean in Israel? The skeletons are layers of paint, and the barbed wire won't cut. No one in Balata would paint such a thing on the door to his home. Barbed wire, death, torture…Israelis might see this as art.

I knock on the X till the door opens. A woman in shorts, tall and pretty, leans away from me, then forward, and cranes her neck for a closer look. A bird has a keen eye as it waits for a worm to rise from the earth. Maybe I should be afraid, but I'm not. I stand as tall as I can and tell her my name.

Up goes her brow. "And I know you?"

"Not yet."

She glances down the alley. "Are you lost or something? You need help?"

I see a man behind her in an alcove.

"I'm not lost, but maybe you can help me. I'm looking for a former soldier named Jonathan."

Her head tilts till her ear almost touches her shoulder. "Jonathan? You know him?"

"Not yet."

Her lips twitch. "Who are you?"

"I already told you my name is Amal."

She takes a loud breath and calls over her shoulder. "David, we have a guest."

He's bent over a table, tinkering with something. "Wait a second."

"All I know is her name."

So now this man, chubby and squat, comes to the door. He squints as if his eyes are weak, or as if I'm made of fog and he needs to reshape me, compress me, into something solid. He parrots one of the questions the woman asked: "Are you lost?"

Maybe I am, but I refuse to admit it.

"Should I call a taxi?"

"No, sir."

"Please don't call me sir."

"I'm sorry."

"And skip the apology. Just tell us why you're here."

My mother makes a basket of her arms when she's searching for words. I open mine, but for a little while nothing falls in. Confused or curious, they lean toward me—huge and strange and almost near enough to touch. My left foot rises a few centimeters as if I'm about to step forward on a wire.

"I am…Balata. I am from Balata Refugee Camp."

David grunts. "Balata?"

"Yes."

"Well, okay, that tells us something. But why are you here?"

I could ask the same question, but I hold back. "Are you a former soldier?"

He hesitates. "Yes."

"My friend Tali told me about former soldiers who started a group called Machine. They put on performances in alleys or warehouses. They never advertise or post schedules. By chance, I saw one of their shows in Florentine."

His eyes narrow. "Maybe you got lucky and maybe not."

"I saw a man in a mask blow fire through a spout, a sort of nose. And I saw—on a computer screen—glimpses of where I'm from."

"Balata?"

"Yes, and the Qalandia checkpoint that I passed through nine days ago. And a tank rolling over a tree…a body near a dirt road."

"I'm sorry if—"

"None of this was new to me. I was only surprised because I saw Palestine from here."

I look past them, but I feel their eyes on me. When I'm on a wire, walking, I don't see my audience, or need to. I have no more words in my basket, but I have poise. It is their turn to search for words.

I hear David swallow. "How did you find us? Who sent you?"

"A taxi driver."

"That would be Raja, I suppose. Or Ahmad."

"He didn't tell me his name."

"You're looking for Jonathan but he doesn't live here."

"Yes, but sometimes he comes to a café in Florentine that is also a bar. A friend told me he lives in a warehouse."

"And who is this friend?"

I begin to smile. "His name is Mazin. He's in a circus and so am I."

They don't know what to do with me, so they let me in. David gets me a glass of pomegranate juice from the fridge. It is good and cold, but I'm surprised the woman didn't serve me. I perch on a stool and look around the studio. A dismantled TV clutters a work table in the alcove. The shelves along the back wall contain construction supplies: screws, bolts, gears and pulleys, computer parts, spools of wire, liters of oil. I ask David if he sometimes helps Jonathan make machines.

He shrugs. "You seem sort of fixated on Jonathan."

"I'm just curious. Do you work together sometimes?"

"Yes, but let me ask *you* a few questions. Are you really from Balata?"

"I've lived there all my life."

"And somehow you got permission to visit Israel?"

"I have an artist's permit to stay in Tel Aviv for twelve days."

"You're an artist?"

"Yes, but not a painter or sculptor or anything. I'm an aerialist."

He hunches on a chair in front of me. "A *what*?"

"An aerialist, a wire-walker. I'll perform with The Flying Kids of Tel Aviv in Ha'yarkon Park on the last day of July."

He and the woman look at each other. I try to find simpler words, but I can't. I'm an aerialist. I could prove it if they'd let me rig a wire or two across this room.

David rubs his forehead. "Okay, you're an aerialist from Balata Refugee Camp. There's no other possibility."

I feel my face get warm.

"Relax," he says. "I'm not teasing."

The woman whispers something to him in Hebrew.

He answers in English. "That's what I was about to say. She'd come up with a more believable story if she wanted to lie."

Now the tall woman bends over and takes my hand and tells me her name: Shirel Keret. She and David are about the same age, mid-thirties, and I assume they are married. Shirel is pale and beautiful, with dark hair braided all the way down her back and tied with a gold ribbon. I wonder if she too is a former soldier, though I can't picture her aiming a rifle at me, or even at some Arab man crossing a street or an alley. Like a pleased mother or auntie, she smiles down on me until David asks if I'd like to see a show in Jaffa tonight.

Shirel smooths a hand in front of her as though to bury the invitation. After speaking with David in Hebrew, chiding him, I think, she asks where I'm staying tonight.

"Nearby," I say. "With my friend Tali and her mother."

"And Tali's mother knows you're wandering around alone at night? Shouldn't you be in bed?"

"I'm not tired."

"Did Tali's mother give you permission to—"

"No, but please don't worry. I've never been to a place as safe as Florentine."

Shirel tries to tell me that Florentine and Tel Aviv and Jaffa and Israel are not as safe as they appear. I know better than to argue with a motherly sort of worry. I let her lecture me, run out of words, find a few more, and then she and David converse in Hebrew. I lower my eyes but keep my chin up whenever they look my way. *I am from Balata.* I need them to see this. They shouldn't have to look more than once.

Shirel asks how old I am.

I lied earlier to the taxi driver, but to her I tell the truth: "Sixteen, almost seventeen."

"I don't think we've ever had children at a warehouse show."

My voice wavers a little when I tell her I'm not as young as I seem. No one in my alley is young.

"Your alley?"

"Balata," I say. "I've already told you and your husband where I live."

They exchange glances.

"We're not married," says Shirel.

"Just friends," says David.

Shirel winks. "Sometimes not even that."

Just now I don't care what they mean to each other as long as they take me to the show in Jaffa. I look up at Shirel, then David, and say, "Can I please come with you tonight? Can I see the show?"

David says, "You're from Balata, so nothing we do will shock you."

I wish I could hug him the way I sometimes hug my grandpa.

"But I hope you'll see at least one or two things in a somewhat different way."

Shirel speaks to him in Hebrew, on and on, and all he does is nod. At last she turns to me and says, "You need to tell us where you're staying, the exact address. The show will last half the night, but we'll have you home within an hour."

She meant to say, "Tali's home," or "place where you're staying," but I don't mind. It isn't enough for me to tell Shirel the address. She makes me write it on a slip of paper, then enters the address in her phone. She bends down and I smell her hair, her shampoo, jasmine, I think, or something as sweet. There's a quickness about her, in her eyes and body, and she would be as slender as a wire-walker if her breasts were small. David hasn't married her, but I bet he'd like to. Thirty-five and single? She has no husband to serve, no children, so tonight she's adopted me.

33

THE SOUNDS OF THE SEA

Neither of these Israelis owns a car. The bicycles leaning on the wall near the skeleton door will take them to Jaffa. There is no bike for me, so I tell them I can run faster than they can peddle. I remind them I'm a circus girl, and then I go further—"I *am* a circus. I can ride on Shirel's handlebars."

David squeezes a box of computer parts and other gear into the basket of his bicycle. "Be patient," he says. "We'll find you something to ride."

He has an alley friend whose daughter is small like me and I can borrow her yellow bicycle shiny as a candle flame.

My hair is covered now, because Shirel gave me her helmet. This pretty bicycle has blinking lights, front and back, and a lamp for a headlight. David, in the lead, has no helmet or lights, and sometimes he rides no-handed. Maybe machine artists and wire-walkers take few precautions. When I, too, lift my hands from the bars, Shirel the Worrier says, "Keep hold of your bicycle, *steer*." I obey, though this is in no way dangerous. I could ride this bicycle on a wire.

We ride south on the Promenade beside the Mediterranean Sea. My grandfather hasn't seen Jaffa since he was a small boy, and he hasn't left Nablus since his release from jail in 2001. I am determined to be his eyes, his ears, and when I return to Balata we will drink tea at night and I will tell him what I remember. I haven't brought his phone because he worried it might be confiscated at a checkpoint. "You won't need it anyway," he told me. "You have eyes, you have memory, and these—for the most part—are beyond their control."

I will bring my grandfather the sounds of the sea. The waves roll in and out like the breathing of a thousand giants, a steady soughing and singing over sand and rock. I can breathe a giant's breath if I must. My grandfather barely remembers his birthplace, so I'll lean into his ear and swish my tongue and blow and blow till he hears the sea and the shore.

The sound of a wave, a single giant, is wild, almost out of control, and so am I. Riding toward Jaffa, I imagine breathing into the dark of my grandpa's ear. I'll need to blow hard to get past all the hair in there. The sea is untamable, wild in each wave. Yet there's something inside her body as calm as a lady in her sleep.

Shirel asks me what I'm saying.

"Nothing." I smile, but this is not true. I was practicing, making sea sounds, remembering the sea for my grandpa. Maybe Shirel thought I was speaking in Arabic. I said, "Nothing," because hours sometimes pass before the right words find me. Listen. The sounds of the sea well up from inside and could be no other way. Who could argue with a wave? I envy the sea that never need words or reasons, that never lies to anyone, stranger or friend.

❧

Jaffa is a church tower, a cross, a minaret, and a terrace of buildings, many levels, rising step by step from the sea. We turn away from the shore and peddle up hills, narrow streets, lanes too narrow for cars, then enter an alley and stop. Palm trees and other trees turn the walkway into a tunnel. The darkness calms me. And over here, between high branches, a bough of stars.

David pushes open a door twice my height and as wide as my mother's kitchen. Shirel and I follow him through a foyer and into a large hall. Here and there, like stars about to blink out, bare bulbs hang by cords from the high ceiling. Why am I happy to wander in shadows, to hear a language I don't know (Hebrew), and to be with people I don't know? Is it possible to travel farther from Balata? I glimpse maybe twenty Israelis in the aisles between the sharp angles of machines.

After we park our bicycles, Shirel takes my hand and says, "Stay with me, okay? A few minutes of this will probably be more than enough."

She pulls me one way while David goes another, his arms full of gadgets and gears, metal tubing. The innards of machines.

34

EXHIBITS

Shirel leads me down an aisle between six robots wrapped in desert-brown blankets, their heads peeking out. They look like oversized soldiers asleep on their feet. Cube heads, jutting jaws. Big ears. Teeth. A tall man rips a blanket off one of them and its mouth gapes open. The breathy yawn means there's a speaker down its throat.

The robot points toward the end of the aisle. He speaks in Hebrew, then English: "Don't look at me; look where I'm pointing." A circle of bars surrounds a dollhouse on a pedestal. The bars start spinning the wrong way, counterclockwise, and burst into flames.

Shirel holds me near, but I'm more fascinated than afraid. Who set the fire? What makes things move? Maybe machine artists, unseen, monitor computers, press buttons, turn levers, and use propane (I can smell it) to destroy and reveal. The roof of the house catches fire, peels away, disappears. There's a room with a bed, a baby in a crib, a green chair, a man and woman lying face-down on the floor. The bars press inward and—whoosh—all is gone in a breath. Smoke rises through an open skylight. A house of paper has burned. No flesh smell in the air.

The robot says, "Arson attack in Duma. Three Palestinians die after a settler fire-bombs their home at night."

He turns to another robot. "When was that exactly?"

"Late July, 2015."

They sound bored, but everyone in my alley knows of this attack. Duma is near Nablus. A mother, a father, and a baby burned to death. A four-year-old boy survived.

Now the other robots stir, toss their blankets aside, but Shirel leads me away before I can watch them perform. "Seen enough?" she asks. "I can call a taxi and have you home in a few minutes."

"What about the bicycle?"

"David will come back for it tomorrow."

"Can I stay a while longer? Just five minutes?"

She squeezes my hand. "Okay, but I really don't know why you need to be here at all."

Shirel worries that a high-wire walker from Balata Refugee Camp might see or hear something unsettling. She doesn't seem to know I was born unsettled. I'll soon return to Balata's alleys where I'm expected to remain the rest of my life. I know a few things Shirel will never know: Who is the most daring person in this audience? *Me*. Who is the quickest? *Me*. Who is not afraid to be afraid? *Me*. Who has the wildest patience? *Me*. So I wait for her to relax, loosen her grip on my hand, before I slip away.

I picture Shirel turning in a circle as she calls my name. I put more distance between us as *Amal, Amal*, echoes through the hall. I am not disrespectful of elders. I am not rude. If Shirel were given one chance to visit a museum, or see a machine art exhibit in a forbidden country, would she waste her time? Would she be good?

In an alcove where the light is dimmest, I find side-rooms with their doors ajar, cautious invitations. I sidle into one, pass through a slit in a curtain, and join a small crowd gathered around a boxing ring. Show-goers lean on the ropes and heckle the two man-sized machines who pummel each other with pillows. One fighter hides his face—all but his eyes—with a checkered black and white kufiyah. The other one looks silly in an oversized helmet that rattles his metal skull every time he gets slugged with a pillow. Feathers float, dozens of them, maybe hundreds. Some have stripes, rainbow colors. I snatch the first pretty one that comes my way.

Instead of fists, pillows.

Thump.

The kufiyah slips down and covers the Palestinian's nose.

Thump.

The Jew's helmet flies off. The moon is less bald.

Thump.

Such a soft war a breeze on our skin.

Thump.

Feathers fly. I catch another rainbow.

Double thump.

Triple thump.

The pillows are the pale yellow of clouds I have seen over the Mediterranean Sea.

A small sign—*Courtesy of Banksy*—hangs by a string from the ceiling.

I take pictures in my head and say to myself, *I'll show these machines and this boxing ring to my grandfather. I'll show him this pillow fight and maybe he'll see it in my way and* his *way*. Here's what I think about words and pictures. If you love someone, if you want him to see what you've seen, you try out this word and that word and keep going till you find the ones he needs. The words settle inside him and stay a while.

The fight ends when the robots slump down, too tired to continue. They lean on one another, shoulder-to-shoulder, and now some machine artist in the control room pipes in gasps and sighs, the strain of catching one's breath, drawing the air into the lungs and belly. Machines can sound as human as anyone. I'm listening to recordings, yes, to speakers hidden in metal throats or chests, but am no less amazed. If I could live two lives in one, I would be a wire-walker and a machine artist. Is it possible to master more than one marvel at a time?

❧

The next exhibit invites viewers to enter a destroyed village. I pass the ruins of miniature homes, a few walls still standing. At the end of a lane, I reach an area that smells of soil and grass. Little palm trees—plastic, I suppose—rest on a bed of earth. I touch the grass, the soil, surprised they are real.

A searchlight sweeps over the upper floor of a two-story home, faces in windows. The palms are on one side of the house, a row of orange trees on the other. This house begins to talk. *Bismillah arrahman irrahim …Bismillah arrahman irrahim.* One by one, each person in a lighted window gives her or his name: *Adnan, Faris, Fatima, Yousef, Aisha, Maryam.* Midget robots call to each other. *Allah yerda alek (God bless you)… Allah maek (Go with Allah).* I hear each word, though the speakers in their throats must be small as thumbnails. The prayers and well-wishes are echoes I have listened to since the morning of my birth.

A tall machine carrying a shovel and a rake rolls out from behind a curtain. Its head swivels, its mouth flaps, but there are no words, only small sounds that remind me of crickets. It is no louder than a bush at night till the engine revs up and fans blow and in comes a storm that shall have its way with us. The machine has webbed feet like those of a lizard, metal columns for legs, and its chest seems to swell as it raises the shovel in one hand, the rake in the other. Someone tall, human, steps in front of me, blocks my view, but it doesn't matter. I can close my eyes and see the house and the people and the trees and the earth being shoveled and raked into shreds. Dust is everywhere. These high-powered fans that blow a storm, half choke me, are part of the exhibit. Palestinian robots pray their last prayers in a playhouse. The one real thing is the dust I breathe. Machine artists, or their helpers, hauled in soil and set their fake house and fake Palestinians and trees on a bed of earth before they shoveled and raked them to death.

The machine speaks Hebrew, but also some English.

I strive for historical accuracy. I throw a fit after every targeted assassination or major battle and call it rabies.

The men in the audience laugh or chuckle.

The machine says, *O, really? You wouldn't laugh if you were me. And maybe you are.*

I bump into someone, but I can't see a face. The overhead lighting is for the exhibit rather than the audience. I don't know what anyone else feels. People speak, if they speak, in Hebrew. What I hear most, though, is *O*, maybe the only sound we share. Sometimes *O* is sad or surprised. Sometimes it is tired or bored or disgusted. *O* can mean anything. My throat feels achy when I make this sound.

I pass back down the lane, enter an arena, and join the watchers crowded around a dais, a cage. A thin man, not a machine, stands behind bars. A black and white kufiyah covers his hair, his face, and is wrapped tight around his neck. The bars of the cage start spinning. The man stretches himself, becomes skinnier, taller, one arm pressed flat to his chest and the other straight over his head. He throws something, maybe a stone, before the bars catch fire. A whooshing sound, not loud, the flames spinning round and round this skinny Arab who has a choice—stand still or burn. Time is long, a second is long. Someone beside me says, "Some night he'll take this too far and kill himself." Another person answers in Hebrew, but then I hear a name: *Jonathan.* So this is Jonathan? The wizard of machinery? I want to see his face.

I'm ambushed before I can see anything else. Shirel grabs my elbow from behind and turns me around.

"You didn't hear me calling? You know how long I was looking for you? You have any idea?"

I do.

"You've seen enough of this show."

No, I've *lived* enough of this show, but I can't expect Shirel to understand. The machine artists know where I'm from, and this—I can't explain it—gives me hope. Shirel wants me to be safe. She's good the way my mother and my aunties are good. As for me, I didn't become an aerialist by being good, didn't get to Jaffa and Tel Aviv by being good. This doesn't mean I'm bad, but just that I'm somewhere in between.

Shirel takes out her phone and calls for a taxi. "I'm going with you," she says. "I'll see you to your door."

Maybe half way to Tali's, after she calms down, I ask her about Jonathan. Who exactly is he?

"A guy," she says.

"Yeah, but—"

"He has certain frustrations, so he makes machines."

I think about this. "They're not just any kind of machines."

"No, they're not."

"Jonathan's a former soldier, yes?"

She nods.

"Was he ever in Nablus?"

"He doesn't talk much about it."

"But you're his friend, yes?"

She hesitates. "His girlfriend."

"Really?"

"We've been together almost three years. I have only one boyfriend at a time."

I nod, as if we live in the same world. I don't care if Shirel has three boyfriends. For me, though, it would be impossible to have even one. Mazin? I'm not supposed to think of him till I marry him, if I do marry him. I want the world to be different before I marry a trapeze artist. If the world becomes half as pretty as Mazin, then I pray he asks my grandfather for permission to take me as his wife. One boyfriend at a time? No, I want one husband for life.

I ask Shirel if she and Jonathan can come to my show on July 31st.

She looks at me in the dark of the taxi.

"Circus," I say. "But I won't be the only one to perform."

I ask her for a slip of paper, a pen. She digs them out of her purse and I write my invitation on my knee as we roll down a wide boulevard toward Florentine.

Dear Shirel and Jonathan,

Please come and see The Flying Kids of Tel Aviv on July 31st at six p.m. in Ha'yarkon Park near the Yitzhak Rabin Centre.

O, the machines! They are fascinating, sometimes scary. But I love the boxers and the rainbow feathers.

Thank you, and see you soon!

Amal Tuqan, Wire-Walker

I ask Shirel for her phone number so I can remind her and Jonathan of the performance.

She looks at me as if I'm a pest.

"I won't bother you, I promise. I'll leave one voicemail if my friend Tali loans me her phone."

35

FATHER

A wire-walker, a thief—who is more silent? I ease the creak of a door as if I've oiled the hinges. My steps wake no one but the air. I glide across wires this way.

Tali's a sound sleeper, but any carelessness may wake her mother. I wire-walk through their home and sit in a chair before a blank TV. The light from a street lamp seeps through the curtains. I am not ready for what my grandfather calls "the mercy of sleep." There is more light than shadow when I close my eyes.

I must have a million pictures in my body, and movies too. A man on a dais escapes the flames whirling around him by standing still and straight. I know how hard this is because of my training. I could wire-walk till you got weary of watching, but if you were to say to me, "Enough, hold still," I would fall like a stone. Even a wire cinched tight sways with the weight of the walker. The aerialist needs to lean, bend, waver, to keep her balance. The man circled by fire has a dais, an island in the air. And he will live if he keeps his poise.

Jonathan, once a soldier, is now a machine artist. A bystander said, "Some night he'll take this too far and kill himself." But is this what he *wants*? He designed a machine with three parts—a cage, a dais inside the bars, and a ring of fire. He pretended to be Palestinian, hid his face in a kufiyah. Is he serious? What does he want?

I turn on a small lamp. Practice for The Flying Kids begins at eight a.m. Tali and her mother will wake at six thirty, maybe sooner. Will I sleep tonight? Will I find a way to make myself tired? My body is a river with strong currents. Electric. Gymnastic. So I do a hand-stand and begin practice in the middle of the night.

Bone whispers, small clicks in my shoulders. No other sound till the blood rushes to my head. Yalla. I come back to my feet by easing forward in a summersault, no noisier than a cat springing from chair to floor.

There are books in this wide room, hundreds of them, maybe a thousand. I bet my grandpa had at least as many before the Israelis ransacked his library and took everything but my grandma's cookbooks. I may never love books as he does, but there's something wonderful about words printed on pages and pressed into bindings that stay put till they are dust. A book is like a body, but can live hundreds of years. New copies can be printed, so that if some die others are born. Books can sail on ships, fly on planes, travel to any part of the world. My grandfather's library had books from South Africa, Morocco, Chile, Spain, Canada, Japan, and India. I wish I could have seen his library, not just heard about it. Did the Israelis read any of the books they stole?

I take out a circus book and look at pictures of tumblers, trapeze artists, high-wire walkers, jugglers, clowns. Tali has written her name inside the cover. I hesitate, then trace the letters with a finger. Are we true friends? Tali and me? I eat her food, sleep in her bed, but do we know each other? Florentine is light years away from Balata. Tali will never wish to visit my home or live a single day in my skinny alley. Besides, it wouldn't be safe for her. Not even my grandfather and my uncles could protect her for long.

There's a whole shelf of circus books, and other shelves with books about theater and film, music and dance, European literature, American literature, Judaism and Buddhism, poetry, and I don't know what else. Many books are in Hebrew, but I'd say at least two hundred are in English. I'm stunned to find books about Palestinians mixed in with European novels. I rub my eyes to clear them, then trace a finger over spines and titles and names of authors: *Palestinian Walks* by Raja Shehadeh, *So What, New and Selected Poems* by Taha Muhammad Ali, *Peace and Its Discontents* by Edward W. Said, and *Men in the Sun* by Ghassan Kanafani. Tali once told me her father had read many books by Palestinians, and now I believe her. I'm startled by the possibility that he wanted to know us. I doubt Tali has read a single chapter from a book by a Palestinian author, but this library is not yet dust. These books may live for five hundred years.

I wait in silence for I don't know what. The bookcases are towers to my smallness. I would need to leap, make noise, to reach the top shelves. Did Tali's father need all these books? Her mother? Does she need each one? Maybe some books just fill up space, sort of like furniture. Or maybe they are loved.

I have too much energy, so I do another hand-stand. I quiver down the length of me as blood rushes to my head. My ears feel warm, my hair too. I'm made of sparks, small fires. Jumpy and warm. It's good to have an athlete's body, except when it's too powerful to sleep.

I return to my feet with a summersault, my face to the window. Something catches my eye—the gold handle of a cabinet between an arm chair and the sofa. *Open it,* I tell myself, *no one will mind.* In these next three days, before I return to Balata, I will believe what I wish to believe.

I open the bottom drawer of the chest and find a thin book beneath a white shawl. The cover is a photograph of Israel's flag, white and blue with the star of David. *Unforgotten (1988-2008)* is in Hebrew and English. I sit on the floor near the lamp and leaf through it. Every man, woman, and child I read about is Jewish and dead. A girl, Shira Levinson, lived only three months. Killed. She and the others in *Unforgotten* died in a span of twenty years.

There is a photograph of each one, a brief biography, and quotes from family members who survived the victim. If Palestinians made a book called *Unforgotten (1988-2008)*, there would be more names and pages, a book too wide for my hands. The Israelis would censor such a book because of the Holocaust. Our deaths are as small as onion seeds while theirs deserve special publications, monuments. I am sad, though, as I look at people who died too soon. Some show a smile, a wink, and a few wave as if their goodbyes are temporary and they will be home by morning. They appear—I need to hunt for the word—undefeated. Palestine's *Unforgotten* would have stern faces, few smiles, if any. But we would not name a book *Unforgotten* because our dead are too many to remember. How many from Nablus died between 1988 and 2008? I don't know. We remember best the martyrs we see daily, their photographs and slogans pasted to walls.

I scan the names in the index. There are two Glazmans, Edith and Jacob. I go to Jacob's page and see a stout man, smiling, waving a cap in the air as if to greet a friend. I read the story of his life. One page, large print. I'll forget some of the details in the coming days, but I'll remember a face like Tali's. I'll remember how he died.

Jacob Glazman taught world literature and drama at Ironi Aleph High School in Tel Aviv for nine years. On the night of September 3, 2008, he and his wife were passing a popular café in Neve Tzedek when a bomb went off. They were unhurt, merely stunned, but Jacob went into the café to offer assistance to the wounded when a van driven by an Israeli Palestinian crashed through the front wall and into the crowd.

Two were killed, including Jacob Glazman. He was thirty-one years old.

Amos Glazman, Jacob's brother, remembers him as "a man who lived partly in the world and partly in books, taking the best of each and sharing them with his family, his students, and this city he loved—Tel Aviv. Jacob had a passion for theater and circus arts. He was more alive than any man I've had the pleasure to know, and was always working on multiple projects. He had begun to organize a youth circus for Israelis and Palestinians, and he aspired to train professionals, including his daughter. He taught Tali to juggle when she was three years old. She lost her father at age four."

There was more, but I closed the book, wrapped it in its shawl, and returned it to the cabinet. *Unforgotten.* I am more alert now than when I walk across wires. Did the maker of the bomb, the driver of the van, get what they wanted? I know what I want, but it will never happen. A bandage for every wound.

Now I understand why Tali avoids crowded cafes. I don't think bombers have targeted Tel Aviv in recent years, but she takes precautions. Tali knows more of my world than I imagined. If not for circus, every bridge between us would be sad.

I turn off the lamp and sit in a hard chair, my hands in my lap. Some time passes before I realize I am breathing no more than I must. Maybe someone dying breathes this way, conserves her energy, prays for a miracle. I am not in danger. I am so alive my eyes hurt. I close them, try to see nothing. Have I ever sat so still? Insects breathe deeper breaths.

No house is silent if you listen. Boards, joists, hinges—they talk in their own way. A girl in a chair can be quieter than the floor beneath her. I am funeral quiet. It is the world that moves.

Over the floor, across the hallway, a rib of light under a door. Mrs. Glazman is awake. Maybe she, too, sits in a chair and breathes no more than she must. I didn't hear the click of a switch when her light came on. I want her to know that I, too, am awake.

I rise from my chair and walk into the hall. I stop near her door and cough, not loud. Maybe Mrs. Glazman can be as quiet as a wire-walker or a thief. I listen for her steps, hear nothing. She startles me when she opens her door.

A bedside lamp casts light on her shoulders. She stands over me, a silhouette in a loose robe, the light around her an aura. I don't see her arm coming up till she touches my left shoulder. What can I say to her at this hour? *I was snooping… I found an important book. I read about your husband. I am sorry…* I breathe my insect breath, say nothing. We stand as still as people can stand till she stoops over me and brushes the hair from my eyes. "Please," she whispers, "see if you can sleep. If you can't sleep, rest. This is all we can do at this hour."

She walks with me to her daughter's room, her daughter's bed, and tucks me in. The darkness in her hands and in me are a kind of mercy I have never known.

36

A HAND WARMER THAN MINE

This morning I am lost at practice. Dagan guides me through leg-strengthening exercises because I keep falling from the wire. Miki walks in my place, but she is better on the trapeze with Mazin as her partner. An Israeli boy, Nachum, walks the wire better than Miki. I am better than both of them when rested and alert.

"Two days before the performance," Dagan reminds me. "I don't think you'll be ready."

I promise him I will be. I have not come to Tel Aviv to perform in a circus and make a fool of myself.

That night, as I lie in bed beside Tali, I tell her I'm sorry. We are in shadows, almost invisible. I doubt I could say this in clear light.

"Sorry for what?"

"I know this isn't easy."

She turns on her side to face me. "What isn't easy?"

"Just my being here."

"No, you're welcome. I thought you knew this."

"I do, but…"

"What?"

"You and your mother…"

"Well?"

"You've been very kind."

The important words stay inside me. Who killed Tali's father? Was it someone like Issam, a boy overcome by rage? My brother's angry enough to kill any Israeli, Tali and her mother included. I don't know how to stop this, or how to stop Israelis from one day killing him.

I say, "My father died when I was four. I don't know what happened."

She seems to hold her breath a long time. "You once told me you tried to visit his grave but the road was blocked."

"Yes."

"I almost felt like you blamed me, as if this were my decision."

I will never see the faces of those I blame.

"What was wrong with you in practice today? You didn't look right."

"I had trouble sleeping last night."

"My mother takes sleeping pills. I don't think she'd sleep at all if not for the pills."

I'm sorry Tali has no father and her mother has no husband. I may never know how my own father died, but I know about Jacob Glazman. My mother and my grandfather told me my father died bravely. Maybe—like Tali's father—he rushed to help the wounded only to become one of the dead.

"Amal, is something wrong?"

"No."

"You feel so quiet."

I stare at the ceiling, almost no light.

"You need to get some sleep, okay?"

"Yes."

"This means no worrying. Leave the worrying to my mother."

Or mine, I'm thinking.

"Tomorrow you'll have a good practice."

"I hope so."

"I didn't know you were a worrier."

"Me either."

"Try to get some sleep."

I touch a hand warmer than mine. I wish I were brave enough to ask Tali to hold me. I believe she would say yes. And I would hold her back and fall asleep and maybe we would surprise ourselves and wake in each other's arms at first light.

37

CAT GIRL

I have a stage name—Handala's Sister, The Cat Girl of the Balata Camp. Coach Dagan thinks the name is long, but I disagree. I tell him about the real cat, orange as a flame, who patrols the rooftops of my alley. "This cat can balance on a thread," I tell Dagan, "a strand of silk," though I've never seen this feat. How do I know what's possible? I don't. I believe this cat is more talented than Phillippe Petit in his prime.

I cannot tell Dagan of the original Handala, the creation of Naji Salim al-Ali, a cartoonist assassinated in London at the order of Israeli intelligence. We do our best to avoid politics and disharmony at circus, but as I practice, do tumbling exercises, walk across wires, someone is being hurt, someone is dying, someone at a checkpoint wants to kill those who control the roads, the cities, the towns, the fields, the water in the ground, the traffic in the sky. What can I do? I want no one to lose a father, a mother, a brother, a sister, a child. I want no one to lose a home, a tree, a neighborhood, an orchard, a farm. More is lost every day, I know this. I am Handala's Sister, The Cat Girl of the Balata Camp. I want to walk a wire from my father to Tali's father. I want to walk among ghosts on a thread, a strand of silk, and weave things together. But how do I begin? And who among the living will notice the design if I find the thread?

Two hours before our performance, I borrow Tali's phone to call my family and my friend Maysa. Mother's voice is all worry. She wants me home, that is all. Home. Her voice shakes. She still can't believe I'm among Israelis in a strange city, a strange land. Each night I lie in bed beside Tali the Juggler. I can't tell my mother how good she smells. Jasmine, cinnamon. And I don't know what else.

Grandpa Saeed laughs when I tell him my stage name. He gets quiet, though, when I ask about my brother. "Not home," he says finally. "It seems he only comes home to eat and sleep."

He calls across the alley to Maysa. Soon I see her face on Tali's phone, more happiness than worry, more light than shadow. Sometimes people who love each other don't talk much. Tonight, when I climb to the high-wire, perform solo, in a spotlight, and then with another aerialist, I will walk for everyone. Somehow it feels more powerful to fold these words inside me, as under a wing. Besides, I think my best friend knows why I walk.

I also call Shirel to remind her to come and see The Flying Kids of Tel Aviv in two hours, yes, two hours, and bring Jonathan and David and any of the machine-artists who want to see "the best circus in the Middle East."

I may be telling the truth, but Shirel laughs. I hate to beg, but once, no twice, I say, "Please come, please come. I promise you won't be sorry. I've worked for this chance to perform in a professional circus since the day I was born."

38

PERFORMANCE

Circus is made of fire colors. Under the red dome of the tent a banner in gold—THE FLYING KIDS OF TEL AVIV! Coach Dagan checks and rechecks the rigging, the high wires and trapezes, the net I hope I will never need. My heart thumps. How many people crowd the bleachers that rise row by row toward the walls of the tent? Several hundred? A thousand? I shade my eyes, look around, but I can't find Shirel or any machine artists beyond mats and equipment and the ring lit in gold.

Jugglers, tumblers, clowns—they are in lights. Tali and a Palestinian boy I secretly call Cutie play catch with knives, soft blades, maybe rubber. They start slow, but soon six knives spin round and round, higher and higher, as in a whirlwind. They are almost the length of swords, with blades streaked red, fake blood. Tali and Cutie catch four of them, toss them aside, and as the last two arc down they swing their arms behind their backs and catch the blades in their teeth.

In row one, behind a bench for the coaches, Tali's mother claps twice. She stays seated as the man beside her (Tali's uncle Amos I will find out later) gives his niece a standing ovation. As far as I know, this is the only time Mrs. Glazman has left her home since I arrived. If she's not in her kitchen, preparing food, wiping counters, staring out the window, she retreats to her room. Door closed.

Now Tali and Cutie juggle sticks of fire, but soon the clowns block my view, plus acrobats tumbling over the mats, doing flips and turns in mid-air, and dancing, leaping frog-like, in time to calliope music, or what Tali calls "showboat tunes." Maybe at circus she forgets she has no father. On the wire, I often forget mine because what I'm doing needs everything I can give. Maybe it would be more difficult to concentrate on my work if I still remembered his voice, his touch, or the way he held me when I was small. I wish I could miss him more than I miss him. I don't know enough to bring him close.

Can I tell you how beautiful Mazin is on the trapeze? No, but you know I must try. Think of sun and sea, in the warmth of a bird. In his green costume, he shines as bright as the spotlights on him and Miki, his trapeze girl, though she is not, I pray, his girlfriend. I don't mind if his face is upside-down or right-side up; he shines the same either way. He swoops and rises, and here she comes, in her red costume, swinging toward him, then away, in a circus sky over a gold ring. I envy this girl who soars to some precise pocket in the air, a place only she can see, before she lets go and flies to Mazin who catches her wrists and swings her in a wide arc toward the roof of the tent. Danger is beautiful. Some in the crowd ululate. Others gasp. But there is more. Miki flies free of him, soars, and loops into a full flip before she snags the bar of her trapeze with one hand. What does she do with her other hand? She waves, casual, as if to say, *I could do more if I wished.* I am willing to believe her. She and Mazin have mapped every centimeter of circus sky, every centimeter of themselves. They draw maps in the air, maps in their minds, and follow timetables that tell them when to fly alone, when to join, and at what height. My grandfather might see this as basic math with arcs and tangents and obvious equations. Still, I know these artists practice obsessively and fly through the sky every day of their lives.

Coach Dagan introduces the Israeli wire-walkers. A heartbeat later, as I light up a ladder toward my perch, he says, "And there goes Handala's Sister, The Cat Girl of the Balata Camp, a.k.a. Amal, who comes to us all the way from Nablus!" I think he repeats the same words in Hebrew. My heart speeds up as when soldiers search our alleys, our homes, and speak to us in a language we rarely understand. Nonetheless, I'm confident of my art and the ways of my body. I imagine those who love me are watching: my grandfather, my mother, Uncle Sami, Maysa and her mother, and every aunt and uncle and cousin and neighbor who lives in my alley, plus my first teacher, Handala the Cat. The only one missing is my brother who hates me. I glance down at Tali, then her mother. Those who love me a little or a lot will help me to keep my balance. If Dagan knew this, he might ask the equipment manager and his crew to take away the net.

I stand still and straight on my perch, and Nachum, my performance partner, has his own perch on the far side of the wire. Now the music, an oud and a drum, a slow rhythm, signal me to glide toward him, a spotlight following me from above. I slow-dance, wriggle my hips (I hardly have any), while Nachum weaves, wobbles, and pretends he's about to fall. Slow, seductive, he walks toward me till two spotlights are one. I feel the wire with the arches of my feet and breathe through the soles. Nachum crouches, makes himself small, and the moment he tucks his chin to his chest I jump over him and fly a color too high over the rainbow arc I see in my mind. Bye, Nachum. I lean back to slow my descent, then straighten to catch the wire with my right foot and—a drumbeat later—I come home with my left. Only Coach Dagan and me know I flew too high and almost lost myself. Sometimes my legs are scary strong. No lie. I could sail over a rainbow if we had one tonight as a prop in our circus sky.

After the last act, Tali introduces me to her uncle Amos. He looks much like his brother, Tali's father. He shakes my hand and calls me "a phenomenon, a daredevil on the wire." Yes, I am brave as I step or fly through the sky, but I'm not brave now. I know how Amos lost his brother, how Mrs. Glazman lost her husband, how Tali lost her father. I wonder if anyone under this tent has not lost someone dear.

Walking a wire, jumping over a boy, mean nothing to the dead. Maybe, though, the joy of circus brings comfort to those who must learn to live. Mrs. Glazman pats my left shoulder, a gesture so small I barely feel it. She is a butterfly, but sad, slow, more shadow than light. I want to take her hand and say, *Don't fly away. Please stay a while. You're beautiful. I wish we could be friends forever.* Instead, I talk nervously about "Tali and the Palestinian boy," the way they tossed knives back and forth, then "snatched them right out of the air with their teeth!" I would like to do more than entertain her. I remember the way she comforted me when I couldn't sleep and she tucked me in her daughter's bed as if I too were her child, as if I too belonged in her home.

We are moving down an exit aisle, Tali first, Uncle Amos last, when I hear my name, turn, and see someone near the top row of the bleachers waving her arms. She's a small bird in the distance, so I need a moment to shade my eyes from the overhead lights and recognize Shirel. The man at her side, tall and thin, might be Jonathan.

I say to Uncle Amos, "Excuse me, go on ahead. I'll catch up with you." I am, once more, a performer. Circus-fast, I fly up the stairs of the bleachers before he can respond. Show-goers on their way down make way for me. A few applaud as if this is the encore of my performance. Walk a wire, fly up stairs…befriend a machine-artist? What else might I accomplish in the few hours before I return to Balata Camp?

I don't know what to say when I reach Shirel and the machine artist, if that's what he is. The first thing I notice is his hair: not long, not short, not combable. Shirel surprises me with a hug that lifts me off my feet. She calls me "a prodigy, Wonder Woman-in-training," and other nice things. She is warm and soft and smells of coffee. "Just one complaint," she adds. "You took my breath away when you leaped over that boy!"

Now she sets me down between her and this man. "Jonathan," she says, "this is Amal. And what was the stage-name the ringmaster…?"

"Handala's Sister, The Cat Girl of the Balata Camp."

Jonathan winks.

"You think my name's too long?"

"Not at all."

His hair, spiky and stiff, reminds me of a broom. A broom with black bristles instead of blond ones. My uncle Sami is tall, but Jonathan is taller. A handsome machine artist with grease under his nails.

"You were good," he says, and I know he means it. "How did you learn?"

I tell Jonathan I walk wires almost every day of my life. "An obsession," I say, "that has stayed with me since I was small."

I'm too shy to ask how he became a machine artist, where he learned his skills, and what he hopes to accomplish. Shirel saves me from my awkwardness by praising the circus. "We need more of this," she says. "I mean, joint projects, Palestinians and Israelis, here and elsewhere." I've heard Israeli idealists on TV, on radio, but this is different. Shirel put Palestinians before Israelis in one sentence. I hope this wasn't a slip of the tongue.

I tell her and Jonathan I leave for Nablus, the Balata Camp, tomorrow morning, but maybe we can write back and forth so we won't forget each other.

Shirel says, "I won't forget you jumping over that boy any time soon."

"Yes, but what if I need to tell you something? What if it's important?"

They glance at each other.

"You have the internet in Balata?" asks Jonathan.

"We do."

He hands me a business card. "Feel free to write to us any time. Google 'machine art occupation' and tell us what's important."

"Thank you."

"Any chance you'll visit us again?"

"I don't know. If The Flying Kids want me back for another performance, I'll need to apply for an artist's permit."

"You'll be back," says Shirel.

"You really think so?"

"Someone will be sane enough to know you're a gift."

Tali's calling my name, so I bow to Jonathan, let Shirel hug me, breathe in her coffee smell, and light back down the stairs toward the arena and the exit gates.

Tali wants to know why I flew up the stairs of the bleachers. "Why so fast? Who *are* those people?"

"Just some fans. They enjoyed our performance."

"But someone called your name. How does she know you?"

"She just does. Can't I know other people?"

"Amal, that's not what I'm saying. How could you have met anyone outside the circus since we've been together all this time?"

I don't have an honest answer. I can't tell my friend I snuck out of her home late at night and rode a bicycle to a machine art exhibit in Jaffa. Mazin once told me everyone knows Jonathan, or knows of him, and most Israelis hate him. Can I bear to lose my friendship with Tali? No, I don't think so. If I love her already, if she loves me back, any stitch that binds us is fragile and deep and will hurt if it breaks.

Before we leave the arena, Tali turns toward the bleachers and shades her eyes to block the glare of overhead lights. Would she recognize Jonathan? Maybe he always wears some sort of costume when he performs as a machine artist. Tali gives up after a few seconds. I believe her eyes are less keen than mine.

39

GIRLS SMELL GOOD

Tali and I stay up late. After her mom goes to bed, we sit at the kitchen table, side by side, but I already miss her. All around her there are pleasant smells that I must remember so I can bring some hint of her back with me to the Balata Camp.

Cinnamon.

Cardamom.

Jasmine.

Rose.

❧

I ask Tali if she uses perfume.

"Sometimes."

"And now?"

She blushes a little. "Yes."

I tell her she smells like many different things.

"Just one perfume."

"Jasmine? Rose?"

"It's called Ocean Flower."

I think the name is wrong, but I keep quiet. Cinnamon. Cardamom. Jasmine. Rose. Maybe the perfume, in its glass bottle, smells like someone's idea of "Ocean Flower," but Tali smells better. She adds to the ocean cinnamon, cardamom, jasmine, and rose. Maybe it's impossible to describe how any girl smells with a word or two. A wide word like *ocean* buries all else.

My father smelled of tobacco. I want to ask Tali what her father smelled like, but I'm afraid I'll sound strange. I am so sad about Jacob Glazman because I know his daughter and his wife. If I were the "Wonder Woman" Shirel said I am, I would breathe into his lungs, wake his heart, and return him to his home. I would bring my own father back, too, but then I would have to ask him how he died to begin with. A violent death? A war death? A car crash? Someday I have to know. I will remember him better if somebody is brave enough to tell me the truth.

❧

In bed, after Tali starts snoring, I hold her hand. *Be my friend forever. Keep a light on in your heart.* Maybe she'll remember me by my smell, though it can't be as sweet as hers. That's okay. My sweat smells sort of good, except when I'm scared or angry. If I'm lucky, I smell like a tree after it drinks from the earth. An olive tree, maybe. But not sour like an olive on the tongue. More like the leaves, and the skin of the bark cracked open in light. No perfume for me, or any girl in Balata except on her wedding night. I can't find exact words for what Balata girls smell like, but I hope we smell like trees so young they're just beginning to send out roots, search for home. There's no room for trees in Balata, but there are some in Nablus. I have smelled olive trees and olives, and of course Tali has too. Maybe I smell sort of tree-like. I sure hope so. My friend will remember me if it's true.

Part Three

Balata

40

MOVIE THEATER

I envy spiders, birds, angels, insects with wings. An aerialist in a professional circus walks on a wire about one centimeter wide. I practice on thinner wires, and this one's so delicate it almost disappears in the gray light of my alley. So here I am, my first morning home, playing on a spider-wire that stretches from my window to Maysa's window. There are two things for an aerialist to practice—walking and falling. I am one meter over the earth.

I'm about to step on Maysa's windowsill when the wire gives way. A spider can spin silk from her belly and glide to earth in silence. The best I can do is spring cat-like, almost silent, and raise a feather of dust.

"Maysa! Maysa!"

I call to my dearest friend till she comes to her window. Maybe she sees the joy in my face, and the sorrow too. It is complicated to be home.

❧

In the early evening, Tali sends me a link—*The Flying Kids perform in Ha'yarkon Park*. I call out to my grandpa and my mother, "Hurry! Come see the circus in Tel Aviv!"

I also invite Maysa and a half dozen girl cousins to gather in the alley around my grandfather's phone. Minutes later, it's as if we've entered a movie theater to stand before a screen the size of my palm. I am in charge. I hold up the screen, run "the projector," and I pray my audience will catch at least a glimpse of the first professional performance of my circus career.

Maysa and my cousins cheer when I dance out on a wire and fly over Nachum! After I play this twice, I tell my audience the truth: I almost fell because I had too much energy and jumped almost a full meter higher than I needed to jump.

Grandpa says, "My child, let me tell you a secret. If I become any prouder, I'll bust the buttons of this shirt!"

My grandpa's chest is a washboard of bones. There are no muscles to swell outward and bust buttons. He praises me because he loves me. But it is also true I am worthy of praise.

My mother complains about clothing "too snug at your hips, your waist, your chest. *Everywhere.*"

She will worry no less if I remind her every stitch of me was covered, except for my face. I would walk naked if I could remain decent. The less that separates me from the wire, the air, the world, the more at ease I become.

Issam is gone, we know not where, but my mother and Grandpa Saeed and Maysa and some girl cousins watch a replay of The Flying Kids of Tel Aviv. I introduce the performers, so they get to know Tali and Cutie, Mazin and Miki, and they see Coach Dagan and Coach Mousa shake hands or clap each other on the back each time we succeed. My mother sometimes looks from the screen to me as if to ask, *But who are you, child, and what have you become?* Well, for one night I was a star in a Palestinian and Israeli circus. Although I performed well on the wire, I'm nowhere near my limit. I'd say I came within a cat's whisker of falling when I jumped over Nachum. If that had happened, I would have said farewell to my stage-name: Handala's Sister, The Cat Girl of the Balata Camp.

41

NIGHT

In bed, when all is still, I lean toward my mother. She smells of garlic and onions, sweat and stew, and something I can't name except to call it the dust of Balata, smudges of earth on her neck, her face, her clothes. I must remember these smells if I leave her again. I will love her always whether or not she understands why I walk across wires and into the sky. She rests a hand on my stomach as though gravity may not be enough to keep me from flying from our bed.

A loud blast wakes us before the first call to prayer. I feel her hand, still on my stomach, and a moment later I light to my feet. Another explosion, muffled, and one more—loud. My mother grabs me from behind and says, "Down, down. Lie down on the floor."

If we die this morning, she will go first. My mother has made of her body a cave, a shelter, and I am beneath her. If our ceiling falls, if other ceilings and walls and four stories of cousins come tumbling down, a wire-walker may survive in the rubble. Do I deserve this care? I don't know. I wish I could make of my own body a shelter for my family, for four stories of cousins, and for all the alleys of Balata. I am small. We all are. I sometimes wonder how any of us survive.

We suffer one final explosion, far off, before my brother opens a window and curses the Israelis. Cousins shuffle about in the rooms above us. My mother lets me up from the floor.

The kitchen is six steps in front of us. Grandpa slumps in a chair and grips the edge of the table. "Just harassment," he says, "stun grenades. Some lieutenant decided to wake us before the first call to prayer. Now we can be especially alert in our ablutions and praise."

My grandpa winks in the dark. We are shadows within shadows. I need no light to see his face. I catch his wink, now his smile, because I know him. My mother, another shadow, prays aloud for our safety. It seems everyone's talking now—four stories of cousins, men and boys leaning out windows, opening doors, glancing up and down the alley.

Curses, moans, threats. Where have the Israelis vanished? What do they *want*? In Balata, words are angry or they are prayers. Sometimes they are both, but they are not weapons to steal sleep from our enemies. I'm not saying Balata is innocent. I'm saying we have few weapons we can use on a given night.

Grandpa tells Issam we must save our energy "for things we can fight."

My brother stands at the window, his hands on the sill.

"The Israelis haven't woken us in several weeks," Grandpa continues, "so I sort of expected them." He shrugs. "I wonder if they know how predictable they've become. At regular intervals, they demonstrate a presence to remind us of their power, of what they can do to us if they wish." He opens his hands on the table. "They lack subtlety, dismiss every nuance. We're the ones who have to be subtle to find ways to resist."

Issam responds with silence. Resist? Maybe he would be happy for a moment if he could kill someone, and happier still if he could kill many. I sometimes fear my brother as much as I fear the soldiers who enter our camp at will. The alley outside our kitchen is a bit wider than the lid of a coffin. Grandpa wants Issam to be subtle, but I have another idea. I want him to surprise us, surprise himself. Scream. If I could make my brother obey one command, I would say, *Scream, Issam, scream till there's some room inside. Or till we hear an echo over Fire Mountain.* No one can hold for long what my brother holds in his body. The sky can. The sky has all this room. Issam thinks I've wasted my life as an aerialist, but he is wrong. I wish I could teach my brother to sometimes forget our few atoms of earth and see the way the sky opens on either side of the wire.

I receive an email from Mrs. Glazman minutes later. My heart races, then quiets. I sit at the edge of my bed.

> Dear Amal,
>
> Your few days in my home and my daughter's home leave more than a pleasant memory. Although our conversations were minimal, mere fragments, I'm grateful that words are not all that makes the world. I must tell you I struggle with language, whether spoken or written. How to match the world I've witnessed with words, honest

words—this is often beyond me. I hope this at least partly explains my reticence and retreat into silence. My hesitance to speak in no way reflects a lack of care or respect for you.

So, please know you have friends here, Tali and me, and I'm sure every performer and coach in The Flying Kids is grateful for your visit. Friendships that span both sides of the Green Line are rare, almost unheard of, which is all the more reason to reach over the divide word by word, or—if you can imagine—the goodwill that resides in silence.

I read her message twice. *How to match the world I've witnessed with words, honest words—this is often beyond me.* Mrs. Glazman and I share a struggle. Helicopters buzz over the Balata Camp. A baby cries. What should I say?

I want to walk across a bridge of words the way I walk across ropes and wires. But words are more delicate than the art I practice. Words—even one sound—can mean so many things.

Dear Mrs. Glazman,

I am closest to home while walking on a rope, a wire. Words sometimes throw me off balance, but I like them anyway. One thing for sure—I already miss you and Tali and The Flying Kids. You were so kind to invite me into your home where I learned…

I delete where I learned because I was thinking of Jacob Glazman. I sit still, eyes closed, then tell her what I can.

You were so kind to invite me into your home, into a new world. I am better because of you and Tali, I mean a better person. And here, in Balata, I can see over the rooftops all the way to Florentine.

Your friend always,

Amal

42

TULKARM

The electricity blinks off in the afternoon but returns in the evening. I sit in our alley with Maysa and my grandpa and his miraculous phone, our occasional window to the world beyond Fire Mountain. I say, as casual as if I'm offering tea or a tray of sweets, "Want to see a machine art exhibit in Jaffa?"

My grandpa winks. "Machine art?"

I nod.

"How can I resist?"

So once more, as when I showed them and my mother and some girl cousins my performance with The Flying Kids of Tel Aviv, I am the stage manager of Balata's movie theater, the operator behind the projector. I google *machine art occupation*, hit the link, and tilt the screen so my audience can see. "Wait," I say, and hit the link five or six times. We stare at a blank screen, a checkpoint in the ether. I shake the phone, turn it off and on, but we are alone. No window to the world tonight. The sky over Fire Mountain has invisible gates that open and close for reasons others may understand.

Maysa, who sits cross-legged near our drawing of Handala, tries to lift her heels to her shoulders, her ears. Her breath sounds like a bellows as she pulls the air toward every muscle and joint that hurts. "Keep trying," I say, "keep trying." Her left heel finds a niche in her right shoulder, but her right hangs awkwardly in the air.

I help her by raising her right heel to her left shoulder and holding both heels in place so she can begin to relax in this pose.

My grandpa applauds. "I prefer circus to machine art any night."

He has never seen machine art.

"Well done," he says to Maysa. "You look like you could fold yourself into a ball and roll away."

❧

Sometime in the night, I wake from a dream and remember only its colors. Streaks of red and orange vanish as I open my eyes. I lie still and listen to my mother breathing. She has the best thing I can wish for her at this hour: the comfort of sleep.

I go out to the kitchen, pour a glass of water, and sit at the table with Grandpa Saeed's phone. I hear him snoring behind a half-shut door, but I sense an absence: Issam. Where is he? Wandering the alleys, meeting with friends, oiling weapons, making plans? All I know for certain is that my brother is not home at this hour.

I again fail to open the link—*machine art occupation.* Israeli authorities might have disabled it, or set up a checkpoint in the ether. The best I can do is open a page titled *war-time remembrances of a machine artist.* I'm a bit like Maysa the contortionist as I bend over the table, straining to read the small print in the light of the screen.

Tulkarm (2002)
Jonathan Geffen: corporal, team leader

All Palestinian men have received a notice to report to a soccer field. If there is any confusion as to who is a man and who is a boy, look for a moustache. A kid with a bit of fuzz over his lips—round him up.

Our mission will dovetail with other missions. Homes emptied of men will be searched for weapons and explosives. Perhaps evil is simplicity. Choose a path and refuse to waver. If something strange should appear—complex, inexplicable, or needing further investigation—shoot to kill.

Night 1 of 2

I cannot count the number of moustaches in this stadium. They have no weapons, except perhaps those hidden in homes and fields and alleys. If they lack bread, let them eat cake. And if they are cold, let them use each other as blankets. Searchlights brighten the arena. There is no mission, spoken or written, that says destroy sleep. We erase the night because we can.

Ten p.m. I can't remember if the Palestinians have eaten. They have no access to toilets, bathrooms, so maybe they should fast. The Israeli Occupation Forces will need at least forty-eight hours to search every home in Tulkarm. Via radio, we learn some fertilizer has been discovered. The moustaches could use this for flowers, farms, bombs, gardens, graves. They wish to grow things and they wish to kill. This is all we know.

Night 2 of 2

No stars over the arena. Searchlights brighter than sun on snow. We are sentries of impotence. Now and then a few Palestinians raise their fists, shout curses and threats, but their rage means nothing. They stink. They are filthy. They shout at night-blind stars, or at God the Avenger, also unseen, impotent as they are. Allah this and Allah that. We've heard this before and shall hear it again. The voice script of hell.

In the small hours, one of us breaks. Corporal Shalev tosses his helmet to the ground, then his rifle, his glasses, and—as if he is a colonel—he announces the operation is complete. He grins as he smashes his glasses with the heels of his boots. Myopic, damn near blind, he looks around and says, "I can still see," and starts to tear at his eyes. Three of us stop him from harming himself. He doesn't cry out, doesn't say anything except, "Aktion, aktion," in a whisper. We let him fall when he goes limp, face-down on the sidelines. *Aktion* is not from our language. *Aktion* is German for mission, Nazi mission, and most of us know this word. Sergeant Klein, standing over Shalev, appears ready to bash the corporal's face with the butt of his rifle. I step between them and say, "He's already hurt." This is my one brave act as a member of the Israeli Occupation Forces. I say to Klein, "Easy, easy. Give him some room."

We didn't injure or kill a single Palestinian. After forty-eight hours or so—I can't remember exactly—we let the moustaches return to their homes. Each man and his family will hate us forever. Most of them won't try to kill Israelis, but some will. And all of Tulkarm will rejoice whenever a terrorist succeeds.

Corporal Shalev was the sole fatality. Three nights later, back at base for a physical and psychological examination, he put a bullet through his head. I didn't know him well.

My mother has only a few words of English. In the morning, after the first call to prayer, I ask my grandfather to translate the report and read it to her aloud. My mother takes the story with eyes half open. Corporal Shalev is in a grave, as are countless others. I realize how afraid I am to die in a war. If I fall from a wire, okay, I've lived my life to the finish. But if I die in a war, if anyone dies in a war, there is always a question:

What could she have done, what could he have done, if allowed to live? Corporal Shalev, for instance. He had help pulling the trigger. I don't know how many fingers it takes to kill a man.

Many words ago, I told you I can stand at my kitchen window, extend my arm between iron bars, and touch the wall across the alley. How long is my arm? Not long. Still, I sometimes need this closeness, especially when I sit between my grandpa and my mother, elbow to elbow at the kitchen table. Is there a better smell in the morning than grandpa's cardamom and coffee? Well, I'll admit the Mediterranean Sea smells more wonderful, though it's light years away. And my friend Tali smells of cinnamon, cardamom, jasmine, and rose.

My grandpa invites me to sip from his glass. He thinks Corporal Jonathan will soon be in jail if he isn't more careful about his "public remembrances."

"But he's no longer a soldier," I whisper. "He's a machine artist."

"An unusual occupation won't help this young man in a court of law. He's taking a risk putting this sort of narrative online."

My brother, still asleep, didn't hear the first call to prayer, and Grandpa chose not to wake him. I may never show Issam the *war-time remembrances of a machine artist.* My brother, who entered the world a few minutes before me, who opened his eyes before I opened mine, shuns me as if I'm a leper. Besides, the story of "the moustaches" herded like cattle into a soccer field would only add to his hate.

I send Jonathan a message to thank him for having the courage to post his account of Tulkarm and Corporal Shalev on the internet. Minutes later, he writes back:

> You're welcome, my circus friend. Machines are my main medium, but words are another way to wrestle. The writer Zvi Kolitz referred to Jacob of the Old Testament as not only wrestling with an angel but 'wrestling with God.' Much of Israel is in the grip of religion, which—in part—explains my disdain for any blind or feverish faith. Nonetheless, in machine art, or in words of remembrance for Corporal Shalev, there may be something of a prayer. If so, I too wrestle with God. I wrestle to strip myself down to the essentials—empathy and imagination. I'm fearless as I make machines or design stage sets for warehouse shows. Only when I pause does depression

and hopelessness set in. Is it the same for you when you step down from a wire, lead a normal life?

Salaam, shalom, Jonathan

I remember the way he "wrestled" in Jaffa by enclosing himself in a cage of iron and fire. Someone in the audience whispered, "Some night he'll take this too far and kill himself." I didn't shiver when I heard this, but I shiver now. I hope Jonathan wrestles God with machinery, with words—with whatever it takes—for one hundred years. Please, no war death for my friend. Let him die with a full heart in his home by the sea.

43

MRS. GLAZMAN'S "DISCOVERY"

On a Sunday night, sleepless, I send Tali the story of Corporal Shalev and Tulkarm. An entire week passes before she calls me on Messenger.

Why did you send this to me?

I thought you should see it.

That's not a real answer.

Yes, it is.

She shows me one eye. I can't decide which one, big and brown and pretty on the screen of my grandpa's phone.

Tali, remember when we first wrote to each other? Two months ago?

A silence.

You read my blog about Balata and circus and sent me messages. We called each other and sometimes we argued. We became friends through arguments.

Did we?

My heart quickens. *You decide.*

My screen turns gray, fuzzy. Maybe Tali has closed a shade or turned off a light.

My mother was the first to read your blog. You're her discovery.

I don't understand.

Maybe she doesn't either. She spends much of her day lying in bed with a handkerchief over her eyes. She sees odd things in shadows. She sometimes thinks we—I mean she and I—should try to make friends with strangers.

My screen flickers. I see a shape like a tea cup, a table knife, then nothing. Am I a stranger who became a friend, or a stranger forever?

My father had Palestinian friends, circus friends, in Jaffa and elsewhere. He's gone, I barely knew him, but my mother sometimes tries to figure out what he would want from her, from his daughter, so she found you one night when she couldn't sleep.

I strain to see Tali, her face, an eye. Anything.

My mother read about Balata, a "sort of ghetto" she called it, and then she made me read your blog, or part of it, maybe because you and me are circus girls, and in circus there are no strangers.

Tali, please—

My mother doesn't talk much. One day I counted her words: twenty-six. When she does speak, I listen. She asked me three times to write to you "in an honest way."

I hold my grandpa's phone close to my face. Here, Tali, I'm right in front of you. Did you write to me in an honest way? Words are difficult, but I believe you tried.

I see something now, her hair, I think, the way it falls in a wave and frames one side of her face. An eye appears. She doesn't blink. Neither do I.

How do you know Jonathan?

I tilt the phone so she might see me in profile. *Did I say I know him?*

Well, you sent me his… She can't find the right words for Jonathan's war-time remembrances. She shows me her lips, plump and pink, and a moment later her jaw, her chin, the shadows on her throat. *Jonathan makes everything so stupidly simple.*

It seems you *know him.*

Just know of him. He's the robot who makes machines.

She asks again why I sent her the story of Tulkarm.

Sleeplessness and love. I can't say this, so I wink.

Well?

We've argued before. Why is this different?

It is.

How?

You know me now, or should. You stayed with my mother and me for twelve days. Jews don't have horns, cloven hooves.

Tali, I never—

Tulkarm is not Treblinka. It's not—

I know, I know.

Do you?

I sometimes feel I'm a hundred years old.

I swallow. No, I don't know the Holocaust, but I will not let her bend me unless she bends too. Jonathan wrestles God with words and machines. I wrestle Tel Aviv Tali with the stories that reach my alley. Does Tulkarm deserve a moment's remembrance? Do any of my people matter? I need time to think of one true thing that won't bend me too soon. *Tali, I love your mother.* Surprised by my words, the strength of my voice, I tell her again, slowly. It's almost a miracle to say something altogether true.

The face on my screen gets smaller and smaller. Fade-away Tali, stingy Tali, offers me a speck of herself. *Well, that's nice, but…*

What?

I still don't know why you sent me some story from 2002. I wasn't even born yet.

That's not the point.

You think Israeli soldiers just happened to round up all those men for no reason?

Why not? They sometimes round up men in Balata for no reason.

The Passover Massacre in Netanya. Have you heard of it?

No.

I didn't think so. I was foolish to ask.

I know what's going to happen before it happens. Click. Gone. Tel Aviv Tali won't wrestle. *The Passover Massacre in Netanya. Have you heard of it?* I know exactly what I need to say. *Well, why would I have heard of it? Netanya—where is it? Most camp people lack knowledge of geography. My grandfather remembers the geography of Jaffa, the family home, the sea. He remembers Cairo where he taught physics at Ain Shams University. Kids like me, though, or anyone born in the camps, know best the narrow passageways that lead from under our feet to the nearest checkpoint.* I say all this and more in my head, wrestle my own self and almost believe she hears me. Tali can't hear a word. No one can. Maybe people try so hard to talk to God because the world is deaf.

44

NETANYA

I mope around my alley, then walk to the house half fallen near the south end of the camp. Two walls, no roof. No barrier between me and the sky over Fire Mountain. Maysa is my practice partner, but tonight I slipped past her door and kept going. I want to walk alone on the wires until I gather my wits, conjure a plan. I don't know what comes next for Tali and me.

I rig two wires, attach them to rebar, plumbing. I loosen my limbs with stretches, acrobatics, then hop on the lowest wire. I angel-walk, wings for arms, no balance pole, but soon I fall with the weight of a human. When I walk well, the boundaries between the wire and me, the earth and sky, almost disappear. I fell because I was thinking of Tali and how afraid I am to lose her. Does she need me as much as I need her? And what did Mrs. Glazman hope for when she asked Tali to write to me "in an honest way"?

I sit amid the bones of this house and listen. Voices wind their way through alleys. The loudest belong to mothers calling their children home. If words don't say much, listen past them. Not only is it time for bed; let it be morning and all of us well, or at least alive. Still, I love the sky and the dark between the stars. I can see constellations from this roofless home. Every star has what I have lost—balance, faith. A wire-walker may forget where she belongs in the sky or where she's going, but no one will ever watch a star walk the wrong way through the night. I have seen stars fall, though, in flares beautiful and frightening. As if every friend they had died or disappeared.

I hear my mother calling my name, calling me home, but she is several alleys away, her voice faint. I squat in the ruins and google *Passover Massacre in Netanya.* I don't wish to learn what I must learn. I open my eyes just wide enough to read.

On March 27, 2002, Abdel-Basset Odeh, a suicide bomber disguised as a woman, carried a suitcase packed with explosives into the dining hall of the Park Hotel and killed thirty mostly elderly Jewish vacationers celebrating Passover. Operation

Defensive Shield was the Israeli response to this and fourteen other suicide bombings in March of 2002. Between March 29th and April 21st, IDF soldiers invaded the six largest cities in the West Bank: Ramallah, Tulkarm, Qalqilya, Nablus, Jenin, and Bethlehem. For every dead Israeli soldier, there were sixteen dead Palestinians during Operation Defensive Shield.

Tali was unborn in 2002, same as me.

I write my friend or acquaintance an email I will never send:

> 16 to 1. I think the ratio has gotten worse for Palestinians since I was born. Please don't imagine that by mentioning this I want any of your people to die or in any way suffer. I'm ashamed of what happened in Netanya. I'm ashamed and afraid it could happen again and again till all of us are dust. Tali, you said to me, *Tulkarm is not Treblinka.* Does suffering have to be Treblinka, Auschwitz, etc., to be important? I believe the beginning of something, the shadow of something, was enough to disturb Corporal Shalev. Tali, what do you need from me? I'm sorry for what happened to your people in Netanya and Treblinka and everywhere, and I'm especially sorry for the loss of your father. I hope you're at least a little sorry for what has happened and keeps happening to Palestine. I think your mother knows about us, but you haven't really tried.

I pray for Tali to call me or text me. What good am I at prayers? Not good at all, but that doesn't stop me from trying. *Inshallah, inshallah.* I count the days…two, three, four, and check my grandpa's phone over and over. Does Tali need me half as much as I need her? I am too proud to call her first.

45

TANK

We bake in summer. I'm not talking about putting bread in an oven. Our alley is the oven. We have no trees. We fall in love with clouds, the darker the better. We dream of ice. No one moves at midday. We sit. We lie down. We keep quiet. Or most of us do.

I'm almost asleep when I hear my brother through the wall that divides our rooms. Issam has his own phone, though I don't know who paid for it. I press my ear to a sheet of plywood and hear whispers, silences, the fragments of a message: "They'll come on Friday, patrol Faisal Street… No, not there. South of the graveyard at 7:10 p.m."

The Israelis have given themselves permission to enter Nablus and its camps at any hour, so why so exact? *They'll come on Friday…7:10.* How does Issam know this? And who told him? Faisal Street, a main artery through Nablus, is wide enough for tanks.

Maybe nothing will happen. Nothing's better than everything else I can think of. *Inshallah, give us nothing on Friday. Give us nothing for days, nights, weeks, or the rest of our lives.* If the muftis could hear my mind, they would accuse me of blasphemy. They can't hear me. No one can. Besides, I know things they're afraid to admit. I'm not the only one who asks Allah to give us nothing. We've seen too much of everything else.

It seems Issam and his cohort(s) have a plan, so I have mine. On Friday night, I decide to practice my art about one hundred meters south of the graveyard. I have no cousins on Faisal Street, but Maysa does, and some of them allow me to string a wire across the road between third-story windows. I'm guessing Issam and his cohort(s) will wait in the shadows of tombs, their eyes on the road. If they harm one Israeli soldier, how many Palestinians will die? Twenty? Thirty? My performance may delay the patrol so the timing of any ambush or bomb will be amiss.

Maysa plays the ringmaster of Faisal Street. Everyone who lives in or near the camp knows I was in Tel Aviv and saw the sea and performed with The Flying Kids, so I have an audience, mostly children. I stand at the sill of a third-story window while Maysa, on the sidewalk beneath me, claims I can walk on air.

Vehicles drift by: cars, vans, pickups. The drivers glance from the road to the wire, but no one stops. I'm almost ready to walk when I notice a young man in a doorway staring at me with such hatred that I blink, step back from the sill. Something inside me clicks. This stranger appears as familiar to me as my own brother, as certain cousins and neighbors. I remember what I've known for most of my life: Those who are loved most are in graves or prisons. And here I am, a circus girl, who received permission to spend almost two weeks in Tel Aviv.

I wear my grandfather's watch. I've never strapped a watch to my wrist, but tonight I count minutes. At 7:06, the young man disappears.

I call to two girls standing beneath the wire, "Move back, move back! I will crush you if I fall!"

This is not true, but it builds suspense. I don't weigh much more than my balance pole. Besides, a wire the width of a finger is all the earth I need.

I step out over the street and stand almost still. I'm about eight meters in the air, high enough that a tank or almost any military vehicle can pass beneath me. I don't want to go to jail for blocking the road. Only the Israelis may block a road, or open it, as they wish.

I soft-step to the other sill and perch in the open window. How easy to please these children! They cheer and look up at me wide-eyed as if beholding a miracle. I'm not a miracle. I'm a will. My steps are as natural as theirs, only more practiced. I learned to walk on wires because… because what else *is* there? This is how I live.

7:08. I wait for a patrol that may never come. My brother expects the Israelis at 7:10, so I will perform till at least 7:20. Once more, I begin my slow walk over Faisal Street. Some of the children make squealing sounds when I play-act, sway back and forth, as if I might fall. I know almost exactly where I am on the wire. There is always an almost inside me. Nothing—not even my next breath—is 100 percent sure.

An orange taxi skids to a halt a few meters past my wire. The driver calls out his window, "Soldiers, soldiers!" and speeds away.

I am half way across Faisal Street, where the wire sags, when I hear the rumble of machinery. Soon I see a tank on my left, a massive barrel protruding from its gut, and a machine-gun in a turret behind and above the barrel. Three jeeps trail after it, then two trucks, and a smaller tank secures the rear, its barrel pointing away from us. My audience scurries toward doorways as bright lights flood the road. I leave my eyes half-open to see my path across the wire.

I feel more than see the disappearances. No faces in windows, no children along the street or in doorways. Only Maysa watches me from beneath an eave. Except for her, I lose one audience but gain another. The Israelis have me in their sights. A beacon flashes. I am blind. I'm fine for three or four steps, but then my mind skips ahead of my body. I come down with my right foot in the sky. I stagger, toss my balance pole, and catch the wire in both hands.

I dangle over Faisal Street. The lead tank had stopped, but now it lurches forward, followed by the jeeps, the trucks, and the mini-tank at the rear. I hear shouts over the noise of machinery. Maysa, opening her arms and running toward me, says, "Let me catch you, let me catch you!" I have a better plan.

The tank keeps coming. Its barrel pivots from me to Maysa, from Maysa to me, and scans windows, doorways, walls, roofs, sky. Seven soldiers emerge from jeeps and trucks. They move forward, slow, slow, weapons pointed at homes. My arms are strong. I could, if I wished, lift myself back to the wire. One soldier trains his rifle on me and barks something in Hebrew. Maysa says in Arabic, "Help her, help her. Get her down."

Minutes later, the tank is beneath me, its barrel angled almost straight up and extending to within one meter of the wire. One of the soldiers, a translator, speaks Arabic. He tells me to grab the barrel and slide down, but I say, "Not yet, not yet." I lift myself to glance at my grandpa's watch: 7:16. I could hang here well into the night if no one shot me. I call this part of my act The Stall.

7:20. They are learning how strong I am. Monkey-like, I let go of the wire and drop down to grab the lip of the barrel with my left hand, now my right. I could swing myself onto the barrel, slide down to the hatch, but I linger. *Never before*, I say to myself, *never again. This can only happen once.*

I ask the translator and the tank commander and his soldiers in Arabic, in English, and with a few words of Hebrew, to please lower the barrel of the tank till it is parallel to the road. I apologize, insincerely, for the inconvenience. They don't know I want the barrel parallel so I can continue to perform.

Minutes pass before the commander stops mumbling and gives what sounds like an order. He behaves as I wish him to behave. Confusion takes time. I wonder what my brother is doing. He and his cohort(s) may have to wait for another night to execute their plan.

After the barrel is parallel to Faisal Street, the commander expects me to drop down safely. He hollers, gestures for me to let go, but I use both arms to lift myself and clamber onto the barrel. I sit a few moments, swing my legs to loosen them, and then I rise, stand, arms wide, and begin to walk. Once, in the house half-fallen where Maysa and I practice, I fantasized walking on the barrel of a tank. As expected, the surface is slick, oily, but wide enough for a stroll. I mosey toward the turret, jump, turn in mid-air, and light back the other way. "Circus is universal"—I learned this from Coach Dagan. Three soldiers start clapping, cheering me on, till their commander tells them to shut the fuck up.

To hell with your tank, I'm thinking. Did you use it at Tulkarm? Did you use it to round up the moustaches, the Palestinians? I strut and style till the tank operator begins to lower the barrel. I am quicksilver. He's trying to throw me to the ground, but I half walk, half leap, onto the tank.

I stand beside the machine-gun and bow without deference. Earlier, the children thought they'd beheld a miracle, but my performance was ordinary until the tank arrived.

Two soldiers start talking with Maysa, and several others disappear through a doorway. A soldier climbs out of the hatchway of the tank, pulls my hands behind my back, and cuffs me. Another soldier, not much older than I am, whispers, "Assif, assif," (sorry). Me too. But I am in no way broken till I turn and see a soldier cuff Maysa and press her against a wall.

46

INTERROGATION

The room is clean and white and smells of disinfectant. I sit on a metal stool in front of a desk, a woman in a green uniform on my left, and a fat lady, doughy and round, a balloon or a baby in her belly, sits across from me in an oversized leather chair. Name. ID. I won't give much else.

I ask the fat lady why I was arrested.

She corrects me in Arabic: "You've been detained, not arrested."

"For being a circus performer? Is this a crime?"

"You haven't been charged with a crime."

"Where's my friend Maysa?"

She waves a chubby hand, a teacher wiping a chalkboard clean. "We never detain anyone to listen to questions."

"Do I have the right to speak with a lawyer?"

"You are here to speak with me."

She rests her forearms on the desk. "Why were you trying to delay or distract a patrol?"

"Sayyida, I wasn't delaying or distracting anything. I was practicing my art. I'm a wire-walker in a circus."

"A wire-walker?"

"I just returned from a performance in Tel Aviv."

She raises her chin and looks down on me over the tip of her nose. "You might go home tonight if you answer my questions without diversions. Who gave you permission to practice your stunt on Faisal Street?"

"No one."

"Did you know there would be a patrol tonight?"

"No, I just wanted to practice. I never know when the soldiers will come."

"Where do you usually practice?"

"In alleyways, or the ruins of a house."

She nods. "In Balata?"

"This is correct."

The woman who stands beside me removes my handcuffs, cheap plastic things, and tells me to massage my wrists. I keep still, pretend nothing hurts. I am less stoic when she offers me a glass of water. It is gone in two gulps.

The fat lady pages through a sheaf of papers. "There have been several incidents on the road where you pulled your stunt."

It was not a stunt.

"Rock-throwing and worse. I'm sure you know this."

Then why tell me?

She ruffles the papers. "Some years ago, your grandfather spent more than four months in custody. The fact that we sometimes release detainees without filing charges does not mean they did nothing wrong."

Occupation forces separate right from wrong, Israelis from Palestinians. If they could, they would tell the sun when to rise, when to set, when to separate from our few scraps of earth and shine on their skyscrapers and forests and fields, and the moon would need permission to pass through checkpoints in the sky, as would the clouds and every drop of rain.

"Did your grandfather ask you to practice on Faisal Street at a certain hour?"

"No."

"A neighbor? Or perhaps your brother?"

"Sayyida, no one tells me where and when to practice. Besides, I did nothing wrong."

"You blocked the main route into Nablus for several minutes."

"No, that's not what happened. The tanks and trucks and jeeps could have passed beneath me. I'm a wire-walker. All I can block is a sliver of sky."

47

A CAGE

I bet right now my grandpa is talking with Uncle Sami and other uncles about how to get me out of here. It's not so bad, though, to be in a cage large enough for a lion. I have cage mates, two women and a girl my age, so I say to myself, "Four lions." Okay, sometimes I color my words, add some muscle, because I need to feel stronger. No one here is weak, though. If my cage mates and I stood side by side and hunched over, we would be one big lion. I see us this way as I lie in a cot with a hand over my eyes to block the glare of ceiling lights.

Jonathan described himself as "fearless" when he makes machines or designs stage sets for warehouse shows. Only when he pauses does depression and hopelessness set in. I understand this, but how can I continue my work in prison? What would my grandpa advise? Is there a way?

Earlier, this old woman, fifty or more, told me we're in a holding cell, which means we won't be here for long. Anyone this old knows the difference between holding cells and permanent cells, so I believe her. We don't talk about why the Israelis detained us. The less we know tonight, the less our interrogators will know tomorrow. Maybe tomorrow we'll be released if we know nothing at all.

❧

After resting a while, I rise from my cot and play jump-rope without a rope. If I tell my cage mates the great Nik Wallenda trains six hours a day and so do I, their blank stares will get blanker. I doubt they've heard of Nik and The Flying Wallendas, or Phillippe Petit either. I'd better answer their head-shakes and whispers, though, so I tell them I'm "a circus girl preparing for a performance." This is true because every step prepares me for the next. Walking back and forth on the barrel of a tank prepared me for no-rope-jump rope. I won't get behind in my training because I'm locked in a cage.

The girl my age becomes my friend in minutes. She, too, plays no-rope-jump-rope, and says I'm "more fun than her sisters and cousins."

After she gets tired, she lets me strengthen my legs by carrying her back and forth in the narrow row between cots. I make lion sounds, but soft, almost silent, a lion the size of a cricket. The guards will come if I roar.

I do one-hundred-and-one squats while carrying my friend. She keeps her laughter quiet, a burble in the throat, a quiver in the belly. I know she hasn't been here long because she smells good. After a rest, she sits cross-legged on my back while I do push-ups. As for training, all I'm missing is a rope or a wire. I don't tell my friend I've seen the Mediterranean Sea and performed with The Flying Kids of Tel Aviv because I don't want her to feel angry or jealous. Nothing is fair. The world will have to turn upside-down for her to know the sea before she dies.

The old woman whispers, "That's enough now. We'll all be punished if you have too much fun."

Three days later, I devise a way to practice my balance. My cage mates know by now I'm a professional wire-walker because last night I found the courage to tell them. My friend believed me at once. The women believed me only after we prayed the night prayer, Isha, and I heard one of them whisper to the other after they had settled in their cots: "What reason would she have to lie? Maybe she *is* a professional." There is no maybe, but I can't talk down to my elder. Only here, in writing, I can be blunt: I'm the greatest high-wire walker in Palestine.

My cot has a wooden rod on each side, canvas in between. A few words are enough for the girl my age to see my plan to practice my art. The women are slow, so I need to repeat and repeat as if I'm teaching a new language and introducing words they have never heard.

At last, we are ready for circus. My cage mates stoop, grab the rod on one side of my cot, and up I go on the other rod. The cot stays somewhat steady, except when they giggle or jiggle and I feel I'm weaving my way through an earthquake. How perfect! A stationary cot would be easy to walk, no more of a challenge than the barrel of a tank.

Birds and angels are athletic, but so am I. Arms wide, playing the sway, I cross the rod in four steps, spin a 180, and start back the other way. I will never hear more quiet or beautiful ululations. The women whisper their happiness. The cage shines. I keep crossing the rod, spinning, turning, walking back and forth, back and forth, and I could leap and touch the ceiling if I wished. Sometimes I pray as I'm supposed to pray, but practicing my art, performing—this is the prettiest prayer I know. I've walked wires in Tel Aviv for hundreds of people, but circus fits in cracks and crannies, even cages. To pray with my whole body—this is enough for joy. My new friends mutter and laugh and ululate, but so quiet that I think of Grandpa's whispers in the alley at night.

On day five in this cage, the two women are released and two more arrive minutes later. The girl prisoner, Yara, still keeps me company, but I have no idea what she did to offend the Israelis. She doesn't know about me either, the way I high-wired over Faisal Street and tamed a tank by walking on its barrel, because it's easier this way. Twice my interrogators have asked me to tell them about my cell mates, and all I give them is names. *Ha, ha, ha, I'm wasting your time!* I'd like to spit these words in their faces, but I pretend I respect them. I hope to leave here soon.

Everybody in this cage knows my stage name—Handala's Sister, the Cat Girl of the Balata Camp. Yara, my assistant in training exercises, sits on my back when I do push-ups, and she laughs her sweet laugh, softer than soft so the guards won't come. She keeps telling me I'm "way more fun than her sisters and cousins," and I tell her she's "dear to me" because she is. I wish I could take her home to meet my family the day the Israelis release us. Me and my mates made our cage shine once, but we can't do this whenever we wish. It never helps to force such things. No one shines if they're greedy, or if they think they can shape long strands of time however they wish. I learned this by walking on wires, by falling from wires. Sometimes we shine and sometimes we don't. I try to stay calm when our only light comes from the glare of overhead bulbs.

I would like to film prison life and send a link to Tali and Mrs. Glazman and the machine artists and The Flying Kids of Tel Aviv. Nothing much happens, though, except that sometimes we shine. I need to make this book true, so I will tell you we are dull more often than we are shiny. Maybe the goal of our keepers is to defeat us in subtle ways. I don't think anyone here has been tortured. None of us have marks on our hands or faces. None of us want to come here again.

48

THE SOUND OF A MILLION STONES

I'm released from the Ofer Prison after eleven nights and ten days. The sky is blue. Noisy crows, black and beautiful, fly over a wall and keep going. My grandpa's here, my mother too, and Uncle Sami the taxi driver. This is the first time they've left Nablus in almost twenty years.

I slide into the backseat beside my mother. My grandpa, in the passenger seat, turns to smile at me every few seconds. Uncle Sami checks his mirrors, then drives away slow and careful. Gold dust swirls over the road.

"Is Maysa at home? Is she all right?"

"Her mother and uncles came for her several days ago," says my mother.

"Was she at Ofer?"

"Yes," says my grandpa, "practicing contortion, juggling escape plans." He chuckles. "You are both fortunate to be released."

I tell my family about Yara, who lives in Ramallah and went home three days before me. "She's my age," I say, "and is interested in circus." My grandpa and Uncle Sami laugh when I explain how my prison friend helped me stay in shape by sitting on my back while I did push-ups. My mother thinks this is silly, not funny. She wouldn't believe that Yara and two women and me made our cage shine a short while. Maybe this doesn't matter. I love her whether or not she sees how beautiful we are.

I ask about Issam. My mother gives me a look that informs me I should have asked about my brother's welfare the moment I was released.

"He was detained," says my grandpa, "but only for around twelve hours."

"For what?"

He raises a hand, palm up. "Does it matter?"

Sometimes it does, but I don't wish to contradict my grandpa. "No," I tell him. "I'm just happy he's home."

Grandpa tells me several of Maysa's male cousins who live on or near Faisal Street were also detained. "Nothing was found in their homes," he says, "or at least nothing we know of. The Israelis became very cautious after they saw you walking over Faisal Street, trying to divert them."

"Who said I was trying to divert them?"

"Child, you know how they think. Nobody needs to say anything to raise their suspicions. They expected there would be an ambush, a bomb, some sort of trap. Sometimes they are right."

Issam must have disappeared into the alleys while I performed for Israeli soldiers, but I wish he'd seen me strut along the barrel of a tank, the tank commander and his minions beneath me. I might have saved my brother's life, or those of Israelis. I can close my eyes and feel the hardness and width of the barrel on the soles of my feet. No path on earth has been easier to walk.

My mother says, "You need to be more careful. Why were you practicing so far from home?"

"I'm sorry."

"You were a long way from where I expect you to be."

My mother keeps a map of our world folded in her heart. One step beyond our alleys is off the map.

In whispers, as if someone could eavesdrop, she tells me the Israelis found explosives on Faisal Street. "Maybe one hundred meters from where you practiced," she adds. "I'm surprised they didn't charge you with a crime."

I look out the window. "I don't think they have a law that says, 'No circus on Faisal Street, no high-wire show.'" I try to smile. "I did nothing wrong."

Grandpa Saeed tells me the same soldiers who detained me found a bomb about an hour later. "They brought in robots," he says. "They saw a spot in the road that was dug up, so they let their machines take the risk."

Uncle Sami, one hand on the wheel, says, "A friend who lives on Faisal Street told me they brought in two robots, but lost one." He smiles at me in his rearview mirror. "I heard the explosion from more than a kilometer away. It was like the sound of a million stones thrown all at once."

49

TRAINING REGIMEN

Before the heat of the day wrings the rivers from our bodies, Maysa and I practice in the ruined house at the south edge of camp. Other girls join us, mainly to watch, though one tries to juggle stones, and another tries to copy me as I walk-slide down a strip of iron to a broken floor, the concrete smashed into bits. The ruins are a spider web of ropes, wires, rebar. The lines I've threaded through holes in the walls are set at different angles, none of them parallel to the ground. After Fadwa, the girl trying to copy me, falls for the third time, I tell her she would have no trouble walking back and forth on the barrel of a tank. "Don't be discouraged," I say. "You can be a circus girl someday if you learn to walk through this house."

All the girls want to know about Tel Aviv and Jaffa. While I rope-walk, wire-walk, rebar-walk, I talk about beaches, about young women almost naked, and "young men almost all skin, with just these little patches of cotton or something over their privates." The girls giggle. Not me. The shake of it would ruin my balance. I smile as I talk about Tali, a great juggler, but I don't mention I stayed with her and her mother. The wire and I wobble some when I begin to tell my audience about Jonathan and the machine artists. I go silent when I realize my words are a great distance from the machines, the artists, and the harder I try to bring them near the farther they recede. Words. Sometimes they have pulses, sometimes not. Today I'd rather walk on rebar, slippery and bent, angles shifting, than scavenge the rubble for words.

My brother comes up the alley kicking a soccer ball and peeks through a gash in a wall. I want to know about the smile on his lips, what it means. Did he plant another bomb on Faisal Street? Will he hate me forever for visiting Tel Aviv?

Tali left me no messages while I was detained. Now she won't answer my emails or take my calls. I'm confused. I miss Tali, but I'm angry too. I said to her in an email, *I don't understand your silence. Why should those few words about Tulkarm end our friendship? If you hate me, you don't know me, and you don't know what you mean to me. What more can I say?*

I did not beg her to respond. I refuse to beg. I carry my grandpa's phone with me. I am available.

❧

I'm sitting with Maysa in her doorway when Issam comes up and calls me sister. This delights me like a burst of rain over the camp. Sister is a beautiful word.

"I heard you did one of your circus tricks on Faisal Street."

I nod.

He tries to glare, but a smile breaks through. "You walked back and forth on the barrel of a tank. Is that right?"

"And I jumped on it," I add, my voice even, as if taming a tank and talking with my brother is nothing special.

He stares at the ground, then me. "Well, you finally learned a circus stunt that isn't a waste of time."

I look past him. "I don't do stunts. There are no stunts in circus."

"Then what are there?"

"Skills. Art."

He chuckles. "Okay, okay. But you finally did something good."

I wish my brother a long life because he will need a long life to understand circus. No one's in charge of me when I'm on the wire, except sometimes the wire. No one's in charge of Tali when she and a Palestinian boy juggle fire in Tel Aviv. No one's in charge of Mazin when he swings on the trapeze and catches Miki in the light of a red tent. My brother's body has less room than stone, steel, rebar. I don't know how to scrape a spark into it, how to light a lamp. *Brother, I pass through checkpoints on the wire. I will keep walking till I pass through every barrier, every cage, and I wish you would follow, or even lead.* I hold my silence because Issam would understand nothing. Checkpoints, soldiers, guns, tanks, planes—I will slip past them all before I die. Circus loves me. I love it back. No magic, Issam. My body is a flame.

❧

Late at night, while my mother sleeps, I slip out to the alley because I feel something's about to happen. Clouds are low. Wind grazes our roofs, a patter of rain. Storms don't come in summer, so maybe I await a miracle. I sky-watch a long time. Sure, I'd like to see cloud mountains sweep over the camp, but this—a gap between walls, a narrow path for the eye—is also a gift. More rain now, and I catch a few drops on my tongue. It falls from clouds and tastes shiny as me.

I feel it down the length of my spine—the electricity of a storm. All is dark before sparks fly. Bursts of light, wire-walker paths, zigzag over the camp, and I'm both here and there, walking in my alley, drinking rain, and riding over the roofs to wherever the paths lead. Sometimes the dark is so dark the light must break it open. Cloud mountains flash and boom, a flicker of suns. I walk zigzag paths and drink rain and wonder at the light. I wish I could say, "Here, Issam, this is for you too," and teach my brother to walk, stay upright, play the sway, and do better than survive.

Two more flashes and the clouds sail east. I will see a star soon. I will carry the smell of rain to bed. Never in my life have I seen a summer storm, so thank you, strange clouds, for getting lost in the sky and giving us bursts of rain and thunder and light.

50

CAREFUL

This morning I hear from Tali, not in words but photographs, grainy videos. Holocaust highlights. She'd hate me if I muttered these words, "Holocaust highlights," but these videos and stills belong in Germany. Let the Germans post the photographs on lamp-poles in Berlin, Munich, Hamburg. Palestinians had nothing to do with the Holocaust.

I write:

> Sometimes I'm furious because you don't know me at all, and because you don't know your own country, or even yourself. Israelis are free to live as they please and harass whoever they please and imprison and destroy whoever and whatever they please, day or night. Your politicians and generals draw maps with bulldozers and bombs and blood not theirs, and maybe they won't stop till every grain of sand is secured, fenced, guarded by sentries, and by armed robots, too, because the Holocaust gives Israel the perfect excuse to commit every sin and forgive itself in advance.

I almost touch *Send.*

I go back to bed after I finish my morning chores. My chest hurts. The bones ache, as if bruised from a fall. I drift off, dream a short while, and when I wake I know some of my words are false. I don't know how to make every word mean what I need it to mean. Does my grandfather? Does anyone? I see Jacob Glazman, his photograph, and wonder if my words—even if they stay inside me—can harm someone. Maybe I love Tali despite everything. It's easier to love Mrs. Glazman and Jonathan, and of course Mazin of The Flying Trapeze. I love my grandpa and my mother and Maysa, and try hard to love my brother. These simple words are true, yet they take so long to find me. It may be impossible to make a book in which every word means what I need it to mean.

Three days later, I write to Tali on Messenger:

I am sorry. The pain is sometimes too much. The only time I am free is when I'm on a wire or a rope, though I know I can fall. And you? I'm afraid you won't believe me, but I remember your smell and I miss you so much. You smell like cinnamon and jasmine and cardamom and rose. (*I won't admit I love her until I'm confident she'll believe me.*) Honest, Tali. You smell like cinnamon and jasmine and cardamom and rose.

I touch *Send.*

51

MAZIN

One afternoon, the alley almost hot enough to steam, Grandpa is napping, Mother is upstairs with Aunt Salma and other cousins, and I am alone. I sit at the kitchen table with Grandpa's phone when I receive a text from Mazin. *Can I call you on Messenger?*

My mother would not allow this, nor would my grandpa.

My response is *WHEN?*

Seconds later, Mazin the Magician, the trapeze artist, appears on the screen of Grandpa's phone. I'm the only traveling girl in Balata. I've seen the Mediterranean, the shine and swell of waves, but I may never decide who is prettier—Mazin or the sea. What can I say to him? A sudden breath blows out of me and I belch like a frog. Mazin laughs, but not to make fun of me. The scar on his left cheek closes like lips when his smile spreads wide.

We talk circus. At the close of each practice, The Flying Kids form a pyramid, the tallest and strongest boys at the center, the lighter kids balancing on their shoulders. "I'm in the middle," says Mazin. "I'm right where the coaches want me to be. Miki—because she's the lightest girl—stands at the top."

I don't care to hear about his trapeze partner, Ms. Miki. I'd like to boast about delaying an Israeli patrol, walking on the barrel of a tank, but our conversation may be monitored. I'm trying to believe I have at least one small chance to return to Tel Aviv and perform with The Flying Kids.

I tell Mazin I see circus everywhere, even in the ruins of a house. I'm learning to walk on rebar, slippery and bent, and a spider-web of ropes and wires, none of them parallel to the ground. He calls me Spider Girl. Yes, I'm thinking, Spider Girl, Cat Girl—I'll have many stage names over the years. I think he's lost his mind, though, when he tells me I'll be invited to perform with The Flying Kids in mid-October in Ha'yarkon Park.

"Mazin, you forget where I live. Months or years may pass before I can leave the camp."

"Don't be so sure. Tali's mother watched us practice today, and I heard her talking with our coaches."

"Mrs. Glazman?"

"Yes, they have to listen to her because her husband founded the circus. She knows our legal team, too, the lawyers who can fix things. You will hear from them this week."

I have lighted on a wire I can't quite see. "Mazin, you're sure of this?"

"One hundred percent. Besides, it's not only Mrs. Glazman who's trying to help. All our coaches are for you."

"And Tali? Did she say anything?"

"I don't think so. All I heard was her mother and the coaches."

"But Mrs. Glazman's so quiet. She speaks in whispers."

"Not always. I heard every word."

I am the quiet one now. I remember Tali telling me I'm her mother's "discovery," not hers. Mrs. Glazman was the first to read my blog, my circus notes, my Balata notes, and she decided her daughter and The Flying Kids should give me a chance. Mrs. Glazman may be stranger than all of us. A terrorist killed her husband. Why would she wish to help any Palestinian? Why has she chosen me?

I ask Mazin to describe the sea today.

"Hot," he says.

"What else?"

"Blue-green. Quiet. Not many waves."

"Did you go swimming?"

"Not yet."

"What beach do you go to?"

"Alma Beach," he says, "or sometimes Banana."

I wink. "Banana?"

"That's what it's called."

We talk in whispers till he says, "My uncle's here, I better go," and we have no time for proper goodbyes. What I want, what I really want, is to perform with The Flying Kids, walk the beaches of the Mediterranean, swim with Tali and Mazin in the sea, and marry that pretty boy someday.

I lie in bed and close my eyes. A curtain separates this room from the nook we call the kitchen. Sometimes my life is simple. I want Mazin to want me. I've wanted other boys to want me a little, but it would be haram (forbidden) to let them know. Now I don't want just any boy. I want a trapeze artist. I want Mazin. I am certain he knows.

There is a place in the throat so hard I could mistake it for a bone. Adam's apple, they call it, though it could be Eve's apple. Either way, it feels harder than fruit. I touch myself here and think, *Does he love me yet?*

I unbutton my blouse. My ribs feel harder than my Adam's apple, my breasts as firm as the muscles of fish. Mazin lives far away, but I like missing him as I touch myself, my hands light, the way my feet are light on a rope or a wire. A girl's not supposed to think of her body, but I have one. Sometimes I don't know my own beauty till I touch myself.

I pretend to sleep as I hear my mother coming down the stairs from Aunt Salma's kitchen, snickering at something her sister has said.

52

TALI AND ME

Tali Glazman finally sends me an email.

> My mother says you're a nice girl, she insists you are, so I must forgive. Do you understand us? NO, NO, NO, NO, YOU DON'T. My mother says, "Forgive anyway. It'll hurt worse if you don't." In regard to hurt, my mother is a foremost expert, a scholar. She could write many books.

Tali includes a quote from an Auschwitz survivor because she thinks I need an education:

> "We must be listened to: above and beyond our personal experience, we have collectively witnessed a fundamental unexpected event, fundamental precisely because unexpected, not foreseen by anyone. It happened, therefore it can happen again: this is the core of what we have to say. It can happen, and it can happen everywhere…
> Everybody is somebody's Jew."
> —Primo Levi

I write, *Maybe Palestinians, camp kids, are the Jews of the Israelis*, but I don't touch *Send.* I write, *Regarding hurt, displacement, every Palestinian is a scholar, crazy with knowledge*, but I don't touch *Send.* I write, *I won't touch my body today because I'm angry and sad,* and I won't touch *Send.*

The next day, after practicing circus in the ruined house, I lose my anger and a smidge of my sorrow. I write, *I miss you, Tali, and I miss your mother and The Flying Kids. Here's what I believe. We should be friends no matter what happens here or there or anywhere in the world.* I read these words in silence, then aloud, and they are true. I touch *Send.* I touch it twice. I wonder if we'll ever know each other well enough to share words we're afraid to touch.

Part Four

Tel Aviv/Jaffa

53

AISHA

Tali's mother and the coaches of The Flying Kids, plus some Israelis I don't even know, used their pull to get me a six-day permit, what Tali calls "a cultural permit, an artist's permit." I will once more walk the high-wires of Tel Aviv.

Tali has forgiven me, or claims she has, but she will not share her bed "this time around." An old Palestinian coach, Mousa, arranged for me to share a room with his niece Aisha in South Tel Aviv, less than a kilometer from Jaffa. Aisha is twenty-three, dark and pretty, but she has a boyfriend, not a husband. Her father has vanished and her mother seems to have lost control of the family. Aisha has sisters, fourteen and sixteen, but only her mother wears hijab.

Her home, in a dead-end alley, is almost as small as a Balata home, but open a window and you will smell the sea. My first night here, after the lights are out, I breathe the good smell and wait for a dream of Mazin and me. I wake sometime in the night, the room dark, and my dream—whatever it was—has vanished. I hear whimpers, sighs, and then a name: "Zahra, Zahra." Aisha keeps her sorrow quiet till shudders shake the bed.

I hold her shoulder. "What's wrong?"

"Nothing."

"Who's Zahra?"

"You don't know her."

"If there's any way—"

"You can't help. No one can. It's too late."

It is too late. Aisha, after she calms somewhat, tells me she lost her best friend less than a year ago. She turns so that my hand slips from her shoulder. Her friend died in Istanbul on New Year's Eve.

Zahra was her name. On holiday, with money she earned as a waitress in a café in Jaffa, she went to Istanbul with two other girls to celebrate the New Year. They went to a nightclub popular with foreigners. "I imagine they were having a good time," says Aisha, "though of course

I don't know. Did they have drinks? Did they dance? Did they talk to any men? I don't know. All I know is that one minute before midnight a fanatic burst into the club and opened fire with an automatic weapon. Eleven dead, Zahra included. Her friends survived, but one of them never leaves home."

My eyes close. "I am so sorry."

"Yes, so am I, but sometimes I'm more furious than sorry. Today I'm with some cousins, we're having lunch, and I start talking about Zahra, how I wish she were with us, how I never stop missing her. They miss her, too, or two of them claim they do, but then Maha, this big mouth, says Zahra and those other girls shouldn't have been in that club, what were they doing there, what did they expect to find?" She turns to face me. "Amal, I hardly know you. You're in Uncle Mousa's circus. This doesn't tell me much, does it? Are you like Maha? *Are* you?"

"Not at all."

She struggles to breathe. "Honest?"

"Honest."

"Because if you're *that* kind of girl, weak and cruel and pious…" She rises on her elbows, then slumps back in bed, exhausted. "Sometimes I am so tired of this world."

I am not that kind of girl, but how do I explain? I learned kindness from my grandpa, and also from my mother. What sort of girl am I? I'm a wire-walking Muslim girl from Fire Mountain. My stage name is Handala's Sister, The Cat Girl of the Balata Camp. I can't reveal these sweet sides of myself point-blank because I just met Aisha and she'll think I'm crazy. I'm not weak. Vulnerable, yes, but not weak. When Uncle Mousa decided I should stay with her, share her bed, she could not refuse. Aisha has a right to know me, but what can I say?

I smile in the dark. "I'm nothing like Maha, I promise. And I think you're right to say she is weak."

"My other cousins aren't much better. They just stared at their plates while Maha blabbed and blabbed. They didn't say a word."

"And what did you say?"

She ruffles her pillow. "I'll tell you, but first I need to hear what *you* would say. Would you just sit there, stare at your salad, or would you say something that matters?"

"I don't know. Sometimes words are hard to find. Sometimes they don't help."

"And sometimes they *do*. What would you say? *Any*thing?"

"I need a moment."

"Take it. Tell the truth."

I need more than a moment. I need a fat minute or two. Aisha huffs a breath. "Wait," I say, "*please*," and watch another minute roll by. I've never met Maha, but maybe this doesn't matter. I know many camp people, women and men, young and old, who have firm ideas about how to live each moment of our lives. My grandpa sometimes refers to them as a group, "our not so friendly morality police."

"I would tell Maha she has no right to blame Zahra for her own death. She is not a judge."

Aisha exhales noisily. "And what else?"

"I'd tell her it is better to keep quiet than to judge."

Aisha sighs and I'm sure I've disappointed her, but then she giggles. "Keep quiet? Well, that's a good start for Maha. You want to know what I told my cousin?"

"Yes."

"I told Maha, I told her four times, 'Shut the fuck up, shut the fuck up, shut the fuck up, shut the fuck *up*!'"

I lie still. My heart plays drums on my ribs, four booms, echoes—*Shut the fuck up!* I want to comfort Aisha, but how? She starts laughing. I touch her shoulder, wait for words, but maybe she needs something else. I fill my lungs, my stomach, and now I laugh, too, for Zahra, I guess, and for every girl who can't laugh anymore, or never could. Do I have a new sister? I miss lying near Tali, smelling her, I miss Mrs. Glazman, but Aisha is surprising, so am I, and in this way we are more than friends or cousins. We mourn Zahra, dead Zahra, so, yes, we're sad, but we laugh because she'd want us to, girls not hemmed tight, hardly hemmed at all, and our mourning and sadness and strength are for her and how many others? Walls wider than those in Balata mute some of our laughter and sorrow. Aisha's mother, in the next room, might hear a rumble in her dreams, a sound not so different from the blowing sea.

54

CIRCUS PRACTICE

No trapeze artist in the world is more beautiful than Mazin. Look at him with his green tights, long legs, long arms, jaw-bone scar, and black hair like the crest of a bird. Before climbing the ladders to the trapezes, he and Miki, his lucky partner, use bungees to feel the spring and strength of their arms and shoulders. Miki's too elegant to sweat, but Mazin seems to have leaped in the sea and rose with the sun.

Balata girls don't look at boys, but I'm far from home. I notice smiles not for me—Mazin for Miki, Miki for Mazin, round-trip. Even a camp girl knows when smiles mean something extra. Remember the day Mazin surprised me, called me on Messenger? All my longing moved through me, earthquakes and shyness, a heart-drum in the belly, a warmth spreading out, and I wonder, I still wonder, does the earth feel this way when dark clouds bring hope of rain? Now I know Mazin never needed me as I need him. Maybe he called Miki the next day, or walked on the beach with her, or swam beside her in the sea. I'll never know exactly when their smiles began to mean so much. I just know they're in love.

Why did I ever imagine Mazin might one day be my husband? A girl from Balata is a stranger elsewhere. I'll be a wire-walker with The Flying Kids for five more days, but Miki lives in Tel Aviv, her forever home, and no one can pack her on a bus, drop her at checkpoints, ferry her to a camp, and close the gates. Fair or unfair—it doesn't matter. Does Mazin think I'm pretty? I am, I am. But he'll never look at me long enough to see.

I have my art, ropes and wires, the sky I walk through, nothing more. Coach Dagan has a saying for his aerialists: "Steady the mind with the body, move with care." I know this method, but I can also *think* myself warm, strengthen and balance my body with no movement other than breathing. My grandpa Saeed taught me this, so maybe it's scientific. I don't know if other aerialists can think themselves warm.

Today I can't think *period.* I tell Coach Dagan I have a bellyache and I'm dizzy and need to sit. He brings the trainer and she's really nice and checks me and finds nothing wrong and gives me shoulder rubs to relax me and Pepto-Bismol chewies for my gut.

❧

But something good happens at circus. During a break, Tali pours two cups of water and offers me one. If you wish to stay friends with someone in Israel or Palestine, give her water. This is better than signing a truce.

I thank Tali in my language and hers, then ask about her mother.

"Better than usual," she says. "Maybe because you're back with The Flying Kids."

Mrs. Glazman is a mystery. She helped me to come here, she needs me somehow, though I don't know why. I believe she would welcome me into her home again if this were acceptable to Tali. Maybe I'm lucky to be with Aisha and her family, where I don't have to guard every word and feeling. I would like to think of Tali as a sister, or a close cousin. My grandpa would say, "Be patient," and maybe Mrs. Glazman would say the same.

But I need to be sure of something 100 percent. "Tali," I say, "I've been gone for several months. Mazin and Miki, are they…?"

She half smiles. "You want to ask me something?"

"I think they've changed since…"

"Are they boyfriend and girlfriend? Is that the question?"

I nod and blush.

"They've decided to restart the peace process on the trapeze," says Tali.

Sometimes I hate sarcasm.

"And why not?" she adds. "Nothing else has worked too well."

❧

That night, watching the news with Aisha and her mother and sisters, we learn that two Israeli women were killed in East Jerusalem hours earlier. IDF soldiers, off-duty, were walking on a sidewalk when a truck roared up, jumped the curb, and pinned them to a stone wall. They were nineteen, three years older than me.

I need water. I drink three glasses, then go to the bathroom to be alone. I can picture my own brother as the murderer, skinny Issam using a truck as a weapon, a machine as powerful and fatal as a suicide vest. I want to stop him, stop the soldiers, too, from taking more of our land, our homes, but how? I want to call Tali and her mother and tell them I'm sorry. I want to call the mothers and fathers of the soldiers and let them scream at me if they must. Once, at night, Mrs. Glazman said, "I wish, I wish," but couldn't finish. Maybe we are partners searching for words that can come true before words are dust.

The great Phillippe Petit strung a wire between the Twin Towers of New York City and walked out some six-hundred meters over the street. In 1974, long before 9/11, before Arab hijackers, mostly Saudis, turned the towers to smoke and ash, Petit performed the most unforgettable walk in history. I love him, his craziness and courage, but sometimes the wire that meets my feet is thinner and wobblier than those of any Frenchman. Petit had less to think about. He was able to concentrate and see only the wire, or better, to see the narrow path through the sky and the whole sky, above and below. Coach Dagan often reminds his aerialists "to take a laser-like focus, to see and feel the body and the wire, nothing else." I never contradict my coach, but there are other ways to walk. I'm at my best when aware of the void.

All through the night I dream wild dreams and wake many times. In the morning I almost hope Miki marries Mazin and gives him babies and they live many years and become grandparents and great-grandparents because no one should die too soon. Maybe these trapeze artists have a future. Maybe they can say, "I wish for a family, for children, for grandchildren, for the sea and the shore," and maybe, in Tel Aviv, they can have everything until they die.

55

MACHINE ART EXHIBIT

Aisha, my sister-friend, has an iPhone, and lets me play with it after dinner. I google *machine art occupation* and see a notice for a show in Jaffa tomorrow at ten thirty p.m. Why so late? Circus practice begins each morning at seven forty-five.

I ask Aisha if she's ever seen a machine art exhibit. She looks at me.

"Former soldiers make machines, all sorts of robots. They put on shows."

"I've heard of them."

"Will you go with me to a show tomorrow night in Jaffa? Ten thirty?"

"My mother will never let me take you anywhere at that hour."

"Maybe you can talk with her."

"No, talking won't help. Our only option is to slip out of the house."

Over the entry to a warehouse, on a catwalk shielded by glass, two machines stand over us, heads swiveling one-hundred and eighty degrees. The tall one speaks Hebrew, the short one a mix of Arabic and English. They order us to stay in line, keep our arms away from our sides. No bunching up, no pushing. Advance one at a time.

Aisha says to me in Arabic, "Why program robots to be assholes? There are enough assholes."

Before I can shrug or nod, the short machine turns to us. "Palestinians may enter on the left."

"What?"

"Palestinians may enter on the left."

The voice is so sweet I remember Maysa. The machine says, "This way, at your leisure," and a door swings open. A lady robot, in a traditional Palestinian dress of many colors, greets us in Arabic and waves us forward with the flutter of a hand.

Remote control. I whisper these words because they are generous only once. The robots must have miniature microphones and computers in their throats or chests. By remote control, Jonathan or other artists can play track one or track two, etc., and a robot may say different things to different people, make different gestures, behave as the artist wishes. I don't understand the mechanics, which makes this fascinating, sort of like walking wires through changing winds. Maybe the artist who controls the robots at the entry, the mock checkpoint, is monitoring a computer on the far side of this wall. I notice the eye of a camera mounted to the ceiling. Maybe everything, everywhere, is seen. And for once the eye is kind.

I glance back at a long line of Israelis waiting to enter. One by one, they step forward to be frisked by a machine twice my height. Long arms with creaky hinges fold over each person, and hands painted red pat the rib cage, the armpits, the small of the back, the blades of the shoulders. Aisha says, "This robot's a cutie," but she's not serious, only amazed. A woman her age, in a pink skirt, a low-cut blouse, wriggles and giggles as the machine has its way with her. Tickle? Stage lights erase shadows. I see bracelets on her ankles, and dragonflies, spiders, tattoos on her calves. She enjoys the frisking because she is safe.

In a dark corner of the warehouse, Aisha finds a bartender robot bending over a table, his limbs angular like those of a grasshopper, his head a box with painted eyes (blue), a hook nose (brown), and curvy lips (pink). Iron or steel can smile forever. A snake (green body, red tongue) coils around a leg.

Aisha studies the diagram wired to the bartender's sternum, then presses his belly button. His arms jiggle, his right hand comes up, and a few ounces of red wine pour from his forefinger to a paper cup.

Aisha sniffs. "Pinot noir?"

The bartender nods.

Red arrows on a cement floor lead to an amphitheater. Aisha and I join maybe a dozen show-goers, all Israeli, I believe, before a stage littered with brooms, dustpans, handles of doors, keys and key chains, overturned chairs, the fender of a car, a cracked mirror, a poster of Abu Ibrahim, a martyr from Jenin. Hooded figures appear on one side of the stage, faces veiled. Maybe they are human. They don't creak like machines as they approach the debris.

A red-haired man, flesh and blood, skips across the stage and warns us in Hebrew, in English, in stiff Arabic, in gestures, "Stand back, stand back, better safe than dead!" Moments later clicking sounds, a whoosh of wind, and four machines rise from the wings, soldiers skeletal and tall, with long-barreled rifles on their shoulders, bandoliers drawing Xs on their chests. They find their places on one side of the debris while the hooded ones seem to watch from the other. I say *seem* because their eyes—if they have them—hide behind the mesh of niqabs.

The tallest robot has the insignia of a captain on his left shoulder. His uniform clings to the iron of him, or the steel. The hooded ones breathe through veils. They must be human because every sound they make rises from somewhere soft.

The captain points a finger whittled to a thorn. "Bring forth the pebble-thrower." The hooded ones look up as if a prayer or a prophet might appear beneath the roof.

Captain: "…small boy tossed pebbles at jeep…big boy…stone at drone." Static erases words, but not the message. "Bring forth…*sons*. The debris…need clear path though village…Bring forth…yes, Pebble Boy, Stone Boy…clear debris…no time for…shithole village. Bring forth Pebble Boy, Stone…No, fuck it…bring forth boys, sons…*any* two...no matter…I…count to ten."

He looks up, so I look, too, at a drone hovering over the hooded ones, a flying camera smaller than my fist. The captain repeats himself. The same words, the same static, but louder, faster, his mouth flapping, jaw joints clicking. Pebble Boy and Stone Boy or any two sons must clear the path, haul away the keys and key chains and brooms and dustpans and overturned chairs and the car fender and the cracked mirror and the poster of Abu Ibrahim. A nest for IEDs? Harmless rubble? Little boys will provide the answers. Neither the captain nor the men he commands will risk their lives in "shithole village."

Sometimes Israelis bring in robots to clear away suspicious packages or barricades. This takes time, though, and delays their mission. Once, in Balata, an Israeli lieutenant forced Khalil, a twelve-year-old boy, to haul away tires and broken furniture and cinder blocks from the entrance to the Camp. When his mother raised a fist and began yelling at the lieutenant, two soldiers held her and gagged her till the entrance to Balata was clear. No IEDs, no body parts to collect. But Khalil cried after he finished his work.

Stage lights come up on the women. Soon, above them, we see bubbles, dozens of them, each about the size of the drone still hovering. No niqabs now. Bare faces, eyes, cheeks, even *necks*. These women are not the work of machine artists. Flesh and blood, they behave as they wish. Each has a bubble bottle, a wand, and lungs to blow. The captain calls once more for Pebble Boy and Stone Boy or any two sons to clear the debris from the path though the village. The women blow bubbles—red, orange, yellow, green—almost a rainbow. Most show-goers laugh, or at least chuckle. I only smile because this is the war I have always known: iron against bubbles, steel against bubbles, crazy arsenals against bubbles, Israel against Palestine, Goliath against *us*. Yes, we have some guns hidden in our camp, a few bombs, too (I know this without having seen them), but mostly we have bubbles, or things like bubbles—old tires, broken furniture, things we can stack between ourselves and the soldiers, and we have pebbles, stones, the spit in our mouths, the wind in our throats. We have no bubble bottles or wands, though I wish we did. The captain gives an order. The drone flits this way and that and pops bubbles. I want to watch till the end, but Aisha says, "Quite fantastic, isn't it? But I need more wine."

She finds two robots in an alcove, one dispensing white wine, one red, and chooses the latter.

"My mother would scream," she says, "if she saw me now."

Mine too, but my secret life is not yet a sin.

An usher, a woman robot in a green dress and matching scarf, says, "Don't just drink for free, see some art," and directs us to Exhibit #3. Dozens of TVs, all tuned to the same channel, are mounted on a wall and form a tower that rises higher than the minaret near the Balata Camp. A silent film, in black and white, shows in slow motion. I scan the TVs, then settle my eyes on a screen wider than the others, a few meters from the rafters, but angled toward the floor.

Four soldiers point their rifles at a man as he steps from an orange taxi and raises his arms over his head. He must be sixty years old. One soldier hops in the taxi and drives off while another twists the prisoner's hands behind his back and snaps on plastic cuffs.

Subtitle: Penalty for driving on Israeli road near the settlement of Elon Moreh

The TVs show a parking lot jammed with seized cars and pick-ups, a pack of settler kids closing in on the orange taxi. They howl and curse (muted, with close-ups of mouths spread wide); they throw stones and smash windows (muted, with glass shards like diamonds in sun); they kick the tires before they slash them (muted, no thudding sounds or bursts of air); they beat the taxi's body with tire irons (muted, except for my head, the pulse at the temples). At last the biggest boy holds up a hand like a policeman halting traffic. The frame narrows and soon there is only his hand on TV, on *all* TVs. The orange taxi is dead. Soon this whole parking lot will die. The picture widens to show the settler kids and their leader moving as a pack to the next vehicle in the lot.

Subtitle: Nine days later

The old man, released from detention, comes to the lot to retrieve his taxi. Three soldiers greet him, one hands him his keys, then leads him to his car. The taxi driver raises his arms and howls (muted), and the soldier un-holsters his pistol and shoots in the air (muted). On each TV, the driver grows smaller and smaller till he's the size of this period. The moment he disappears the screens turn so white and bright Aisha and I must turn away.

She sips her wine, then drains it. "You know what I've always liked about the Israelis?" I have nothing to say. "They know their grapes."

One corner of the warehouse opens to a garage with a banner strung from the ceiling—PRAYERS IN SESSION. Flapping flags—blue, white, red, green, yellow—spin round and round on a wheel powered by some sort of engine. Each color bleeds into the next. A bright wind, a rainbow fire. Aisha finds a note tacked to a pole: *Tibetan Prayer Wheel Powered by Small Jet Engine & Biofuels.* The engine, about the size of two of me, is enclosed by a cage so no one can reach with a hand or an arm and get mauled by a blade. The garage opens to an alley. A series of metal tubes carries the exhaust outward to the night.

We dream when we sleep and some dreams follow us when we wake. Maybe machine artists woke one morning, pulled back the curtains to the world, and decided to color their prayers bright and power them to a jet and fly them to God special delivery. *Look, God—fast prayers, shiny prayers. Pay attention.* Maybe the artists wonder if only fast prayers can save us. I understand the rush. No one in Balata is too young to think about the end of the world.

Aisha and I back away from the Prayer Wheel and drift in a kind of fog. She needs another drink, but can't find a wine robot. The warehouse is shadowy away from the exhibits. My sister-friend believes that I, sober, know where the bartenders are, but I am lost.

I lead her to a halo of light, an exhibit titled *Almost Home, Train #9*. A man (Aisha thinks he's a machine but she's wrong) lies face-up on a platform the length and width of his life, its iron wheels half-hidden in the rails of the world's skinniest train-line. The man's mask reminds me of Florentine graffiti—a pink snake crawling from the skull of a beetle. Maybe the life beneath the snake and the insect, the white shirt and shiny green pants, is Jonathan.

The train and its passenger begin their ride. The track stretches some twenty meters. Near one end a gold hoop arcs over it, the world's skinniest bridge. Before the train slips though, there's a rushing sound, the hoop hisses, sparks, and bursts into flame. The train shifts gears, speeds ahead, and the passenger—too fast and thin to burn?—flies horizontal under the bridge.

He has just begun. The train shunts along the rails, a back-and-forth bullet. The man shines as he blows through the fire feet-first, face-first, feet again, on and on. He threads a hole in the sun just wide enough to slip through without burning. But how many times can he do this? I'm not a Prayer Wheel, but I can pray fast. No words, just a strong light in the throat and heart. I edge nearer to the man and the train and the fire till Aisha tugs my arm from behind. "Little sister, what are you *doing*? Get away from those tracks!"

So I step back, shine my prayers, and wait. Minutes later, I cheer with everyone else when the burning bridge darkens and the train lurches to a halt. The man jumps to his feet and styles like he's in a circus, one arm raised high before bowing, the arm a wing to swoop down, shine shoe-tops with a swift hand, then up again, both arms skyward, and the rest is momentum—the light of him pouring over us. I can see though his mask. Jonathan played with death, and maybe I'm the only show-goer who in some way understands. On the high-wire I like to experiment, see how close I can come to falling without falling. And sometimes I let myself fall to practice this, too, so I can learn how to land, how to roll, how to lessen the hurt each time I fail.

Aisha says, "Okay, I think you've seen enough."

No, I haven't. I seldom contradict my elders, except in silence. How can I see enough? How can *anyone* see enough? Are there eyes that can see everything? I don't think so. And we all die too soon.

I squeeze her hand. "Please," I say, "one minute. I need to say hi to Jonathan."

She leans in to see me better. "*Who*?"

"Just a friend. He once saw me perform with The Flying Kids."

Now Jonathan removes his mask. Maybe Aisha will be less anxious to find a wine robot or an exit because this machine artist is pretty. I'm shy, but I walk my wire, go up to him, and I wish I could do what I sometimes do for my grandpa—kiss the back of his hand and bring it to my forehead to show respect.

Jonathan recognizes me. He shakes my hand, calls me "my circus friend," and I call him "my machine-artist friend." He laughs as if my words are medicine. "Thank you," he says. "That's the sweetest thing I've been called all year."

"And the circus?" he asks. "Will you perform again with The Flying Kids? Can I come?"

"Yes! And I hope Shirel can come too. Where is she?"

He gestures behind him, toward the shadows. "She's here somewhere, but she doesn't like to watch when I do anything with fire."

I turn to Aisha, who shadows me like a guardian, drunk though she is. I tell Jonathan that she and her family are my hosts. I call Aisha "my sister-friend," and other nice things. She and my machine-artist friend shake hands.

Jonathan asks me when and where I'll perform with The Flying Kids. I start telling him when he steps back, screams, "Down, get down!" but I stay where I am, befuddled. Two shots ring in my ears. I think it's part of the show, a bearded man with a pistol, but then the blood drains from Jonathan's face and he falls backward. Three men wrestle the shooter to the ground, strip the gun from his hand, and it makes no more noise than a can clattering across the floor. The men hold his arms, his legs, his shoulders, and he spits in their faces, curses, tries to break free. Someone kicks him in the ribs. Jonathan, on his back, head turned, calls, "Don't do that, please." Blood spurts from his left shoulder, his forearm. "Just get an ambulance here."

56

ONE CAN BE A BIG NUMBER

I wake from a dream of machines and stage lights and bursts of gunfire.

Aisha gathers me in her arms. "Can you hold me too?"

Soon I dream quieter dreams.

❧

My life is simple math: 100–99=1. I control almost nothing, but I can speak in my heart the names of those I love. It makes no difference who comes first or last, so just listen:

Jonathan, my wounded machine-artist friend;

Maysa, my forever friend;

Handala the Cat, the Sentry of the Balata Camp;

anyone who whispers, *Can you hold me too?*

Grandpa Saeed, my first and best teacher;

Layla, my worried mother;

Issam, my furious brother;

Uncle Sami, who drives a taxi when he has gas money;

Mrs. Glazman, who would hold me and be held;

and Tali, though she may never speak my name in the light of her heart.

Mazin? No one's more beautiful, but it's too late to hold him and be held. I'd be sadder except that day or night, awake or asleep, I love many people and also a cat. The life of a refugee is a life of subtraction (100–99=1), so I've made 1 a big number. At first light I hug Aisha, smell her winey breath, somehow pleasant, and soon I will walk the high-wire with The Flying Kids. Here is my plan: I will walk till I die and love who I can. I hope someday I'll be an old grandma with rickety bones and good balance, but the world will decide how far I walk, how long I love.

57

A RISK

The Flying Kids have a two-hour break between morning practice and afternoon practice. Tali and I walk on the Promenade, then sit on a bench and watch the sea. No one in Balata will see what I see—beach girls almost naked, boats with white sails. A mother breastfeeds her infant under a parasol.

I ask Tali about her mother.

"You'll see her when we perform at Ha'yarkon Park. She misses you."

"I miss her too."

Tali half smiles. "Maybe I'm jealous."

"What do you mean?"

"My mother wrote you a letter. I think it's around twelve pages."

My heart speeds. "For *me*?"

"Yes, but the letter's unfinished. Everything is unfinished."

I stare at her.

"Those are my mother's words."

The sea would be less beautiful without the darkness beneath. Somehow I know Mrs. Glazman, though so little has been spoken. Maybe she is attempting the impossible: to make every word of her letter true. I try to make this book as true as my life, as other lives, and deaths, too, but it is always, at best, a walk unfinished. I hope Mrs. Glazman gives me an unfinished letter instead of waiting forever for perfect words.

Tali has a sack lunch and offers me a sandwich. "My mother made this," she says, so how can I refuse?

The first time I was in Tel Aviv I learned to say taim, tasty. Today I have a gift of black bread and yellow cheese, chopped cucumbers, pickles, olives, a bit of onion and mint. Thank you, Mrs. Glazman. Some people say I love you with food.

Tali tells me about a gangster movie she watched last night. "Not an American film," she says. "Chinese with subtitles. I think the Americans make the best gangster films, especially the ones that take place in

Chicago in the 1920s." She shrugs. "James Cagney's my favorite actor, but he's been dead a long time."

Everyone in those films has been dead a long time, but the world still has gangsters. Maybe Tali is addicted to violent films that seem to happen far from home.

Soon I'll return to Fire Mountain, the Balata Camp. I may never have another chance to show Tali who I am and where I come from. I want more from her than a casual friendship, a polite shying away from controversy. Tali and I will never know each other well unless one of us takes a risk.

I tell her, in whispers, about the shooting I witnessed last night in Jaffa.

"You were *there*?"

"Yes."

"So Jonathan got shot? You're saying someone shot him?"

"Twice," I tell her. "In the shoulder and forearm."

"Well…" Maybe she wants to say he deserved it, but she stops herself. "I thought warehouse shows were for adults."

"Yes, but I'm not a child, am I?"

She flicks a hand. "Whatever."

"Besides, I went with someone in my host family, a chaperone." I look toward the sea. "I want to visit Jonathan after practice. My host family thinks he's at the Sourasky Medical Center."

"They *know* him?"

"No, but I do. He saw me perform once."

She squints. "So how many warehouse shows have you seen?"

I hesitate. "Two."

"That's crazy. You have a secret life, Amal."

"Not really."

"You want me to go with you to the hospital?"

I look at her hard. "Are you serious?"

She twists her hand to the left, as if opening a spigot. "You can see into this whatever you want. Maybe you'd rather go alone."

58

HOSPITAL

Bandages and a sling, a needle in an arm.
Pink orchids and sun on a windowsill.
Pain bearable at a glance.

Shirel, in a bedside chair, holds Jonathan's hand. They say a cat has nine lives because he's clever. I hope a machine artist has one thousand and one.

Half reclining in his bed, Jonathan raises his unwounded arm. "Ahlan wa salan," he says. "The circus has arrived."

Yes, the circus can go anywhere a body goes. I could have walked high-wires to the hospital, Tali could have juggled, but we took a taxi and pretended to be normal. Normal's okay if it doesn't last too long.

I introduce Tali as "the greatest juggler in The Flying Kids, maybe the greatest in the Middle East."

Jonathan wags his head. "Here's to the greatest."

Shirel says, "We remember you, Tali. Jonathan and I once saw you and Amal perform."

Tali offers such a thin smile that I wonder if she practiced in a mirror. Her lips could squeeze the green from a blade of grass.

I ask Jonathan who brought the beautiful flowers.

"My mother," he says. "She went home to get some sleep."

Shirel tells us Jonathan spent almost four hours in surgery last night.

"Nothing to worry about," he says. "I think I'll be back to work in two or three months." He slurs his words, maybe because of medication. "The guy who shot me wasn't a stranger. I'd seen him at other shows, but he didn't worry me."

"Maybe he should have," says Shirel.

"Israeli artists, poets, writers—I always thought we were superfluous."

Shirel squeezes his hand. "You *are*."

"No, not entirely," says Jonathan, his grin loose and clown-like. "The guy who shot me has religion on his side. He also has friends in high places, and enough money to buy prime real estate in heaven."

"Jonathan—"

"He and his consortium helped bankroll three settlements in Palestine, and have plans for a fourth." He pats the bandage on his left shoulder. "This hurts a bit, but I'm delighted they see art as a threat."

Shirel rolls her eyes. "Jonathan, these girls didn't visit you to hear all this."

"How can you be sure? They, too, are artists. We inhabit similar worlds."

I tell Jonathan he needs to leave the hospital soon if he wants to see The Flying Kids perform in Ha'yarkon Park at twelve noon on Sunday.

"I expect they'll send me home tomorrow or the next day."

"Where's home?"

Shirel says, "You don't want to know."

"Yes, I do."

Jonathan says, "We live near Lewinsky Park, the bus station."

"South city," says Shirel. "A warehouse."

"It's perfect," says Jonathan. "But don't visit at night."

I ask Shirel to write the address on a napkin.

"Be careful," she says. "The neighborhood's a bit rough."

Tali sits in the chair near the window, the sun, the bouquet of orchids. We are fatherless and always will be. This, in part, is why I love her. Even if it's foolish to love because of loss.

"My neighborhood can also be rough."

We look at her.

"So what's the point? Are we wondering whose life is hardest?"

Shirel says, "No, that's not—"

"My father's gone. He was murdered when I was four. I wouldn't want a medal to place on a mantel."

Jonathan coughs. "Nor would I."

"I'm tired," says Tali. "Sometimes I'm so tired."

"Me too."

"I mean, there's no control. Things just happen. I can't make them un-happen."

"I know this well," says Jonathan.

"And I'm not sure why I'm here."

She's here to say these things. She offered to come with me because of pain. I'm not sorry I let her shadow me. I'm sorry for bigger things.

Tali rises from her chair. "Okay, so it's too bad you were shot. I'm not happy you were shot."

Jonathan winks. "Thanks, Tali."

"But I don't know why you do what you do."

"Sometimes I don't either."

"I mean, the machines, the pop-up shows in alleys—everybody knows about them. Everybody knows about the warehouse shows even if they haven't seen them."

He nods. "Have you seen one?"

"No, I don't care to."

"Fair enough."

"And the stuff you write—it's so upside-down. Amal showed me your post about Tulkarm."

His eyes shift from Tali to me and back again.

"No one died there," says Tali. "No Nazi said, 'This way to the gas, gentlemen. Just follow the man or child in front of you.'"

I hold up my hands. "Tali, wait."

"No casualties, none. And those people wouldn't have been herded into a soccer stadium if there hadn't been so many suicide bombings in Israel."

"This is somewhat true," says Jonathan.

"The Passover Massacre in Netanya, you've heard of it?"

"Of course."

"We didn't kill anyone in Tulkarm."

Jonathan rubs his eyes. "Well, this much *is* true. That post about Tulkarm, I was…I was simply trying to remember what happened."

"Simply?"

"Yes. But I'm not so stupid as to believe I can say everything with words."

Tali slumps back in the chair near the window, the flowers, the sun on her shoulders. She shakes from grief, rage, confusion, and I don't know what else. She speaks in English, in Hebrew, of how her father died, and maybe the words I can't translate make no difference because I read about Jacob Glazman in a small and difficult book—*Unforgotten*. Tali struggles to remember him, but he remains a blur, which makes the loss more difficult. *Unforgotten?* Maybe her copy of the book should have blank pages. My father could vanish in a similar book.

I'm thinking, *Go ahead, Tali, scream*, but her voice turns so soft it startles me. I lean in to catch each word.

"Why should anyone need to point out the obvious? Jews are Jews, the same as any other time. Many people wish to kill us. I mean many, many, *many*—all across the world." She glares at Jonathan. "So who gave you the right to turn us into abusers? As if it's our fault that we want one safe place where no one will harm us." She sits straighter. "I want to live in a country where no one tries to kill me or my mother or my uncles and aunts and cousins and friends and neighbors and *everyone*. My father…" A finger draws an X in sunlight. "He's dead forever, isn't he? I'll never see him again."

Quiet words reach farther into me than screams. Tali keeps shaking. I touch her hand. Cold sweat.

Jonathan lies motionless.

Shirel says, "Tali, I am so sorry."

Jonathan sighs. "Yes, yes," and presses a hand to his heart. "I wonder, though…I wonder if I can say something."

"Jonathan—"

"The settlements, the annexations…they kill people too. I see them as a nod to corrupt politics and biblical imagination. Will we be safe soon, and holy? Will we be happy if we take everything, leave only ourselves?"

Shirel turns to Tali. "He's on medication, quite strong. For pain."

"Yes," says Jonathan, "for pain, and there's enough to go around. They don't have opioids for Gaza, pain with ten thousand teeth. A ghetto for the ages? Guinness Book of Records? Or runner-up to Warsaw?" He scratches his left cheek, leaves red marks. "But never mind the complexities. Shirel's about to remind me this is not the time to discuss sensitive matters."

"This is correct."

"Tali, all I need to say is I'm sorry for what happened to you, your father, your mother—*everyone*." He braces himself with his good arm and sits almost straight. "You won't believe me, but I would give my life for your father to live. Maybe you think, 'This guy's meandering, drugged to the gills,' but I wonder, I sometimes wonder…what do I do with my life? What is it *for*?" He swallows hard. "And I wish I were as handy with words as I am with machinery. On a given day, all I see is the bare structure and motion of the world, the tendency to self-destruct."

Shirel spaces her words and syllables as if talking to a baby: "Jon -a-than that is e-*nough*."

He nods. "Yes, yes. Sometimes a mere glimpse is enough."

My heart pounds. Twice, at shows, I have watched this man almost immolate. He sees how close he can come to fire before he retreats to safety. Many hate him, including, I suppose, Tali. Yet I know Jonathan better than I knew my father. Surely, Tali would understand this. Jonathan is here, in this well-lit room. Unlike our fathers, he's not a blur, or a patchwork of words our mothers and relatives have knitted in set patterns or printed in a book called *Unforgotten*. Jonathan, machine artist, *present*. Love him or hate him, he's here. So are we.

Sometimes light makes no sense, nor flesh. Tali, pudgy and sad, head bowed, shines in the sun. Light comes whether or not we make sense of it, the same as flesh. Smells come, too, and these are pleasant. I'm near enough to Tali to breathe her smells of cinnamon, cardamom, jasmine, rose. Sadness, grief, confusion—she still smells pretty. Nothing needs to make sense.

Most things are painful or pleasant.

Flowers, spices, wounds, words.

This is the world.

59

THE FLYING KIDS

I could jump rope on the wire till the sun goes home. Skip, fly, the rope a blur. Have you seen the Palestine Sunbird catch the light on her wings? Dark and shiny she is, same as me.

I trade my rope for a balance pole nine meters long. Now my arms are longer than two homes in Balata. I walk till I stand over the center of the ring and begin a routine Coach Dagan calls, *Slide, Glide, Open the Scissors.* Acrobats wing open their legs on rubber mats. A few might learn to do this on a wire if they practice several years.

I swing my left leg behind me and ride the wire backward on the arch of my foot. My right leg, knee cocked, holds all but a few feathers of me. I don't need to flex many muscles. I let gravity take me down, down, to where my right leg slides forward, my left all the way back, and I'm spread-eagled, both legs level with the wire. I wobble some, but my balance pole, held at the waist, steadies me. Everybody but Coach Dagan call this the splits, not *Slide, Glide, Open the Scissors.* Whatever. No one needs words to see beauty and poise.

Maybe a thousand people have gathered in the red tent in Ha'yarkon Park. High over the ring, I'm safer than a machine artist performing in Jaffa. No one will shoot me from the wire. If I fall, I have a net. Coach Dagan calls to me over the cheers and chatter of the crowd. "Okay, one, two, three—stand." I feel like a saint on my wire in the sky. I breathe a breath for everyone and rise faster than you can say *Palestine sunbird, fly.*

The hardest thing to learn is stillness on the wire, or even on earth. If I could learn stillness, I would master everything else. Only my grandfather might understand my longing. I wonder, though, must there be movement while we live? The nearest I come to stillness is when the breath I breathe for everyone vanishes in light.

Tali rides a unicycle while juggling knives. Later, she and this Palestinian boy I secretly call Cutie play catch with broken bottles. Tali drops one, then Cutie drops two. Out rush the clowns to sweep away the glass.

A skinny clown begins to tie a tourniquet on the neck of a fat one. They wrestle and make wild gestures at each other and the crowd. I can feel Tali steaming, furious with herself for dropping a bottle. Her mistake led to Cutie's mistake. The rhythm gone, her partner dropped two bottles. The audience is nonetheless entertained. A jangle of snorts and laughter fill the tent as the fat clown snatches the tourniquet, blows his nose, and offers the soiled rag to a beautiful woman sitting beside the ring.

I'm almost afraid to watch. In spotlights, on trapezes, Miki and Mazin swing over the ring, and when she lets go, becomes an angel, he becomes a god, a stream of light to catch her before she falls. Moments later, he releases her to fly faster, higher, back to her trapeze, her home in the sky. I'm not so jealous that I wish for her to fall and break her neck. Tali, mockingly, once told me they'd restarted the peace process on the trapeze. Is the world so strange that anything can happen? Maybe peace will come two Flying Kids at a time.

We end the show by forming a pyramid, three tiers of kids, with me and Miki, featherweights, standing on shoulders at our shared summit. I scan the crowd for Jonathan and Shirel. I called them last night on Aisha's phone to remind them of the performance and Shirel said they were coming. Tomorrow I return to Balata. Will I see them again?

Coach Dagan makes a wavy motion with his arms. "Okay, style and shine, lower the beam."

This means show's over. Miki and me slide down backsides, then other kids slide down, and in the space of three drumbeats from a clown, everyone's back on earth, styling and shining and bowing to applause.

Mrs. Glazman and Tali's uncle Amos wait beside the ring. Aisha, my sister-friend, is here, at the first circus of her life. While they praise me and a few other Flying Kids hanging around, I almost cry because I may never see my friends again.

Mrs. Glazman looks up, as if searching for something near the dome of the circus tent, before she surprises me with a hug. Sometimes my heart has to seize up before it opens. I stiffen a few moments, then rest in her arms, as in the shade of a tree.

She releases me. "I'd hoped to give you a letter today, but I'm unable to finish."

"That's okay."

"Sometimes I wait half the night for a single word I can trust." She blushes. "I realize how silly this sounds."

"Not at all."

"Be patient," she says. "I'll send you my letter in an email if I find the right words."

Tali watches us from the center of the ring.

I wave and smile for her.

She hesitates before she smiles back.

We speak each other's name, not loud, but important.

This is all the medicine I need for now.

Many times, awake or in dreams, I'll see our names over the ring, shiny as a circus, no space or comma between us, no period at the end.

TaliAmal

Mrs.GlazmanTaliAmal

60

MY SISTER FRIEND AND CHAPERONE

I count the hours—sixteen more in Tel Aviv-Jaffa. Aisha takes me to a café where she orders fizzy water spiked with vodka, lemonade for me.

She leads us in a toast. "To Amal Tuqan and The Flying Kids."

I drink with a smile.

"How do you do it?" she asks.

"Do what?"

"Keep your balance."

I shrug. "It's what I do."

"That simple?"

"Yes."

❧

On her second vodka, my sister-friend tells me she'll miss me. I'll miss her, too, and tell her so. I name a few others I will miss: Tali and her mother, Jonathan and Shirel.

"Who's Shirel?"

"Jonathan's girlfriend. She's nice."

"A machine artist's girl had better be nice."

"No, I'm serious. I invited her and Jonathan to the performance. Shirel told me they were coming."

"Well, the guy just got shot a few nights ago."

"That's what worries me. Maybe she had to take him back to the hospital."

"Let her worry about him. Let his mother worry."

"I'm sure they do. But can I use your phone to call Shirel?"

She winks. "Anything for…what did the ringmaster call you? Your stage-name?"

"Handala's Sister, the Cat Girl of the Balata Camp."

She leans back and laughs. My stage-name isn't funny, it's who I am. But I wish I could say something every day to hear laughter shiny as a coin.

❧

I dial the machine artist's girl three times. All I can do is leave messages. *Call me, call me, call me. Tomorrow I return to the Balata Camp.*

I try the Sourasky Medical Center. A receptionist tells me Jonathan was discharged two days earlier. By now, he could be anywhere.

Aisha needs to meet her boyfriend, Khalid, in about an hour. "I already told him about you," she says, "and you're welcome to join us. We'll walk on the beach, then get something for dinner."

"I can't.

"You have a better plan?"

"I'm afraid something happened to Jonathan."

"Well, he has some wounds to recover from. If something else happened, there's nothing we can do about it."

"I know where he lives, a warehouse near Lewinsky Park. Maybe I can find out what happened."

"No, I can't let you go there alone. The neighborhood's rough, and I promised to meet Khalid."

I melt an ice cube with my tongue. "Can all of us go?"

"Not a chance."

I remind Aisha of where I'm from: the Balata Camp. I know rough neighborhoods better than they know me.

She shakes her head. "I know you're brave, habibti, but you don't know Tel Aviv. You don't know Lewinsky Park."

"Maybe it doesn't matter. I can take a taxi to the warehouse. I won't walk the streets at all."

"I don't like the idea of you going there alone."

❧

On her third vodka, Aisha decides I won't need a chaperone "in daylight hours." She'll loan me her phone, plus taxi money, and I can go alone to Lewinsky Park if I call her boyfriend every thirty minutes. She fidgets with her phone and shows me how to bring up Khalid's number. She makes me promise to meet her at her home before dark.

I refuse her offer of money. "The Flying Kids paid me a stipend," I say, and wave some bills.

"You're sure you have enough for a taxi both ways?"

"More than enough."

"I shouldn't be jealous. A circus star deserves better pay than a housekeeper."

"We both deserve decent pay."

"Well, you're my darling," she says, and kisses my cheeks, twice on each side. "Call every half hour and be home before dark."

61

SUITCASES

This alley is four paces wider than my Balata alley. At the far end, a homeless woman and two children squat near a tent. The sun lights the woman's hands as she peels an orange. Razor wire stretches across the top of a wall.

She tears at her small sun with her thumbs. The brightness makes me squint. I would offer a basket of suns if I could. She licks her fingers, divides the orange between her children, and saves a slice for herself.

My mother would do the same.

My taxi driver waits at the corner. I bang on a warehouse door, press my ear to the metal. No voices inside, no steps. I play drums on the door till the metal turns warm as my hands.

I'm about to go back to my taxi when I see Shirel and a stranger turn into the alley. Shirel walks with her head down, but her companion looks every which way, makes sweeping gestures with her arms, and wags a finger at the sky as if it has wronged her. I hear three words of Hebrew I can translate: *police, prison, disaster.* The stranger is barrel-thick, with dyed red hair, red lipstick, jowls, belly fat. And tall enough to throw shade like a tree.

"Shirel?"

I'm near enough to touch her elbow before she sees me.

"Child, what are you—?"

"You didn't answer your phone."

"The police have my phone. They also have Jonathan."

My breath catches. "What do you mean?"

"They arrested him."

I shake my head, as if I could clear it. "But Jonathan's hurt. They can't arrest him."

"They can and they did. They let us visit him for about an hour."

She wraps an arm over my shoulder and turns to her companion.

"Amal, meet Leah, Jonathan's mother."

I gape.

"Leah, are you listening?"

"Not intentionally."

"Amal is a circus star from Nablus."

"Congratulations," says Leah.

"Thank you."

"Now that we've survived the formalities, let's go inside and have a drink."

Shirel winks as if to say, *Don't worry about Leah. She was rude the day she was born.*

The warehouse is a mess. Shirel leads us to a cluttered counter, several stools, two of them overturned, and motions for us to sit. I turn a stool right-side up and offer it to Leah. She ignores me and roots through cabinets for wine.

The police who arrested Jonathan destroyed some of his creations. The guts of machinery litter the floor: spliced cables, spools of wire, motors of various sizes, batteries, electrical switches, screws, bolts. TVs and computers are scattered over shelves and tables. The far wall almost disappears behind robots, junked appliances, parts of cars and trucks, sheets of metal, and contraptions I have no name for. The Prayer Wheel and jet engine from the recent show in Jaffa stand near the captain robot who wanted Pebble Boy and Stone Boy or any two sons to clear the debris from a path through a village. Wine robots and usher robots look lonely with no one to serve.

Shirel brings me a glass of water. "No wine for you, if Leah finds any."

"That's okay."

Leah, moments later, calls, "Mazel tov, an open bottle. Cheap pinot noir." She dusts off two cups with a sleeve of her blouse.

Maybe I'm smiling. This is Jonathan's *mother*? Her belly is three of his, her voice five of his. She's a bulldozer with painted lips.

Leah pours wine for herself, then Shirel. "To my son," she says, "to our prison system." And drains her cup.

I spot stacks of suitcases in a corner between the wine robots and usher robots. Why so many? I count thirty-one suitcases, shades of gray, which is why I overlooked them at first.

Leah follows my eyes. "If you're lucky," she says, "this will be your last glimpse of my son's suitcase project."

"Suitcase project?"

"Yes, Jews have a long history with suitcases. Perhaps you've heard."

Sometimes I'm afraid I've heard too much.

She fills her cup. "Do you know some children of Holocaust survivors still keep packed suitcases beneath their beds or in nearby closets?"

"No."

"I did this myself till four or five years ago when I began to relax."

Shirel apologizes for not having any food on hand. "Empty fridge," she says. "Jonathan will probably eat better in jail."

Leah lifts her cup in both hands. "Let's drink once more to our prison system. Can you imagine a son who forgets to eat? Who won't let his mother feed him?"

She does not expect an answer.

"Why eat if you're enjoying yourself as a lunatic? He's in jail, doesn't know when he'll get out, but all he can talk about is machines, technical issues, scenarios—his suitcase project. He's already made some very small robots for his suitcases. He needs to make dozens more, and scour junkyards for the right parts. 'The smaller the robots,' he says, 'the bigger the story.' As in, history made simple, the Holocaust for Dummies. Maybe my son can condense it to one sentence. Jews arrived from Europe with the remnants of their lives packed in suitcases, but since then more than five million Palestinians had to pack *their* suitcases."

Shirel says, "Leah, please. He knows it's more complicated."

"Does he? His suitcase project has a simple title: *Shared History, Help Yourself.* Some suitcases will open to destroyed Arab[3] villages, others to refugee camps, others to barbed wire, a row or two of Auschwitz bunks, others to Jews and Arabs in the same suitcases!"

"Does she need to hear this, Leah?"

"And this shared history will be audience friendly, hands-on. Open a Jew's suitcase, activate sensors, enjoy the show. Miniature robots may emerge from compartments, serve as tour guides." She flicks a shoulder. "Jonathan says every machine he's made in recent years is more complex than the average Israeli sunbathing on Banana Beach."

Leah raises her cup. "So here's to smart robots, simple sunbathers, and—once more—our prison system. Jonathan? He's not my fault and never was. Yes, I birthed an idiot genius. Maybe we can blame the father, dead twelve years. The only time Zev was happy was when he was dying

---

[3] Jewish Israelis often refer to Palestinians by a more general term—Arabs.

of cancer. The world? Zev couldn't take it. He was weak. He left all the burdens to me."

She pauses to breathe, drink, sigh. Shirel rubs her forehead. My breath is small. Leah takes most of the air.

"Jonathan's my Einstein gone to the devil. He's never been weak, only crazy. He knows he could make millions in any tech company in the country. If he wanted, he could become a doctor, devote himself to medical research. My son's smart enough to cure anything but insanity. Instead, he collects gadgetry, rubbish. Meet the Jewish junkman of lore, hording debris his fellow citizens toss in the trash." She smiles, or else her lips twitch. Teeth a red smear. "Look at this rubble! This isn't just any junk; this is my son's *home*. Why should he live in a mansion when he can build his own original junk-cart?" She sips from her cup, burps. "And worst of all I love the idiot and he knows this and torments me nonetheless."

Leah is loud even in silence. She rests her forearms on the counter, leans forward, and takes up twice as much space as Shirel and me.

I ask when Jonathan will get out of jail.

"No time soon," says Leah. "They'll make an example of the idiot to deter other idiots."

"But he just got shot. He needs medical attention."

"You think I didn't tell them? You think I didn't remind them three thousand times?"

Shirel rolls her eyes.

"The good news is that my Einstein's in fine spirits. He all but ordered us to leave so we could come back to his junk-cart to take inventory and tell him how many of his computers and robots are still alive. That's his word for them—*alive*. He acts as if everything in his cart is a child who might be kidnapped. You know what he told me before we left? You know what he said right to my face?"

The jinn might be swift enough to slip a word in edgewise.

"He said, 'Mom, I'm no longer depressed.' This means he was depressed when he *wasn't* in jail." She throws up her hands. "So what's the reason for his brush with happiness? Well, the schnook wouldn't have bloody wounds if his art meant nothing, wouldn't be behind bars if his art meant nothing." She cackles. "Maybe he'll feel he's done something marvelous the day someone shoots him in the head."

The widest sky lacks room for all her words, but I will take a few for remembrance. She loves her son but wants to "punch him in the face." She says, while looking straight at me, that "Jonathan has more respect for Arabs than for his own people. How did this happen? Somebody tell me." (I could begin if she would let me.) "Who doesn't want peace? Every schnook wants peace, but there's no peace and no hope for peace. Once you know this you can be tough, do what needs to be done. Is this paradise, or is this the world? We aren't in heaven yet. Some Jews don't believe in heaven. Maybe everything's a story, and *this*"—she opens and closes a fist as though to clamp the world in a vise—"is where the stories end."

But Leah keeps talking. Other stories might end, but not hers. I half-listen, then trail after Shirel when she wanders off to do inventory. Some of Jonathan's computers are gone—four laptops, one desktop—and several robots are missing. "They took the EO robots," says Shirel, "plus the checkpoint robot, the frisker."

"EO robots?"

"Three of them. They handed out fliers. If you were at the show, you got one."

"I didn't."

"They were behind the checkpoint. After people were frisked, these other robots handed them info about the movement to End the Occupation."

"But my friend and I didn't get frisked. We were welcomed by an Arabic-speaking robot."

"Smart robot," says Shirel. "Bilingual. But either David or Eden was sitting at a computer, monitoring the gate, working the controls."

Shirel leans over a desk strewn with papers and makes notes on a clipboard. "He's going to be upset that his frisker and EO robots are gone."

"I still don't understand why he's in jail."

"Fire safety violations," says Shirel, "plus the politics of occupation. They may charge Jonathan with sedition."

I would stay with Shirel and comfort her, but no comfort is possible in the presence of Leah. I call Khalid's number, speak with Aisha, then call for a taxi. I shake Leah's chubby hand before I leave. Shirel waits with me outside the warehouse till the taxi pulls into the alley. I ride with the windows open, the wind and sun on my face.

Part Five

Vest

62

BALATA

The machine artists' website is down. I can't reach Shirel by email or text. Is Jonathan still in jail? Is Leah still talking? I hear her ("Do you know some children of Holocaust survivors keep packed suitcases beneath their beds or in nearby closets?") as I do my chores.

I gather dirty clothes in the room Issam shares with our grandpa. I stoop to snatch a shirt from under the bed and spot something in the shadows. Belly down, I can't snag it with a hand. I snake under the bed and drag it out.

I'm surprised by the weight of the package. Duct tape bunches the contents in a square. I jiggle the package, listen. My mind moves fast before it stills.

I slip into the kitchen, grab a pair of scissors, and retreat to the room I share with my mother. I cut through layers of tape, brown paper, plastic. The vest is the color of sand.

I strain to see numbers in small print. Friday's date is written where the wearer's heart would be. Today is Wednesday. Issam, you wish to die so soon?

Many mornings ago, I loved him enough to die for him. My brave brother raced down our alley to a wider alley to hurl stones at a flash of wings. Fighter jets swooped over our roofs with a roar that seemed loud enough to destroy the world. Issam's stones rose in the light, landed on roofs, but the rage kept flying, keeps flying, never stops searching for targets. Where will I hide the vest? Can I delay a plan, interrupt death? How?

Grandpa Saeed and Uncle Sami are playing backgammon in the alley. My mother's upstairs, drinking tea with Aunt Salma and Aunt Lena. Issam? He's with those who break apart their anger and share it, pass it around, before they share bread or even air. Will he become a martyr on Friday? Who will he kill besides himself?

I hide the vest under the bed I share with my mother. I return to my chores, gather shirts, pants, underwear, robes, and carry them to the spigot in the alley. I wash clothes in a daze and hang them on a line that stretches from my front door to Maysa's door. My eyes walk the stripe of blue over our alley, but the sky belongs to planes, helicopters, drones, Israelis. I understand my brother's rage. We have no sky, except for what I reach on ropes and wires.

I curl up on Mother's side of the bed, eyes closed. My brother wants to kill Israelis, especially those in settlements, or the collaborators among us, those who work for the Israelis, the servants and slaves of the occupation. Who will he target? A bus taking Palestinian workers to Elon Moreh, to Har Bracha, or to Israel? Issam would kill Jonathan and Shirel if he could. He would kill Mrs. Glazman, Tali, The Flying Kids, and sweep their blood to the sea.

But what if the vest disappears? Is there a hole, a crevice, where it will never be found, where it will disintegrate like the flesh of a corpse? If Issam has no bomb, no mission, those who supplied him with explosives will consider him a traitor. They will punish him, maybe torture him back to the fold. My brother may become more desperate to die for something, anything. I am trapped. If I tell my mother and grandfather what I've found, they too will be in danger. The vest is mine.

I roll out of bed, take off my blouse, and do what I do best: walk. Six steps one way, six the other, on feet more at home in the air. I have given my life to learn to walk one clear line above everything. Look at me, look at me. I have failed.

I strap on the explosives. Over my bra, my stomach, a bomb. I put on a different blouse, sack-like, shapeless, and walk outside.

Grandpa Saeed and Uncle Sami hunch over a tray table, a backgammon board, and glasses of coffee. My brother, at breakfast, told our grandfather a lie: "I have a day-job in the market." Issam's probably making his martyr video or receiving final instructions from those who assist with strategy, execution. Taking a vest home—this has to be unusual. Maybe there's a fear that the place where bombs are made will be raided. I don't know if Balata makes bombs. The camp is a honeycomb of rooms, cages. My brother may be nearby, or in the home of men I'll never know. What does he feel—fear, pride, joy? Is there a thrill in being almost dead?

The wind blows dust over our roofs. If I'm lucky, it will blow a storm, make me invisible. I drift down the alley to the ruined house where Maysa and I train for circus. Handala the Cat perches on a nearby roof. I will watch for any twitch of his ears, flick of his tail. He will warn me in silence if someone nears.

I slip inside the ruins, comb it with my eyes. A twisted section of rebar about one meter long is knife-like at one end. I stab the earth over and over, more stone than soil. Sweat burns my eyes. I toss my knife aside when I see this is wrong.

Maysa's cousins live near the ruins. If the Israelis find the vest, bulldozers will come, new ruins will appear, and anyone old enough to grow a moustache will be jailed. How far must I walk to bury the vest? The Jordan River? The Arabian Desert? Only a jinni might shrink herself, grow smaller and smaller, wander unseen. My mother, who begs me to eat more, says I resemble the wires I walk, but she exaggerates. At best, I can squeeze into crevices, nooks and crannies, or the dark under Issam and Grandpa's bed where I found a nightmare in a package. I wonder what my brother dreamed last night when his death lay beneath him. What will he dream tonight if his death disappears?

I pat my chest and stomach, the stiffness of the vest. I edge near a wall, a window, and see Handala the Cat seeing me. The wind sings over the roofs.

I stroll down the alley as if on my way to visit relatives. Handala strolls, too, four stories above me. A few women and children greet me from doorways, as we all know each other. I hurry on, before they can ask where I'm going. The bomb I carry is about the weight of three bricks. No matter. I could carry it to the other side of the world if there were no checkpoints or oceans in the way.

I slip from alley to alley, exit the camp, turn left on Al-Quds Street, and join other walkers. I glance at passageways, balconies, rooftops. There is no sign of Handala. I walk and walk, the sun on my back, my shadow dark before my feet.

63

MOUNT EBAL

I pass a store selling sodas, candy, a bit of fruit, and keep going. A man older than my grandpa, standing in a doorway, greets me and asks if I'm lost. I must appear dazed. I pause, gather my poise, and tell him I'm on my way to visit my aunt.

Many steps later, I know my destination: Mount Ebal. Up the slopes, beyond the houses, there are quarries, caves, and hopefully no Israelis. I've never been there, but my grandfather told me about the caves, and Uncle Sami mentioned a picnic area from which you can see all of Nablus in the valley between mountains. He takes passengers there in his taxi, though not very often. One has to be rich to ride so far.

❧

Mid-morning, I find the road that snakes up the mountain between stone houses. The wind sings louder as I climb. Dust whirls counter-clockwise. My clothes take on the color of the road, the houses, the ridges far above. The mountain seems to have lost some of its flesh. A mirror might show me I've lost some of mine.

Mount Ebal, can you hide me for a time? Can you hide a bomb forever?

I listen for words in wind and dust.

The mountain won't speak.

It doesn't know me yet.

❧

I spy an orange cat before he darts behind a bush. There are many cats in Nablus—orange, black, gray—so I doubt this is Handala. Maybe he's a younger brother, Handala II, the Sentry of Mount Ebal. I don't need arak to water my hope. My face softens. My first smile while carrying a bomb.

"Handala, Handala II?"

No answer.

He doesn't know me yet.

❧

The wind lessens, the dust clears, before I reach a guard post, a parking lot, and a picnic area near the crest of the mountain. The guard, Palestinian, looks over the valley, but it wouldn't matter if he saw me. There's a food stand, tables, shelter from the sun. Men smoke hookahs, women too, and three boys run around kicking a ball. Tourists have come here, a half dozen Europeans or Americans, and the taxis in the lot are probably waiting to take them back to their hotels.

My eyes widen when I see my city—all of her—for the first time. Patches of green surprise me: trees, bushes, gardens, on the slopes of Mount Jarzim. I find the Old City beyond Martyr's Square and City Centre Mall. The Balata Camp is a smear of beige and gray, a shimmer of roofs. Opposite my perch, overlooking the valley from the south, an Israeli military post stands near the crest of Mount Jarzim. Guards can use binoculars or the scopes of rifles to scan streets, mosques, meeting places, the Balata Camp, the other camps, and Mount Ebal. Maybe they monitor drones, too, the cameras that scan every patch of earth.

I hunch down and think. I need food, water, but I have no money. They sell oranges here, and other fruit. In Tel Aviv, I spent half the stipend I earned with The Flying Kids and brought the rest home to my mother. I wish I'd saved a few shekels for myself.

I greet two women smoking hookahs. Well-dressed, in wrinkleless robes, black hijabs, they look down on me. I ask in my gentlest voice, "Could you please tell me if the quarries, the caverns, are nearby?"

The younger one flicks a hand toward a gravel road behind me. "Back there somewhere, I don't know."

I go up to the food stand and ask the man behind the counter.

"Not far," he says. "Maybe a fifteen-minute walk."

I ask for a glass of water.

He pauses. "You have money?"

"No."

He's at least forty years old, but the way his eyes dart makes me think he's searching for his boss.

"Well," he says, "water used to be free. Same as air and light."

I sit in the shade of an awning and drink a tall glass of water, a slice of lemon on top. The sky opens over the valley. I want to believe I can save lives, including my own. An angel could ride a rope of wind into the blue and disappear.

I walk up a gravel road, a narrow rib of the mountain. The call to prayer and the sun tell me it is midday. I turn toward Mecca, quiet my mind, and bow three times. I want to believe someone or something other than the Israeli Occupation Forces and their drones watch over us. I doubt I can carry this vest alone to the place where it dies.

I move up the mountain till I find the first caverns. I walk in and out of stone shadows, empty and clean. Nothing here would conceal a bomb for more than a day. I need a quarry with steep walls, a shelf or a cave far above, and crevices, cracks, footholds, a stone path rather than a wire daring me to climb.

The orange cat crosses the road some ten meters ahead. I creep forward so as not to scare him, but he darts past a boulder and disappears.

Minutes later, I find what I'm looking for: a deep quarry carved in the mountain, walls too steep to climb unless you're a funambulist. Pitch black, some fifteen meters straight up, a cave cuts into the stone.

I sit under a small tree, my back on the trunk. Before I can study the mountain, chart my path to the cave, tourists arrive, three westerners speaking English, led by a Palestinian guide. We exchange nods, greetings. How heavy my chest strapped with explosives. My rib cage collapses each time I exhale.

The guide gives me a look as though to say, *What are you doing here alone?*

I give him a look as though to say, *I'm preparing to bury a bomb, Mr. Guide.*

I doubt he sees the glint in my eye.

He turns to the tourists. "This quarry, one of many on the mountain, may date back several centuries. No one knows when it was dug, or by whom. Most of Mount Ebal is limestone. Workers must have had ladders or special equipment to mine the stones far above us. It would be impossible to scale these walls."

He knows nothing about circus arts. A funambulist can do things he'll never imagine even in dreams.

He asks if there are questions or comments.

A guy in a red cap, his belly hanging like a laundry bag over his belt, says, "Last night I heard gunshots from my hotel room."

"Perhaps you heard a wedding."

"Or Arabs shooting Israelis."

A pistol, a keen eye, an escape—give me these and I'll blow the cap off his head, the buckle off his belt.

"You ever hear of any fighting on this mountain?"

The guide rubs his moustache. "Yes, but not in the past few months. Part of my job is to know which area is safe and which isn't."

The guy winks. "I hope you guessed right today."

"Sir, in all respect, I prefer not to guess. On most days I end my tours at this quarry. The Israelis control security on Mount Ebal. If Jewish visitors wish to see Joshua's altar, a short distance beyond the crest, soldiers protect them. They also protect the settlement of Elon Moreh, a few kilometers to the north."

They also enter Nablus and its camps whenever they wish, open and close roads whenever they wish, conduct raids whenever they wish, arrest and set free whoever they wish, create new boundaries whenever they wish. Maybe there will come a day when all Palestinians will be contortionists on wires.

As the tourists and their guide start back down the slopes, I mime my right hand into a pistol. Pop, whiz. Pop, whiz. I picture the guy's cap flying down the valley, his belt flying, his pants falling, and then he keels over, rolls, disappears down the mountain in a rumble of dust.

I stop my mind by letting the fat man go. Fantasy can kill me. I have no time for distraction. The bomb on my chest—the weight of it—shortens each breath.

I turn to the quarry, the cliffs, and draw a map in my mind. Niches in stone may serve as footholds. The zigzag lines between them may serve as wires leading to the cave.

My grandpa once told me that concentration must be effortless before the first step, but this is not always true. Sometimes I must *take* the first step to calm my mind and body and feel the wire from beginning to end.

I'm almost brave enough to climb when more tourists arrive with a different guide. My brother would kill them with the bomb I carry. I only hate them for being here. I will wait for night when, inshallah, the tourists return to their hotels, the Israelis draw nearer to Elon Moreh, and their drones—which may see most of Nablus and its mountains—aim their lenses anywhere but here.

Darkness is many hours away. I lie down, face to the sky, bomb on my chest, and wait. Sometimes my eyes close. Sometimes they open to blue light around the mountain and me. Is this the longest day of my life? The sun moves slowly, carefully, as if following a snail over the blue. Sun, snail, sky—I lack your patience. I have walls to climb, a bomb to bury. My chest itches under the vest.

I feel years older when I hear the call for Maghrib, the sunset prayer. The muezzins from the minarets of more than one hundred mosques call toward heaven, and the sounds rise up the ribs of the mountain and into the sky. I wish I could follow, bury the bomb in space! Words and their echoes pass through me, keep going, and maybe I'm hearing the adhan the way the mountain hears it, the shudders of praise and yearning bouncing off stones. The sky begins to darken. The picnic area and parking lot should be empty now. Maybe Israeli soldiers patrol the crest of Ebal, or the road to Elon Moreh. I hope I have a friend on this mountain. I watch for the orange cat. Nothing moves, except a breeze blowing from the south.

I unbutton my blouse, remove the vest, and strap it to my back. On my chest, it might butt against outcroppings, ledges, and throw me. On my back, it will serve as ballast, help me plant my steps. I put my blouse back on as night draws near.

The guide said the mountain is mostly limestone. I try to crumble a fist-sized stone. I am strong, I use both hands, but it won't break. This tells me the stone wires I walk will not give way.

A trace of skylight is enough to climb by. The walls of the quarry stand almost straight, but there are niches, grooves, places for my feet, grips for my hands. Any cat or goat could climb the first five meters or so. Once I'm well up on the face of the cliff, I meet a challenge. No one but me or Phillippe Petit or The Flying Wallendas would step to a ledge thinner than the wires we walk. I hear my grandfather's voice: "Concentration must be effortless…" My heart bumps my ribs, then settles. I test each foothold before I lean into the climb.

The mountain, the cliff, the weight on my back, the void beyond the weight—take me beyond thinking. I press against stone, the warmth of my body a kind of suction. A bird chitters in the near dark, maybe a swallow. I hear how keen she is. A rustle, a burst of wings. Gone.

She is above the mountain, unseen. I have no wings, only hands and feet, the brightness of my body. Ledges too narrow to walk let me walk.

If I live, I will puzzle over their kindness, but for now I walk, climb, zigzag, the bomb on my back a ballast as I rise. I'm three or four steps from the cave when a searchlight passes. No need to pause. The light, many meters below me, shines on a tamer rib of the mountain. Tonight only the first stars or a drone may find me. I love the moon, which I seldom see from Balata, but I'm grateful she shines on some other side of the world.

I pull myself onto the lip of the cave and lie on my stomach. My blouse clings to me. I've watered the bomb with sweat.

I can't see into the dark, so I crawl, touch my hands to the walls to learn their shapes. The cave goes back about four meters before the walls narrow. I poke around, find a crevice, V-shaped, perfect. I remove my blouse, now the vest, and shove the latter as far back as I can. Only an earthquake might cause it to explode.

Finished with my work, I take a moment to gather my strength. I see a way up rather than down, a small climb before I crisscross a steep slope and return to the gravel road some twenty meters ahead.

I'm bleeding from my hands, my left knee, my elbows. I feel strong, though, almost too strong, so I remind myself I'm human. I cannot fly down the valley between mountains to my alley and my home and the bed I share with my mother. She is awake now, praying. Or pulling her hair. I'm sorry she suffers, but the mountain and I saved her son, my brother, for at least one night.

❧

The parking lot is empty, but someone—probably a Palestinian policeman—stands in a dimly lit guard house. I leave the road, glide past bushes, boulders, light without the bomb. When I can no longer see the guard station, I return to the road. The night is clear, the air cool. The stars—a great bowl of them—are beautiful and frightening. I'm not sure how alive everything is, what has eyes and what doesn't. I hear something off to my left. A cat—I can't see what color—seems to look at me before it walks off, disappears.

I have seen the stars over the Mediterranean Sea, over Jaffa. Grandpa has too, when he was a child in the city of his birth, but most of my people have only seen the sky over our alley, the stars a thin line like soldiers in formation. Now I lie flat, press my cheek to a stone, as a searchlight sweeps over. I wonder who has a better view of me, the stars or the Israelis? Maybe I will escape my enemies because the light around me and inside me is unlike any they are trained to see.

On the edges of my city, amid stone houses, a man older than my grandfather appears terrified when he sees me.

"Child, you look like you could walk on air."

I show him my bloody hands so he will know I'm human.

"But who are you? Where have you come from?"

"Balata. I got lost on the mountain, but I know my way home."

He asks a young woman to fetch me water, and a beautiful girl brings me bread, a slice of cheese. I had forgotten hunger and thirst.

I bleed on bread.

64

ALIBI

What can I say in my alley? I tell my mother, my grandfather, my cousins, my friend Maysa, I hiked up Mount Ebal and got lost. I wanted to see the view from the picnic area where Uncle Sami sometimes takes riders. "We have no view from here," I say, and point to the sliver of sky over our walls.

I would tell the truth if truth were safe. The mountain knows me. The dust knows me. The sun and stars know me. A bomb knows me. I buried death in a cave.

Handala the Cat watches from our rooftop. He might be the only one in Balata who would understand.

❧

Issam is not home, praise God and His prophets. My mother sits me at the kitchen table and brings a basin so I can soak my hands, wash my wounds.

"Who did this to you? What happened?"

I like stories and they like me. I tell her I fell three times in the night. "You won't believe how steep the mountain is, or how beautiful. The Israelis have searchlights, but they can't erase every star."

My mother hugs me, then shakes me. Water spreads over the table. She wipes it dry with a towel.

"How could you just walk off like that? How could you?"

"I'm sorry."

"And look at you. Your clothes are torn, you're bleeding."

"I'm fine."

"Did someone hit you? Did soldiers—"

"No, there weren't any soldiers. I wandered safe paths. I saw Fire Mountain beneath me, all of Nablus. I never knew how beautiful we are."

My mother raises an arm, but decides not to hit me. "Let me find bandages for your wounds."

65

FRAGILE

I lie beside my mother in our narrow bed. Neither of us can sleep, so I whisper stories about the mountain, the picnic area, the women and men smoking hookahs, the stars over Nablus, the people who gave me food and water. "I wish I could show you the quarries near the crest, the caves carved in limestone. Some are so deep a girl almost disappears."

She pinches my arm. "You have too much imagination."

No, I'm thinking. I need more to make the world new.

I'll never tell her that Issam wants to kill himself and others, or that he may kill his own sister for interrupting his mission. Those who trusted my brother with death may be more brutal than the Israelis. Ignorance will be a blessing for anyone facing questions in the coming days.

❧

Late in the night, I hear Issam enter our home and shuffle about in the room he shares with our grandpa. I know his steps. I brush a hand through my mother's hair and tell her I love her. She may lose both her children at once. I tell her I love her three times to make sure she believes.

Has Issam ever loved anyone? We have heard our mother half speak, half sing, a proverb: "No one's dearer than one's child to the heart, except the child of one's child." Issam wants death for himself and others. His child is desperation. There are many such children in the camps.

My mother yawns. She, too, has recognized Issam's steps. She pats my arm and says, "God willing, I can sleep now. Both my children are home."

I hear whispers, Issam and our grandfather. I can't make out words, only hissing sounds—like water beginning to boil.

I remember my mother's questions when she washed my hands, my wounds, in a basin: Who did this to you? What happened?

The world did this to me, to her, to Issam, to *us*. Insects are fragile in the shadows of shoes. Some go insane.

I doubt my brother knows the vest is gone.

Tomorrow he will come for me.

66

ISSAM

After breakfast, I pretend to be sick so I can go back to bed. I need to lie still, wake my imagination, save my life. My body is flesh, bones, blood, and light. These walls hold some darkness. I light a lamp under my skin.

I remember the night I walked above Faisal Street on the barrel of a tank. The past is the present. Then and now, I strut and style, shiny as a fish riding a wave, the sun painting rainbows on her scales. I make myself a promise: *I was born into a war, but refuse to die in it.* That's what I meant to tell the tank commander and his soldiers. That's what I tell myself today.

I walked, I walk, on the barrel of a tank.

I wake to sour breath on my face.

"Where is it?"

My brother hunches over me.

"Where's what?"

"Don't play with me. Where is it?"

"High on a cliff."

"What?"

"Near the crest of Mount Ebal."

Mother must be upstairs with Aunt Salma. Grandpa must have wandered down the alley to play backgammon with Uncle Sami. Issam and I have never been alone in this room.

"I'll give you one more chance: where is it?"

I stand to face him. Issam is big, he's almost a man, but I'm an athlete. Every muscle of mine is ten cats stronger than his.

"I told you it's near the crest. A cave some fifteen meters up the walls of a cliff."

"You expect me to believe this?

"Yes."

"A circus story? You wire-walked up a cliff?"

"No, I walked stone paths. Some were narrower than circus wires."

He grabs my shoulders and shakes me. "It would be easy to—"

"But you wouldn't find your vest, would you?"

He squeezes till my bones hurt. "You know what we do to traitors, collaborators?"

He knows I know.

"Once more—where *is* it?"

"High in a cave on a—"

"You're lying."

"I can prove it."

"Shut the fuck up."

He scans the room, the corners, the shadows. He roots through drawers stuffed with clothes, empties them, tosses gowns on the floor. He calls me filthy names as he stoops to check beneath the bed. He whispers because walls are thin, people are many. He tells me I had no right to interfere, no right to do anything. (No one in Balata has rights, but it won't help to remind him.) He calls me the same filthy names. It would be easier for both of us if Issam could shout, *Whore, cunt, bitch!* He haunts the quiet with whispers. He promises to kill me unless I obey.

"Tomorrow morning, after Grandpa's in the alley with his coffee, you'll put the package back where you found it."

I breathe in. "I'll need more time."

"No, you won't. I don't believe you carried it all the way up Mount Ebal."

I show the blood on my hands where stones made their marks.

"So you cut yourself? So what?" He jabs a finger near my throat. "Storytime's over. Do what I said."

He's about to leave when I call to him. "Issam?"

I speak to his back.

"I understand. I think I understand."

He turns. "Understand what?"

"I hate how we're forced to live. I'm trying to change it."

He smirks. "So now you're one of us? Fedayeen?"

"In my own way, yes. I'm the girl who walked on the barrel of a tank."

Issam clears his throat. I raise a hand, ready to catch spit or bile, but he turns, says, "Don't betray us," and is gone.

67

SEARCHING FOR MIRACLES

In the early eve, when the air begins to cool, Maysa practices contortion in the alley. Sitting cross-legged, erect, she lifts her feet until her heels rest in the hollows of her shoulders. She's been trying for months to loosen her spine, the hinges of her hips and knees, and hold this pose for one minute. I count the seconds and applaud at sixty. "Sababa!" Maysa deserves a circus tent full of admirers, but at least she has me.

I slip inside and send a message to Tali: *I miss you and your mother. I miss The Flying Kids. If I never see you again, please know you are dear to me.*

I say to Aisha, *Thank you, sister-friend, for your kindness, your trust. Maybe I understand how hard it is to lose Zahra, your cousin, because*—I can't tell her I may lose my own life soon—*I too have lost those I love. This is what I think, though. Zahra would want you to live and not stay sad forever. I never met her, but I believe she was a generous girl.*

She texts me minutes later: *Maybe you'll be happy to know I haven't had a drink today. And, yes, you're right—Zahra was a generous girl.*

The machine artists' website is down, so I can't reach Jonathan. Shirel doesn't answer my text, so maybe the authorities still have her phone. If Jonathan's out of jail, maybe he'll complete his "suitcase project." I imagine Maysa, a small, bendable girl, folded in a compartment. Jonathan sometimes mixes live performers with robots. I wonder, though, how would she breathe?

Tali texts me back: *The next time you visit Tel Aviv and The Kids, maybe you can stay with my mom and me. She's still trying to write you a letter, explain some things, but she can't get it "right." Maybe someday you'll receive a masterpiece, a few pages she has written and rewritten for months, years. She prefers silence to words. We don't speak much, and she won't show her "work-in-progress" even to me.*

Is your mom a little bit strange? I know it's selfish to hope she is.

There's all kinds of strange. It's simpler to say, *Yes, yes, yes, she is.*

My mother builds small nests. I'd like a feather of distance between us in our bed, but tonight she holds me in her arms. Her body says, *Child, you're not going anywhere. Don't even try.*

Maybe it's midnight, still no sleep, so I dream while awake. I see myself growing thinner, lighter, to slip free of what keeps me here: rib cage, skin, mother's arms, walls, alleys, Issam, the camp, the Israelis and their world. I see myself climbing Mount Ebal again, but this time I pass the quarry and the cave, rise over the crest, walk onward and outward, beyond Joshua's altar and the settlers of Elon Moreh. I've never seen the Jordan River, but give me a chance and I'll cross it, cross many rivers, skirt villages, cities, military installations, and keep going. The work of a funambulist is to walk in the sky on a rope, a wire, a prayer. I'm an athlete, but I'm also a crazy girl searching for miracles. I cannot fly from my rib cage, skin, or Mother's arms any time soon. But the fantasy gives me a buoyancy I may need at the break of day.

Issam will need a weapon to finish me. Awake or in dreams, I know this much: No one in Balata can kill me with his hands. Only Handala the Cat is faster, stronger. I mean, kilo for kilo. I'm way bigger than Handala. Ten cats could slip under my skin.

68

MAPPING

My mother rolls on top of me when the noise begins. "Lie still, don't move."

The bed shakes when helicopters whoosh over our roofs.

She prays in my ear. All I can do is receive: my head, my body, a prayer. Balata has shields. Prayers and skinny alleys keep away tanks, Humvees, jeeps, anything wider than the wing-space of arms. Drones small as sparrows appear, as their pilots wish. And sometimes soldiers come.

I see all around because war is the same show over and over. Several tanks wait near the exits of the camp to prevent escape. Helicopters hover over alleys, shine lights, watch for movement, and drones make Balata Camp movies. Machine art, Jonathan's remembrances, show scenes that repeat themselves in Palestine, though this one may surprise him. I'm in a bunker made of Mother. Her body between me and the war.

Tanks can't reach us, but soldiers can. They smash doors if no one answers, so we listen for *knock, knock, knock*, fists louder than prayer. My mother begins to rise until Grandpa Saeed peeks into our room: "Let me take care of this; just stay where you are."

But soon two soldiers crowd my mother and me. The taller one, in Arabic, orders us out of bed. We have no head coverings. My mother—after hiding her hair with her hands—tells me to do the same.

The soldier who speaks our language has a radio transmitter and a phone. The other one steps past me and sweeps a hand under the bed.

We need to show our IDs. The light on our interrogator's helmet almost blinds us. My mother shields her eyes with a hand, covers her hair with the other, and bows toward a shelf.

He studies the documents, our photographs and names and numbers, and enters the data on his phone. Something similar is happening in every home in our alley. The Israelis have a name for the operation: mapping. They last mapped our alley about a year ago. They keep track of who lives here, who might be visiting, who is new in each household, who is dangerous, dead, jailed, or vanished. The best time for mapping is the middle of the night when most of us are home.

Jonathan could create a model of the alley, add robot soldiers and refugees, or show raw footage of the war, mapping operations on multiple TVs.

Soldiers of low rank seldom have phones to record data. This short one who accompanies our interrogator searches for weapons, shines a light into drawers, corners, baskets, canvas bags. Just as Issam did, he dumps head scarves, robes, blouses, and pants on the floor. He growls something in Hebrew as he scatters my circus tools—ropes, wires, leather-soled slippers—on the bed.

The interrogator asks in Arabic: "What's this stuff for?"

I tell him.

He leans in. "You're in a circus? Balata has a circus?"

Wherever I go is a circus.

"Answer me."

"Yes, we have circus in our alleys and in a ruined house at the south edge of camp. I've performed twice with The Flying Kids of Tel Aviv."

If he believes me, he doesn't care one way or other. He informs my mother and me that our alley, our particular home, has been linked to terrorism. "Normally," he says, "we just take our census and leave, but tonight you'll have to answer a few questions." He shrugs by way of apology. "Tell the truth and you'll be home in a day or two."

He presses buttons on his phone. Two more soldiers somehow squeeze themselves inside, turn my mother and me around, bind our hands behind our backs, and push us into the kitchen where my grandpa perches on a stool, hands cuffed.

The Israelis will map second-story homes, third-story homes, fourth-story homes. They will clump around in heavy gear (rucksacks, ammunition belts, rifles, tear gas canisters, gas masks, grenades), and interpreters will ask questions. The only change they'll record is a new cousin, Abdullah, three months old, who was unborn the last time soldiers counted us at night.

I hear Hebrew, a loud voice, in the room my brother shares with our grandfather. Issam replies in Arabic: "Sifr, sifr, sifr." He claims his ID number is zero, zero, zero. He's shoved outside and into the kitchen.

His breath smells like vinegar. He wobbles, almost touches me, hands cuffed.

A tall soldier points a pistol at his chest. Issam may have lost his ID, or hidden it, a serious offense either way. All he will say is, "Sifr, sifr, sifr." The soldiers who cuffed me and my mother take turns shoving him. Does Issam think I turned him in, brought this upon us? Brother, your bomb is in the mountain. If the Israelis know it's yours, they did not learn this from me.

The tall soldier's helmet scrapes the ceiling as he shoves a hood over Issam's head. I'd never seen the Israelis use hoods while making arrests. Blindfolds, yes, many times. Either way it is night inside.

Issam, muffled, almost muzzled, says, "Zero, fuck you."

Our mother, who doesn't understand basic English, whispers prayers while a soldier blindfolds her and pushes her against a wall.

They blind my grandpa next, now me.

Wherever I go is circus.

I could walk a rope blind out of this camp.

69

THREE DAYS LATER

A female guard who looks young enough to join The Flying Kids stands at the door. My interrogator, slouched at his desk, face dark with stubble, yawns without covering his mouth.

But something new has begun. Last night they let me sleep and fed me when I woke: rice porridge, a chunk of bread, an orange. My interrogator, an Israeli who speaks my language, leans back in his cushioned chair and asks if I'm comfortable. My answer means nothing, but I say, "Yes, thank you." My chair is metal, my hands cuffed. I swing my legs because today they are free.

Interrogators have fake names, Arab names. The man in the cushioned chair calls himself Abu Ali. He asks the same questions he asked yesterday and the day before, and I provide the same answers: some truth, some lies, nothing to implicate my brother. Ali knows what's coming. He mocks me by drumming his fingers on his desk to match the cadence of my words.

I ask if he can tell me where I am, the name of the prison.

"A name means nothing."

"But—"

"You are where you belong."

A nod to the female guard is her signal to leave the room. Ali's assistants, Abu Abed and Abu Nihad, arrive moments later. They are large men who would need to duck and turn sideways to enter my home in Balata. They stand near my chair, one on each side, and greet me as if we are friends. Yesterday they questioned me—often shouting—for seven hours. Abu Nihad threatened "a strip-search, a complete examination." But so far only female guards have forced me to stand naked and exposed.

Abu Ali tells me what he already knows: my brother has training in explosives; he wants to kill Israelis, make a sport of it; he will never get out of prison. I believe he's lying. He wouldn't keep asking questions if he knew all this.

He leans over his desk. "Issam's your twin brother, but I have a hunch you're different. Or at least less dangerous."

"Neither of us is dangerous."

"Yes, I knew you would say this, but would you like to go home, see your friends? Would you like to perform again with—what's it called—The Flying Kids of Tel Aviv?"

"I would."

"I hear you're famous. The wonders of the internet allow anyone in the world to watch your performances on YouTube."

"Sir, I don't know who watches me."

"Thousands have watched you walk back and forth on the barrel of a tank. Are you aware of this?"

"No."

"I suppose there are many things you'd rather be unaware of. Your brother, for example, has training in explosives."

"I don't believe this."

"Yes, you've mentioned this how many times? Nine by my count, or is it ten?"

"I don't know."

"But let's bypass your brother for now. Your mother remains in jail, in solitary. You'll both be released if you cooperate."

He tells me this every day.

"Your grandfather is not well. Old people in prison—they tend to deteriorate."

"We are innocent."

"Really? Would you make this claim under oath?"

"I would."

"We believe one of you—perhaps all of you—know something about a bomb."

He leaves the room and I'm alone with Abu Abed and Abu Nihad. At first they comfort me, ask if I need anything, and Abu Abed—because my hands are cuffed behind me—holds a glass of water to my lips so I can drink.

Abu Nihad asks if I slept well.

Fuck you, I'm thinking. "Yes," I say, "thank you. I feel stronger today."

Abu Abed asks the same questions Abu Ali asked. I insist on my innocence, my family's innocence. "I'm sorry," I say, "but I'm afraid someone gave you false information. Someone is telling lies."

Abu Abed and Abu Nihad take turns shouting. They want to break my skull. Their breath is hot. They smell of onions. I start shaking, gasping for air, which makes them think I'm about to unravel. They quiet down, talk to me in whispers, and I apologize many times for being so useless. I seldom beg, but I say, "Please, please, how can I give a confession when I've done nothing wrong?"

70

NIGHT

I am led to a cell with two doors, the second one a step beyond the first. After removing my handcuffs, Abu Abed says, "Duck," shoves me through, and the doors click shut. My eyes grow big, big, but no light comes in. I feel around for a blanket in a corner, a bucket of water, half-filled, a hole in a cement floor. Everything is cement, cement, cement. Except for the hole, the stink coming up, I am sealed.

I do a humpback walk, three steps forward, three back, my head brushing the ceiling. *They will kill me before they break me.* I pause when I hear this inside me. Am I as brave as my words, or are they just words? How dead are the dead? Can they celebrate their bravery when they're gone?

Minutes later, maybe hours later, I run my hands up and down walls, hunt for cracks, and find something else. A metal sphere the size of a thumbprint is over the door. A listening device? A way for my captors to monitor what I might say to myself? I sit cross-legged and think.

Out loud, but not too loud, I pretend to talk truth to myself. I'm innocent, my family's innocent, my four stories of cousins are innocent, but I don't say Balata's innocent because they know better. Is anyone listening? I call out, moan, and repeat my story in whispers. "I'm innocent. My family's innocent. Abu Ali wants me to confess to lies. How would this help? *Who* would this help?"

Big breaths like sobbing, but I'm not. I say I miss Tali Glazman, Mrs. Glazman, and The Flying Kids of Tel Aviv. The weeping's for show, but the words are real. I miss my Israeli friends. I miss the beach, the sea, the sky that goes forever. I remember the night Tali and her mother grilled a fish for us, tossed in handfuls of pine nuts, roasted garlic, a splash of lemon. I thank them out loud. I remember coconut-almond ice cream for dessert.

Inside, unheard, I tell the truth to my brother: *Issam, I carried your bomb to a mountain because I don't want you scattered like red seeds in places where nothing grows.*

I have fewer words for my captors: *Zero, fuck you.*

I sit on my blanket and begin to practice contortion. I've never developed this skill, but I discover I can sit cross-legged and lift my feet to within a few centimeters of my shoulders. Maysa would applaud.

Hunched over, I begin to walk. Picturing a line on the floor that divides my cage, I take six steps forward—spin, breathe—and six steps back. I keep going till my neck hurts. I sit on my blanket near the door.

Every Palestinian, whether or not she's been detained, knows that a confession—for an interrogator—is better than a dead body, a slack tongue. I wonder, though, if a cell this small, a dark this dark, is unusual. Abu Ali and I share one thing: patience. He could have me killed—drain the blood, cut the breath—and call it suicide. In a minute, maybe less, a corpse. Confessions take time.

What can I tell Abu Ali that won't harm anyone? What will he believe?

I remember my first performance with The Flying Kids when I wore one of Palestine's colors—green. Mazin flew the same color on the flying trapeze, and Miki, his partner, now his girl, wore red. Other performers wore orange, yellow, blue, indigo, violet. I try to fix in my mind the brightest color: Mazin and me the green of a rainbow in Ha'yarkon Park.

Later—can't say how late—I am blind. How did they squeeze so much dark in one cell? Sitting cross-legged, I gather my blanket, fold it in my lap, unfold it, on and on, in the longest night. Some of the loose threads come apart in my hands. My blanket may be older than me.

71

STAGE-MASTER MACHINE

Two clicks, two doors, open on a beam of light. I go from darkness to blindness. I can't see past the skin of my eyes.

Abu Abed and Abu Nihad coax me from my cell. My sight returns, but what about my spine? I'd expected to see female guards rather than junior interrogators, Abu Ali's assistants. I hunch like an old woman as Nihad cuffs my hands behind me. Huge and pale, he has red hair and blue eyes. Abed is almost dark as me.

I might give something dear to see a stitch of sky, day or night, but I know where I'm going: a windowless room. Abu Ali slouches at his desk before a laptop computer. The dirty stubble on his chin looks the same as before. Is it possible I was in the dark only a few hours?

I sit across from him in a metal chair bolted to the floor. A calendar taped to my side of the desk predicts the future. Xs cover numbers 1 through 31. No month or year is given. Nor would they matter to anyone in jail for life.

Ali slides a photograph across his desk. "How's your eyesight?"

I look at the Xs. "It's okay now."

He holds the photograph near my face. "Still okay? Any issues?"

A girl my age, her limbs twisted in painful positions, is tied to a metal chair.

"You know of shabeh, I assume?"

I tell him I do.

"There are numerous positions. What you see here is among the least painful."

I look away.

"If we keep this child bent over in her chair for four or five days, what will happen?"

I pretend ignorance.

"She will never walk normally again."

She might become a contortionist. They've bound her hands and feet to the chair's legs in a way that forces her to lean forward, open her thighs, twist her knees. Every bone, every muscle, is off balance. None of this is new to me. Everyone in Balata knows of shabeh.

Ali says, "Hold still, please."

He takes my photograph with a cell phone.

"A visual reference," he says. "Before and after."

He leans in for a close-up.

"You'll decide what you look like when we're finished here."

Abu Abed straps me to the chair. This is not shabeh, not yet, for I can sit almost straight, roll my shoulders, jiggle my feet. I could sit this way a long time without being damaged much.

Abu Abed and Abu Nihad shout at me in Hebrew. My ears become sirens. They want to open my skull, pluck out the words I refuse to speak. *I found a bomb under the bed shared by my brother and grandfather.* I say nothing, but they wouldn't hear me anyway. Abu Ali plugs his ears with his thumbs.

All at once silence, or am I deaf? I hide a smile when I hear my breath.

Abu Ali motions for Abu Abed and Abu Nihad to leave the room. I suppose every interrogator has an Arab alias. If, in court, I complain that one Abu or another abused me, I will be told no such person exists.

Abu Ali has a soothing voice, which no one should trust. He tells me everything done at this facility has one purpose: to save lives. (He means Jewish lives.) He tells me they treat prisoners well, feed them well, give them medical care, except in extreme conditions. If, for example, they have reason to believe someone has training in explosives, or is ready to explode (suicide bomber), they have a mandate to use every means possible to extract information from him and his associates. He asks me what I know that might save lives.

I envy a girl in Balata who can't speak, whose tongue has one job: rest.

"Maybe we should start with family history," says Ali. "Our records show your grandfather was a physicist, and something of a scholar. Old men rarely cause trouble, but perhaps he's passed on his knowledge of explosives to his grandson, or to a nephew, a cousin, or even—I suppose—to you."

I shake my head.

"You disagree?"

"My grandfather would never harm anyone."

He smiles. "Really? Is he a saint?"

"That's not what I'm saying."

"He was detained a number of years ago, and there are still unanswered questions."

"Abu Ali, excuse me, but the questions are yours, not mine."

"So he's innocent? That's what you're saying?"

"That's what I *know*. My grandfather would never make a bomb."

His eyes stay on me a long time. I slump down because I don't want to taunt him, suffer more than I must. I'm the girl who walks the high-wire. I'm not easy to scare, but I have limits. Ali wonders what I can and can't endure. He waits for…not the scream, but the words that follow. I am a quiet girl.

For the first time, I see a man I wish to kill: Abu Ali. Maybe my brother's smarter than me because he didn't have to face torture before he realized the Israelis have the power to do anything, everything, and can dispose of us one by one or all at once, when and where they wish. A vest? It looks less savage from here.

"Would you like to see more photographs?"

Silence.

"It's up to you. If you prefer to close your eyes, I'll do my best to describe them."

My eyes are open. The Xs on the calendar are machine-made, identical.

"Can you lift your head a little?"

Not yet.

"The girl in our first photograph is too dirty to be touched. This is why a stick was used to encourage cooperation."

Flash.

I look up and he takes another picture of me.

"As for our second photograph—not of you, but of her—there's blood where there shouldn't be any. We're still trying to determine if she harmed herself."

Jonathan could program a machine to speak this way, casual and informative, as if describing scenery. A stage-master in complete control, pressing this nerve, that nerve, metal to flesh.

I lean forward to see this girl through my eyes rather than Abu Ali's. Something dark—maybe blood—stains her thighs. Bound and gagged, she tilts forward and would fall face-down if her chair weren't bolted to the floor. Whether or not the photograph is fake, I know they could do this to someone, anyone, *me*. Maybe my only way out is to be as crazy as Ali, but smarter. What I know is fantastic. He thinks he can shock me with his power, his cleverness, his evil. I can shock him by feeding him a rag of truth.

I begin to tell my torturer about my journey on Mount Ebal. He interrupts, imagines this is small talk, but I know which word will silence him: *bomb*. So, yes, I found one, a bomb in a vest, beneath a tree when I stopped to rest. What could I do? If I turned it in to the authorities, they would demand an explanation. Who gave it to me? How many people are involved? What organizations do they belong to? I would face interrogation, torture, until I told lies and sent innocent people to jail the rest of their lives.

Abu Ali grins. "So you just happened to find a suicide vest on Mount Ebal?"

"I did."

"Someone dropped it along a trail? A moment of carelessness?"

"Sir, it wasn't along a trail. It was beneath a tree, partly hidden by rocks."

"And you poked around and found it?"

"No, but I saw it. I'd never been more terrified in my life."

He laces his fingers, twiddles his thumbs.

"Should I give you more time to create a plausible story?"

"I'm telling the truth."

"Okay, then, let's fast forward to the epilogue. Did you leave the vest where you found it?"

"No, sir. I was afraid those who hid it would return and carry out a plan and kill innocent people."

He yawns. "So you're a good Samaritan?"

"I'm Palestinian."

"Well, that gives me a ray of hope. Only a Palestinian can answer questions such as, Where's the vest now? Where exactly?"

"Near the crest of Mount Ebal. I climbed the walls of a quarry and left it in a cave."

"So someone else can retrieve it?"

"No. Only I can climb those walls."

He smiles. "You're the bomber?"

"No, no—that's not what I'm saying. The vest will never be used."

I want to spit at him when he snickers. I hate this Abu's face, the pouch under his chin the size of an egg, jowls like mush. I doubt he could hike one kilometer on Mount Ebal. All he can do is threaten people from a cushioned chair.

"You're from Balata, yes?"

He knows where I'm from.

"Your home is how many kilometers from the crest of Ebal?"

"I don't know. I walked a long time."

"You didn't get a ride?"

"No, sir, I didn't need a ride. I'm an athlete."

He sits back in his chair, hands folded on his belly.

"Who are you protecting? What's his name?"

I shake my head.

"Your people aren't worth the effort. Look what happened to your father."

My heart stops, then pulses in my ears.

"They betrayed him, didn't they?"

"I don't know what you're talking about."

"Maybe no one told you. Maybe they were ashamed."

"Abu Ali, my father died when I was four."

"Yes, he died by his own hand. They forced him."

"I don't—"

"It's true. Ask your mother. Ask your grandfather."

I shut my eyes.

"He was a brave man, your father. So let me tell you why he took his life."

I lean forward till my bindings stop me. I have a word to shut him up (*bomb*), and he has a word (*father*) to do the same to me. Anyone who says *your father* stills my tongue. Maybe every word is a lie, but the Shin Bet know many things about us, they study us, and Abu Ali could—if he wishes—toss me a rag or two of truth.

Years ago, when I was small, my father worked in an olive orchard a few kilometers from Nablus. Abu Ali knows a bus took him back and forth to work, to the trees, but his main job was to maintain and repair farm equipment. The bus traveled farther north with six or seven other laborers who were helping to build a better road to the settlement of Elon Moreh. My father was part of the resistance, though Abu Ali is unsure which faction he had joined.

"Anyway, it was summertime, mid-July, when your father got wind of something big. The road laborers, those working for the settlers, were despised by their own people. Collaborators, traitors—you know how people are judged."

He waits till I nod.

"Over the years, I've come to see fanaticism as a disease, a contagion. It spreads faster than any plague under certain conditions."

He should know.

"Your father heard of a plot to kill the laborers and several leaders of Elon Moreh with one blast. Two of the laborers were from Balata, and he knew them well. Your father made a fateful choice. He tried to persuade the bomber—let's call him Zuhair—to reconsider his plan. This man wanted what many want: paradise. He was ready to blow himself up, take a few Arabs with him, plus the settlers who hired them, put bread on their tables. Zuhair became furious that someone would question his will. We don't know who your father spoke with next, but Zuhair was arrested three days before he could carry out his plan." He burps, shakes his head. "His family and extended family believed your father informed, and perhaps he had. We're still not sure this is true."

Silence.

"Did you love your father?"

I nod, but this is what I would say if words were safe. *Fuck you, Abu Ali. In a machine art exhibit, you would be the one called Sadist. You will rust someday. Your hands, your voice (soft but like a knife) will touch no more nerves. You will send no one to hell other than yourself.*

"It seems your father was a decent man. He risked his life to protect others, avoid senseless violence."

(This may be true.)

"Of course Zuhair's tribe believed in retributive justice. The cycle—I've seen it more times than I've seen the sunrise—goes like this. There's betrayal, or the perception of betrayal, followed by a form of vengeance more brutal than an eye for an eye, a tooth for a tooth. Zuhair's grandfather gave your father a choice: he must take his own life, or sacrifice someone in his immediate family." He shrugs. "Perhaps we should give Zuhair's grandfather an A for originality. The common practice is to kill the collaborator, spare the family. Am I right?"

(He is, but I keep quiet.)

"Meanwhile, in his last hours, your father denied he betrayed anyone.

His claim, whether true or false, meant nothing to Zuhair's grandfather. Honor, *tribal* honor—please tell me if something's more precious in your world."

I walk across his words the way I walk across wires. He wants me to implode, scream, call him every vile word I can think of, and in the meantime to reveal something, *any*thing—maybe the fact that I know nothing of the story he is telling. Sorry, Abu, my first language is silence. Palestinians are often forced to sign confessions written in Hebrew. If this fake Abu lets me write my own confession, I'll reduce the script to contortion, letters too small to read. Or make two or three indecipherable marks on a sheet of paper and leave the rest blank as a razed field.

"Are you listening?"

"Yes, sir."

"As far as we know, your father had twenty-four hours to choose. If he lacked the courage to take his own life, you or Issam or your mother or grandfather must die. Your father haunted himself with questions: 'Who do I love most? Who do I love least? My father? My wife? My son? My daughter? Myself?' Few Arab men would sacrifice their father, their only son. Am I right? So that left three options: you, your mother, or him."

I can take this. If I live one word at a time, one moment at a time, I might survive. Abu Ali, the Shin Bet, the prison, the image of my father holding a gun to his head—none of this kills me yet. If Abu fucks me with a stick, maybe I can take that too. The thought of his hands, though, his sex… Here is the wire I will not cross.

He fingers the soft flesh under his chin. "You seem distracted today."

(Not at all. I want to murder him.)

"Earlier, before I changed the subject, you were telling me about a recent hike on Mount Ebal."

(That seems a long time ago.)

"You found a vest, a bomb, that just happened to be there. And because you're a good Samaritan blessed with athletic skills, you scaled a cliff and left it in a cave where it will never harm anyone."

(I wish I had it now.)

"And when do you say this remarkable thing happened?"

"I can answer if you tell me how long I've been here."

He scratches the stubble on his chin. "Not long. Four days, maybe five. I can't remember off-hand. Numbers are irrelevant here."

I tell him I found the vest on Mount Ebal the day before soldiers raided my home, my alley, and maybe all of the Balata Camp.

"What date would that be?"

"I don't know."

"So the vest is yours? Are we wrong to believe your brother was the carrier?"

"It belongs to neither of us."

"Then whose is it? Was it issued to a friend, a cousin?"

"No."

"Have you ever tried it on, strapped it to your chest?"

I hesitate. "I had to, but I carried it on my back when I scaled the walls of a cliff. The weight on my spine helped me to balance on ledges."

"You expect me to believe this?"

I look at him hard. "You don't have to believe my words. I can take you to the mountain."

He chuckles. "A guided tour? A change of scenery?"

"I'll show you the ledges I walked, the walls I climbed."

"Fascinating."

"If you wish, I will retrieve the vest."

He sweeps his desk clean and says, "Excuse me for a minute. I need to rearrange some files."

He turns in his chair, stoops, and turns on a machine. I can't see what he's doing. A grinding sound, a high screech—maybe he's shredding photographs. He speaks to me over the noise.

"You could be hurt far worse than you imagine. You could be ruined if you're lying."

"And you?"

He looks over his shoulder, winks, and the machine goes silent.

"You would be wise to think of yourself today."

72

RETURN TO MOUNT EBAL

Praise Allah and the prophets Abu Ali is not among my escorts. Near the crest of Mount Ebal, I walk with twelve soldiers under the open sky of an afternoon. A jeep follows in our wake, and three more are some thirty meters ahead of us. Machines rattle the earth while the sun makes a spark of me. I walk in mountain light, yellow and gold.

The soldiers, sweaty under their heavy gear, drink lots of water, and nibble snacks for energy. When we reach the quarry, the man in charge, a lieutenant, refuses to believe me when I tell him I carried the suicide vest some fifteen meters up the walls of a cliff.

I say to him in English, "Sir, if you remove my handcuffs, I will show you how to climb."

He shouts at me in Hebrew, and then his translator, an Israeli soldier several years older than the others, shouts at me in Arabic. "The lieutenant wants you to shut up. If you were to climb these walls and fall, break your neck, break even a finger, he'll be the first to be blamed, then his soldiers. Human rights groups, certain media outlets—they'll skewer us. And if, by some miracle, you scale the walls and reach the cave, then what? If there's a vest, as you claim there is, you could strap it on, jump from the cave, and blow us to bits."

"This is"—I stop myself from smiling—"paranoid."

"Not at all. Thousands in Nablus wish us a speedy death."

The Israelis see danger everywhere. I'm not sure what prison I was in, but they ferried me here, blindfolded, in a helicopter. I kept trying to see beneath the cloth, or through it to hills, trees, roads, villages, landscapes. They darkened my eyes, but I tasted the sky of Palestine. Would they remove my tongue if they knew?

Now the lieutenant gets on his radio and barks at someone on the other end. He speaks Hebrew, but I can make out a few words—*Arab girl, mountain, bomb*. Everyone speaks some truth whether or not he tries.

I hunch down beside the tree where I rested before I climbed the walls of the quarry. I've told the translator I found the vest in this area, half-covered by stones, but neither he nor the lieutenant believes me.

They also don't believe I climbed the walls of the quarry without assistance. The translator, who called me a liar four times, insists no one can "scale these stones without proper equipment and a team of professionals." I'm sorry, but he is what I will call an asshole. I *am* my proper equipment. I *am* my team of professionals. I would like to show Mr. Translator and the lieutenant and the rest of these non-circus clowns what I can do, light up these walls, retrieve the bomb they're after, hand it over, though no one could find a safer place for it than I have. Today my talents count for nothing. I weigh forty-two kilos, but if they could see what I'm made of, where I'm from, they would notice nothing small about me, or at least nothing less determined than mountain and sky. They would see me wherever they look.

Three drones hover over us. The smallest is the size of the one Jonathan made for a machine art exhibit in Jaffa. I remember the robed women—human, not machines—removed their veils to blow bubbles, and the drone chased the colors, red, yellow, green, and sometimes a bubble got caught, *pop*, and vanished in stage lights. I smiled as the crowd laughed, as I'm smiling now. The translator, who's almost as tall as the tree that shades me, wants to know what in hell I'm so happy about. "Nothing," I say, and put away my smile before he hits me. I cower a bit, pretend I'm helpless. The smile he thinks he erased—it's under my breast bone, wider than before.

Now the two larger drones hover while the small one flits around inside the cave. The lieutenant bends over the screen of a hand-held computer. He's nodding, jabbering, telling whoever's listening at the other end what the little drone sees when it shines its light. I don't understand much Hebrew, but I know there's a suicide vest in a crevice, V-shaped, at the back of the cave.

The lieutenant comes over to where I'm sitting. Fast words to the translator, not loud, though, and then he bends down for a better look at me. The vest is where I said it would be.

The translator says, "Who helped you climb these walls?"

"No one."

The lieutenant cackles.

The translator says, "You're a…what's the word?"

"Funambulist. You can also call me a high-wire walker."

"Yes, we've been briefed on that, but..." He looks at the walls of the quarry. "None of this makes sense."

Hours pass. The sun is low in the west when a helicopter hovers over the cliff and a robot the size of a small dog is lowered by cable to the mouth of the cave. By remote control, or some device a machine artist would understand, the robot unhooks the leash. He—most machines look sort of masculine—stands on his hind legs.

The small drone's in there, too, because he's equipped with cameras, eyes, which become the lieutenant's eyes via computer. The translator isn't watching me now. Monitoring the computer screen, he and the lieutenant stand side by side. Quiet, slow, I get up and peek between them as the robot bends down to lift the vest by a shoulder strap. I sit under the tree again. The robot and the drone will work together. I know how this will end.

In the last light on the mountain, the helicopter hovers near, lowers a harness by cable, and the robot grabs on and descends to earth with the suicide vest. I wish Jonathan could see this. The robot drops the vest and up he goes, into the sky toward the door of the chopper. The lieutenant approaches the vest because he knows the detonator is unattached to explosives. I could've told him this long before the little drone sent him pictures. The lieutenant takes off his helmet and wipes his brow. No one but me sees the first stars over Mount Ebal.

73

THE GERMAN SHEPHERD

Abu Ali keeps asking about my brother. "Is he a member of Al-Aqsa Martyrs' Brigade?"

I shrug. "I don't know."

"Where did you find the vest?"

I've told him a hundred times.

"Perhaps your brother's mission wasn't to blow himself up, but to deliver explosives to someone who would."

I lose a breath, get it back. Sit still.

"Your brother will turn seventeen in a few days, which is a bit young for a bomber. Do you agree?"

"Sir, I don't know what you're talking about."

"Detainees often claim to be disoriented, confused, before they speak clearly."

"I'm not confused."

"No? Disoriented perhaps?"

"No."

"How long would you be in jail if convicted of possession and concealment of a suicide vest?"

"Have I been charged with—"

"No, we're in no hurry to press charges. Our first priority is to build a solid case."

He leans back in his chair, rests his hands on the shelf of his belly. The shouts of Abu Abed and Abu Nihad are easier to bear than the quiet cruelty of my primary interrogator. Ali turns to the computer on his desk, taps a few keys, and smiles. "Normally," he says, "a detainee in isolation spends twenty-three hours a day in her cell. Your case, I'm afraid, calls for more stringent measures. We'll let you decide how long you wish to go before you see the sky."

They've locked me in a different cell. No windows, a slot for food, and a yellow light that hurts my eyes. I sit on a mattress beside a toilet that smells worse than sewage. Maybe Abu Ali wants me to wonder what I'll smell like when I'm dead.

I don't know what time it is, day or night, when I hear a dog sniffing at the door. The yellow light blinks on and off. A guard, female, says something in Hebrew, and the dog barks and snarls. Knees folded to my chest, I squeeze myself into a corner. I can't lean on these walls for long because the surfaces are rough, full of sharp edges. Maybe Abu Ali designed this cell.

The door stays closed. I hear the click of the dog's claws on concrete as it moves away. The yellow light stops blinking. The guard—must be the guard—makes a popping sound. I think she popped bubble gum. She rattles a chain and walks away, steps heavy. I picture a fat lady wearing knee-high boots. I start smiling when I can't hear her anymore.

Maybe it is morning. I'm strapped in a metal chair when Abu Ali tells me my brother died in custody last night. I sit very still. He expects me to cry, tell him something new, but I know his tactics. He comes around his desk and touches my left shoulder. "I'm sorry," he says. "Your brother went berserk, attacked his jailors, and they had no choice."

A female guard stands at the door. Is Issam dead? In one important way, Ali and I are equal. Every word he speaks could be true or false. All I believe now is the pressure of his hand.

I crane my neck to see the guard. She looks neither friendly nor unfriendly, but I doubt Ali will violate me in her presence. She's older than my mother, hips wide, and I hope she has a daughter. I like how soft she is in her middle. She wouldn't look right if she held a rifle in her arms.

Ali returns to his side of the desk and slouches in his chair. He groans, scratches his whiskers, and takes out his phone. He looks at it a while, maybe reading a message, then presses a key. A dog starts barking, snarling. "Remember this?" he asks. "Meir, a German Shepherd, was on duty last night."

He plays the recording three times. "You only know Meir by his sound. Would you like to meet him?"

The guard turns away when I glance at her.

"You'll have to choose," says Ali. "It is standard procedure to allow detainees to determine their own fate."

I give myself to one moment at a time. Ali doesn't know how I live.

On the wire I take one step, just one, now another, another, because all the way across, at each juncture, there is only one. Ali will break me if I forget my training. He doesn't know the wire. He doesn't know Balata. He doesn't know me.

He leans over his desk. "Did I tell you your mother's still detained?"

This may be true.

"Your grandfather also, though he's not feeling well."

I close my eyes.

"This is quite simple, isn't it?"

I wait.

"Everyone goes home if you tell the truth."

Two vents near the ceiling blow cold air. I curl on the mattress and see how small I can make myself. I believe my brother is alive.

I hear the dog in the night, if it is night. I am frozen. He pants, sniffs under the door, but doesn't bark. I hear human footsteps, a guard, I suppose, maybe the wide-hipped mother. I don't think she'll let the dog hurt me. She'll keep Meir on a leash.

The door stays shut all night, if it is night. I don't see the German Shepherd, except in dreams.

74

RELEASE

I am stunned when two guards remove me from my cell and take me outside to the recreation yard. The light is so big I could be in heaven. If the Israelis fly all their planes through the blue, shoot their rockets and missiles and bullets, bulldoze our trees, smash our homes, turn our mountains into dust, the sky will return for everyone who survives. Do my enemies have a strategy? Maybe they're giving me a glimpse of the sky so I'll panic the next time they cuff my hands, chain my legs, tie me to a chair, or throw me in a cell. I walk the cement paths, eat dust and light. A feast compared to prison food.

In a jeep, blindfolded, feet chained, hands cuffed, I'm going somewhere fast. The male soldiers in front jabber in Hebrew. Are they taking me back to Mount Ebal, or to a prison farther from home? Israel is the god I despise. They could bury me today, in an unmarked grave. Or set me free.

Maybe a half hour passes before we reach a town or a city. I doubt this is Nablus, but I hear Arabic beyond closed windows. I lean toward a door, my face in the sun. Am I in Palestine? If I'm near my home, is anyone home?

My ears tell me there are other jeeps, Humvees, a convoy. A radio transmitter crackles, sends out messages in Hebrew. A helicopter passes low, now another. Soldiers are machine people. Maybe Jonathan knows them best.

Office. No cuffs, no chains, no blindfold. Two men dressed as Palestinian policemen stand over me. Are they Israelis in disguise?

One of them gives me a glass of water. "Your mother and grandfather are here."

He'll need to prove it.

"Relax," he says, and motions to a cushioned chair. "No one's going to hurt you today."

He asks me to sign a document.

"Is it written in Hebrew or Arabic?"

He hesitates. "Can you read English?"

"Yes."

"We have the English version in our files."

Your release depends on your compliance with three conditions:

1. *You are hereby prohibited from leaving Nablus for one year;*
2. *you are prohibited from visiting Mount Ebal or Mount Jarzim until further notice;*
3. *you are prohibited from approaching within one hundred meters of Joseph's tomb until further notice.*

Other restrictions may be implemented, with or without notice to you or your legal guardian(s), at the direction of Israel Security Agency.

I have no interest in Joseph's tomb, which is near the Balata Camp. If Israeli pilgrims visit the site, soldiers provide security, drones keep watch, and to all this—and the conditions above—I say, *Zero, fuck you.* The tongue I speak with is reasonable (*Thank you for the translation*); a more honest tongue is silent. I think of my brother as I sign the document. If he's alive, what conditions would allow his release?

I'm led down a corridor, through a metal door with an eyehole, down another corridor, through another door, and into a lobby. My feet stop, even my heart stops, when I see my mother, my grandfather, because I need stillness to believe we are again a family. My mother draws me to her thinness. I don't understand her body. How can someone so bony become soft to comfort me? Abu Ali's a liar. I confessed to nothing, but she's out of jail, my grandpa's out of jail. Is my brother alive?

This is my first question.

My mother shudders. "Yes, but he's still in prison."

"Where?"

"Megiddo," says my grandpa, "or maybe Ofer."

"They haven't told you?"

"They keep us guessing."

"And where was I all this time?"

"Hasharon Prison. You were in Israel."

"For how long?"

"Seventeen days."

"And now?" I ask. "Where *am* I?"

"Tulkarm," says my grandpa. "You're almost home."

My uncle Sami sits on the front bumper of his Hyundai. He opens his arms and I run to him, kiss his right hand, and bring it to my forehead.

"I wanted to go inside," he says, "but they wouldn't let me. These are our own police, but they said, 'Two family members at a time.'"

In the back seat, my mother keeps touching my cheeks and lifting my chin to look into my face and claim me once more as her daughter. I try not to think of Issam as I lean into her warmth and her words: "I prayed and prayed I would see you again."

As we leave Tulkarm, Mount Jarzim shows green on the horizon. The Israelis decided I'm unwelcome there, unwelcome on Ebal, too, but I'm on my way to the only home I know—Balata. I miss my skinny alley and all the pictures children painted and drew on bullet-pocked walls. I miss Maysa and Handala the Cat, my four stories of cousins, and the house half fallen where Maysa and I practice circus skills. I'm behind in my training. Tomorrow I'll return to Nik Wallenda's regimen—aerobics, wire-walking, strengthening exercises, six hours a day six days a week. If I never leave home, never perform again, I will not give up my art.

The last time I saw my mother an Israeli soldier was covering her eyes with a blindfold. "Mom, were you in prison while I was in prison? Seventeen days?"

"No, three days, almost four. I don't know why they kept you so long. And Issam…we're still not sure where he is."

I'll never speak of the suicide vest, the mission I interrupted, but I need to compare notes. "Were you interrogated? Did they ask about our family, our cousins?"

"They couldn't stop asking. At first all their questions were about Issam. They tied me to a chair and tried to convince me he has training in explosives."

"They believe that?"

"They seem to. Later, they asked about you, and described you as 'potentially dangerous.'"

"That's crazy."

"I know it is. That's exactly what I said."

I ask my grandpa if he too was arrested.

"I was detained," he says, "but they were more lenient than expected. They held me for six days."

"Were our cousins detained?"

"Yes, a few of the men, but they were released by morning."

"The Israelis have no proof of anything."

"No, but they like to make up stories. This gives them an excuse to do as they wish on a given night."

My mother clutches my hand. "I won't sleep till Issam is home. If I have to pray forever, I'll pray forever."

Our hands are sweaty.

"You and Issam just had your birthday, seventeen years old. Instead of a party, prison. I won't rest till both my children are home."

She and my grandfather are safer than I am. If they are detained again, they will not be burdened with knowledge. I wish part of my memory could be erased. An empty heart and mind is precious in prison. I fear the Israelis know I have secrets. Maybe they released me at this time because they want to see where exactly I go, who I talk with. Maybe I'll stay home. Maybe I won't even visit my four stories of cousins. If my mother allows it, I'll set up ropes and wires in the room we share. I don't need to walk across the sky to practice my art. To balance one centimeter over the earth requires the same skill as walking a wire between the crests of mountains. Nik Wallenda wire-walked across the Grand Canyon on a summer day. I might do the same in winter if they gave me a chance.

75

BALATA

I have text messages from Aisha. I also have messages from Tali who says three times, *Text me back so I stop worrying, ok?*

I tell her the camp had no internet for more than two weeks. I tell the same lie to Aisha. The Shin Bet may be monitoring my grandpa's phone, so I claim my family is well and the camp is calm. How much can I say before the Israelis put me in a cage or tie me to a chair? I might get my friends in trouble, too, if I write something that upsets them. I send messages that mean nothing. Maybe everyone knows how.

I won't try to reach Jonathan or Shirel because they have enough trouble. If Jonathan's out of jail, I wonder if he agreed to certain conditions. Maybe the authorities insisted that he stop making machine art, or at least stop all street performances and exhibitions. He may have to go underground to keep working. But who would see his creations besides Shirel and a few machine-artist friends?

My second day home, I receive an email from Mrs. Glazman that includes an attachment—unfinished letter.doc. I remember her telling me she sometimes waits half the night for a single word she can trust. I envy her patience. Sometimes I hunger for words as if they are food, air, light. I can't say I trust every word I've written. I can only hope most of this book is true.

> Dear Amal,
>
> I have no choice but to send you these scraps of an unfinished letter. I have torn up perhaps three hundred pages, and I have to admit there's some pleasure in hearing paper rip. Words being shredded—at least it's honest. These few have survived on my computer. I hope I'm not making the wrong choice by sending them to you.
>
> Whose family history is pretty? After World War II, my father, Tali's grandfather, was three years old when he arrived at a displaced persons camp in Cyprus. His mother, Tali's great-grandma, died in the camp soon after, for reasons unrecorded. She'd survived the

Rovno Ghetto in western Ukraine, but I have no record of how she ended up in Cyprus. After the war, there were hundreds of DP camps across Europe. Amid the chaos and trauma, I doubt she herself could have traced her path to the island. She wanted to take her son to Palestine or the United States, but immigration restrictions were severe at this time. Her husband died in Auschwitz. I don't know how she and her three-year-old escaped.

My mother was born in Kaunas, Lithuania, in 1940. Her father, my grandpa Joseph, was once so distraught about anti-Semitism in Lithuania that he applied for citizenship in Germany. He was, of course, denied. Born in Kaunas, he died in Treblinka. His wife, my grandma Tzipi, is a rarity. She died of natural causes (lung cancer) in 1941. Cigarettes saved her from the gas.

My mother never spoke of how she survived Europe as a little girl. I suppose someone sheltered her in a cellar or an attic, or gave her a non-Jewish name and hid her in the open. She and my father met in Haifa and married in 1969. A few years later, they moved to Tel Aviv, where my father began his career as a professor of comparative literature. I have inherited his melancholy, but not his brilliance. They are both gone now, of natural causes. I find this remarkable. No one tried to murder my parents even once.

I will tell you about my husband—Jacob. I don't know where his energy, his zest, came from, or why he fell in love with me. He had my father's passion for literature, but no trace of sadness. Jacob was too smart to try to separate me from my melancholy. Instead, he took me to beaches, to theater, to art galleries, to dance performances, to concerts, so that perhaps something larger than a husband (e.g. beauty, culture) might reunite me with the world. Can some smidge of sorrow evaporate into joy? Well, not very often, but then came Tali. That so much beauty could come out of me—I am still in awe.

There would be no point in telling you how my husband died, but I will tell you how he lived. He opposed the occupation of Palestine and tried—in large ways and small—to correct a disaster. Jacob could not understand why the Jewish people, who suffered more than 2000 years of persecution that culminated in the Holocaust, would—willingly, systematically—displace others, and make their lives difficult or impossible. His parents and mine, to survive, had to come here, but Jacob never forgot who they and other refugees displaced. Palestine has been shredded. This includes you, Amal, your family, your relatives, the Balata Camp, the other camps, the diaspora, the ongoing catastrophe. When will it end? Who will end it? And how?

Jacob had given up on adults, or most of them. He taught high school drama and literature, and every project he put his heart behind brought Palestinian youth and Israeli youth into the same arena. His religion, if he had one, was the arts—theater, literature, poetry, music, circus, etc. Did Tali tell you she's been juggling since she was three years old? Jacob founded The Flying Kids of Tel Aviv when she was one.

Several months after my husband's death, I cleaned out his desk and found these words of Professor Yeshayahu Leibowitz on an index card which I tore in half. "A state ruling a hostile population of 1.5 to 2 million foreigners would necessarily become a secret-police state, with all that this implies for education, free speech, and democratic institutions. The corruption characteristic of every colonial regime would also prevail in the State of Israel. The administration would suppress Arab insurgency on the one hand and acquire Arab Quislings on the other."

Leibowitz wrote this in 1968, about one year after the Six Day War. He repeatedly called for Israelis to refuse to serve in the Occupied Territories, and warned that Israel was turning its soldiers into "Judeo-Nazis," writing that if "the law…can allow the use of torture as a way of getting confessions out of prisoners, then this testifies to a Nazi mentality."

Amal, my views often differed from those of my husband. Jacob and I used to argue about everything, but over time—and despite his loss which I still can't bear—I've drawn closer to his heart. The index card torn in half—I eventually taped it together and keep it in my own desk. At this point, most Israelis seldom, if ever, consider the fate of Palestinians. As a nation, we have backed away from our deepest truth: The Holocaust ends when the suffering ends. During World War II and the early years of Israel, many of those who arrived in this land once shared were dazed, broken, unable to see beyond the miraculous fact that they survived the mass graves. One could not have expected them to see the suffering of those they displaced, or even murdered. These "first citizens" are mostly gone now. Nowadays Israelis have immersed themselves in a malaise of conscience, an unwillingness or inability to see the suffering of the Other. My efforts to find words, meaning, seem almost irrelevant. I live in a nation that sees nothing beyond the edges of its skin.

Tali, who will celebrate her seventeenth birthday next month, will soon be called to serve in the Israel Defense Forces. I don't know how to prepare myself for this, especially if she agrees to serve in the Occupied Territories. Her father was not a normal father, and I would be naïve to expect her to understand him at this time, or to understand whose steps I follow. Sometimes—to be honest—I feel like a ghost, almost gone from this world—but I will never abandon my daughter. Forgive me if you can. Perhaps I have said too much about what I know, what I feel, of "the situation" that both separates and binds us. However inadequate my words, I wish you and your family peace in these difficult times.

With love and kindness,

Rebecca Glazman

I was not a crybaby even as a baby. The sounds coming out of me now are like those of a small animal. My mother's upstairs with Aunt Salma. Grandpa Saeed and Uncle Sami are drinking coffee in the alley. I sit on the bed I share with my mother and wonder at my tears. My cries are those of a mouse, but I don't need them any louder. I like hearing small things. I have ears in my heart. *Will Tali soon arrive in Palestine as a soldier? Will Mrs. Glazman be able to prepare herself? Will I?* I hear Mrs. Glazman's worry. I worry, too, but quieter. I hear someone upstairs pouring tea in a glass. I make almost no sound when I cry. This is so I can hear.

I write her a love letter, though I must be careful. *I can't begin to tell you how grateful I am for your kindness. Your husband lived a beautiful life.* (She doesn't know I know how Jacob Glazman died.) *I will always remember and honor every word you've written. I love you and Tali and The Flying Kids. I wish I could say more.*

I hope Mrs. Glazman won't get in trouble for writing her letter. Words are safer for her than for me, but I think she took a risk. I'll show her letter to my grandpa, and translate it for my mother. I would translate it for four stories of cousins and read it in every alley of Balata if words were safe.

76

PRACTICE

One rope extends from the headboard of the bed I share with my mother to a pipe set in cement. Another crosses diagonally over the first and is attached to metal hooks driven into walls. My mother says I've turned our room into a spider's web, ropes everywhere, but there are only two. I take them down before we sleep.

Maysa wants to practice in the house half fallen at the south edge of the camp.

"No, I'm not going there anymore."

"Why not?"

"You're a contortionist. You could practice your art in a box."

She takes my hand and traces a line on my palm. "Did they…did they hurt you?"

"No, they just kept asking the same questions."

"What questions?"

"Nothing important."

"You almost never leave home."

Maysa can't match the contortionists in The Flying Kids, but she can twist herself into a snake that touches its head with its tail. The floor is cement, so I bring out my foam pad for her, the one I use for acrobatics. Face down, she stretches to her full length (she's not long), then rises like a snake preparing to strike. Her belly holds all of her as she lifts her legs, too, and her calves and thighs arc over her spine. Head to tail, she seesaws, reaches back to grab her feet and touch the soles to the top of her head. Reduced to simple lines, she looks sort of like this: δ

Sometimes—and now—I help her hold the pose to condition her joints and muscles. Maysa is the best contortionist in the Balata Camp. If she had professional coaches and extensive training, she could match any girl in The Flying Kids.

Tali's text begins and ends with a smiley face emoji.

> The Flying Kids will perform in Haifa the second week of December. Maybe you can get permission to join the troupe!

I use the same emoji.

> I don't think I can come this time, but I appreciate the invitation. All is well here. My friend Maysa and I practice circus every day.

Tali, still smiling:

> I think you'll get a permit if you apply. Coach Dagan and the office staff have connections. My mom knows a few people, too. Don't let her "sweetness" fool you. She's a bulldog in a dress.

No emoji with my words:

> Thank you so much, but I think I'll need at least a year before I apply. You won't believe me, but I can see your smiley face—you, not some emoji—from the stool where I sit.
> Love, Amal

77

MY FATHER

Grandpa Saeed calls me into the alley at dusk. He sits in a plastic chair outside our doorway while I squat beside him. He wants to know when I last looked at the sky.

I'm not sure why anyone looks. A hint of light over our walls is all we can see.

"When's the last time you sat with me in the alley?"

My shoulders bunch. "Before my detainment."

"You don't have to tell me what happened in Hasharon, but I insist you leave your room, come out to our alley, go to school, return to life. You understand?"

I watch an ant crawl over a pebble. "I'll go to school tomorrow."

"I want you and Maysa to practice your circus skills right here, in this alley. No one has confined you to a cell."

I nod.

"Amal, look at me."

I obey.

"You mustn't be defeated. You mustn't let them take more than they already have."

I will never speak of the cages the Israelis make for girls like me, the chairs they strapped me to, or the girl Abu Ali described as "too dirty to be touched." My grandpa knows about such things anyway. All I suffered and much worse has been suffered by many. I wonder, though, if Ali told the truth about my father. Did he really kill himself? I need to separate story from truth.

"One of my interrogators told me my father prevented the deaths of both Palestinians and settlers, but maybe he was lying."

My grandpa closes his eyes.

"Is it true? Did he save lives?"

His eyes, his mouth, stay shut.

"I need to know my father."

Grandpa nods, but keeps quiet.

"I hardly remember him at all."

Mothers sometimes rub the wrists of children, the inner sides, to calm them. Grandpa does this to me now, his touch warm, but I won't be distracted. "Please," I say. "I believe I deserve to know."

He lets go of my wrists. Down the alley, two men are smoking hookahs and playing backgammon. Someone's forearms rest on a windowsill, hands sticking out between iron bars. I follow my grandfather into our home.

I make mint tea for us. At the kitchen table, in whispers, he tells me some of what Abu Ali told me. Several men from the camps, including two my father knew well, were hired to help widen the road to Elon Moreh.

"A man your father called Abu Z decided to stop this. Z would blow himself up, blow up the traitors who worked for the settlers, and—inshallah—kill some settlers, too. I don't know how your father learned of this, or how much time passed before he tried to dissuade Z from going through with his plan. One of your father's friends, Ahmed, was among the laborers. His daughter suffered from asthma and other ailments. Months earlier, she almost died when the Israelis gassed the camp. Ahmed needed money, medicine. Had his hatred for the settlers been greater than his love for his daughter, he would've spat on their road rather than widen it. To choose where to work, to live, to debate something of relevance, is rare. Tomorrow your mother may wonder whether to buy four oranges or one pomegranate. Oranges cost less, are more easily shared. As for Abu Z, he was arrested before he could carry out his plan."

I close my eyes. "Did my father work for the settlers?"

"No, he was less desperate than his friend. He worked on a Palestinian farm that no longer exists."

"Did he warn the settlers—?"

"No one knows. He may have because he wanted them gone, not dead. Your father said to me once, 'Every time there's a bombing, Israel's leaders mourn the dead on one side of their hearts and celebrate on the other.'"

"I don't understand."

"The violence, the dead—*their* dead—give them permission to do as they wish, with the world's blessing. Imagine a man in a box, no room to stretch, so he grows smaller, or tries to, until the day he blows himself up, scatters in all directions." He spreads his arms. "Whoosh. He divides himself, leaves the box by exploding *out* of it, and maybe he kills a few of his enemies, which gives Israeli leaders permission to come after us, *any* of us, and to lock us in jails, innocent or not, and to plow our trees and crops into the earth, or to annex us, to take our hills and vineyards and fields to be *their* hills and vineyards and fields, to erase Palestine hectare by hectare. The few Israeli leaders who have wished for peace since 1948—you can count them on one hand. The endgame is to force us to emigrate, and if we can't—if no nation will have us—Israel will expand, it will annex, it will take more, and comfortable homes will be built on our graves."

I may forget the words of a man who shouts, but whispered rage, my grandpa's rage, goes into me. I've always admired him for his poise, but tonight—remembering his son, my father—he reminds me of my brother. I love them both, but my grandpa has surprised me. I see his rage for the first time. Maybe it was always here, but I didn't know where to look.

I let some quiet seep in before I tell him Z means Zuhair.

"What makes you say this?"

"My interrogator told me."

"And you believe it?"

I glance at the barred window. "Maybe I do."

Abu Ali was enjoying himself when he told me my father tormented himself with questions: *Who do I love most? Who do I love least? My father? My wife? My son? My daughter? Myself?* Maybe Abu Ali was telling a story, or maybe not. Lies, truth—he could hurt me either way.

I look up at my grandpa. "Was my father told he must take his own life or that of someone in our family?"

"He never heard the word *or*."

"What do you mean?"

"To kill me or your mother or your brother or you—is that a *choice*?"

"No."

"I've never heard of a more cruel ultimatum. Normally, only the collaborator is killed. The family, though shamed, lives on."

"So it's true, then? My father took his own life?"

Grandpa breathes in, shudders.

"But who told you? How do you know?"

"Your father told me. He left a note. He wrote all this down before…"

"He killed himself?"

He rubs his eyes, nods.

"How? How did he do it?"

"A gun."

"And you didn't stop him? You didn't—"

"How could I? I knew nothing till he was dead. *Nothing*."

"I don't understand."

"You will if you wait."

He tells me, with pauses, that the Palestinian police found my father's body near the crest of Mount Ebal, near one of the quarries, and one of them gave him the note that explains everything but the identity of Abu Z. The note, "printed neatly," according to my grandpa, claims that Z came from outside, but what does that mean? Another camp? A nearby village? Another country? Grandpa presses his thumbs to his temples. "Z's a letter in the alphabet," he says, "nothing more. In this way, your father made sure the only death would be his own. Had he given us a name, a *real* name, retaliation would have been possible. Abu Z? Good luck trying to find his people. They could be anywhere in the world."

I sit upright. "Why didn't you tell me all this before?"

"Because our lives can get harder."

I need to think on this. "How?"

"My son may have informed. Mere suspicion is enough to cause us some trouble."

I'm shaking a little.

Grandpa touches his chest. "Those related to an informant have a lot to prove: loyalty, for example, love of Palestine, or the *idea* of Palestine." He sighs. "I didn't want to burden you with this knowledge, nor did your mother. I'm sorry, but there was no other way."

I tell him I understand, but I don't. Was my father an informer? Was he brave? Is it possible to be both?

"When Issam gets out of jail, don't speak a word of what I've told you."

My brother will never get out of jail if the Israelis know what I know.

"He might see your father as a coward, and this—I promise you—was never true for a single day of his life."

We are quiet a long time.

"Can you show me my father's note?"

He leans forward and opens his hands on the table. "I already have, because I remember each word. Your father asked that I show it to your mother, then destroy it. The note was brief, and this was his only request. I have nothing to add."

78

A FRIEND FROM OUTSIDE

Grandpa is at the table when I wake before the first call to prayer. A small lamp is on. Maybe he has sat here all night.

I sip his coffee, surprised by a hint of sweetness.

"Sugar," he says. "Have some more."

I lean into his warmth. This may be the best part of our day, a cup of coffee with sugar. I'm glad for this, but I can see my grandpa is very tired.

"Last night I spoke honestly," he whispers, "but I don't want you to think that I've lost hope, that our efforts mean nothing. The fact that you're no longer detained relieves your mother and me of an enormous burden. We'll be a family again when Issam returns."

I change the subject because Issam may spend the rest of his life in prison. I want my grandpa to remember better times, so I talk about cousin Ghassan, the green kite he made when he was nine years old. "He somehow found the right-size sticks," I say, "and the prettiest paper. We flew the kite over the entrance to the camp."

Grandpa makes more coffee, adds a pinch of sugar. We drink it together. My mother's still asleep.

I've been waiting for the right time to show him Rebecca Glazman's letter. If I'm not in prison or in Israel with The Flying Kids, my grandpa's phone stays with me. I wake it up now, click what needs to be clicked, and the first words—*Dear Amal*—light the screen.

"I've told you about Tali Glazman, my best friend in The Flying Kids." I place the phone in my grandpa's hands. "Her mother wrote me a letter that I want you to see."

My grandpa reads English as fast as anyone in our alley. He can finish a newspaper over a cup of coffee, but with Mrs. Glazman he slows down, moves his lips over the words, and sometimes he pauses, his face soft, surprised, a little confused. This sad letter tells him a woman from outside is our friend. Mrs. Glazman offers hope.

I may tell my grandpa how she lost her husband, how Tali lost her father, but not now. Fajr, the call to prayer, is far louder than our whisperings. Mother's awake now, as are four stories of cousins—everyone preparing to pray. We wash our faces, arms, hands, feet, and rinse our mouths. Water sounds calm us. The prayer before the prayer.

79

ALLEY CIRCUS

After school, my grandpa tells me tonight is circus night in our alley. He wants me and Maysa to put on a show.

I step back. Maysa and I haven't talked about this. We haven't rehearsed. I tell my grandpa we may need a week or two before we're ready to perform.

He often listens to me, but not today. "A week to prepare? Two weeks? When's the last time we had entertainment in Balata?"

I remember walking on the barrel of a tank, but that was outside the camp.

"Your uncle Sami and I have already spread the word through the alleys," he says. "Your audience will arrive after the sunset prayer."

My grandpa looks at me. "Any questions?"

I shrug.

"I'll ask your uncle Sami to sink some new hooks in the walls, so you can string a wire between second-story windows."

I think about this. "Third story would be better."

"Yes, but we don't have a net, only arms to catch you."

"I won't need either."

"There will be cousins under you. If you won't need them, your mother will."

"What do you mean?"

"The appearance of safety will prevent a heart attack."

I make tea and sit with my grandpa at a small table in our alley.

"Just one thing," I say. "I can't use a balance pole here, not even a broomstick, because there's barely room for my body."

"You need a balance pole?"

"For style, yes. I learned to wire-walk without a pole, but tonight I need one."

Grandpa raises his glass. "By all means, then, for style."

I point down the alley. "Remember the morning Issam raced down our alley to that wider alley and threw stones at fighter jets?"

My grandpa's eyes shine. "Oh yes."

"Right there," I say, "where the alley widens, is where Maysa and I will perform tonight."

Grandpa stands and tries to see what I'm seeing. "Okay," he says, "but that alley's not much wider than our alley."

"It's wider than a broomstick, which is all I need."

He chuckles. "And Maysa?"

"She's a contortionist. All she needs is space to breathe."

We finish our tea and wander down our alley to the wider alley where Uncle Zaki lives, a few cousins, too, and several of Maysa's relatives. My grandpa speaks with other grandpas, and with Uncle Zaki, and soon Maysa and I have a place to perform.

After Maghrib, the sunset prayer, circus. Many children have come, not only those who live nearby but those from other neighborhoods, other camps, those for whom circus is a dream. In every window, from the first story to the fourth, a candle burns, so the alley glows, as in moonlight. Showgoers line the walls or watch from windows. My mother, in the shadow of a doorway, calls, "Careful, be careful." I haven't even begun to perform.

Uncle Sami helped me string a wire diagonally from my uncle Zaki's third-story window to Maysa's aunt Samirah's window some twenty meters down the alley. Perched on Zaki's sill, I style and shine, and wave to the kids with my broomstick balance pole. A real balance pole won't work because our circus ring is skinny. Waiting in the alley, all along the path of the wire, many cousins have gathered. Tonight, if I wish, I can fly down the walls in candlelight. In lieu of a net, cousins. No one can be harmed with all these arms in the ring.

Maysa is in charge of "stage lights." Above me, from a fourth-story window, she shines a flashlight on the sill where I stand in my leather slippers, my green pants, and long-sleeve blouse, my broomstick pressed to my waist. My grandpa, near my "net" of cousins, films me with his phone. Uncle Sami's down there, too, sitting on a stool and banging a drum, a metal tub, the heartbeat of a giant. This life is so big! All I love goes with me as I step on the wire between windows in the alley where we live.

Half way across, I sink to one knee, raise my right arm, and point my broomstick toward the sky. The kids are calling to me. Still kneeling, I sway with the sway of the wire, my broom like a finger. Below, above, all around—candlelight and cousins. Our strip of sky isn't so dark. There's a pink smudge up there, a yellow streak, and three stars. I point and say, "Look, look," because I want the kids and everyone else to see these colors, these stars. The skinniest wire, the skinniest alley, can open to something big.

I think of the one who is missing—Issam. If he were watching from a window, would he stop suffering for a moment? When's the last time he saw a bit of sky, a few stars? I may never know if I fear my brother more than I love him. Would he be happy if he were here?

My broomstick, painted green, is brighter than the trees painted on our walls. Kids are calling to me, saying things like, "Show us some moves," or, "Show us a trick." Circus, or *my* circus, isn't about tricks, but I decide to give them what they want. I rise from my knee, call, "Yalla!" swing my broom over my head, and jump in the air. Remember how I jumped over Nachum during my first show in Ha'yarkon Park? Well, this time I yelp and squeal as I jump over an imaginary boy. A clown on a wire, I wobble, pretend I'm about to fall, recover, strut back and forth, over confident, before I fake another fall, swing my broom this way and that, as alley cousins open their arms. My mother calls, "Enough, get down from there," so I fake deafness, too. I need to show these kids how to wire-dance, or fancy dance, which means I shake what I can, then twist, leap, turn around, and dance the other way. This is easy in the shine of things, and so is the watching. Everyone at this circus shines no less than the girl on the wire.

I end my show with a leap to where I began—Uncle Zaki's windowsill. When I turn, the first one I see is Handala the Cat watching from the eave across the alley, his eyes half closed, his paws tucked under him, his stillness a gift. More than I, he rests in the shine of things. His whiskers silver in candlelight.

Contortion. Maysa lies face-down on my foam mat in the alley, her arms stretched in front of her. She was in charge of "stage lights" when I performed, so now I shine a flashlight from my window perch while my grandpa shoots video up close. Maysa can bend every which way. In one motion, she swings her torso and legs upward and toward each other, and in the next breath she reaches back to grab her feet, seesaws on her belly, and touches the soles to the back of her head. I lead cheers. I'm proud of Maysa because I know how hard she's worked to master this pose. The audience sees something like this in the beam of my flashlight: δ The round bottom—that's her belly. She rocks back and forth, sort of like a cradle, then holds almost still.

Her mother stops the performance because she thinks boys are staring. Well, maybe they are, but Maysa's clothes are loose as mine, nothing showing. She allows her daughter to juggle oranges, so the boys watch oranges instead of Maysa. Handala the Cat sits on the eave, his paws tucked beneath him. I study his stillness and think of my brother. If Issam could see us tonight, would it ease his pain? Would it calm his heart?

Listen, brother. We've made our own circus, maybe the first ever in candlelight.

80

ISSAM

I no longer wish to practice my art in the room I share with my mother, nor would my grandfather let me. Each day after school, I train with Maysa in the house half fallen at the south edge of the camp. We are each other's assistant. I help her to hold difficult poses, contortions that stretch her joints, especially her knees and hips. She sometimes helps me by shaking the wire I walk, as if a huge wind is blowing. The greater the sway, the greater the challenge. I believe we're both improving as artists. My grandpa thinks we should perform in our alley every Saturday night, but Maysa is shy.

Wednesday. I'm walking a wire strung between sections of rebar when my grandpa, who limped two-hundred meters to get here, pokes his head in the ruins, waves a piece of paper in the air, and calls to me, "Your brother, your brother's coming home!"

I stand almost still on the wire.

My grandpa has tears in his eyes. "He was in Megiddo Prison, but now he's in Ofer."

I jump from the wire.

"He'll return to Balata on Thursday afternoon."

I pretend to share my grandpa's joy, but my brother and I have secrets. The morning before soldiers stormed our home and detained us, Issam promised to kill me unless I returned his "package" the next morning. Will he still want his vest? I stole my brother's death, but now the Israelis have it. Does this make me a traitor? My grandpa's tears are happiness; mine are fear.

Ululations greet Issam in our alley in mid-afternoon. A one-person procession, he waves to cousins and neighbors crowding windows and doorways, mothers holding up babies, and our grandpa limps forward to hug him, kiss him, while our mother weeps. Issam refuses to rest in our grandpa's arms. He walks tall, or tries to, but has to drag his left leg because the knee will not bend. His cohorts, those who trusted him with a vest and a plan, whatever it was, may be among us today, as well as the informer who told the Israelis whose homes to raid and who to detain. I stand behind the barred window of our kitchen. I don't think my brother sees me yet.

Gifts of food arrive. Trays of kanafeh, chocolate-covered almonds, a small mountain of chicken and rice, bread warm from the ovens. My brother's alive because of me. Those he would have killed along with himself are also alive, though I have no idea who they are. What do you want now, Issam? A bigger death? Will you kill me if I stand in the way?

81

EQUATIONS

We are silent for three days, my brother and me. Sometimes he walks to the house half fallen and watches with the children and a few adults as Maysa and I practice our routines. A thought can move a foot, a bone, and a collision of thoughts is a wire-walker's nightmare. I rise fast after each fall. If I learn to walk well for Issam, not even a strong wind will throw me from the wire.

❧

On his fourth morning home, before I leave for school, he corners me in the kitchen. I've finished the dishes and other chores. Our mother's upstairs, gossiping with Aunt Salma, and our grandpa has wandered down the alley to play backgammon. I sit at the table, a math problem in front of me. Issam looks over my shoulder and sighs.

"A difficult equation?"

These are his first words to me.

"Grandpa told me you were in jail for seventeen days."

I close my eyes. "Yes."

"Did they hurt you?"

"A little. But mainly there were threats."

I cannot say strip-search in front of my brother. I cannot speak of a girl "too dirty to be touched," a girl Abu Ali or some other Abu might have violated with a stick. All I can tell Issam is that the interrogations were terrifying and my captors threatened to ruin me if I refused to cooperate. I dare to look at him. "They couldn't break me," I whisper. "If they had, you'd be in jail the rest of your life."

His eyes startle me, a spark of something besides rage, a hint of—what is it, gratitude? I glance out the barred window to our alley. People are about. We are silent when someone passes. It is almost time to leave for school.

"They wouldn't let me sleep," says Issam, and the softness in his eyes disappears. "They beat me, they enjoyed themselves, so they did it over and over."

"I'm sorry."

"They asked the same questions at least a thousand times. At night, in bed, I still hear them."

I sometimes hear Abu Ali, his voice like a needle.

Issam whispers, "I want to kill them all."

I look down at my math homework, though I may as well be blind. I tap the eraser end of my pencil on the table until my brother covers my hand with his.

Issam sits beside me on a stool. "Let me teach you some prison math," he says. "Two equations written in pencil on a wall."

He takes my paper, my pencil, and begins to write in the space beneath my name. My pencil sounds like a claw.

My brother hands me my paper. "There," he says. "Nothing you shouldn't already know."

The Gilad Shalit Prisoner Exchange of 2011
1 Israeli POW = 1024 Palestinians held in Israeli prisons
1/1024th of a Jew = 1 Palestinian

One of his front teeth is missing. Issam winces, works his tongue in the gap, and smears blood on his lips. His smile is insane.

"Israel writes the equations," he says. "Our lives are cheap, but this helps us with prisoner swaps. In 2011, one Israeli soldier held in Gaza for five years was released in exchange for one thousand and twenty-four Palestinians." His smile widens. "And I almost forgot—eight corpses have been returned to Jewish families over the years. Our grandpa, a scientist, is good with equations. Maybe he'll know how to fit the corpses into the scheme." He wipes his mouth. "The best I can do is round things out. While alive, I'm 1/1024th of a Jew."

He tosses me my pencil and I catch it.

"My friends think the Israelis found the vest when they raided our home," he whispers. "If I tell them the truth, you'll be worse than dead."

I sit straighter.

"So where is it, sister? Did you think I'd forget to ask?"

"I told you what I did with it."

"Save your stories for children. I don't want to hear how you carried the vest up the slopes of Mount Ebal and left it in a cave."

I look at him hard. "I didn't tell you a story."

"Then it's there? It's still *there*?"

"Yes," I lie. "But in fragments."

"What—"

"I broke it. I smashed some parts, scattered the pieces."

He grabs my left wrist and squeezes.

"I'm sorry, Issam. I didn't know what else to do."

Once, in prison, when Abu Ali threatened me, I wanted my brother's vest to silence him, to blow him and every interrogator and myself into a million merciless pieces. 0 = 0. We would vanish into nothing. The interrogations would end. Yet I wanted my life moments later. Would Issam understand this? I want us to live.

My brother softens his hold on my wrist. "You made a mistake, but so did someone else."

You, I'm thinking, *you*.

"Someone in the camp told the Israelis which home to raid and who to arrest. In all, they detained twenty-three cousins, but I was the target."

He lets go of my wrist.

"Issam, at least we're alive."

He licks his lips, swallows. "And this makes you proud? We're alive for *what*?"

"To stop doing the same thing. To do something different."

"Like what? A circus stunt?"

"No, listen to me, *listen*. Every time there's a bombing, what happens? Israel's leaders mourn the dead on one side of their hearts and celebrate on the other."

"What are you talking about?"

"The violence, the dead—*their* dead—give them permission to do as they wish, arrest us, bulldoze our homes, take more of our land, with the world's blessing."

"You sound like someone I met in prison."

No, I sound like our father, but I won't tell Issam he took his own life and might have been an informer.

"And what if this prisoner's right?" I ask. "Then what?"

Sick smile, Issam. Did you practice in a mirror?

He bends over and underlines one of the equations: 1/1024th of a Jew = 1 Palestinian.

"This was in 2011," he whispers. "We're worth less now."

Everyone in Balata would agree.

"So are we on the same side, sister? Are we?"

Silence is almost yes.

"Careful," he says. "There's no way you'll survive another mistake."

However long I live, I will have secrets. I never told Abu Ali whose vest I found, or where I found it, but I led an Israeli patrol to Mount Ebal and gave them what they wanted. A traitor? In Issam's eyes, in Balata's eyes, yes. In my grandfather's eyes, in my dead father's eyes, no. In Jonathan's eyes, in Mrs. Glazman's eyes, in her dead husband's eyes, no. There is another equation: 1=1. If I didn't know this, all I would want for Balata, for Palestine, is a vest and a target, a gathering of Israelis. Sometimes nothing makes sense but nonsense. A prayer wheel in Jaffa powered by a jet engine. The flags—blue, white, red, green, yellow—spin so fast the colors bleed. A machine artist prays fast. Me too. I can't tell my brother about Jonathan or Mrs. Glazman because he won't listen. What is left for us? Fast prayers, flags and colors. I wonder how much time we have.

82

GO OUT AT NIGHT AND COME HOME WITH ONE WORD

We survive Monday, Tuesday, and now it is Wednesday eve. My family and four stories of cousins wait for sleep. I lie near my mother, my face to the wall, and listen to Grandpa Saeed lecture Issam about fatherhood, the future, our family's future. A wall as thin as a blanket separates our rooms. They, too, are in bed, and I picture my brother face-up, eyes closed. Grandpa turns to him, his voice loud for this hour. We have heard this lecture before.

"Of course you'll have children," he says, "and grandchildren. You're Palestinian. This is how it is."

Issam mumbles.

"No, I'm not rushing anyone," says Grandpa. "I finished my undergraduate degree before I married your grandmother. Did I tell you she couldn't have more children after she birthed your father? Despite the challenges we face, we have to build what we can—family, children, grandchildren. You know what would make me happier than anything?"

Issam coughs, grunts, whispers.

"No," says Grandpa, "it's impossible to return to Jaffa someday. I'll die here, in this alley, because I have no choice. If you think I've given up, you're wrong. Nothing could make me happier than to hold your child in my arms, or your sister's child. A newborn tells us with its first breath—don't give up, you must never give up."

Issam makes shushing sounds, sort of like a baby.

Grandpa chuckles. "Yes, some Israelis probably *would* sterilize us if they could. Our greatest poet, Mahmoud Darwish, speaks to them directly: 'I am an Arab... / I have eight children, and the ninth is due after summer./ What's there to be angry about?'" Grandpa laughs. "So make them angry, Issam. Someday you'll be a husband, a father, a grandfather. There is no other way."

But there is a way to make some of them angry and others dead. A boy can trade marriage and children for ten thousand kites made from his own flesh. *Boom.* He rises from the camp, the alleys, and he says with his last breath what a newborn says with his first—*don't give up, you must never give up.* I'm shaking a little. I can't think of a way to save my brother or myself or anyone. Like Issam, I want no children till the war is over. When will it end? Some say on Judgment Day, when the world ends. When I hear people speak of the Last Days, I see blood in every home. Is this what we want? Is this what *God* wants? I don't know. Maybe he'd rather watch a circus by candlelight in our alleys, or in a red tent in Ha'yarkon Park. People who talk about Judgment Day scare me. This means I have cousins who scare me, aunts who scare me. Wide awake, the world is a dream.

Sometimes I can feel the hour, as if I carry a clock inside me. A door opens to the alley at around three a.m. Issam, who has been home all day, who didn't go to school, is going somewhere now. He drags his left foot, which sounds like a broom trying to quiet the dust on its bristles. My mother rolls on her side, her forearm over her eyes. I rise when I'm certain she's asleep.

Our alley is dark, except for a dim lamp at each end. I pass near barred windows, the homes of cousins and neighbors. I hear shooting in the distance, automatic weapons, then small sounds, maybe mice or insects. The quickness in me, the tingling—this is how I feel when I walk across a wire.

I give my brother some distance. I can't hear him or see him, but I know he's leaving our alley for other alleys. I can sense him the way I sense when rain is coming, or the way I sense where to place my foot on a wire, eyes open or closed. Crossing from alley to alley, I pause for each sound, maybe someone turning over in bed, someone snoring, or a breath that might stretch itself into a word. I need words. Sounds, stirrings—they don't tell me enough. I lean on a wall, a shadow inside a shadow. I turn when I hear someone behind me, steps too light to be human. I'm ready to bolt until Handala the Cat brushes my legs.

He's purring before I pet him. I love this boy in every whisker. I'm about to pick him up when we hear a voice, then two voices, above us, near a window on the second story. A chair—or something hard—scrapes across the floor. I hear one word: *Friday*. Maybe Handala hears more, but he can't tell me. He draws into himself, legs taut and ready to spring.

Voices quiet as drizzle. Issam, I'm thinking, if this is you, *speak*. But what would I do with words? If my brother says, *Vest, bomb, rifle,* I can't steal death a second time. The vest I carried to Mount Ebal—now the Israelis have it. My brother would kill me if he knew. Some in the camp might torture me first. Maybe I'm brave the way my father was brave. He is dead. I don't want to join him till I'm very old and have lived my life to the end.

I hear my brother. Not his voice, but his left foot dragged across the floor. Handala hunches in a doorway. A muffled groan from the second story, no words, or none I can hear. My heart races when Handala flicks his tail against my calves. Am I as lost as my brother? I don't know yet. Handala nudges me, then slips away, and I'm too frightened to do anything but follow him home through our web of alleys. At my door, I pick him up and pet him and listen to him purr. Pleasure calms me. I wish I could carry him to the bed I share with my mother and sleep without dreams.

83

FALL

On Friday afternoon, I slip away with Maysa and some girl cousins to the house half fallen. No clouds over the ruins today. Maysa helps me string a wire between two pillars that will hold up the sky and me. No beams, no ceiling—just my few kilos and blue light coming in. I hope Issam will not find me here. Handala the Cat sleeps in what was once a kitchen. He's made a nest of some rusty plumbing torn from a wall, softened by weeds.

I warm up with fast walks, back and forth, pillar to pillar, while Maysa sits near Handala and lifts her feet till the soles touch her ears. Sababa! The cheers of cousins wake the cat, who opens his eyes a slit, then covers them with a foreleg. I jump on the wire and call, "Earthquake, sailor at sea!" I sway as the wire sways, and twirl my green broomstick, my Balata balance-pole. I'm half way across, in a patch of sun, when I hear my brother, not his voice but the drag of his left leg, the humph of his breath. He peeks in through a hole in a wall, smiles, waves, and disappears down an alley. I catch my breath and keep walking. That smile—sweet, sudden—could mean anything. Am I forgiven? Will I die soon? And what about him?

I shimmy down a pillar. I could catch up to Issam in a few seconds, but I stay where I am. That smile slips into me like a new muscle. I hunch down near Handala and sit still. I feel calm, alert, and there's a brightness in the air.

I want to rest now, but one of my girl cousins asks me to get back on the wire so she can watch me and learn. Okay. She's seven years old, so I can't tell her a wire-walker learns many things by keeping still. I shimmy up a pillar, some three meters, and rig my wire loose. I wave to my seven-year-old student and start toward the other pillar. The wire swings as if the wind is howling, but this is what I want. My student thinks it's funny how I twirl my broom and tilt one way, then another, to keep my balance. Way inside me there's a pocket of stillness—there has to be or I wouldn't have a chance. I'm almost to the other pillar when I see out the corner of my eye Handala the Cat, his ears pressed flat to his skull, his eyes open a slit. He's still enough to feel something coming and then it comes—a loud boom, another, and gunfire, maybe on Al-Quds Street, or further to the east. I am more there than here. I flail, lose my stillness, paddle the air, and a short fall—three meters—seems to take minutes. I hit hard on a block of concrete and something snaps, a bone, but I don't know it's mine because there's no pain, just this ball of light in my head, my chest, and a racing in my heart as loud as the booms I heard earlier. My first thought—he's dead. My brother's dead. Do I want him dead? No, no, no, no. Yet I don't know how both of us can live much longer than today.

Maysa and my cousins are over me like a blanket. My seven-year-old student says, "Your ankle…there's a bone sticking out."

Maybe so, but I don't yet feel the pain.

84

MARTYRS

My left ankle is broken, but I will walk wires again. While Grandpa Saeed and my mother and me listen to a doctor tell me what I can and can't do in the coming months, Uncle Sami slips into the room, calls my mother aside, and tells her, in whispers, her son is a martyr. My mother tries to scream. The silence is worse, her mouth opening and closing. My grandpa presses his hands to the sides of his head.

Hours later, Uncle Sami learns that his son Ghassan and our cousin Naji are also dead.

Planes come the morning the martyrs are buried. They buzz rooftops in Balata and other camps, and deafen us as they pass over the cemetery where we gather near graves. My ankle pulses as if my heart is inside. The diving jets, the fever pitch of noise, shake the living, the dead, every bone. My mother and my aunties wail, but I can't hear them. I balance on one leg and bend down for a stone. *I love you, Issam.* I hurl this hardness as far as I can into the sky.

They come for me at night. No knocks at the door. Snapping sounds, broken hinges, and they are in. The lights on their helmets blind my mother and grandpa and me. Circled by soldiers, we are squeezed into the kitchen and one of them says in Arabic, "Stay quiet, stay quiet. Nothing bad will happen to you."

A soldier whose face I can't see gives me my crutches. He says in Arabic, "Go, go, and don't say a word or your mother and grandpa will be harmed."

My mother shrieks. "You can't take her, you *can't*. I have no other child."

She keeps pleading till they gag her. Whirring sounds, insect sounds. She tries to shout and bite her way through cloth.

Soldiers escort me into the alley. My grandpa says, "Wait, please wait," and limps ahead of us. "Take me," he says to the soldiers. "If you must detain someone, if you have orders, take me."

A soldier pushes him aside with the butt of his rifle. I wish I had the bomb I carried to Mount Ebal.

85

DETAINMENT

Is this an interrogation room? A photograph of a sheik riding a camel, a sand dune and a blue sky in the background, is taped to a file cabinet. Other photographs—the dome of Al-Kebir Mosque in Nablus, an orange grove under a green mountain—almost fill the wall behind a desk. A female guard leads me to a straight-back chair across from a man who introduces himself as Abu Hasan. He has a thick black moustache and wears civilian clothes, dark slacks, a wrinkled beige shirt, the collar open to the hair on his chest. The guard chains my right ankle, the unbroken one, to the leg of the chair, and takes my crutches. Abu Hasan, in a cushioned chair, rests his hands on the pouch of his belly. The questions begin after the guard leaves the room.

"How many times have you been detained?" he asks in Arabic.

I need a moment. "Three."

"Do you know why you're here tonight?"

I shake my head.

"Several weeks ago, a suicide vest was issued to your brother."

I look at the orange grove, the green mountain.

"The last time you were detained you told my colleague, Abu Ali, a fantastic story. Walking on Mount Ebal, going nowhere in particular, you found the vest issued to your brother, strapped it on, scaled the walls of a quarry, and left it in a cave."

I nod.

"You later led an Israeli patrol to the cave and the bomb was recovered."

"Yes, sir."

"So, then, you told a partial truth to my colleague. You knew where the bomb was, but no one believes you found it beside a mountain road near the crest of Mount Ebal." He leans over his desk. "Your brother was barely seventeen years old when he died. You're his twin, am I right?"

"Yes."

"No one wants to harm you."

Silence.

"You're a nice girl, it seems."

A longer silence.

"But we'll ruin you unless you tell the truth."

(I will never tell the full truth. If the Shin Bet learn I found the vest in the room shared by my brother and my grandpa, my grandpa will spend the rest of his life in jail. Truth, lies, stories—nothing is safe. The morning I found the vest I wondered if I would have to cross the Jordan River, the Arabian Desert, to bury it in a place where it would never be found. The cave high up the walls of a quarry—it was the best I could do. Soldiers or settlers would have spotted me had I strayed beyond Mount Ebal.)

I look at Abu Hasan and claim I've already told the truth and have nothing to add.

He rubs the hair on his chest. "I'll give you a chance to reconsider. How about if I count to three? One, two—"

"Sayyid, I've done nothing wrong. *Nothing*."

"Who issued your brother the vest?"

"I don't know."

"Was he a member of Al-Aqsa Martyrs' Brigade?"

"I have no idea."

He yawns, scratches his belly. "The Popular Front for the Liberation of Palestine?"

"I don't know."

"Islamic Jihad? Hamas?"

"I don't know."

"And you? Are you a member of any organization?"

"The Flying Kids of Tel Aviv."

His laughter sounds like hiccups. "You'll never see Tel Aviv again. Your future is more or less sealed."

(I'm still a Flying Kid.)

"The last time you were detained, we released you because we wanted to see what you would do, who you would speak with, and who you would contact via social media. The same is true for your brother. We now think we've accounted for all of his associates but one."

(Jonathan could make a robot who demands complete control, who wants to have eyes everywhere, and ears, antennae, and weapons pointing in all directions. The robot would enjoy telling a girl that he watches over her day and night, monitors her actions, her speech, her messaging, her tweets. Maybe, though, a smarter robot—small as the girl, but clever—would smash it, rip away its power source. Black out. Sorry. Countless sensors die at once.)

Abu Hasan stands, rests his hands on his hips, and peers down on me. "Let's start with a bit of background," he says. "Six nights ago, you left your home in Balata and followed your brother through alleys. Drones recorded your movements, so you would be unwise to deny this."

(I glance at the picture of blue sky, a sand dune, a sheik on a camel.)

"This was a fateful night," Abu Hasan continues. "Your brother was told that Jewish tourists would visit Joseph's tomb on a certain day, a certain hour. We relayed this fiction through an informer. As mentioned, your brother's associates have been accounted for, except for one. Do you know who's missing?"

"No, sir."

"Why did you follow your brother through alleys?"

"Because I was scared. I didn't want Issam to die. I didn't want him to hurt anyone."

He leans over his desk. "No one needs to hear what a nice girl you are. Were you part of something? A plan?"

"No."

"Your brother wasn't very smart, was he? We fed him a lie and he believed it. We added several layers of security around Joseph's tomb because we expected more than three boys, three rifles, a Molotov cocktail. They never had a chance to carry out their attack."

He comes around his desk and stands at my side. "Why did you follow your brother through alleys six nights ago?"

"I already told you."

He places a hand on my left shoulder. "Same question."

"I wanted…I wanted my brother to change. I wanted him to resist in other ways."

He smirks. "Resist? Resist *what*?"

I look past him to a spot on the ceiling.

"I hear you have Jewish friends in Tel Aviv. Do they help you to resist? Do they help people in Balata to resist?"

I shake my head. "No, sir."

"Your circle of friends includes Jonathan Geffen. Is he your best friend?"

I shrug.

"Or is Rebecca Glazman your best friend?"

I have many friends in Israel. I could say Mr. Geffen is my best friend, or Mrs. Glazman, but I won't give Abu Hasan a name.

"I have friends everywhere," I tell him. "And you?"

86

REFRIGERATOR

Two female guards lead me to a small room with bright overhead lighting. Cold air streams down from vents in the ceiling. One of the guards says something to me in Hebrew. She takes away my crutches before she and her partner back away and shut the door.

I balance on my right leg, the good one. I cannot sit down in this cold. I hop around, my arms fanned to my sides to brace the walls. No bed, no blanket. Who taught the Shin Bet this torture? It's simple, so maybe they thought of it themselves. A small room, bright light. And a coldness I can fight only for so long before I collapse in a corner and pull my knees to my chest.

I can see my breath. I watch my hands turn blue. I begin to shake them to get the blood moving when the noise begins. My captors play for me recordings of war planes. These may be the same planes that swooped over Balata and other camps and the cemetery where Issam and our cousins lay buried. I plug my ears with my thumbs, but it doesn't help. Winter winds, white light, the roar of jets. Can my brother see me? I'm a white bomb waiting to explode.

87

A LITTLE LIKE MERCY

Abu Hasan questioned me nine times, had me taken back to the refrigerator nine times (he calls it "the air-conditioned room"), but now I'm in a quiet place where no one harms me. There's no window in this cell, only a vent. A yellow light in a metal cage sometimes blinks off and on, but the walls aren't so bright that they hurt my eyes. Best of all, there's no soundtrack of jets swooping down and the air blowing from the vent is warm. The toilet smelled bad at first, but now I don't smell anything. I have my crutches and have walked many kilometers in this cell about the size of the room I share with my mother. My ankle's had time to heal. I can swing my leg back and forth without much pain.

Maybe it's morning when they feed me. The door has a slot wide enough for a tray with a slice of bread, an orange, and watery soup. I can't see the person who passes me the tray, but I say, "Thank you" in Hebrew. I want my jailer to speak so I will hear a voice other than my own. "Thank you," I say again, as her steps move away.

I think I've been in prison for eight or nine weeks. I haven't seen Abu Hasan or any other Abu or interrogator in a long time. My great fear is that they'll take me back to the refrigerator. Torture is simple. They can turn on some lights and machines and walk away. Jonathan would understand what I went through. He could make robots to show an audience in Florentine or Jaffa what can happen to someone like me. I was afraid I would die. I was afraid I would live but lose my mind. You know what helped me to fight? I remembered walking on the barrel of a tank over Faisal Street. I'm alone now, but to strut and style, to humble every man with a gun, everyone with power—that's why I was born. I don't think I'm finished. I know my art well enough to hop across the barrel of a tank with one good leg. I'll be a circus girl for however long I live. I'm a little bit broken now, but most of me is here.

Once daily, handcuffed, shackled, I leave my cell and see the sky from the recreation yard. Female guards lead me to my freedom when no other detainees are present. I've tried to speak with them in English, a few words of Hebrew, but they ignore me. I'm beginning to understand the strategy of the Shin Bet. They plan to keep me alive, nothing more, until I break.

They've given me a jacket. Winter in prison. Sometimes the cold steals my few feathers of warmth. The guards refuse to tell me what day it is, what month. January? February? My ankle feels strong now, and I walk as briskly as I can with shackles and crutches. I love the sky, which gives me big breaths to breathe. Blue light or clouds—it doesn't matter. The sky's face keeps changing, mine too. I'm seventeen years old. The sky is millions and billions. My jailers seem unaware of my moments of happiness. I see way more sky from this prison yard than from the alley where I live.

One morning, or maybe night, someone brings me coffee, watery and weak, nothing like my grandpa's, but coffee. I drink it slow the way he does. My mind's clear enough to see him inside me, his wrinkles and whiskers, the shine of his eyes, and I smell him, too, a slight sourness like old bread, but pleasant because I love him. I see us sharing coffee the way we do in Balata when the first light seeps down the walls of our alley. I hear morning sounds, too, my mother and four stories of cousins getting ready for breakfast. Everyone who's alive has reason to move. That's how it is. I'm here, in this cell, but I'm there too. Me and my grandpa drinking coffee real slow.

They don't bring me much food. Sometimes I'm afraid they've forgotten me, so I make a little noise. I never shout or cry out because they might take me back to the refrigerator and drown me in *their* noise. I say hello and good morning and how are you. I mix in whatever Hebrew I can, and lots of English. I'm very polite in case someone listens. I'm always hungry, which means I want to live.

A lawyer visits, or at least he claims he's a lawyer. He greets me in Arabic, gives me his name, and asks how I am and how's my health. I tell him I'm fine. I can't see this "lawyer," who stands outside my cell, shuffling papers, or what sound like papers. He speaks Arabic well, but so do my interrogators. For many days and nights—perhaps months—I've longed to talk with someone, trust someone, but my captors know this and maybe they've set a trap. The "lawyer" tells me that no charges have been filed against me, that I'm "being held in administrative detention pending further investigation." (I already knew this.) He describes my case as "sensitive," and apologizes that he has no idea why I was detained. He gripes about Israeli secrecy, and then he waits, goes silent, maybe because he expects a confession. I tell him what I tell every interrogator: "Sir, I'm innocent, I've done nothing wrong. I'm here by mistake."

The "lawyer" complains that Israeli authorities have refused his requests for access to my file. "Not that I'm surprised," he adds. "This is typical protocol in any case with serious security repercussions. They keep all evidence to themselves."

He can't see me, but I shrug.

He asks, after a pause, "Is there anything you wish to tell me? Any message?"

Message for whom? I'm thinking.

"Just know I'll continue to work on your case."

"Thank you, sir."

"I'll visit again next month if you haven't been released."

I might begin to trust this man if I could see his face.

Part Six

Pandemic

88

DR. BEETLE

Her gown is a green shell. A blue mask hides half her face. Her goggles make her eyes look huge. I'm strapped to Dr. Beetle's table. She whispers to me in Hebrew, then starts cutting through my cast with an electric saw. I shut my eyes till the noise stops. Dr. Beetle uses scissors to slice through the wrappings under my cast. Soon my ankle and foot are bare.

The guard who brought me here sits in a chair on the far side of the room. She, too, wears a mask and gloves, but no gown or goggles. Dr. Beetle replaces my cast with a brace, and gives me a pamphlet that explains with diagrams how to do exercises to strengthen my ankle. I don't understand what she's saying in Hebrew, but when I reach for my crutches she stops me. "No more," she says in English. "Wear the brace when you walk. Take it off when you rest. After two or three weeks, you will no longer need the brace."

Jonathan could use her clipped voice for one of his robots. I like her, though, because she removed my cast without hurting me. Everyone who doesn't hurt me is my friend. I thank Dr. Beetle before the guard leads me away.

Anywhere but the refrigerator. That's why I smile when the guard escorts me to a cellblock. Women lie in their beds, eyes closed. A girl my age walks sideways between rows of beds because the aisle's skinnier than a Balata alley. A woman older than my grandpa stands at the door of her cell, her hands on the bars. Maybe she feels like she's been here for eons. It's this way for me too. The days and nights—they're more than numbers. I don't know how long I've been in prison. I'm walking without crutches for the first time since my brother died.

I'm sad and should be sadder, but I can't help who I am. My ankle doesn't hurt much. I bet I could walk a wire down this corridor if they let me. Yalla! Wherever I go is circus. They won't break me if I remember this.

I'm led to a four-person cell with an empty bed. The guard opens the door, motions, and in I go. A metal plate covers the window at the back of the cell.

I exchange greetings with two women sitting on their beds. The one lying down stares at the ceiling, holding her chest and coughing. The guard says something in Hebrew before the door clangs shut. I'm locked up, sealed, but lucky too. I have a bed, a blanket. No cold air blowing like winter. I remove my ankle brace and curl in a ball. Maybe I'll sleep through day or night.

89

"WHAT IF YOU AND ME COULD DECIDE?"

Maybe it's morning when I wake. A woman older than my mother sits on the bed on my left. I rise on my elbows and turn to her. "Sayyida, can you tell me what day it is?"

She needs to think. "Wednesday, maybe Thursday. They'll bring breakfast soon."

"The month…do you know the month?"

"Child, it's springtime. April."

"What prison is this?"

"Hasharon."

"In Israel?"

"Yes."

A woman who'd been lying face up in the bed in front of me, a bandaged hand over her eyes, groans as she rolls on her side. "You slept a long time," she says. "I never saw anyone look so peaceful in prison."

I'm not sure if this is criticism or praise.

"So where's your family? What village or city?"

I tell her.

She grimaces. "A lot of trouble comes out of Balata."

I bite my tongue.

"*Good* trouble." She winks. "If you know what I mean."

She introduces herself as Imm Waleed. I tell her what is safe to tell her—my name. Interrogators can ask anything about anyone. If Abu Hasan or some other Abu questions Imm Waleed, she'll know my name and where I'm from, nothing else.

She sits at the edge of her bed. "I'm also from a camp," she says, "the Dheisheh Camp. I have four children."

I stare at the ceiling.

"Dheisheh is in Bethlehem. Have you been to Bethlehem?"

I shake my head.

"Dheisheh, Balata—bad things can happen in any camp."

She waits in vain for me to add something.

"I don't know who's taking care of my youngest son," she says finally. "The Israelis shot him while he was standing outside our home."

This may be true, so I tell her I'm sorry.

"Yes, but are *they* sorry? No, not at all. You know snipers sometimes aim for the legs instead of the head or the heart?"

I do, but keep quiet.

"They can kill a child, cripple him—whatever they choose. A boy with serious leg injuries needs his family to care for him the rest of his life." She clucks her tongue. "But what if—what if we could do the same thing? An Israeli boy steps outside and stands in front of his home. Maybe he's watching a bird, a cloud. Should we aim for his heart, his legs? Put down the rifle? Declare a truce? I mean"—she looks straight at me—"what if you and me could decide?"

The woman older than my mother answers for me. "Only Allah can decide who lives or dies. For us, this is dangerous."

"It's dangerous to let our enemies do as they wish. Maybe Allah's ashamed of us."

"No, He's not ashamed. He's only asking us to be patient."

"Yes, I've heard this how many times? We need to wait for The End of Days, which could be any day now."

"Stop mocking me."

"Stop saying the same thing every morning. I'll give you ten thousand shekels if you say something new."

The old woman shakes a finger. "Shekels? Ten thousand shekels? You don't even have one."

Imm Waleed chuckles. "Thank you for surprising me this morning. You said something new!"

I cross my arms over my chest when they keep arguing. They could be collaborators, or could become collaborators after they are tortured. I wonder if anyone in this cell has been to the refrigerator. This is way better, but I'm still in prison and my words are in prison. I can't say who I am or where I've been or what I know. I'd like to tell everyone who's not a spy about Jonathan's warehouse shows, his robot who frisked Israelis at a mock checkpoint, and the robed women who blew bubbles at a drone. I'd like to talk about Maysa, how good she's become at contortion. I remember parts of Mrs. Glazman's letter by heart. *Cigarettes saved her* (Grandma Tzipi) *from the gas...The Holocaust ends when the suffering ends.* I'd like to talk about Aisha, too, and Zahra, her best friend. I'd like to talk about The Flying Kids, especially Tali, and about Florentine and Jaffa and the Mediterranean Sea. Maybe someday I'll burst with words that spill out of me every which way and get me in trouble. *Good* trouble, Imm Waleed might say. But I'm afraid she's a spy.

She tells me, in whispers, a few Palestinians will be going home soon. "They can't keep us packed together," she says, "because of the pandemic."

I nod, as if I know what she's talking about.

"They don't care if we get sick, except that it would cause a scandal."

The older woman says, "You talk like you know everything."

"I know they're releasing a few Israeli citizens, and these include Palestinians. They're also being careful not to crowd us together with sick people. Last night they took Imm Mahmoud to isolation because of her cough, and maybe she has a fever."

"You don't know where they took her."

"No, I heard the guards whispering. They're going to isolate her for two weeks."

"You understand Hebrew?"

"A few words," says Imm Waleed. "Enough to know what happened to our friend."

90

MASKS AND GLOVES

The female guard who cuffs me and takes me to interrogation wears a medical mask and white gloves. Abu Hasan, sitting at his desk, also wears a mask and gloves. The guard motions me toward a chair in a corner. She locks my right foot to a front leg of the chair, then retreats to the far side of the room. I'm about three meters from Abu's desk.

I know this room, but things are missing. The photograph of a sheik riding a camel, a sand dune and a blue sky in the background, used to be taped to the file cabinet. The photographs on the wall behind Abu's desk—the dome of Al-Kebir Mosque, an orange grove beneath a green mountain—have been taken down. The smell of chemicals, or bleach, burns my eyes. I feel naked in this light.

Abu Hasan repeats questions I know by heart. Who issued your brother a suicide vest? Was he a member of Hamas? Was he a member of Al-Aqsa Martyrs' Brigade? The Popular Front for the Liberation of Palestine? Islamic Jihad? And you? Are you a member of any organization? (The Flying Kids of Tel Aviv.) He knows my answers by heart.

"Have you been told where you're going tomorrow?"

I sit still.

"You're going home. You'll be driven to the Security Barrier and—for now—released."

I almost make the mistake of smiling.

"This doesn't mean we believe you're innocent, or that your status has changed. We can detain you again at any time."

I look to the place on the wall where there was once an orange grove and a green mountain. Abu Hasan riffles through sheets of paper as he describes the conditions of my release. Online communications with Rebecca Glazman, Tali Glazman, Jonathan Geffen, or anyone in Israel, are permanently forbidden. If I make any attempt to contact my "former friends," their punishment will be greater than mine. I will be placed under house arrest for one month, and will be prohibited from leaving the Balata Camp for a minimum of six months. I will never again perform with The Flying Kids of Tel Aviv. The only way I'll see Israel again is from the inside of a cell.

"One last thing: Don't take part in conspiracy theories."

I look at him.

"You will soon learn of a pandemic sweeping the globe. The West Bank, due to its isolation, has relatively few cases." His lips twitch. "Several Palestinians have stirred up hatred by suggesting that Israel has intentionally spread the disease in East Jerusalem and the West Bank, but this would be disastrous. Almost half a million Israelis live in the West Bank, plus at least two-hundred thousand more in East Jerusalem. Palestinians work for us, come into our neighborhoods, which means we'll get sick if you get sick. If you're detained for circulating propaganda, I can promise you the consequences will be severe."

I close my eyes.

"Look at me."

I open just enough to see.

"Will you remember what I've told you?"

I hear my brother clearly: *Zero, fuck you.*

I tell Abu Hasan I'll remember each word, and I will.

Maybe he smiles under his mask.

I smile with a face he will never see.

91

ISRAELI CHECKPOINT, PALESTINIAN CHECKPOINT

Over my eyes, a blindfold. Over my mouth and nose—something thinner to breathe through. Someone's cuffed my hands behind me, fastened my seat belt. I think I'm in a jeep. I think it will carry me to a checkpoint where the driver or some official will give me back my eyes, hands, and tongue. I've been ordered—in Arabic—not to speak before my release. I'm going home on a smooth, fast road.

Abu Hasan mentioned a pandemic. I'm not sick and could walk home on a wire if they let me. I hope my grandfather and my mother are well. I hope all of Fire Mountain and Handala the Cat feel as strong as I do. It's too late for my brother, his soul in heaven, if heaven's real, and his body in the earth, which *is* real. What should I do with death? Blindfolded, cuffed, I feel shiny inside. Issam's in a coffin. His body… has every spark vanished by now?

The first thing I see when they give me back my eyes is Mount Jarzim in the east. It looks powerful and lazy, like a giant asleep on its side. The soft light on its crest tells me it is dawn. I'm out of jail, I'm *out.* My eyes reach almost all the way home.

The first checkpoint is just this cement slab protected by Israeli soldiers with rifles and officials with handguns strapped to their sides. The man who drove me here hands a folder to an official who opens it and stamps several documents. Another official orders me to stand "at least two meters apart" from other Palestinians on their way home. All of us wear masks, as do the Israelis, and some wear gloves. Maybe I'm the only former prisoner. The other Palestinians—mostly men in dusty clothes—are probably workers returning from Israel. One by one, they file past the barrier. Only I have to present my ID, lower my mask, show my face, before I cross to the other side.

I know I'm in Palestine when I see our flag mounted in a ring of tires stacked beside the road. It was behind a bush, or I would've seen it sooner. A Palestinian man calls, "Compassion checkpoint...good health checkpoint." Strange words spoken in a calm voice become almost believable. This man could be a physician in his mask and gloves, a medical gown over his clothes. Like the Israeli official, he asks us to stand at least two meters apart. We have to be sprayed with disinfectant before we go home.

I watch how it's done. A man returning from Israel spreads his arms as if walking a wire without a balance pole. The sprayer disinfects the front of him, then the back. He has the man lift his left foot so he can spray the sole. He has him do the same with the right, then waves the man on and calls to the next one in line, "Compassion checkpoint, good health checkpoint." The line moves slow, but nobody grumbles. When it's my turn to spread my arms as if I'm walking on a wire, I notice the sprayer's "medical gown" is a plastic trash bag. I laugh under my mask. He laughs, too, as he disinfects me, front and back, including my ankle brace and the soles of my shoes.

92

MR. MOUSTACHE

Taxis wait for us, some with their engines running. There must be twenty of them lined along the road, but I don't see Uncle Sami or his Hyundai. I have no money, not even a shekel. I wonder how far I am from the Balata Camp.

A Fatah official, sitting at a card table at the side of the road, calls for us to line up for interviews. His moustache curls out the sides of his mask and seems to write in the air as he asks a man going home, "Do you have a fever, a dry cough, fatigue? Do you have difficulty breathing? Aches and pains?" The questions are important. The moustache seems important, too, except the sun has climbed over Mount Jarzim and turned the crest green.

Some minutes later, I tell Mr. Moustache I have no fever, no cough, no fatigue, no difficulty breathing, no aches and pains. He asks if I was employed in Israel, or in prison. Which prison? How long? Did I share a cell with anyone who was sick? He takes notes, writes my name on a clipboard. He looks at me hard when I tell him where I'm from.

"It will be more difficult to quarantine," he says, "but you must. Remember to stay at least two meters away from everyone, including your mother, for two weeks. All those returning from Israel—former prisoners, day laborers—will do the same. If, during quarantine, you experience flu-like symptoms or shortness of breath, contact the local police or a Fatah official to be tested for the virus. An emergency committee in Balata will assist you in every way possible. Did prison officials inform your family of your release?"

"I don't think so. My uncle Sami would be here if they did."

He makes a checkmark on his clipboard. "I'll call the committee chair and word will go out to your family."

"Thank you, sayyid."

"Any questions?"

"No, but…"

"What?"

"I don't have money for a taxi."

He waves a hand. “That’s already been taken care of. Sit in the back seat, as far from the driver as possible. One passenger per taxi. Keep your mask on at all times.”

93

TAXI HOME

My driver's older than Uncle Sami. He plays his radio, talks over the music, and goes quiet to hear announcements. The virus is spreading far faster in Israel than in Palestine. He cracks open the windows to circulate fresh air. We breathe the morning through our masks.

A man on a motorcycle, pulling a cart heaped with vegetables, waves the peace sign as he passes us. My arm out the window, I wave back. I'm hungry for roots, fresh vegetables. I'm hungry for light and the sky is clear.

My driver glances at me in the rearview mirror. "The situation isn't so bad in Palestine," he says. "Being isolated—at least for now—works to our advantage." He chuckles. "Stay at home? Shelter in place? We've been doing this since 1948."

He tells me most of the Palestinians who've contracted the virus are day-workers returning from Israel. "Construction workers," he says, "agricultural workers, plus a few domestics. Israel needs cheap hands and we need a few shekels. What did you do in Israel? Clean houses?"

I wait a moment. "Sir, I was in prison."

"Really? What for?"

I shrug. "They don't need a reason to put someone in jail."

He swerves to avoid a bump. "I've known this since I was twelve years old," he says. "Sometimes it seems they make a game of it, draw names from a hat—sort of a lottery. They've detained me twice, but never charged me with a crime."

He asks how long I was in prison.

"More than four months."

"Well, the world's turned upside down during this time. What's happening in Palestine reminds me of '87, the First Intifada. Back then, we looked out for each other and shared what we could. That's how it is now. Bakers—if you lack money for bread, they'll give you a loaf, maybe send it to your door with a policeman. Your belly's empty? Don't worry. We'll find a way to give you what you need." He bumps a gloved fist on the wheel. "Inshallah, I sort of love this stupid virus. It came so fast no one had time to argue. We look around, see what needs to be done, and *do* it. And let me tell you something else. If we stop helping each other, let them divide us, or let our own factions divide us, my heart will break, it will break. There'll be nothing left of me. Nothing. You understand?"

I tell him I do.

"The Israelis—with their freedom to go anywhere—are vulnerable to the pandemic. You'd think they'd stay home out of fear of the virus. No, they're still harassing us with raids, arrests, and there's a lot of chatter about annexation. They want everything, the Jordan Valley, the farmland, the water. This summer—as early as July—they'll make their decision. I believe—I have to believe—we've already made *our* decision. No more, I say. Not one more pinch of earth. Not one more drop of water. We have to draw a line or we'll no longer exist."

I feel a shiver at the base of my spine when he bangs his fists on the steering wheel. It doesn't matter that he's a small man with small fists. He's strong enough to move the bones that keep me upright. We pass two boys riding bicycles near a dry creek bed. The driver toots his horn and pounds the wheel again. Spring morning. April. Has the world turned upside down while I was in prison? The sun is a crayon greening the trees on Mount Jarzim.

94

MARTYRS ON THE WALLS

My brother, in a green headband, a white T-shirt, brandishes a rifle. The crown of an almond tree with white blossoms rises above his photograph. Maysa and I and many others painted a garden on these walls—yellow suns over almond and olive trees, a fig tree, a stream. Cousin Ghassan's photograph covers part of the stream he helped to paint. Cousin Naji eclipses half of a sun. I slow my walk, but feel nothing. The photographs repeat, dead boys in the alley. The three-meter-tall drawing of Handala is still here, though, and the fig tree. The largest of the yellow suns shines almost as bright as before.

My grandpa and my mother cry when they see me. I can't kiss their hands or come near them. Their faces—like mine—are mostly hidden by masks. I pause at the sight of Issam, another photograph, enlarged, as tall as the fig tree, on the wall where the alley ends.

My grandpa steps into our kitchen, then my mother, then me. It's hard to stay two meters apart. Grandpa retreats to the doorway of the room he once shared with Issam. My mother, crouched in a corner near the stove, motions toward our bedroom. "I'm sorry you'll be alone," she says, "while in quarantine. I'll leave your meals on a tray near the door."

"Thank you."

"I'll stay with Aunt Salma and Uncle Sami till we can be together again."

"Two weeks," says grandpa, "but you'll see us every day. We'll take care of you."

I wish I could care for them.

"Have you lost weight?" asks my mother.

"I'm fine."

"I'll fix you something to eat."

Before she turns to the stove, she folds her arms to her chest to show how near she would hold me if she could.

Grandpa Saeed left me his phone. It's on a shelf near the bed I share with my mother. Grandpa must think I can still talk with Tali, exchange messages, or that Mrs. Glazman and I will communicate, or that I'll reach Jonathan through his website. Maybe Abu Hasan told the truth when he promised their punishment would be greater than mine if we continue our friendship. Can people know they are loved by a friend who disappears? I don't know, but I would send love letters to Israel if I could.

I'm surprised the Shin Bet hasn't confiscated this phone. I do some quick checks and it seems nothing has been deleted. I study the pictures I took of the alley before my brother and my cousins became martyrs. I'd forgotten that Maysa and I painted cucumbers and tomatoes on the walls, vines dark green. I watch a three-minute film I sent to Tali. The garden's still here, and a drawing in blue chalk of a girl on a tightrope, one foot raised. I remember standing on a ladder to draw my portrait. A drone flies over me, two fighter jets (lightning streaks to show their speed), and under the rope there are knives, swords, words of caution—*Keep your balance, please.* Rain washed away the chalk many months ago, but Tali might have saved the film on her phone. Maybe she'll watch it again on a day when she misses me.

My mother leaves a giant bowl of lentil soup and a plate of rice on the tray near the door. I would need to be three times as wide to eat so much. A wire-walker is a beam of light.

Late in the night, I lie awake and remember arguments. Me and Tali on our phones, talking, testing each other, and sometimes running out of words. The time she placed her phone against a table or something to darken my screen. *Here*, she seemed to be saying, *look at this and you'll understand.* I heard my friend breathing. I strained to see her face, an eye, an ear. Anything. The sudden blue on my screen made me blink. Maybe Tali had opened a window in Florentine, or maybe I held in my hand a piece of sky over the Mediterranean Sea.

She spoke her father's name: "Jacob, Jacob."

I hear her better now.

95

FIRST MORNING HOME

My grandpa sets a glass of coffee and an orange on the tray near my open door, then hunches on a stool in the kitchen. It is four a.m. A familiar sound—*zizz, zizz*—tells me I'm home. A drone glides over our alley, a whir of rotors or wings.

I flinch when something lights on the windowsill. Down I go, chin to the floor, but then I see him—Handala the Cat! Three meters away, perched between iron bars, he turns his face so Grandpa can rub his whiskers on both sides. His fur—orange—is a dull flame at this hour. He'll outshine the sun if he crosses our rooftops at noon.

Grandpa turns to me. "Handala missed you," he says. "He came here every morning when you were gone, and again at night."

I hear him purring. "Can I pet him?"

"No, he never comes inside, which is good practice during a pandemic. I'm the only one who pets him now."

I'm jealous of Grandpa because I used to be *the only one*. I've known Handala since he was a kitten and I was twelve years old.

Grandpa tells me he's forgotten how to sleep since the death of my brother. "You must be careful," he says. "I can't bear to lose you. Do you understand?"

"Yes."

"I have no more children to lose."

I know my grandpa well enough to hear him thinking, tinkering. Like static on a radio turned low. He gestures toward the window, the alley, with the flick of a hand.

"We celebrate martyrs more than we mourn them," he whispers, "which makes me a stranger." He sighs. "I failed your brother. There must have been a way to reach him, but I failed."

What way? Issam, with his last breath, broke every barrier, every stitch, every wall in the world. My brother prayed once or twice a day, sometimes not at all, but maybe he believed he would break through death too. A hole in the ground, clothes soaked with blood, a plaque at the graveside, his picture pasted on walls—Issam has become a legend. Maybe there's more life in death than in camp life. Whoever dies fighting the Israelis is forever a hero whether his mission fails or succeeds.

I once stole death and buried it in a mountain. Maybe I saved Israeli lives, even those of soldiers, but Issam found another way to die.

"Did you know we had a traitor in the camp?" says Grandpa.

I sometimes wonder if I'm the traitor.

"Abu Abdullah and his wife and son received a private escort from Balata the night you were detained."

I breathe in. "I didn't know them."

"Sure you did. They lived five or six alleys that way," he says, and motions over his shoulder. "It seems Abu Abdullah was a collaborator for several months, or even years. The night you were detained the Shin Bet came to his home, but not to arrest him. According to his neighbors, he spoke Hebrew with the agents, joked with them, as they escorted him and his family from the camp. Maybe the reward for being a traitor was safe passage to Kuwait or Morocco, or who knows where."

I close my eyes. "Maybe this is a rumor."

"No, you know how it is when Israelis arrive in the night. They back us into corners. They often break things."

"Yes."

"Not so with Abu Abdullah. They treated him with the utmost respect."

Silence. I remember the night I followed Issam through alleys and arrived at what might have been the home of Abu Abdullah and his family. I heard one word—*Friday*—which was the day my brother died. I knew he was there, in a second-story apartment, because I heard him dragging his injured leg. He had two more days to live.

My grandpa sighs. "There are things I may never understand. The Israelis sometimes arrest whole families, but you were the only one taken into custody after Issam and our cousins were martyred. Your brother was supposedly the ringleader. He and our cousins had planned an ambush at Joseph's tomb and hoped to take hostages, bargaining chips in a prisoner exchange." Grandpa rubs his eyes. "A dream, no chance of success, but they went through with it. Abu Abdullah must have told the Shin Bet you were in on it, or that you knew something else."

I remember what Issam taught me about the math of prisoner exchanges:

1 Israeli POW = 1024 Palestinians held in Israeli prisons
1/1024th of a Jew = 1 Palestinian

The only equation that could have saved my brother is 1=1.

My grandpa talks about the pandemic. Like the taxi driver who brought me home, he tells me our isolation has protected us. "Greek tourists brought the virus to Bethlehem," he says, "and they were quarantined. Old men like me have been quarantined since 1948."

I let some silence seep in before I ask if the Israelis have intentionally spread the virus in Palestine.

He stiffens. "Where did you hear this?"

"An interrogator at Hasharon said a rumor was circulating. He called it propaganda."

"Well, even an interrogator occasionally tells the truth."

"So it *is* propaganda?"

"Yes, I think it is. The Israelis want at least some of us to stay healthy because they'll need our backs, our cheap labor, when the pandemic ends, if not sooner. They employ thousands of West Bank Palestinians inside Israel, and others in the settlements. There are families in Nablus who wouldn't have food without this work. Right now we're managing to take care of each other, but how long will this last? Our farmers don't have much land from which to feed us. The Israelis control the water, the electricity—everything. Some of our food and other essentials will need to come from outside."

We sit about three meters apart. I can't see my grandpa's face in the shadows. I lean away from the bars on the kitchen window—pitch black.

"Child, what about your ankle? Are you able to walk?"

I know he means wire-walk. "Yes, if I'm careful."

"I remember when you strung wires in the bedroom after your second detention because you were afraid to leave home. This is different. You'll have to stay inside for two weeks."

"A month," I correct him. "I'll be in quarantine for two weeks and under house arrest for a month. I can't leave the camp for at least six months."

He mumbles curses.

"Grandpa, it doesn't matter anymore. I can practice wherever I can string a rope, a wire. In mid-May, Maysa and I will perform in Uncle Zaki's alley. A candlelight circus."

He stops mumbling.

"For now I'll rig the wires tight, with as little sway as possible. I won't practice falling before my ankle is fully healed."

A silence.

"Practice falling?" he asks.

I wait a moment.

"Yes."

96

RAINBOW GIRL

I walk on wires that cross the bedroom at different heights and fasten to metal hooks driven into walls. Maysa, at a safe distance, practices contortion on a mat outside my door. My smile, crooked, is still a smile.

I leave the wires and shoot video with my grandpa's phone: Maysa sitting cross-legged and touching her forehead to the mat; Maysa standing and bending backward till her palms reach the floor and her belly arches toward the ceiling. Like me, she wears drab clothes, a medical mask provided by the Balata Emergency Committee, but notice her form—the arc of a rainbow. I ululate as my friend, her face in profile, smiles upside-down. I tag this film *Rainbow Girl.*

Abu Hasan forbade me from communicating with Jonathan or Tali or Mrs. Glazman, but said nothing about the world. I'm the girl who carried a suicide vest to Mount Ebal. I'm surprised the Shin Bet hasn't come for everyone I love.

Grandpa.

Mother.

Uncles.

Aunts.

Maysa.

Four stories of cousins.

Etc.

I have one move left. The Israelis will watch me, follow me, and maybe watch everyone I love unless the world tips on its side and sees a new star in the sky. Before soldiers raid the camp again and perhaps take me and those I love and this phone and everyone but Handala the Cat, I'll release my book to the ether. I've wire-walked thousands of kilometers, and soon—after Maysa and I finish circus practice—some of me will fly free of the camp. All my words and photographs and films are in one blog. Someone besides the Shin Bet may see a new star in the sky, small but important, and show the star to someone else. What slips free of the alleys, of Fire Mountain—the skinny truths I tell—may protect those I love because they are innocent and always have been. It's a risk, sure, but what else is there? Jonathan made a prayer wheel powered by a jet engine. I walk wires—sky above, earth below. How else can I live? How else is there a chance for those I love?

AFTERWORD

Why I Wrote *The Wire-Walker*

Several years ago, while visiting my hometown in rural Illinois, I read an article in the local newspaper about a circus in the Galilee for Israeli children and Palestinian children. The *News-Tribune* covers Illinois Valley news almost exclusively, so this article stood out. I'd never planned to write about Palestine or Israel. In the end, though, I write about what haunts me, what gets into my dreams and my waking, what refuses to go away.

I visited Nablus, Palestine and Tel Aviv in the fall of 2017 and read more than sixty books about Palestine and Israel before I began writing. The narrator of the first two drafts of *The Wire-Walker* was a white guy modeled after my father, John Janko, a.k.a. "the Twinkie man of the Illinois Valley," because his occupation was to supply local stores with Hostess cake. "The Twinkie man" in my story dreamed big, sort of like James Thurber's Walter Mitty, and his passions were circus and his belief that the arts can inspire peace in places where peace has seldom existed. I placed "the Twinkie man" in the Middle East on a two-week vacation, in Nablus and Tel Aviv, and allowed the novel to unfold from the POV of a white male, an observer on the periphery. These drafts were a miserable failure.

Novelist Rumaan Alam referred to the last ten years of American literature as the "decade of autofiction." The most pervasive question in literature (Who has the authority to write this story?) often leads to a simple answer: autobiography equals authenticity. Nonetheless, a fiction writer—whatever her or his background—has to write from genuine need to produce a story worth reading. Rumaan Alam again: "I don't want to write the book people expect me to write."

I almost abandoned the effort to write about circus in Israel-Palestine, but one night, unable to sleep, I sat down and wrote non-stop for almost six hours. The voice that came to me and persisted was soft, sometimes a whisper, yet clearer than any voice I have heard in my life. Word by word, the life of a sixteen-year-old circus girl from Nablus took over the narration and "the Twinkie man" disappeared. I admire my father, his great open heart, but this was not his story to tell.

Zadie Smith wrote at length about cultural appropriation in the *New York Review of Books*: "…a prominent component of the new philosophy is a performative display of non-interest, a great pride in not being interested in the other, which is sometimes characterized as revenge and sometimes as an act of self-preservation. Full disclosure: what insults my soul is the idea—popular in the culture just now, and presented in widely variant degrees of complexity—that we can and should write only about people who are fundamentally 'like' us: racially, sexually, genetically, nationally, politically, personally. That only an intimate authorial autobiographical connection with a character can be the rightful basis of a fiction. I do not believe that. I could not have written a single one of my books if I did."

Nonetheless, cultural appropriation has persisted for centuries and is not a thing of the past. People who've been colonized and enslaved and oppressed over the years, and the millions who are still colonized and enslaved and oppressed, want to tell their own stories in their own voices. I wrote *The Wire-Walker* from a POV well outside my own not to flaunt the current rules in publishing (e.g., stay in your lane, write autofiction), but to make room for empathy and imagination. Amal Tuqan, the narrator of the novel, builds bridges between disparate peoples and disparate worlds. In the early chapters, she has only an abstract awareness of the Holocaust, but by the end of the novel she sees glimpses of this most profound tragedy through the eyes of someone she loves—Rebecca Glazman. In turn, Rebecca, and to a lesser extent, Tali, her daughter, begin to see the occupation of twenty-first-century Palestine. A funambulist, Amal walks over every barrier set before her, including the barrier that makes a sharing of stories unlikely or impossible.

Acknowledgments

I thank Mahmoud Masri, the founder of the Nablus Circus School, his wife, Lisa, and the current manager of the circus, Mohammed Shafee. I also thank Arnie Kotler, my agent, Nili Belkind of Jaffa, Israel, Eden Fuchs of Tel Aviv, Miki Kashtan, citizen of the world, and Maxine Hong Kingston and the Veteran Writers' Group. A bow of gratitude to Jaynie Royal, and the entire staff at Regal House Publishing. Thanks also to Chanpidor Uong, my wife, and to Sarah Schwartz, Vicki Dern, Ellen Greenblatt, Pat Mayo, and Andy Ross.

Grateful acknowledgment is made to the following for permission to reprint previously published material:

Qiu Miaojin, excerpt from "Letter One" from *Last Words from Montmarme*, translated by Ari Larissa Heinrich. Reprinted by permission of *New York Review of Books.*

Joe Lamb, excerpt from the poem, "A View to the Lake", in *Holdfast* by Joe Lamb. Reprinted with permission from Littoral Press.

Mahmoud Darwish, excerpt from "In My Mother's House" from *The Butterfly's Burden*, translated by Fady Joudah. Copyright © 2007 by Mahmoud Darwish. Translation copyright © 2007 by Fady Joudah. Reprinted with permission of The Permissions Company, LLC on behalf of Copper Canyon Press. The excerpt: "A hole in the wall was enough/ for the stars to teach you the hobby of staring/ into the eternal."

Hanan Mikha'il 'Ashrawi, excerpt from "Women and Things" from *Anthology of Modern Palestinian Literature*, edited by Salma Khadra Jayyusi © 1992 by Columbia University Press. Reprinted with permission of Columbia University Press.

Mahmoud Darwish, excerpt from "Identity Card" from *The Music of Human Flesh*, translated by Denys Johnson-Davies (Washington, DC: Three Continents Press, 1980). Copyright © 1980 by Denys Johnson-Davies. Reprinted with permission of Estate of Denys Johnson-Davies. The excerpt: "I am an Arab.../I have eight children, and the ninth is due after summer./ What's there to be angry about?"

I am indebted to numerous authors whose writings about Palestine and Israel have inspired me over the years.

In This Place Together: A Palestinian's Journey to Collective Liberation, by Penina Eiberg-Schwartz with Sulaiman Khatib
Our Harsh Logic: Israeli Soldier Testimonies from the Occupied Territories, 2000-2010, compiled by the organization Breaking the Silence
The Making of a Human Bomb: An Ethnography of Palestinian Resistance, by Nasser Abufarha
Minor Detail, by Adania Shibli
Speak Bird, Speak Again: Palestinian Arab Folktales, compiled and edited by Ibrahim Muhawi and Sharif Kanaana
Palestinian Walks, by Raja Shehadeh
The Honey, by Zeina B. Ghandour
Apeirogon, by Colum McCann
Life as a Way of Death: Israel Ten Years After Oslo, by David Grossman
Peace and its Discontents: Essays on Palestine and the Middle East Peace Process, by Edward W. Said
Out of Place, by Edward W. Said
The Hundred Years' War on Palestine: A History of Settler Colonialism and Resistance, 1917-2017, by Rashid Khalidi
Mornings in Jenin, by Susan Abulhawa
Seeking Palestine: New Palestinian Writing on Exile and Home, edited by Raja Shehadeh and Penny Johnson
Palestine's Children, by Ghassan Kanafani
Dreaming of Freedom: Palestinian Child Prisoners Speak, edited by Norma Hashim, with a Foreword by Professor Richard Falk; translated by Yousef M. Aljamal
19 Varieties of Gazelle: Poems of the Middle East, by Naomi Shihab Nye
Habibi, by Naomi Shihab Nye
The Flag of Childhood: Poems from the Middle East, selected by Naomi Shihab Nye
Music in Conflict: Palestine, Israel and the Politics of Aesthetic Production, by Nili Belkind
Anthology of Modern Palestinian Literature, edited by Salma Khadra Jayyusi

My Nakba: A Palestinian's Odyssey of Love and Hope, by Samir Toubassy
Occupied Voices: Stories of Everyday Life from the Second Intifada, by Wendy Pearlman
The Butterfly's Burden, by Mahmoud Darwish, translated by Fady Joudah
Selected Poetry of Yehuda Amichai, translated by Chana Bloch and Stephen Mitchell, with a Foreword by C.K. Williams
A Tale of Love and Darkness, by Amos Oz
To the End of the Land, by David Grossman
Occupation Diaries, by Raja Shehadeh
The Lemon Tree, by Sandy Tolan
A Palestinian Teenager, an Israeli Teenager—an Unlikely Friendship, by Amal Rifa'i and Odelia Ainbinder with Sylke Tempel
Three Wishes: Palestinian and Israeli Children Speak, by Deborah Ellis
Salt Houses, by Hala Alyan
We Could Have Been Friends, My Father and I, by Raja Shehadeh
Teta, Mother, and Me: Three Generations of Arab Women, by Jean Said Makdisi
I Saw Ramallah, by Mourid Barghouti
Men in the Sun, by Ghassan Kanafani
A Mountainous Journey, by Fadwa Tuqan
Palestine Speaks: Narratives of Life Under Occupation, compiled and edited by Cate Malek and Mateo Hoke
The Girl Who Stole My Holocaust, by Noam Chayut
Memory for Forgetfulness, by Mahmoud Darwish
Homeland: Oral Histories of Palestine and Palestinians, editors S. Lynd, S. Bahour and A. Lynd
Watch Out for Flying Kids, by Cynthia Levinson
Wild Thorns, by Sahar Khalifeh
The End of Spring, by Sahar Khalifeh
Touch, by Adania Shibli
Ida in the Middle ,by Nora Lester Murad
The Secret Life of Saeed the Pessoptimist, by Emile Habiby
A Woman of Five Seasons, by Leila al-Atrash
A Balcony over the Fakihani, by Liyana Badr

I thank Mahmoud Muna, known by many as "the bookseller of Jerusalem," for his love of books and for his articles, including, "Books, Not Soldiers" (*Institute for Palestine Studies*, 2017) and "The Book for Israeli

Soldiers" (*Haaretz*, 2023). I want to acknowledge the journalists at *+972 Magazine*, who provide excellent coverage of Israel and Palestine.

The following books about the Holocaust informed parts of this novel:

The Diary of a Young Girl, by Anne Frank, edited by Otto H. Frank and Mirjam Pressler
Paper Sky: What Happened after Anne Frank's Diary Ended, by Beth Jacobs
Survival in Auschwitz, by Primo Levi
This Way for the Gas, Ladies and Gentlemen, by Tadeusz Borowski
Rumor and Stones, by Wayne Karlin
Blood Memory by Gail Newman
Postcards to Hitler: A German Jew's Defiance in a Time of Terror, by Bruce Neuburger
None of Us Will Return, by Charlotte Delbo

Any shortcomings in *The Wire-Walker* are my own.